A PLACE TO RUN

TRIALS OF THE BLOOD, BOOK ONE

BECCA LYNN MATHIS

First paperback edition July 2019

Cover by Joolz & Jarling

ISBN 978-1-7331626-1-6 (paperback)
ISBN 978-1-7331626-2-3 (hardcover)
ISBN 978-1-7331626-0-9 (ebook)

www.beccalynnmathis.com

DEDICATION

To my family, for putting up with endless hours of my absence as this book took over my life.

To Kevin, my dragon, my love, without whom this book would still be lurking on my computer. Thank you for all of your encouragement and endless brainstorm sessions. You are simply amazing. I am lucky as hell to have you in my life.

To Trishinator, my sister-from-another-mister, you have been my fan club from the start, and I love you for it.

To all of my packmates, near and far.

To my beta readers and editor: Ace, Ivy, Natasha, Lynn, Melanie, Andie. You guys helped make this shine, thank you.

Oh yes, and to Chris, my woofball enthusiast extraordinaire.

SARCINA

EIUSDEM

SANGUINIS

THE BLOOD AND THE PACK ARE ONE

PROLOGUE

MATT

GRACE LYNN CARTWRIGHT. AGE 22. FREELANCE COPY-EDITOR. Consanguinea.

I looked up from my phone. The girl on the arm of the vampire walking up to the Italian restaurant was the same from the picture Sheppard sent me: wavy brown hair, fair skin, round face, big eyes. I looked down at my screen and back to the girl. She was even wearing the same brown leather jacket.

Lord knows she smelled like a *consanguinea*—sweet and heady—but the rotten vampire scent clinging to her was cloying. This was the third time she'd gone out with him in just two weeks. And she had been fed on. Recently. Probably while they were out last night. I scrolled through the contacts on my phone to my alpha's number. He answered on the first ring.

"Is she safe?" He was concerned.

I growled, "You didn't tell me she was his sheep." I should kill that bloodsucker for even touching her.

"I was afraid of that." Sheppard's voice was reserved. He ignored my anger, as usual. "Are you certain?"

"Of course I am," I retorted, my face twisting with disgust.

1

She laughed at a comment the vampire made, squeezing his arm and pressing her body against him.

"This is the third time he's taken her out in two weeks, the vamp's disgusting scent is all over her, and she seems pretty friendly with him."

"Dammit!" Sheppard sighed. "He can't try to turn her, Matt. It would kill her," he paused, "or we would have to."

I knew he'd hate to lose a *consanguinea* that way. With only seven or so born to every generation, they weren't exactly abundant.

I stretched and cracked my neck. "Then I'll step in." I lowered my voice to an almost inaudible whisper, "Killing him here would be easy."

"Matthew," Sheppard said sternly, "people aren't ready for us. Just stay close to her and *keep her safe*." He stressed the last three words needlessly. He had already told me to protect her, and I wasn't about to let that bloodsucker have her without a fight.

Silence fell between us. He knew I was still on the line, but he gave me time to cool. The girl and the vamp had disappeared into the restaurant. I was confident he wouldn't try anything in the eatery for the same reason Sheppard didn't want me storming in there. Our war with the vampires had been raging for the better part of 2,000 years, and so far, most of humanity had remained blissfully unaware of the things that go bump in the night. It wasn't our call to make. Besides, Americans usually choose the nuclear option when presented with a problem they don't understand. They'd kill more of themselves than us, and we were just trying to keep them safe from the vampires who would otherwise wipe them from the face of the planet.

"Fine," I agreed finally, settling into a spot against a corner of the building across the street. I could easily keep an eye on the front door of the restaurant from my vantage point.

"Keep me updated," Sheppard replied and ended the call.

Making a sour face, I stuffed the phone back into my pocket and inhaled the scent of the wet city after the rain from this afternoon. Clearly, he chose the public space to avoid a confrontation with me, but it wouldn't save him if he made a move on her.

So I waited, leaning against my corner. And since the vamp couldn't take her out the back door of the restaurant without arousing suspicion, I kept my eyes on the front.

The younger, bar-hopping crowd started to filter in when Grace and the vampire finally left the restaurant. I pushed off the corner and paced along behind them, blending with the crowd as best I could. The downtown area slowly filled with twenty-somethings looking to drink and party and fuck, their too-heavily-applied perfumes and colognes mixing to a nauseating note. The vampire steered her along with him as they walked down the sidewalk, his arm looped around her waist. She laughed at his jokes and I followed them.

After a short distance, they turned onto a largely empty side street and he paused, looking over his shoulder. I pressed myself into a shadow. I'm not the stealthiest of our pack, but Sheppard had insisted that I be the one to follow and protect Grace. He said I would be the best choice if the vampire decided to fight. He wasn't wrong.

"What's wrong, Frederick?" she asked him.

Frederick. Good. A name to track. He smiled in my direction and then down at her. They resumed walking.

"Nothing at all," he said. "Downtown just stinks of wet dog tonight."

It was all I could do to stay put, but I bared my teeth at his back. "It would be my absolute pleasure to kill you where you stand, blood-sucker, but it would scare your little sheep away and bring an abundance of unwanted attention." His supernatural hearing was more than enough to allow him to hear me, despite the distance between us.

He laughed and pulled Grace closer to him. She welcomed the closeness and looped her arm around his waist as well.

"This is nice," she said wistfully, "I haven't been able to go out much since my friends moved away last year."

His smile was feral, but she didn't seem to notice. "Well, you just call me anytime you wanna go out. My treat."

"I can't *always* let you pay for everything," she said.

He laughed again. "Freelancing is paying you more than beans now?"

"Hey!" she said sharply, stepping away from him and smacking his bicep. That was a dangerous thing for a human to do; the vampire could simply snap her arm for the pleasure of it. "At least it keeps the roof over my head and the lights on!"

Frederick made a placating gesture, but his smile remained predatory. "I wasn't trying to offend you, Grace," he said, looping his arm around her waist again. "I just don't want you to have to stay in all the time. You gotta live a little!"

"Which is why I'm here with you, now," she said, brushing a wayward strand of hair from her face and leaning her head against his shoulder.

They were headed to the Chateau, the club where the vampires met their sheep in the night. Dammit. I couldn't let her go in there, but I certainly couldn't go in there myself without backup. It would take too long for Sheppard and the rest of the pack to get here, and we hadn't made a move on this club yet for tactical reasons. The vampires sorely outnumbered us in there, and there were countless more in the den and tunnels underneath the club. We'd lose nearly everyone if we attacked it straight on, nevermind the amount of sheep that would be slaughtered in the fight.

Frederick nodded to the bouncer, a solid linebacker of a vampire clearly meant to intimidate. He ushered the girl into the club and smiled back over his shoulder at me. The thumping bass got louder, and wisps of fog and smoke curled out of the door as the bouncer pulled it shut again. He smiled at me too.

"Looks like you lost your prey, little wolfie," he taunted. "Best run back to your pack now."

Not an option. Frederick would likely bleed her dry in that club and she'd thank him for the pleasure of it. Balling my hands into fists so tight it cracked the knuckles, I bared my teeth at the bouncer. "Nah. It just turns out that you should've taken the night off."

In just a couple of quick moves, he was unconscious. I threw his body through the doorway as the techno drum and bass thumped in my chest. The whole place stank of fog machine smoke and the rot of vampires. The bouncer's body slid to a stop onto the dancefloor. The patrons, predominately human sheep who had been drugged into elation, ignored the intrusion. The seventeen vampires spread around the club, however, did not. They went unnaturally still as I stepped over the now groaning bouncer.

He was regaining consciousness. Confidence was going to be the only thing that would keep me alive now. So, I kept moving, my steps even and purposeful as I zeroed in on Frederick's location. If the vampires decided to attack, I would die. I'd take maybe as many as four or five down with me if I got lucky, but I would still die.

I stalked to the booth where Frederick and Grace sat with another vampire and his prey. Empty shot glasses were on the table and each of them had a round of a pale green liquid in hand. This was one of only a handful of places in town where you could get real absinthe. Grace and the other woman drank as I approached, but Frederick and his friend sat motionless, glasses still in hand. Both their eyes narrowed and, though they didn't move, I could tell they were ready to fight.

"You must have balls of steel, pup," Frederick said coolly, "to come in here with no backup."

Grace noticed my arrival with a start, nearly dropping her shot glass as she did.

"I'm not here to fight," I said through gritted teeth, despite every cell in my body screaming to do otherwise.

The friend smirked at me. "That's a shame."

Grace turned her face away from me and leaned toward Frederick. Using her hand as a screen, she used a quiet voice. "Look at his face."

No one could miss what she was talking about. Half my face had been torn up in a fight ages ago, leaving deep, nasty scars and a milky left eye. I could only see the most basic of shapes and contrast out of that eye, though my vision out of the right was perfect. I winced anyway, I'd have to stay further out of sight after tonight, assuming she and I lived through this.

Frederick smiled his feral smile at me. "Then what are you here for, if not to fight?"

"I'm here for the girl," I said, nodding to Grace. "She's not safe here, and she's not staying."

All the vampires on this side of the club laughed.

"There are so many beautiful women in this club." Frederick gestured vaguely to the dancers in the center of the club. "Any of them more than happy by now to leave with anyone who's nice enough to them," he said through his laughter. "But you want mine." He sobered. "I think not, wolf."

Grace inched closer to Frederick, pressing her body against his. Her eyes were unfocused and glazed over, pupils so wide that only a sliver of grey-blue iris circled the black. Clearly there was more in the drinks than just absinthe. She giggled at me, "So you're my dad now?" Her speech was slurred. "I don't even know you, man, and you must be on some pretty spectacular drugs if you think I'm going with you anywhere."

Spectacular. Impressive vocabulary for someone so high. Frederick pulled her closer to him, as if it were even possible. She was practically sitting in his lap.

"One of you," Frederick said, pointing at me, "and no fewer than seventeen of us. You're lucky you're still alive."

I gritted my teeth. "You and your brood won't make a move. They all know what Sheppard would do if any of you killed one of his pack."

"You guys are too much!" Grace said, laughing obnoxiously now. Frederick handed her his shot, and she drank it down without even a thought.

I took a slow, deep breath.

"Now, now. Let's not make a scene." Frederick pulled his lips back from his extended canines and brushed the back of Grace's neck with his fingers. She leaned into his touch. My stomach roiled in anger and I closed my hand into a white-knuckled fist.

He blurred with supernatural speed and his lips closed on her neck just behind and below her left ear. It was an uncommon drinking place, but the blood pumped almost as easily there as the more common jugular. In wolf form, I'd snapped the necks of more than a few vamps biting through the vein Frederick drank from now. Grace's dilated eyes fluttered closed and I heard her heartbeat race.

He was actually drinking from her before my eyes.

I heard Frederick's heart start to beat with the rush of power her blood granted him. That heartbeat would fade and stop again as her life-blood diffused through his body, but that would be hours from now.

Red seeped into the edges of my vision. The growl bubbling from my chest was entirely involuntary. My entire body shook with white-hot fury at his audacity. I reached across the cocktail table and grabbed the front of his button-down shirt, pulling him from her and scattering the empty shot glasses, most of which smashed to the floor. The vampires in the club stood as one, but the music continued thumping and the sheep continued dancing.

Frederick licked the last of Grace's blood from his lips and smiled around the club like he had already won the fight. "Let go of me, mutt, or you will die here."

I tried to watch the vampires around the club in my peripheral vision. Not a single one of them had moved from their spot, though they all remained standing.

Something flickered through Frederick's expression. Was that fear?

I pulled his face to mine, ignoring the cloying smell of rotten vampire and the sweet metallic tang of Grace's blood on him. "I'll kill you for that."

"You will try," he said, meeting my gaze. He lowered his voice to hushed tones, "I've never tasted blood as sweet as hers. I will drink from her until she *begs* me to turn her." But his bravado was slipping, I could smell the hints of fear lining the rot of his scent.

Frederick must not have recognized that she was a *consanguinea*. She would never get addicted to being fed upon like most humans; her bloodline protected her. But if I died here, it would be an hour or more before Sheppard noticed my lack of contact, and Grace could be dead by then.

"That will never happen." I gave him a feral smile before releasing him. "Grace leaves with me—*now*—or I will tear your throat out and let Sheppard get his vengeance for my death by tearing this place apart in broad daylight."

He'd lose most of the pack in the fight, but he would wipe out these vampires and their den. My muscles tensed in readiness. My breathing became a deep, even, easy rhythm. The vampires around the club still didn't move. I couldn't fathom why they hadn't, but I didn't try too hard to get into the minds of these slimy bloodsuckers. What I did know is that when they did decide to attack, the fight would be over quickly, and Grace would almost certainly die.

Frederick smoothed his shirt. "You wouldn't throw your life away like that."

I grinned at him, the potential catalyst for my certain death. "Try me, bloodsucker."

He glared at me for a long moment before his eyes flicked around the club at the unnaturally still vampires, ignoring the sheep. His expression fell a fraction before a careful mask went up in its place. Finally, he looked to Grace—who swayed with her eyes closed in rhythm with the bassline. He placed a hand against her lower back, breaking her reverie. "Grace, my dear."

"Hmm?" She looked at him with glazed eyes, but continued swaying with the beat.

"This fine specimen is going to take you home," Frederick said, gesturing with an open palm in my direction. "Try not to miss me too much."

She smiled vaguely, nodded, and clambered to her feet, unsteady.

"The next time a wolf even steps foot in this club, mutt," the friend added. "They will be dead before they even cross the floor."

Anger continued to pool in my stomach as Grace tottered out of the booth. I held out a hand to her, but she missed when she reached for it, tumbling to the ground in an unladylike heap. I knelt and scooped her into my arms, where she laid limply. She continued to breathe steadily, and her heartbeat was strong. Well, good. Then she was unlikely to die unless these vampires attacked, despite whatever she had been drugged with.

I looked to the vampire who had spoken. "The next time a wolf steps foot into this club, the pack and I will be along to burn this place to the ground."

Frederick glared at me, but his voice stayed level, "You'd dare to throw idle threats even now, you insolent mutt?"

I gave him my most predatory grin. "It's a promise, Frederick. Your days are numbered." Turning on my heel, I stalked toward the door, Grace cradled against my chest. None of the unnaturally still vampires made a move to stop me.

Tension knotted my shoulders until we'd made it safely into the back alley. The wet and dingy city scent was a welcome relief from the stink of the vampires. Letting out a breath, I closed my eyes in a silent prayer of thanks. That could have gone south fast, but somehow, we'd both made it out alive.

I set Grace on wobbly feet. She grumbled, but managed to stay upright—if just barely.

"Come on," I said, placing an arm around her waist. "Let's go." The stench of vamp clung to her, prickling at my nose.

We had to take the alleys to get back to my car without attracting too much attention. She looked like a strung-out coed, and I wasn't intent on explaining to law enforcement that I hadn't drugged her myself.

She mumbled something about Frederick being a jerk to not take her home himself.

"You'd be better off staying away from him," I said softly. "But I'd be surprised if you remember any of tonight." With any luck, she'd forget my face too and I wouldn't have to worry so much when tracking her. "Just don't throw up on the upholstery."

I scooped her into the passenger seat of my pride and joy—a cherry red '69 Chevy Camaro Z28 with a pair of thick black racing stripes flowing back over the top from the hood to the trunk of the car—and buckled her in before getting in myself. The engine roared to life and I backed out of the parking spot.

"Mm, that V8 engine purrs like a kitten," she mumbled, stroking the door panel.

She was appreciating my car now? I don't think she heard anything I had said to her.

"Maybe I'll drive you around town sometime when you're sober," I told her.

She grunted and fell quiet for the rest of the drive. Her breathing was slow and deep, though her heart raced faster than I thought it should.

Thank God her keys were in her little purse on a string. Inside her tiny, second-floor apartment, I put her to bed, removing her shoes and leaving a glass of water on her bedside table. The pinprick bite marks on her neck had already closed. They would be nothing more than puckered little scars by morning. "Damn bloodsucker," I grumbled.

I crept out of her apartment only to realize that there was no way I could safely lock her in. I was going to have to keep watch until dawn from the parking lot. Fine.

Downstairs, I moved my car, backing into the empty spot next to her little purple Honda. It was within easy view of her front door. I reclined the driver's seat and crossed my arms over my chest. It had been foolish of me to confront Frederick in the club, but the vampire had left me no other option. I got lucky. We should both be dead. Sheppard was going to be livid when he heard about tonight. Frederick and his brood weren't long for this world.

1

CONSANGUINEA

IT REALLY SHOULD HAVE OCCURRED TO ME THAT RUNNING ALONE IN THE nature reserve might not have been a good idea—even if it was daytime, and even if I'd been running the trails solo for months. But humans are creatures of habit, and I am certainly no exception—my morning run couldn't wait.

Colorado Springs in November was probably colder than most people were used to, but I grew up here. To me, the day was brisk, but clear. I wore layers, but otherwise ran light. I had at least remembered to bring my phone with me, but it was no secret that cell service was unreliable at best on the wooded trails. I didn't like foregoing music while I ran, but since I didn't have a running buddy, it was probably smarter. Most of my friends had signed onto the military and been shipped off to basic training or wherever else they ended up. So, I ran the trails alone, without music, and let my mind wander.

I thought about how sad it was that there were no wolves in Colorado. At least, the editorial piece I had just edited about the Wolf Management Plan seemed to indicate that was the case. I mean, sure, there were coyotes all over The Springs, but I'd heard they could and would live practically anywhere. And there was a wolf sanctuary outside of Manitou, where they rescued wolves and wolf-dogs and educated whoever they could get to go out there and donate. There had been increasing reports of wolf sightings in the northern areas of the state, but here? No wild wolves.

My thoughts were interrupted by something huge crashing through the underbrush toward me. It had black fur, sharp teeth, and yellow eyes. Forgetting all knowledge that running from predators only provokes them to chase you, I turned on my heel and headed toward civilization, ignoring the winding trails altogether. Big mistake, of course. I had only taken a handful of steps when the creature tackled me full force, knocking the wind out of me as I fell across a tree stump that marked a bend in the path. There was a meaty snap that must have been my femur breaking as pain exploded through my right leg and stars swam in my vision. Jaws clamped around my wrist, crunching through the bones, and I wailed.

A wolf's howl sounded elsewhere in the woods and I started to shake as more adrenaline pumped into my system. Well, at least I was wrong about the wolves in Colorado. Barring some sort of divine intervention, I was about to be a hungry wolf pack's next meal. The thing let go of my wrist as I cried out in pain and brought my one good arm up to protect my face. In a momentary flash of clarity, I remembered that going fetal and limp is supposedly one of the best ways to survive a bear attack. The creature was certainly huge enough, and while it more closely resembled a canine, I hoped the theory would still hold true. Through the pain, the best I could manage was to curl around the mess of blood, bone, and muscle that used to be my arm and squeeze my eyes shut.

The creature's claws tore at the arm covering my face as it tried to get a grip on my head, attempting to drag me out of my half-balled position with a mouthful of my hair. Warm liquid slithered down the back of my neck. Blood? Drool? Despite my heart pounding in my ears and the adrenaline racing through me, I tried to go limp. I hoped that if I could make myself boring enough, maybe it would go away. It was a delusion. I fought against my own body, my muscles tightening when I tried to relax them. Tears streamed across my face and into my hair.

When it let go of my hair, sharp teeth scraped against the bones of the ankle on my already hurt leg and dragged me out of the fetal position. My head was swimming from the pain, but I finally managed to be limp. I could hear nothing but the crunching scrape of my body against the brush and my heartbeat pounding in my ears. The terrible yellow-gold eyes of the wolf-thing met mine and I knew I was going to die.

The fucker. Rage filled my chest.

I was not going to go down without a fight. Yelling my anger, defiance, and pain at the creature as more adrenaline surged through me, I took a kick at its head with my good leg. My heel connected with an eye socket and the creature yelped and backed away, shaking its head. I sucked in a lungful of air and put just enough weight on my good leg to start a scrambling, crawling search in the underbrush for a branch I could potentially use to beat the huge wolf.

That's when a flash of brown and black fur slammed into the side of the first creature. It was another huge wolf. I must have somehow managed to get in the middle of a fight for territory. Or the newcomer was interested in picking off an easy meal now that the first had weakened it. Well, not today assholes. I was not going to be taken down by a couple of wild animals, no matter how large they were.

Scooting away from the two wolves, my eyes finally landed on a sturdy fallen branch just an arm's length away from me. One more pain-filled shuffle across the floor of the woods and grasped the end with the only hand that could close around it. Clutching it to my chest, I tried to use it to get upright, but renewed pain crackled through my right leg and I crumpled to the ground again.

I don't remember how I managed to get to my feet, since I couldn't put any weight on my right leg, but I did. Snarls and yelps came from the masses of fur and teeth and claws behind me, but I tried not to look back for fear that it would draw attention to my getaway. Blood poured from a wound on my right side, drenching my shirt and the waistband of my sweatpants. That couldn't be good. Where did that even come from? I pressed a shaking hand to the wound to try to stop the bleeding and started making unsteady progress away from the fight. I tried to stay quiet as I attempted to even out my breathing and my racing heart. I've seen enough zombie movies to know what I must have looked like dragging my useless right leg the way I did. If I survived this, maybe I would look back on this mental image and laugh. At the moment, my vision tunneled into darkness and I closed my eyes for a moment just to catch my breath.

When I opened them again, I was face down in the dirt and leaves. Furrowing my brow in confusion, I tried to push up with my good arm and saw bare feet and ankles in front of my face. I almost laughed at the absurdity of it. Who the hell comes out to these trails barefoot? Uh oh. Senselessness from lack of oxygen to the brain was setting in. I blinked to try to clear the black from the edges of my vision, but that only made everything foggy. I had fallen from my adrenaline high, and every inch of me screamed in its pain report.

As I tried to look up, to see who these bare feet belonged to, a man's arm scooped under me. I fought against the blackness, but my eyes rolled back into my head as it overtook me.

2

"THERE'S ONLY FIVE DAYS BETWEEN NOW AND THEN." A MAN SPOKE somewhere in my vicinity, his voice gruff and matter-of-fact. A vague sensation of softness surrounded me. I smelled something wet and metallic, as well as some sort of animal. Someone was grilling nearby, I could smell the smoke and the meat, but that didn't make any sense to me either. Who grills outside of a hospital?

"And if she wakes up," came another man's calm reply, "she'll make it. She's not the worst I've seen survive."

I groaned as sensation floated back to me. Everything hurt, but I managed to open my eyes. Well, one only half opened—it was clearly swollen, and likely black and purple as well. I could see the night sky through a window. Paisley wallpaper lined the walls of the room, and golden light from a lamp on the bedside table bathed the room in a soft glow. The sheets of my big, plush bed were white, the blanket was warm, and the pillow was soft. It felt homey and welcoming, a stark contrast to my own experience with hospitals.

A middle-aged man wearing a pair of jeans and a white t-shirt sat in a chair next to the bed. His shoulder-length sandy blonde hair was brushed back, and he regarded me with golden-brown eyes. No lab coat. No name badge. Nothing beeped in time with my heartbeat, and no IV line ran to my arm.

This was not a hospital. My heart started to pound in my ears.

Another man with short blonde hair and a vicious scar across the left half of his face pushed off the door frame and stepped into the hallway beyond my field of view. No lab coat on that one either. My pulse kicked into high gear and I shifted under the blanket. It hurt, but at least I confirmed that my arms and legs were not restrained—that was a good sign. Maybe these guys rescued me? But why didn't they take me to a hospital?

"What—" I croaked. My mouth was so dry that the sound was barely more than a whisper.

The seated man handed me a glass of water from the bedside table, and I gulped half of it down before I tried again.

"What happened?" I asked, pressing the glass to my lips for another sip.

"A werewolf," he replied, closing his hand into a fist. "A crazed werewolf."

I nearly choked on a gulp of water. "That's not funny at all," I managed to get out. I cleared my throat and tried again. "A werewolf? Really? That's just folklore and stories. Besides, it was broad daylight." And maybe I'd read too many books like that one with the sparkly vampires. The werewolf stories were always my favorite, though.

He raised an eyebrow at me. "You know, all legends have a hint of truth to them." He rolled with it, and he looked me square in the eye like he was telling me I had cancer. Sick bastard.

I squirmed and looked away.

"It's no joke," he continued. "Human lives are too short to joke about something so serious." He said 'human' like the nature of it simply didn't apply to him.

My heart continued its nearly frenzied pounding in my ears. Using my uninjured arm, I propelled myself up on the bed and winced with pain. That was a mistake. Every movement I made pulled at fresh scabs. Everything itched where it stretched, but worse, it all hurt in that dull ache sort of way that makes you wish it would just stop

16

throbbing for a moment so you could go back to sleep. I bit my lip to stifle a groan and tasted blood.

"That thing was nearly as big as a bear." My head started to feel too heavy for my neck. "And Colorado hasn't had wolves for decades."

"No one believes me the first time." Nodding, he pursed his lips. "I'll have to show you then."

When he stood, my eyes went wide. I took a breath to scream, but he turned away from me and walked over to the door. "Jonathan, we're ready for you," he said in a patient tone.

It felt almost fatherly. Weird.

I narrowed my eyes as well as one can when one of your eyes is nearly swollen shut. A huge wolf-thing like the creature on the reserve padded into the room. As if my heart wasn't racing fast enough, a chill went down my spine. I took a breath to try to stay calm. "Jesus—"

"I take that to mean a creature like this is what attacked you," White t-shirt said, gesturing with an open palm.

The creature next to him was pale grey with black blending in on the face, ears, and tail. Its disconcertingly human green eyes were flecked with gold and it regarded me with what I was sure was quiet amusement. It reminded me of a raccoon in a way I couldn't quite explain.

I slowly bobbed my head once. "Just what kind of dog *is* that thing?!"

The creature sighed.

White t-shirt shrugged. "He's a werewolf, like I said. Jonathan, if you could please rejoin us and show our doubting guest."

I swear the thing nodded as every part of it started to contort. Its legs elongated, and its torso changed to be more upright, above the hips. The grey fur on its head gave way to a dark goatee and dark brown hair that fell to broad shoulders. As fur became skin, I realized that if there was a man under all the fur and claws and teeth, he was going to be naked. I turned my head away.

"No use being shy about skin anymore," the naked man said with an amused chuckle. "People clothes don't fit wolves."

I heard clothes rustling and turned back when I heard a zipper.

Scars crisscrossed his entire torso, and I looked to my own bandages. I was pretty sure this is what it looked like to be run over by a cheese grater. I kind of felt like I had too. I smelled steak and potatoes and wood and warmth and wet metal and my stomach did *not* feel capable of holding down food. Black started creeping into the edges of my vision.

"Oh, Shep, she's got a ways to go, this one," Jonathan said as the glass of water hit the carpet with a dull thud.

I didn't even remember dropping it.

"She'll make it." White t-shirt looked at me, concern plain on his face as he eased me back onto the pillows.

How did he get across the room so fast?

"Jonathan's the joker of our little pack." He pulled the blanket back into place around me, brushing wayward strands of hair out of my face. It reminded me of the way my father used to do it when I was a child, hiding in my parents' bed from thunderstorms. "I'm Sheppard, the pack alpha, and this is my home. Believe it or not, you are perfectly safe here."

Yep. Blackness won that round, but I must not have been out for long, Sheppard was still standing over me when it cleared. He was looking at me expectantly.

Oh yeah, he had just introduced himself.

I wasn't sure I was ready to tell them my real name. I wasn't fully certain I should even trust them. But something in my gut felt a sincere truthfulness to everything they'd said. It was strange and disconcerting.

"Call me...Lynn," I said. That's a better name for them to know me by. Sheppard raised a brow, but nodded. I tried to narrow my eyes again to read his face.

"Pack doesn't keep secrets, it goes deeper than family or blood. You'll see," Sheppard said.

"I'm not in your pack." God, I was just a girl who clearly didn't show the best judgment with her choice of running locales. What the hell did he mean by pack anyway?

"Well," Sheppard pursed his lips. "Maybe not, but you *are* a were-wolf now, and there's no getting around that."

"What? Not a chance!" There was no way. Okay. So maybe hottie with the scarred torso over there was a werewolf. And maybe so was Sheppard. But not me.

"It's true," Jonathan said softly.

"Thank you, Jonathan," Sheppard said, his tone clearly meant to quiet any more comments from Jonathan. "Go get Kaylah for me, would you?"

"Sure," he said, ducking his head as he left the room.

"You are a werewolf, Lynn," Sheppard said. "The sooner you can make peace with that, the better."

I rolled my eyes. Maybe only one of them rolled. The other ached bad enough that I couldn't tell if my eye had actually moved. "Sure I am." But the cold chill on my spine and the pit in my stomach told me that I was simply lying to myself. I couldn't pinpoint or explain how on Earth I knew it, but I could feel the truth of his words. I believed him.

"I have already proven to you that werewolves are real." He leaned closer to me and dropped his voice to conspiratorial tones. "I can prove that you're one too, you know."

His golden-brown eyes bored into mine, making me uncomfortable, but I fought the urge to look away.

"How many have been in this room today before you woke up?"

"Four." I answered without even thinking.

Sheppard raised an eyebrow. "And how do you know that?"

That was a good question. I frowned and picked at my thoughts. "I...smelled that they were here."

Sheppard crossed his arms in satisfaction and sat down in the chair.

I scrunched up my face. "Okay." I took a deep breath. "Let's say I believe you—since I'm clearly in no condition to argue the point. How is that even possible? I should be dead, shouldn't I? I mean, if it wasn't for the other," I eyed Sheppard, "wolf that jumped in, I'd be lunch meat."

Did these guys save me? Why did I feel so safe here?

"That's how it works. A bite from a werewolf isn't enough. It has to almost kill you to get the werewolf healing to kick in." His expression turned somber. "Trust me. There was a point there in which you stopped breathing."

Holy shit. He was serious. And—somehow—I could feel that he wasn't lying.

A waify woman with long platinum-blonde hair and crystal blue eyes came into the room holding two plates of steak and potatoes. She smelled sweet and faintly of flowers. My mouth watered at the sight of the food; I may have thought my stomach couldn't handle it, but God, was I ever hungry. She handed one of the plates to Sheppard and gingerly placed the other on my lap. As I shoved two large pieces of potato in my mouth with the fork, she crinkled her nose and eyed me.

"Those bandages need changin'," she said with a southern drawl that was thick as molasses in the winter. "You'd best eat up quick t' give yerself some fuel."

Sheppard nodded. "Kaylah's right, you've got an awful lot of healing to do and less than a week to get it done."

I nearly choked on the piece of steak I was chewing on. If I didn't die from the pain suffusing throughout my body, I was going to die from choking on stupid bits of food and beverage while they all enjoyed their little werewolf game. "A week?!" I knew that both my right leg and left wrist were broken, there was *zero* chance they'd be healed in a week.

"Five days to the next full moon," Sheppard said. "The legends and stories get that part right at least. It's the full moon that pulls the change from you. . . at least the first time."

My plate was empty. How was my plate empty? Kaylah gently took it from my lap.

"I'll be back with more, hun. Don't look so disappointed, there's plenty where that came from." With a wink at me, she left the room.

A clock ticked from somewhere within the house and I looked to Sheppard. "So, this is your house." I am a stunning conversationalist, just ask me.

His smile was gentle. "This is my home. Also known as pack central. We usually have at least three wolves in residence here aside from me, and everyone is welcome."

"Everyone in your pack at least," I guessed.

"And some," he made a vague gesture in my direction, "who are not. The world at large isn't ready for werewolves. We are very much still creatures that go bump in the night." He stood, empty plate and dirty fork in hand. "Which is why you couldn't go to a hospital. They wouldn't know what to do with your recovery." He crossed the room to leave, "I suspect you'll want some privacy while Kaylah helps you with those bandages."

I let out a breath and relaxed back into the pillows.

A dark-haired head poked into the room, and amused green eyes met mine. "Kind of a lot to take in," Jonathan said, stepping into the room. He now had a black shirt on with a skull and crossbones on it along with the jeans from earlier.

I pulled the blanket up to cover more of my body as I realized the wet metal I was smelling was me and all the bloody bandages.

"No kidding," I agreed as he sat down on the edge of the bed. I tried to pull my feet up and over to give him room, but only managed to wiggle one foot a little in the direction I wanted. It hurt. I winced.

The right corner of his mouth quirked up. It gave me butterflies. Dammit. "It's a wonder you can move at all. I saw you when Matt and Sheppard brought you in. You were definitely lunch meat then."

I frowned.

"But you've come a long way in just a couple of days," he said. "For what it's worth, I think you'll be fine."

My not-swollen eye threatened to bug out of my head. "A couple of days?" Good lord, that can't be true.

Jonathan nodded. "They brought you in around midday the day before last."

I mouthed 'day before last' and lifted the blanket and sheet to look at my mangled body. The sweatpants and tank top I wore wearing were not mine, but they both had bloodstains that matched where my injuries were underneath them. Who had changed my clothes? Did it matter if I was next to death?

Sheppard's words echoed in my head. 'There was a point there in which you stopped breathing.'

Oh my god. Did I really almost die? I met his eyes again. "Oh sure," I said. "I'll be just fine." Why are all the hot ones crazy?

Jonathan gave me an impish smile. "What's really gonna get your goat is how fast you'll heal after your first change. We're just this side of bulletproof, y'know." He waggled an eyebrow and his voice dropped to conspiratorial tones. "Besides, this pack is a sausage fest, you *gotta* be just fine!"

"*JONATHAN!*" Kaylah was back with so much steak and potatoes I wasn't sure how she managed to get it all onto the plate, and I was certain there was no way it was all going to fit in my belly.

Jonathan flinched and winked at me. Turning to Kaylah he shrugged as he stood. "I'm just saying, Kaylah. You and Chastity both have mates. That leaves four of us out in the cold."

The sound that came out of me was more snerk than laugh, but even that sent ripples of pain throughout my body. Biting down on another groan, I closed my eyes and took slow breaths until it subsided. "It's alright," I managed. "At least he hasn't tried to grab my ass."

"*Yet.*" Jonathan grinned. "Mostly because you're laying on it. But also, because it was probably run through a meat grinder." He pointed a finger at me, wiggling it up and down. "Like the rest of you."

"Enough!" Kaylah exclaimed. "*Git!*" She mimed kicking him as he hurried out the door, stealing a potato off my plate as he went. Rolling her eyes, she smiled at me. "He's a joker, but he's got a heart of gold. Our pack just wouldn't be the same without him and his brother Jamie." She handed the plate to me. "Go on an' eat up. We'll change your bandages as soon as you're done and then it'll be more rest for you lil' lady."

I shoved potatoes and bits of steak in my mouth as she went in and out of the room gathering washcloths, bandages, cortisone cream, and alcohol. The more she gathered, the more I was sure that every single bit of what was coming was going to make me wish that thing had just killed me instead. As I shoved the last couple of bites into my mouth, she disappeared again and came back carrying a mug of something that smelled sweet and bitter all at once. It overpowered everything except the wet metallic smell of my wounds. She placed the mug on the table next to the bed.

"Unfortunately, there ain't a painkiller out there that works worth a damn fer us." She nodded at the tea. "But that'll help afterward." She shut the door to the room. "You got all a them wolves on edge with all a yer bleedin'." She took the plate from me and set it on the table next to the bed.

"They'd mostly prefer to tear me up than see me get better?"

"Gracious no!" Her genuine shock caught me off guard. "Sheppard named you pack, girl, whether you take it or leave it, and pack looks out for each other. Good *night* where'd you get such a cockamamie idea?!"

Maybe it was all the books and stories that portray werewolves as hyper-violent creatures. But if Kaylah and Jonathan and Sheppard were all werewolves, those stories were far from the truth of things. And why shouldn't they be? They're just made up stories, aren't they? But how much of it was true?

Deft hands started unwrapping the bandages on my leg. Some of the gauze stuck to the underlying wounds and I bit my lip, wincing.

Don't scream. Just don't scream. Keep breathing. That's it. Air in. Air out.

Kaylah unwound another bandage from the worst of the wounds on my leg. Pain shot up my leg and through the rest of my body. I tasted blood in my mouth from biting down so hard on my lip.

Kaylah clucked her tongue and looked at me disapprovingly. She thrust a wad of gauze at my face. "Bite down on that or you won't have any lip left by the time I'm done wit' ya."

I did as she said.

"Now, sure those wolves ain't all gonna love ya just 'cause Sheppard tells them to, but they're all pretty friendly once you get t' know 'em."

23

Another bandage free and I bit harder on the gauze. It soaked up the saliva in my mouth, and the wad was so big I had to breathe hard through my nose to keep from passing out.

She worked quickly to get all of the bandages off, but it was the scrubbing of the tender fresh wounds underneath that really made me realize I had no idea what pain I was capable of surviving. Blackness loomed at the edges of my vision, but each time Kaylah had another quip to add about one of the wolves. I'll admit that I didn't catch a word of what she said, but her southern drawl bit through the worst of the pain. It distracted me enough from her work, but my conscious mind retained none of it.

Then it was done, and she handed me the mug of strange tea. It was warm as it slid into my belly. She slipped from the room with a bag full of dirty bandages destined for the trash.

"There's lots of books out there about werewolves and vampires," I blurted out when she returned. "They tend to be some of my favorites." Rambling counts as conversation, right? "They make for a great escape from a world that's just a little too real when you're eating cups of noodles three times a day because your rent just ate your entire paycheck."

Sheppard appeared in the doorway, his football player-like frame took up almost the entire space. "Those books get quite a bit wrong." There was something about the tone of his voice—something he wasn't saying.

"Let me guess. The vampires are real." I tried to make it sound like a question; I doubt I succeeded.

He smiled softly and nodded. "And they outnumber us ten to one easy."

Kaylah sat in the chair next to the bed as he stepped into the room.

I took another sip of tea. Tense muscles I didn't know existed began to relax as the throbbing subsided. "Why?"

Sheppard shrugged. "Not many survive an attack like you went through. And if they manage to, well, they're so bad off, they don't survive the first change. Even fewer are born a wolf."

"And makin' a vamp ain't nearly so hard as makin' a wolf," Kaylah added. "Just takes an exchange of blood."

"Wait," I said. "You can be *born* a werewolf?!" Not many of the books I'd read mentioned that sort of thing.

Sheppard's entire demeanor changed. The very air in the room felt charged with something I couldn't even begin to describe. "I was."

I took a sip of my drink and became very interested in what the inside of my mug looked like. The hazy orange-yellow tea swirled in my mug, my own reflection distorting on the surface of the liquid.

"Get some rest," he said. "We'll talk more tomorrow."

I drained the last bit of tea. Kaylah took the mug from me as I relaxed back into the pillows. Something here felt right—felt true. Unlike the invading blackness from before, a different sort of peaceful darkness overtook me, floating me away from consciousness.

3

DAYLIGHT STREAMED IN THROUGH MY WINDOW WHEN I WOKE AGAIN. My arm and leg still ached, but most of the other injuries didn't hurt anymore. Blinking a few times, I rubbed my eyes, momentarily surprised that they were both normal. No swelling. As I sat up, everything pulled tight and itched a little, but the itch was bearable and was followed by only a dull throbbing ache. I looked around the room. The chair was still next to the bed and a glass of water sat on the bedside table. I drained half the glass as voices drifted from elsewhere in the house.

A gruff male voice exclaimed, "I'm just not taking everyone else in there, leaving one of our own wounded and bedridden here!"

It sounded like they were in a large room downstairs. I frowned. Were they talking about me?

"She shouldn't be wounded and bedridden! You were supposed to keep her safe!" I was relatively certain that was Jonathan, and—by the sound of it—he was pacing around.

I huffed out a breath. The bedridden part was going to change. Despite the splint tightly wrapped against my right thigh and another wrapped against my left forearm, I took a deep breath and swung my legs off the bed. Using the chair for support, I put weight on my one good leg. It held.

"Don't start in on that," the gruff man warned. "Crazed wolves are damn near impossible to predict, aside from the rampant violence they cause, and I'd been tracking that one for days."

I started hobble-hopping across the plush carpet, using the chair and walls for support as I moved toward the door.

Jonathan was still moving around as he spoke. "And then you found a cave with three caged wolves. We have to *do* something about them!"

As I reached the door out to the hallway, I realized that making it that far had been the easy part. I was on the second floor of the house.

"I'm not saying we don't," the gruff one agreed. "I'm just saying that we have to plan it out. Those cages are up front in a cave with walls covered in blood. *Wolf* blood. It'll be hard enough to concentrate as it is. There could be any number of anythings beyond that front cavern —including swarms of vampires. There's just no way to tell with all the wolf blood, and there is simply no way that I'm taking a newly turned pup who can't even *walk* in there without a plan!"

I winced at the thought of trying to make my way down the stairs, but I wasn't staying in bed any longer. It was only a step or two to the top of the stairs, and since the living room had vaulted ceilings, I could see Jonathan and the man with the scarred face squared off downstairs.

"Hey," Jonathan said, an immediate shift in the tone of his voice and his body language. "Check it out. Four days later and she's up and moving!"

A smile lit up his entire face. Probably half of Colorado too. He moved to the stairs, probably with the intention of helping me down. Great. I tried not to roll my eyes.

The banister was on my left. Leaning heavily against the wall to my right, I tried to get down a single step. I basically had to hop, but I did it. Four days? It was just two yesterday? Had I really lost a whole extra day? When I tried the next step, my heel caught just the edge and I skidded down the next handful of stairs before I caught myself on the railing, bumping both my injured arm and leg in the process. Grunting, I bit my lip to stifle crying out.

Jonathan was first into my field of view, green eyes filled with concern. He wore an olive-green shirt with loose-fit blue jeans. He nodded to scar-face. "You're right though Matt," he said, sweeping me into his arms like you read about in all those silly romance novels. "She's not ready for anything really."

I sighed and pursed my lips. I'm no damsel in distress. Being careful of my injured arm and leg, he stepped down one step.

"I can walk," I grumbled. "I just misjudged that step."

After the next step, Jonathan made a face and put me down. I resumed leaning against the wall.

"Alright," he said quietly, stepping down the next step and turning to face me. "Then we'll take a different approach."

Matt regarded me with one brown eye and one milky one. The scars on his face ran from the hairline down into his burgundy shirt. He jammed his fists into the pockets of his khaki cargo shorts. "Four days until the full moon," he said, his flip-flops clacking as he walked toward the stairs. "Here's to hoping that's enough time."

Jonathan stepped in between me and the wall, looping an arm around my waist and pulling my side firmly against him. "Let's go." He smelled woodsy and almost electric, like a forest after a thunderstorm.

Putting weight on him, we hobbled down the rest of the stairs to the landing, which sat on an angle to the left, facing a sizable living room filled with the sturdy sort of furniture you can't get at that Swedish import store. The stone fireplace on the far wall was unlit and clean of ashes. The clock on the mantel told me it was just about noon. Well, at least I was well-rested. What was presumably the front door to the house was to my right.

As Jonathan helped me to sit on the landing, Sheppard rounded a corner and came into the room. I felt something shimmer through me as he said firmly, "we are not making a move on the cave until after the moon."

Matt and Jonathan each turned their heads down and away from Sheppard. So did I. Why did I do that? Two of those energy bars you take on hikes appeared on my lap. I looked up to see Sheppard towering over me.

"Eat," he ordered.

Putting one of the wrapped bars on the step next to me, I opened the other and took a bite. It tasted just as I expected: cardboard with a faint sweetness of fruit. "Um," I swallowed that bit of granola. "Is there any way I could get a ride to my apartment, please? I'm sure my car's safe at the reserve, and I sure appreciate your generosity here, but-"

"Already got your car here," Jonathan said, smiling. "Your keys were still in your pocket." He fished my keyring out of a bowl on the mantel of the fireplace and tossed it to me. Much to my genuine surprise, I deftly plucked my keys out of the air with my injured left hand. Sheppard eyed me meaningfully. So I was particularly dexterous today despite my broken limbs, I wasn't certain that made me a werewolf. But Sheppard definitely had a point when he'd asked me before about who had been in my room. Today, I could smell that no fewer than five others plus a dog had been through the house recently, present company excluded. And why didn't my wrist ache from catching my keys?

"We'll have to make it a quick trip," Sheppard said. "We can take you by your place to grab some things and then bring you back here. The vampire has been staking out your place."

I smacked my forehead with my hand and grimaced. Apparently the formerly swollen eye was still a little bruised. "I missed Jenny's dinner!"

Sheppard raised an eyebrow at me.

"She just got a promotion!" I explained. "We were going out to celebrate. I'll have to call—" I reached into my pocket, where I usually keep my phone on runs. But these were borrowed sweatpants, and my phone wasn't there. I narrowed my eyes. "Where's my phone?"

"It got destroyed when you were attacked," Matt said, putting his hands up in a placating gesture. "I didn't know anyone even used that sort of flip phone anymore."

"Hey!" I said "Simple and reliable. Don't fix what isn't broken!" I never even wanted one of the smartphones when they came out. It's not that they were too complex, it just felt absurd to carry around an entire computer in your pocket. The guy at the store had laughed at me when I told him I wanted the flip phone, explaining that those were meant for elderly folks. He took my money anyway, though, so who was the real winner?

Jonathan leaned toward me. "Except it *is* broken now. Here, use mine." He handed me his sleek black phone—the latest model, I was sure.

I stared at it for a moment. What was I going to say to her? "Hey Jenny, sorry I couldn't make it the other night, I was attacked by a werewolf and now I am one too? Oh, but don't worry, I'm not crazy, I'm staying with some other werewolves who seem to be keen on taking good care of me?" Yeah, that would go over *real* well.

I smirked and handed the phone back.

"Keep it for now, nothing I can say to her that wouldn't have her hounding me for acting all suspicious."

No one else would have even noticed me being gone, except for maybe Frederick. But he'd been flaky since the last time we went out anyway. Mom was dead, my dad was off in Europe, and my freelance editing was contracted mostly online and through phone calls. I had a working relationship with the local newspaper, but four days without any contact or updates? My replacement probably started yesterday. Besides, since when did I decide I was staying here to recover? I mean, sure, the food's good, but really? I shook my head and sighed.

Jonathan laughed, the sound bubbling out of his chest. "Nice. *Hounding.* I like it."

I smiled. Matt rolled his good eye.

"Alright," Sheppard said. "Let's move while there's still daylight. Matt, you're with us, just in case the vampire's got friends that want to cause trouble. Jonathan, you're in charge of getting everyone here. Now that Lynn is up and mobile, a meet and greet is in order."

He said my name pointedly, like there was something else they had been calling me before now. Sheppard said I was safe here, and— somehow—that felt true, but it was odd to feel so safe around strangers.

I used the banister railing to get to my feet—well, foot, the one wasn't holding any real weight, though it didn't argue about being rested on the ground. I hobble-hopped a step or two toward the door.

Matt pursed his lips. "Just a moment."

He went through the living room, into the dining room beyond that toward the back of the house, and into a room to the left, which I could now see was a kitchen. I heard a door open and shut and then Matt was coming back through the house. He carried a pair of crutches with him and eyed my injured arm.

"Maybe you don't need both," he said, offering one to me and leaning the other against the wall next to the door, "but one will at least keep you independently mobile."

"Thanks," I said around the last bite of the first energy bar, shoving the wrapper into the pocket of my sweats. Taking the crutch, I took a few steps away from the door and back again to get a feel for them. It took only a minor adjustment to the length to get it to be reasonably comfortable.

"Let's go," Sheppard said, opening the door for us.

Past the front door was a beautiful covered wraparound porch, complete with swing and rocking chair. The crutch made light work of the two steps down to the yard and walkway. The huge house was at the apex of a cul-de-sac. Looming in the driveway was a shiny black Dodge Ram. My little purple Civic del Sol was parked in the driveway too with an olive-green Jeep behind it. The headlights of the Ram blinked as the locks clicked open. I smiled, of course the Ram belonged to Sheppard. How appropriate.

Sheppard opened the passenger side door. "You first Matt, Lynn needs to keep that right leg extended."

Not that the splint would let me bend it anyway.

Matt got up into the truck and, along with Sheppard, helped me in. Actually, it was mostly Sheppard, as he scooped me up and paced me in the seat. Sheppard put the crutch into the bed of the truck. While I understood the seating arrangement logistically, it seemed rather silly to put Matt in the middle of the bench seat as both Sheppard and Matt were built like football players.

The truck smelled of warm spicy musk. Almost like incense. It was actually kind of comforting, and I laid my head against the headrest and closed my eyes for a moment.

But as we pulled out of the driveway, something Sheppard said resurfaced. My eyes snapped open and my heart started to pound. "How do you know that anyone has been staking out my apartment? How do you even know where I live?" With a lurch in my chest, it occurred to me that these guys may be the reason I was attacked.

"I've been following you," Matt explained, placing a hand lightly on my uninjured knee.

That sure didn't help any. I set my jaw and squirmed closer to my door. Matt's hand didn't follow me, thank God.

Sheppard made a soft rumbling noise. Did he just growl? "I asked him to. We wanted to keep you safe."

My thin hold on calm slipped free. "Safe from that *thing* that attacked me?!" I exclaimed. "What did you call it? A *crazed* wolf?! I really gotta hand it to you, *great* job there!"

Fear knotted in my stomach. I put my chin in my hand, facing the window, and rested my elbow on the door handle. The doors were locked, and we were on the highway now. Even if I thought jumping from a moving vehicle was plausible, I certainly wasn't going to get away from these guys in my condition.

Matt growled, an intense rumbling sound in the enclosed cab of the truck. "What genius goes running by herself on a nature reserve where cell reception is shit?!"

"It was *daytime!*" I countered, not looking back at him.

"Look," Sheppard said, his calm voice a stark contrast. "Your friend Frederick is a vampire. We were trying to keep you safe from him, and he knew it."

Wait. Frederick? He'd been following me long enough to know about the time I'd spent with Frederick? And he thought he was a vampire? No. He was sure he was a vampire.

"Right," I said with a huff.

Of course Frederick was a vampire. And I'm a werewolf. I rolled my eyes and opened the second energy bar.

The next exit was onto the street my apartment complex was on. A minute more and we were pulling into the parking spot in front of my apartment, the cardboard fruity goodness on its way to my stomach. This was no gated community, and it certainly wasn't in the best neighborhood, but I lived above the leasing office and that seemed to keep the shady characters at bay for the most part. Sheppard got the crutch out of the back as Matt reached over me to open the door. Sheppard leaned the crutch against the truck and picked me up again. He put me down gently and handed me the crutch. I quickly hopped away and up the flight of stairs to my apartment. As I got closer, there was a familiar perfume, the smoky sweet aroma of clove cigarettes, and something else I couldn't place. I wrinkled my nose at the rank scent of it, focusing instead on the familiar.

"They were just here!" I exclaimed, leaning over the second-floor railing to look back at the parking lot. No sign of Stephanie's convertible or Jenny's orange Eclipse.

"That trail's three days old," Sheppard said, catching up to me.

I couldn't believe it. "Jenny's perfume, Steph's cloves, but that last one..." I narrowed my eyes.

"That's vampire," Matt said, crossing his arms.

"Your friend Frederick," Sheppard said. "He came later, about a day ago."

"Uh huh," I said. "And I'm a tooth fairy."

Matt leaned close and dropped his voice, so it was more of a quiet rumble than actual words. "Does that scent—that rank, acrid scent—smell safe to you?"

He was too close for comfort, but I sucked in a lungful, trying to weed out just the unpleasant scent. It smelled like death—like something that had rotted in the summer sun for hours on a wet road.

I looked into his clear eye and shook my head. "No."

"Then whether you call it vampire or something else makes no difference," Matt said, backing away from me. "Either way, it's bad."

Sighing, I shook my head and unlocked the door to my tiny studio apartment. The welcoming scent of my own home engulfed me as I opened the door and stepped in. I breathed it in, allowing it to help release the knot in the pit of my stomach. Sure, my place was a little messy, it always was, but this was my home. Mine. Another step in and a muscle in my shoulder started to unwind. I closed my eyes, taking a deep, slow breath.

Sheppard and Matt came in and closed the door behind them. Matt began moving around the apartment and I opened my eyes. Sheppard leaned against the wall next to my door. He watched Matt, who looked out the huge picture window to the left of the door. It didn't have much of a view, but it sure let a lot of light into my apartment. He pursed his lips and stepped back from the window, visually tracing around the window frame and then walking through my apartment, tracking along the ceiling, down the short hall and into the bathroom. I heard my shower curtain move and then Matt came back into view. I furrowed my brow at him as he nodded to Sheppard. Then I realized it—he just swept my little apartment like the SWAT teams do in movies. Maybe they *were* trying to protect me.

I opened my walk-in closet and grabbed the duffel off the top shelf. Pulling clothes from hangers and drawers, I stuffed a handful of changes of clothes into the bag. Sheppard hadn't mentioned how long they wanted me to stay with them for, but I suspected it was at least till the full moon. That was what? Five days from now? No, wait. Jonathan's comment as I got up implied I had lost two days. Well I certainly had enough clothes in the bag for three days.

Hopping into the bathroom, I caught my reflection in the mirror. The entire left side of my face was still purple, and the pink skin of a fresh scar ran a vertical track over my cheekbone. It must have happened when that wolf slashed at the arm that had been trying to cover my face. Touching it gently, I remembered Jonathan's scars and the way the skin over his stomach muscles looked so touchable.

The sound of my fridge opening made me blink, and I shook my head, realizing I had been smiling. What on Earth was I thinking? I put the duffel down on the closed toilet lid and grabbed my tooth-brush, deodorant, body spray, and comb. Shoving them into the bag, I tried to remember where I'd dropped my purse. . . It was in my car, of course it was in my car. I rolled my eyes again and grabbed my shampoo and conditioner off the shelf above the bathtub. They joined my other belongings in the bag and I settled it onto my shoulder again.

I hobbled over to my bed and plopped the bag on it so I could zip it closed. The rosary my mother gave me swung on the bedpost in the corner of my field of vision. I'm not the most religious person, but my mom had said it was blessed, and I just felt better when it was close. I looped it around my wrist a few times so it wouldn't fall off and shrugged into my favorite hoodie.

Matt had a slice of cheese rolled up and took the last bite of it as I closed the blinds to my window. Joke's on him, I was pretty sure that cheese expired two weeks ago.

"Ready to go?" Sheppard asked.

I took a deep breath. "Okay," I said around a lump in my throat. Why did I want to cry all of a sudden? It wasn't like I was never going to see this place again.

Sheppard nodded and we exited my apartment. "You can shower when we get back."

Locking the door didn't help the lump in my throat either. I guess I really had made the decision to stay with them until I was healed up.

4

———————

Sheppard scooped me back into the truck and tossed my bag in the bed along with the crutch. The three of us headed in the direction of Sheppard's house. My stomach growled as we passed a fast food restaurant.

"Yea, me too," Matt said, patting his own stomach.

Sheppard nodded and turned around. As he pulled into the drive-thru lane, a voice garbled from the loudspeaker. "Can I take your order?"

"I need twelve number sevens, five of the big packs of nuggets, seven large fries, and three large sodas." Sheppard seemed for all the world like it was nothing at all to order enough to feed an army.

"Who's gonna eat all that?!?" My eyes must have been as wide as dinner plates.

Matt raised the scarred eyebrow and looked at me. "You'll likely have three of the burgers yourself since you're healing, then there's the rest of us. This should tide us over till dinner."

The attendant repeated the order back.

"I can't eat all that!" It was highly uncommon for me to eat everything when I got a meal at any fast food place. That's why I usually ordered off the value menu. Well that, and my meager paycheck from freelancing for the newspaper rarely afforded me anything outside of cups of noodles and canned pasta.

"That's it," Sheppard replied when the attendant finished. He rolled his window up and looked at me, "I think you'll find you *can* 'eat all that.' Werewolves have a much higher metabolism than humans. Much of our body's stored energy is used when we change. Once you're back to one hundred percent, I think you'll find yourself not only able to eat, but hungry, any time food is available."

I pursed my lips as the drive-thru attendant handed Sheppard the bags of food. I'm not so sure about that, particularly since there was no way I could afford to eat like that. Sheppard passed bag after bag to Matt, who handed many to me. The drinks soon followed. Once we had everything, Matt fished three burgers out of one of the bags, handing one each to Sheppard and me.

"Mind the upholstery," Sheppard said with a smile as I unwrapped my burger.

I had that one down and was working on a second when we pulled up to the house. The cul-de-sac was lined with cars, while Sheppard's initial spot in the driveway remained clear. When we had parked, Sheppard got out and grabbed my crutch and bag from the truck bed. He came to lift me out of the truck, but I put my hand up, stopping him.

"I'm tired of being carried around like an invalid," I said. "I can do this."

Matt smirked and walked around to the passenger side of the truck.

Sheppard eyed me. "Your leg isn't holding weight and your arm still can't grip things."

"I can do this," I repeated stubbornly from my seat.

Matt handed me another burger. "Better claim it now or you may not get the chance."

Sheppard nodded, "Okay, I'll take your bag upstairs for you."

"I can get it."

Sheppard's eyes narrowed as they met mine.

"I can do this," I repeated, softer this time.

Sheppard sighed. "All right." He shook his head. "See you inside."

I put the burger in my left hand. It might have been unreliable at helping me into the truck or pushing my body weight around, but it could hold a burger well enough. I scooted toward the open door and let my right leg dangle out while I maneuvered my left down. My right foot hit the ground with more weight than I wanted and with a cry I scrambled my weight back onto the bench seat.

Except my leg wasn't screaming with pain, it just ached in a pointedly throbbing sort of way.

Silly girl.

I sat staring out the front window for a moment, thinking. I leaned and rolled so that my belly was toward the bench seat and my left leg was the leading one. When it hit the ground, it held my weight steadily enough that I could lower myself the rest of the way out of the cab without issue. I sighed and looked at the crutch and my bag. I only had one hand that could do anything.

I grabbed the crutch and hopped over to the porch to eat my burger. I put a little weight on my right leg and used the crutch as leverage to sit. My leg throbbed, but it wasn't unbearable. As I unwrapped my burger, I heard voices drifting from around the back of the house. I could smell that a total of eight others had arrived, including the warm scent I had begun to associate with Sheppard and the spicy muskiness I associated with Matt.

I took a bite of my burger. What would I say to them anyway? I had always considered myself an outgoing person, but this was suddenly all so strange. I couldn't think of any way for me to know the proper way to act around a bunch of werewolves. I guess those books I'd read with all the werewolves and vampires were a little useful, but it wasn't like they were reference material. They were just something someone somewhere made up, hoping to entertain an audience.

The front door opened behind me and woodsy warmth broke my train of thought.

"You're right, it's quieter out here," Jonathan said as he sat down beside me, a box of fries in hand. He offered me a few and we ate in a silence that was much more companionable than I thought two strangers could ever know. I found myself relaxing in his presence.

Something else whispered through me and I suddenly found myself very self-conscious. I frowned. It had been nearly five days since my last shower, and I was still wearing the bloodstained sweatpants. I covered a growl of my own with the grunt of effort to get vertical again.

"Let me help you," Jonathan said, supporting my efforts to get up with an arm at my waist as he handed me the crutch.

Settling my weight onto the crutch I sighed, "I'm no whining puppy."

I started hopping toward the black Ram. I heard and felt Jonathan following me. Reaching for my bag on the ground next to the passenger door made the set of scabbed over wounds on my shoulder itch as it stretched. I grunted with the awkward effort, I turned to swing the duffel up on to my shoulder. My face stopped nearly an inch from Jonathan's chest, the scent of him making me lightheaded as his hand gently closed around my own on the handles of my bag. With a start, I realized I could hear his heart thumping in his chest.

"No one here thinks you weak," he said softly. "The strength of will alone that it takes to survive an attack has nothing to do with luck, despite what you may think."

I gingerly pulled my hand free—no, it's more accurate to say that he let me pull my hand free—and swallowed around something that was not quite fear and not quite self-pity. I closed my eyes and tried just to concentrate on breathing. His clothes rustled as he moved and, startled, I opened my eyes to find that I was looking at his back as he stalked toward the house with my bag. What the hell just happened?

"Everyone's out back," Jonathan said over his shoulder.

I shook my head and followed him in silence up the stairs and into the room where I'd been staying.

"I'll send Kaylah up to help you with the bandages." With slow, precise movements, as if he didn't want to spook me, he set the bag down on the armchair in the corner of the room.

I bit my lip, remembering the scrubbing from before. "Thank you, but I can get my own bandages this time, really."

Jonathan nodded and gestured to a room on the other side of the hall from this one. "Bathroom's there, towels under the sink."

Suddenly, I realized I stood between him and the door, effectively blocking his exit. Sheepishly, I hopped out of his way. He reached out and brushed the scar on my cheekbone with his knuckle as he passed me, a smile tugging at the corner of his mouth. I flinched at the touch, but something in my gut squirmed in a way not entirely unlike butterflies do about a high school crush. Only this wasn't high school, and I knew next to nothing about Jonathan.

Sighing, I pulled a change of clothes from my bag along with my toiletries and hobbled into the bathroom. I locked the door and rested my forehead against the frame for just a moment to catch my breath and clear my head of Jonathan's scent. Straightening up and setting my crutch against the vanity, I shrugged my hoodie off. A full-length mirror was mounted on the back of the door, and a wall-to-wall mirror rested above the vanity, bumping right up against the tub and shower door frame. The bathroom was well-lit, and—with all the mirrors—it was possible to see just about every angle of my body.

I swallowed around another lump in my throat and placed my rosary on the counter near the crutch. I found a towel and a washcloth under the sink, as Jonathan said, and put the washcloth in the shower stall. I pulled my borrowed tank top off to reveal fresh pink scars that slashed across and up the right side of my belly to just under my ribcage. I gingerly peeled the bandages of my itching shoulder—more red-pink scars mottled with dark brown scabs.

I frowned and turned away from the mirror as best I could while I worked the rest of the bandages off, including the splints for my left wrist and right thigh. I gently tried the mobility on my wrist and found that so long as I was careful, it was painless. No sudden movements with it for sure, and no carrying any real weight with it, but it wasn't completely useless at least. It had been just four days since I was attacked in the forest. Four days since those bones were destroyed. No human heals that fast. My vision blurred.

I reached over and turned the water on, managing to hobble under the spray of water hot enough to scald before the tears started. Maybe I could have explained everyone's scent and me having a particularly dexterous day with the keys, but no human heals that fast. I remembered the jaws clamping shut, crushing the bones in my wrist. Thoughts swarmed in my head, all wanting attention and answers all at once. There was no telling how I was to live my life now that I was…I sighed. Gonna have to get used to calling myself that sometime, right? And no time like the present, right?

Now that I was a werewolf.

They all seemed to have a pretty decent hold on their humanity. Certainly none of the ones I'd met so far seemed a danger to me. But what was to be done about my old circle of friends? We weren't terribly close, but still, what would I say to them? I lathered my hair.

'The world isn't ready for wolves.' Sheppard's words echoed in my head. What sort of things will I have to hide from my friends if I can't tell them about what I am now? And just what do wolves do for fun anyway? The water turned cold before I'd even realized I'd been in there that long. The warmest I could manage now was room temperature water. I scrubbed at my skin as best I could and turned off the water, my thoughts still swarming darkly.

I stepped out of the shower stall and the savory scent of grilled meat flooded my nostrils, making my stomach rumble. I toweled off and pulled on my favorite jeans and a comfy black top with long sleeves, leaving my feet bare. I skipped trying to replace the splints— there was no way I was going to get them properly repositioned on my own anyway—and combed my hair in the mirror.

I heard movement outside the bathroom door. Sheppard's warm familiar scent mixed with that of smokiness from the grill. I opened the door to find I was face to face with him, his golden-brown eyes boring into me.

"Breathe," he said, quiet command in the word, and I inhaled deeply. "If you try to go meet them like you are right now, they're all going to clamber all over each other to try to make it better. We protect. It's what we do and who we are down to the very core of our being. This is pack." Warmth shimmered in the air. "*You* are pack—but you will have to be there for them too. Pack takes care of pack."

I swallowed around a huge lump in my throat as I fought back the tears again. This warmth, it was how it was always supposed to be, I was sure of it. For a moment, I was certain that everything in my life had led me to be right where I needed to be when that crazed wolf went looking for its next target.

But then I realized that something had been hanging, unsaid, in the air with everyone. "There's a chance I won't survive the change." My heart pounded in my ears.

Sheppard pursed his lips and squeezed my shoulder. "It's true, many can't strike a balance with their wolf." He sighed. "But your wolf's not letting you go that easily."

I felt my eyes go wide and I stared past him. "My wolf—"

He smiled and nodded, placing a gentle kiss my forehead. "You just haven't let yourself quiet down enough to catch her. She's there—a part of you—and she's not going to let you go."

He stepped aside and gestured toward the room I'd been staying in. I picked up the crutch and my rosary, grasping the crucifix tightly and holding it to my chest. My wrist didn't throb. "I'll send Kaylah up with some of her tea. Calm yourself a bit before coming out back to meet everyone."

I nodded slowly. Sheppard left down the stairs and I hopped into my room. I sat on the bed and stared into nothing as I fiddled with the beads on the rosary. My wolf? I felt something stir in my gut. I ran a hand through my damp hair as Kaylah came into the room, a steaming mug in her hand. The smell of her tea made my nose crinkle and she smiled as she handed it to me.

"It's much weaker this time," she said. "Still good enough to calm ya down some."

I held the mug and gently swirled the yellow liquid contents. "So there's..." I did some quick math, "seven werewolves running around in the backyard."

Random shouts and yelling came in through the window, but I couldn't decipher the actual words. I took a sip of the tea, "Sounds like the beginning of some crazy joke."

Kaylah put a hand on my knee and, with her other hand, brushed some of my hair back behind my ear. "I know how you must feel. I still don't really understand what put me here. I just know that this is where I'm s'posed to be." She shrugged. "This is a good pack. Sheppard's a good leader for this pack."

Something haunted her eyes.

"The silly books get that part right at least."

"Hmm?" her eyes returned from the distant place they had just been.

"The alpha, he's the leader of the pack," I said. "The books I read all seem to agree that werewolf packs have alphas who lead them around and tell them what to do."

Kaylah smiled. "He's the leader and the protector of us. Sure, we all go huntin' and do stuff as a pack, but Sheppard's the glue. He keeps us all centered. Which is good since we're all made wolves here aside from him."

I took a big gulp of the tea before speaking again. "So, every single one of you used to be human."

"All but Sheppard," she confirmed. She took my injured wrist in her hands, rotating it around as she squeezed along the bones. It wasn't comfortable, but it didn't hurt.

Apparently, my wrist set to her satisfaction and she put my hand back in my lap as I took another sip of tea.

"None a that now," she said, eyeballing my mug. "Git the rest a that tea down already so you c'n calm yer nerves n' eat. I know yer hungry."

I dutifully gulped down the rest and handed her the empty mug.

She smiled expectantly as she rose from the bed. "Ready?"

I took a deep breath. "Now or never, right?"

A light laugh escaped her as she shook her head. "Nope, it's only now missy."

She helped me to my feet and put a steadying hand on my back as I hobbled with the crutch to the top of the stairs. Splint or no, my right leg still wasn't accepting any real weight. I was surprised at her strength as she helped me down the stairs.

5

KAYLAH'S HELP MEANT THAT SHE HAD MOSTLY JUST CARRIED THE CRUTCH downstairs for me as I leaned on her for support, but she handed it to me once we reached the landing. I looked up to find both the living room and the dining room beyond it empty. No one was seated at the large dark wood table, though its mismatched chairs seemed almost out of place. They may have all been the same color as the table, but no two styles were the same. The large picture window behind the table provided a nearly panoramic view of the backyard, where more than a handful of people played some sort of running game in the light of late afternoon.

Though the neighbors had wire and post fences, Sheppard's property didn't. The back line of his property was open to the woods and rocks beyond. But the view of the mountains was simply stunning. I had been in The Springs most of my life, and still never got tired of seeing the mountains to the west.

We passed through the eat-in kitchen, and Kaylah held the back door open for me. The crisp fall breeze carried the mixed scents of all the pack members, along with the smoky scent of charring meat and the earthy scent of potatoes. My stomach growled again as I stepped out the back door and onto a large patio, where long picnic tables and

45

Adirondack chairs filled most of the available pavement. Someone had set up a couple of folding tables along the house as well, with coolers underneath. Hamburger and hot dog buns filled the tables, along with all the requisite condiments, napkins, and plates. If they didn't shop at a big-box store, they probably cleared out the local grocery store's stock of all of it. Sheppard tended to a grill at the far end of the patio. It was almost as long as I was tall.

The pack raced across the yard, toward a shed on the back corner of the property, chasing someone who carried an old football. They tackled the lanky guy with close-cropped dark hair, tumbling over each other like puppies. They were all in t-shirts and jeans or sweat-pants. It was November. It should have been cold enough to warrant a coat, but even I was surprisingly comfortable. One by one, as they untangled themselves from the dogpile, they stood and watched my approach.

Crap.

I was immediately self-conscious of my hobbling gait and tried to adjust my steps to make it look like I only barely needed the crutch. I suspect I was not terribly successful, but in that moment, a part of me so desperately wanted to belong among them that I didn't want anyone to think for even a moment that I was a liability. I took a deep, steadying breath. They all stared at me, but at least Sheppard was smiling.

Sheppard looked at the pack and then back at me. "Everyone, this is Lynn." He gestured to me. "She is the one I told Matt to keep an eye on."

I still hadn't decided whether I was okay with that fact, despite my disquieting lack of distress about it.

I waved. "Hello." Like I said, I'm a stunning conversationalist. Jonathan caught my eye and winked at me.

"Lynn," Sheppard continued, spreading his arms to indicate everyone in the backyard. "This is the pack. You already know Matt, of course."

Matt crossed his arms and nodded to me.

"This is his mate, Chastity." He indicated the woman next to Matt.

She had burnished auburn hair that fell in spiral curls around her freckled face. Her hazel eyes met mine, sizing me up for a moment before she raised her hand in a quick greeting. She then hooked her arm against Matt's and moved half a step closer to him.

"You already know Jonathan, of course, and Kaylah." Sheppard pointed to a tall man with chocolate-brown eyes and short wavy hair. "That's Kaylah's mate, Daniel."

Daniel's face lit up with his smile as he waved.

"The pup over there is Jamie." Sheppard gestured to the lanky guy who had been tackled earlier. "He's Jonathan's little brother."

Well of course he was, his pale green eyes had the same gold flecks as his brother. He looked distinctly younger than the other wolves, except for maybe the slim guy next to him.

"Hi," Jamie said with a wave.

"And that's Ian, next to him," Sheppard continued.

Ian had mousy brown hair and sapphire-blue eyes. He had a hand in his pocket with the football tucked between his elbow and his body. He raised his other hand in a greeting and smiled at me.

"Food's not ready just yet, guys," Sheppard said. "Couple more minutes still."

It was like the dismissal bell for recess. Ian immediately tossed the ball across the yard to Daniel, who passed it off to Matt. He let the pack stalk toward him, pacing them around the yard for a moment before throwing the ball to Jamie. The pack redirected, and Jamie went down in a sea of arms and legs.

I pulled one of the Adirondack chairs over to watch their game. As I was about to sit down, Sheppard called my name. I turned and before I knew what happened, a hand came between my face and a can of soda. My hand. Cool liquid dripped down my forearm. Soda. I had not only caught the drink with my formerly shattered hand and wrist, but my apparent new-found strength had crushed the can. I dropped the mangled and soggy aluminum and shook some of the wetness off. My wrist ached dully.

Sheppard tossed me a towel and crossed his arms in satisfaction. He looked past me and nodded. I turned to see that it was Matt he had nodded to. Matt had the football in hand. My confusion only built as the pack tumbled into Matt, bringing him to the ground. Jonathan caught my eye and began to extricate himself, but then the football was in his hand and everyone tackled him.

Kaylah took over for Sheppard at the grill and Sheppard joined the pack. Sighing, I toweled off my sleeve and gingerly sat in the chair. My leg actually wasn't hurting much, but I didn't want to chance anything.

Jonathan appeared with a soda in one hand and a beer in the other. He offered both to me. I took the beer. It had been one hell of a day.

"Me too," he said as he exchanged the remaining soda for a beer as well. He only managed to get a single swig out of his beer before the football pegged him in the head. Jamie had a shit-eating grin, and Jonathan plopped his beer on the table, grabbed the ball from where it landed next to him, tossed it quick to Jamie, and then tackled his brother to the ground. It happened in kind of a blur, but they were both laughing, as were Ian and Daniel.

I laughed too and took a large gulp of my beer. It was bitter, but the cool felt nice as it slid into my belly.

I watched the game the wolves played. There certainly weren't teams, and no one kept any sort of score. Everyone just seemed to want to be rid of the ball as soon as they caught it. It was a letdown any time the ball hit the ground because someone didn't catch it. Chastity caught the ball next, and as the pack stalked her, she threw it to Matt. As before, the pack redirected, and Matt went down as the ball popped into the air. He snorted as he got up and jogged after Daniel, who had the ball and was looking for someone to throw it to. I finally started to grasp the game and found that I really wanted to play. Sheppard came up with the ball and suddenly, it was in my hands.

They all seemed to take a collective breath as my eyes widened. I tried to stand without the crutch. To my surprise, my leg held. It wasn't particularly steady, but it supported weight. Four days. Legs normally healed in what, months?

I took a few halting steps onto the grass. My leg wasn't arguing with me and I smiled to myself.

Matt moved toward me and the rest of the pack followed suit.

Like foolish prey, I started to jog, looking for someone to send the ball to. Daniel was out on his own. I tossed it his direction and the rest of the pack veered off toward the shed.

A heavy weight plowed into my left side, knocking me to the ground.

"Whoops," Jonathan said, something preternatural grinning impishly through his eyes.

I was not fooled. "Uh-huh," I said as he peeled himself off me and stood up. The pack ran by as he extended a hand to me and pulled me to my feet. "How's the leg?"

"Passable," I shrugged. "I won't be running a marathon in the morning, but it's holding weight."

"Glad to hear—" the football slammed into his gut, cutting him off. Dodging back the way he came, he ran off as the pack gave chase.

I turned to follow, but my leg gave way. With a yelp, I crumpled to the ground.

Ian jogged over first, his sapphire eyes filled with concern. "Too sharp of a turn without thinking about it and your leg just won't do it."

"So I noticed." I grunted as he looped an arm under me and helped me to stand. "I'd better go sit down."

He nodded as I turned toward my chair. I heard him growl and looked over my shoulder to see he had the ball again. Ian took off at a sprint as I limped back to the lawn chair. I sat down heavily as everyone dog-piled him. From there the game fizzled out as everyone's stomachs seemed to growl in unison—unless it was all of them growling in unison. Either way, the game was called on account of food.

It was remarkable timing, Kaylah had just smushed some of the burgers on the grill with the spatula, making the coals hiss and the fire jump, before she piled them onto a platter. She handed the spatula to Sheppard as she took the platter to the table with the buns.

He then piled hot dogs and chicken onto two more platters, which Kaylah then took to the table along with a foil pan full of cut up potatoes.

As the pack started to get their food, I maneuvered out of the chair and placed my beer down at one end of the picnic table. I intended to just wait till most of them were done to go over and grab mine, but Jonathan appeared next to me with two plates piled high with food.

"I dunno what you like on your burgers or your dogs," he said. "But I figured ketchup was at least a safe bet and maybe it'd save you the trip."

That was pretty freakin' thoughtful of him. I smiled. "Thanks. Ketchup will work just fine."

"Least I could do." He shrugged, taking a gulp of the beer he'd half-finished earlier.

As everyone sat down, I scooped some potatoes onto an empty plate along with a couple of pieces of chicken and a hamburger.

"Guess I wasn't so ready for the game after all," I said.

He smiled at me and took a bite of one of his hot dogs. "Still, not bad for someone who was lunch meat just four days ago."

I gave him a wry smile. "I suppose. People just don't heal this fast is all." I took a bite of the chicken. It was juicy, tender, and full of flavor. My eyes fluttered closed in appreciation.

"Right," Jonathan nodded. "People don't, but werewolves do. Attacks are the way most of the wolves in the world got to be as they are. Made wolves are much more common than born ones." He fell silent then, and I got the feeling he was somewhere else.

The only real sounds then were that of the pack eating, cans and bottles of soda and beer thumping lightly to the table in between bites. But it wasn't awkward at all. I was more comfortable around them than I had felt as a child with my own family.

"So Lynn," Daniel said around a bite of his food. "How did you get attacked anyway?"

"It happened during my morning run on the nature reserve," I answered, shoveling some potato into my mouth. I am such a meat-and-potatoes kind of girl.

Matt rolled his eyes. Well, he rolled the one. I think the milky one rolled too, but I couldn't be sure.

"You do work for the newspaper sometimes," he said. "You should have known better. It's a good thing I was there to save you."

Chastity smiled at him adoringly, her eyes wide like a baby deer, as she rubbed his arm.

"You're a reporter?" Kaylah asked, concern in her voice.

"Oh no," I replied, waving a hand. "I'm just a copy-editor." I took a sip of my beer. "After four days without giving them any kind of notice or updates, it's likely they won't be picking up my services anymore."

At least I wouldn't have to deal with their holier-than-thou bullshit anymore. "Besides, I had gone hiking through those trails for years now and started running them last year. There aren't actually any wolves in Colorado anymore, aside from the ones at that sanctuary outside of town, so I wasn't actually concerned for my safety until the thing crashed into me."

"Well you're safe now," Sheppard said as he went for seconds.

"But aren't your parents worried about you?" Chastity asked.

I shook my head. "Nope. My mother died a couple of years ago. Dad left for Europe after the funeral and pretty much never came back." He certainly wasn't going to be worried sick at me not calling him.

I guess Jonathan had come back from wherever his mind had wandered off to, because he took a bite from the hot dog in my hand as Sheppard sat back down.

"Hey!" I shouted, laughing. "Get your own!"

His face lit up. "*There* it is! You know, that sullen face you seem to get when you haven't figured out all this wolf stuff yet isn't *nearly* as good as your smile."

Something in my gut jumped. "And all the girls just line up around the corner for that stuff, don't they?"

His laugh was rich and full. "Something like that."

Making a face at him, I shoved the last bite of hot dog into my mouth and washed it down with another swig of beer.

He smiled at me then, and I returned the smile as I finished the chicken from my plate.

It would be night soon. The pack filtered back into the house as the light faded. Chastity and Kaylah took the platters into the kitchen. The opening music and explosions of some action movie started in the living room.

The distance returned to Jonathan's eyes. "Jamie and I were attacked on a hunting trip with my dad," he said. "We got a ten-point buck, and my father was cleaning it while Jamie and I went hiking to gather more firewood. That was when we were attacked. It got Jamie first, and I thought he was dead, so I just," he spread his hands, "stopped feeling. Before I even understood what was happening, the wolf was dead with the head of my axe buried at the base of it's skull. It was such a lucky hit, it was like an act of God. Sheppard had tracked that thing for two days. When he smelled the blood, he came running and found us all torn to shreds. My father didn't survive the attack." He drank the last of his beer, took a deep breath, and was back here again. "Which is to say that there isn't a single one of us who doesn't understand exactly what you're struggling with right now."

Something in the sky caught his attention and he looked up, squinting his eyes. "Hey, what's *that*?" He pointed skyward.

As I looked up, I saw him reach to where my beer was and heard the thump of his empty bottle settling onto the table. The joke was on him, mine was empty too. With a smirk, I locked eyes with him. "Darn," I said, my tone flat. "Looks like we'll both need a new one." My heart pounded in my ears.

Without a word, he stood and obliged, digging two more beers out of the coolers under the food table. As he sat back down, I slowly let out a breath I didn't know I had been holding.

My plate was empty, and only a couple of potatoes remained on the plates Jonathan had brought over. Wow. "I don't know how I'm going to get used to eating like this."

He nodded. "We do tend to eat a lot, but we don't have to. I've heard we can go up to two weeks without food if we need to. It's probably not comfortable, though." He smirked. "And you don't really have to worry about packing on extra pounds. Our metabolism just doesn't work the same way a human's does." Color rose in his cheeks. "So your figure will likely stay as great as it is now."

My gut did that squirmy jump thing again and I looked away, sure I was blushing, and drained half my beer.

"I used to dream at night about being a wolf sometimes." I don't know why I said that. It was true, of course. I'd been having those dreams since sometime back in high school. But I don't know why I told him.

"Hm? Was it like this?"

I rolled my eyes at myself and shook my head. "You're just asking because I said something. It's silly."

"No really," he said, touching my knee with his warm hand. "Tell me."

"Not quite like this." I looked at him. "I won't really know, I guess, until the full moon. But I've dreamt of changing, of struggling with it, and the release of just letting go."

I closed my eyes and took in a deep breath of the night air. Something tugged at my gut in a way that hunger hadn't. A finger traced the scar on my face and my eyes snapped open. I didn't flinch away this time.

Smiling, Jonathan spoke in conspiratorial tones, "Y'know, Dreamer, I think your wolf has been a part of you for longer than you think."

6

EARLY THE NEXT MORNING, EVERYONE PILED INTO CARS AN HEADED OUT
to a local diner at Sheppard's behest. The place was full of the smells
of breakfast. Park rangers in full uniform sat with their morning
coffee and newspaper, a few groggy businessmen hurriedly shoveled
eggs and bacon down, and a lone artist sketched on a pad of paper in a
corner booth.

"Mornin' Shep," the hostess said. She was easily past retirement
age, with shrewd eyes and grey-white hair. She had a pencil tucked
behind her ear and the sleeves of her crisp white shirt were rolled up
to the elbows. "Give us a few and we'll have your corner ready. Y'all're
early today."

Sheppard smiled at her. "Thanks Dolores."

A few moments later, we were ushered to a private dining area.
Three wooden tables were pushed together in the far corner with a
red checkered tablecloth thrown over the whole thing to give enough
room for everyone to have a place at the same table. Honey pots and
little pitchers of milk were stationed at intervals on the table and
enough places were set with glasses of water for all, plus a couple of
extras.

"I'll get the steaks on and be right back with your eggs," Dolores said, pouring coffee into everyone's mugs as we took our seats. She eyed me. "Hey there newcomer," she said, an easy friendliness in her voice. "How'd you like your steak, hun?"

I was never the breakfast type. "Just the coffee and some toast for me please," I demurred. They were having steak for breakfast? Crazy —but my stomach growled at the thought.

Dolores clicked her tongue and exchanged a look with Sheppard. She nodded at me. "Medium-rare—got it."

I opened my mouth to object, but she hurried off to help the customers who had just stepped through the door. I looked to Sheppard. "I thought you said the world wasn't ready for..." I lowered my voice to a whisper and nodded my head in the direction Dolores went. "You know."

He laughed as he poured some honey into his coffee. "Dolores thinks I run some sort of halfway house that takes in the strays of society and gets them all set up to rejoin the normal world."

Honey in coffee? I'd never heard of such a thing.

"She's not far from the truth of it really," Jonathan said as I poured a bit of honey into my coffee as well.

I took a sip, savoring the flavor. It was surprisingly good. I added a bit more honey until it was to my liking, and realized I liked it better than sugar.

"I've been coming here for years." Sheppard smiled. "I just haven't bothered to correct her." He shrugged. "No need to."

"Besides," Kaylah said. "The food here is jus' delish. They got themselves a new chef last year, an' he really knows how to fix a steak."

Dolores appeared with plates full of scrambled eggs on a tray. Serving everyone she said, "I'll be back in just a moment with your steaks, don't you worry."

"You're the best, Dolores," Sheppard said.

"And don't you go forgettin' it, neither," she replied, winking at him.

A few moments later, Dolores was back with plates of steaks for everyone, serving Sheppard first and then going around the table. "Now I'll leave you folks alone to chat," she said, refilling everyone's coffee mug. "One of you'uns come grab me when you're ready for the check. And take your time y'all, there's no hurry."

When she was gone, Sheppard looked to Matt. "Tell the pack what you found tracking the wolf that attacked Lynn."

Matt finished a bite of steak. "Nothing good, of course.There's a cave on the northwest corner of the reserve with four crazed were-wolves in cages. I don't know what put them there or who's holding them." He gulped down some coffee. "But inside, it looks like the damn bastards slaughtered one of us and used the blood for paint. It made it impossible for me to investigate further. There could be almost anything going on there."

"We'll have to get the wolves out first." Sheppard finished his eggs. "They may not actually be crazed, just unable to control themselves in that cave thanks to the blood."

I was horrified, and something in me affirmed that those wolves in the cages could not just be left there. "Why would the blood on the walls make things harder?"

Kaylah reached over and put a hand on my knee. "Ain't no concentrating going on when the bloodlust hits."

"We are protectors, Lynn," Sheppard explained. "Down to the core of who we are. There is no denying it. To know that you are walking into a place where your brethren were slaughtered means the chances of you keeping your head and acting rationally are abysmally slim."

"I could smell humans too," Matt said, making a face. "Which means there's a chance that the wolves are being fed human flesh."

Sheppard growled, the sound rumbling deep in his chest. My stomach turned and I dropped my fork.

Kaylah pressed a glass of water into my hand. "Drink, hun. Stay with us." I took a breath and gulped down some of the icy cold liquid.

Jonathan squeezed my hand. I hadn't even realized he was holding it. His woodsy scent cut through my nausea.

"Lean on your wolf, Dreamer," he breathed into my ear. "She knows what to do."

Closing my eyes, I focused on my breathing. In and out. In and out.

"I could hear a generator running," Matt said. "And I'm pretty sure there was a work lamp, so there's definitely power running through the cave."

"What could—or would—hold crazed werewolves captive?" Jamie's eyes were wide. "Why would anyone want to?"

Something thumped against the table. Startled, I opened my eyes. Sheppard had a white-knuckled fist resting on the table. He must have hit it in frustration.

"Vampires," he said, the word more growl than anything. "They're searching for their cure."

"How can you be sure?" Chastity asked around a bite of steak.

"It's the only thing that makes any sense," Sheppard answered. "They think werewolves can bridge the gap. And since crazed ones are so violent by nature, they must figure they're one of any number of missing links."

Matt clenched his fist so hard it bent the fork over in his hand. I had read about the tension in a room being so thick you could cut it with a knife. I finally understood that turn of phrase, but what sort of cure would the vampires be after?

"That explains the rise in the vamp numbers here lately," Ian said. "They need expendable test subjects."

"Test subjects? What sort of cure are they looking for?" I tried not to think about the wolf crunching into my wrist. If it weren't for Matt, I would have been in that wolf's belly. I took another gulp of ice water.

"To explain that," Sheppard said before gulping down some of his coffee. "I'm going to have to go way back to how they first came about." He sighed and looked around the table, his eyes settling on me. "It's the story of how we came to be as well. It reaches all the way back to when Jesus himself hung on the cross."

My eyebrows shot up. Werewolves stemmed from biblical times? That definitely wasn't in any book I read.

"It is told in the Bible and other religious texts that Jesus cried out to God, asking why He had forsaken him." Sheppard ran a hand through his sandy blond hair. "Some scholars say that this is him referencing an earlier psalm, but the truth of it is that it was in his moment of doubt that he was speared by the Romans, who had taken up the dark sport of poking at him while he hung."

How awful. I looked around the table as I took another sip of my coffee. The pack was still and quiet, enraptured by Sheppard's story.

"A few drops of blood landed on the lips of one of the soldiers who speared him. That soldier licked his lips and was forever changed." His smile was grim. "He became a sharp-toothed monster of the night, with talons that could easily rip through flesh. His bite alone was enough to turn a human into a demon like him."

Vampires were actual demons? That had to be a figure of speech. I narrowed my eyes as I shoveled a bite of eggs into my mouth.

"Entire villages were laid to waste in the nights that followed. The demons roamed the night, killing everything in their path: men, women, children, livestock—if it bled, it died." He took a bite of his steak. "Worse, many stood up from their deaths to join the ranks of the demons. What little there was of the church at the time was frantic. They knew they must find a way to put a stop to these creatures and protect humanity."

Well that certainly makes sense. The deadliest weapon known to man at that time was simply a bow and arrow. And if vampires were as dangerous as the pack seemed to think, or even half as dangerous as any of my novels indicated, an arrow was unlikely to even slow them down.

Sheppard took another sip of his coffee. "So, they took the cross, the nails, and the crown of thorns and used what blood they could pull from them to create something that could fight back. Thus, the wolves were given life." He spread his hands wide. "They were faster than their human counterparts, as strong as the demons, and—unlike their prey—able to move about in the daylight."

Ooh! A part the novels got right! Only that was little relief, really.

"But," Sheppard said. "While the vampires were unnatural things that roamed the Earth long after their time had passed, the wolves were not quite immortal—the church did not want to damn them to eternal life without the release and blessing of God's kingdom." He folded his hands in front of him. "The wolves hunted in the daytime—

protecting the weak—so that when night fell and the demons stirred, no more villages would fall."

Something swelled in my chest. As I looked around, the pack all seemed to be sitting just a little straighter in their chairs. Protectors. Each and every one of them.

"As time wore on, the vampires learned to hide themselves better and the wolves found a rift amongst their own kind: some found themselves questioning the church, turning instead to protect the natural balance of things as God had made them; while the others held to a dogmatic, unwavering loyalty to their creators."

"Cool," I said. "So, I get a pamphlet now, right?"

Jonathan elbowed me, his eyes glittering, and his mouth turned up in a smile.

Sheppard blinked at me.

"I just mean it sounds like you drank the Kool-Aid," I said. "Is this what they teach in the werewolf churches?"

I wasn't a regular church-goer, but when my mom was still alive, we had been to mass on the major holidays like Christmas and Easter.

Jonathan's smile had turned to a quiet snicker. Ian and Jamie joined him.

Sheppard shook his head. "I suppose the story does sound like dogma, doesn't it?" He leaned back in his chair. "But it was what I was taught when I was growing up, and it's what is widely accepted as the truth."

And it rang true in me, too. I couldn't explain it, but it just felt like he was right.

"Yea, but now the vampires seek to right themselves," Matt said, agitation in his voice. "And become true masters of their nature instead of being bound to the darkness." His spicy musk scent gained an edge to it that prickled my nose. "They believe they were always meant to walk in the daylight and that humanity is meant to serve them. They assume that something simply went wrong when they became what they are."

I couldn't follow the agitation in Matt. It was almost directed at me. Or it had something to do with me. I couldn't quite pinpoint it, but I felt uneasy and leaned away from him in my chair.

He sat back, crossed his arms, and looked at Sheppard. "But I don't get what the point is in telling *her* any of this." He jerked his chin toward me. "We may just have to kill her at the full moon anyway."

"Matt!" Sheppard's voice barked, but I had already shot from my chair.

"What?!" My eyes must have been as wide as dinner plates.

Matt leaned forward in his chair, keeping his arms crossed. He met my eyes with his clear and milky gaze. "If you go crazy at the change, on the night of the full moon, there's nothing to be done for you. So, there's no point to telling you any of this."

Oh God, he was serious. I don't know how I knew for sure, but I could feel he wasn't lying. I backed away slowly.

Sheppard stood up, his eyes wary and his hands open in front of him. "Lynn—"

"You might have to kill me?!"

I didn't give him a chance to respond, I just ran. Out the door of the diner, out into the parking lot, out to the sidewalk along the street. I needed to get away from them. They might have to kill me? What the ever-loving fuck? What the goddamn hell was the point of making sure I met pack or anything if they were just going to have to kill me? Why save me at all? Tears streamed down my face, but I wiped them with the back of my hand and kept running.

"Lynn!" Sheppard's voice came from behind me. His footfalls echoed on the pavement.

I shook my head and tried to run faster. I had to get away from him—from all of them. He knew where I lived.

"Lynn!" His voice was closer now.

Oh god, I was going to have to figure out a way to get into the witness protection program or something. They'd lock me up in a mental institution and throw away the key. I needed to hide from a pack of werewolves? Really? How the hell does one do such a thing? I wiped at my face again.

"Grace Lynn Cartwright!" Something vibrated in the air, but it didn't matter. I froze.

The footfalls stopped when I did.

I turned around, slowly, and looked the mountain-of-a-man in the eyes. I didn't stand a chance if it came to blows. "How do you know that name?"

Sheppard took a few steps toward me, closing the distance until I took a step backward. Nodding, he stopped.

"I told you," he said. "Pack doesn't keep secrets."

I lifted my chin, maintaining eye contact with him. "Then why didn't you tell me about that?!" I gestured back toward the diner.

He put his hands up in a placating gesture as another vibration wafted through the air. He took a couple more steps and I stood my ground, despite the fear that trailed down my back like an icy bead of sweat.

"I chose not to tell you that," Sheppard said, nodding back toward the diner. "I could have, but it would have changed nothing." He took another step closer. "You were bitten. You will change. You will either make peace with your wolf, or you won't. These are absolute facts, Lynn." He smacked the back of his hand into the palm of the other. "Knowing them doesn't change anything. You're angry, and you're scared—and that makes sense. But don't let that lead you to stupid decisions."

I heard what he wasn't saying. "And running home, away from you and the pack, is stupid because there's a vampire there."

He spread his hands. "You smelled him as well as I did."

I narrowed my eyes and shook my head. "No. You told me that was vampire. But it just smelled of rot, decay, and dead things."

Sheppard crossed his arms and looked at me the way a disappointed father would look at a toddler throwing a tantrum. "And does rot and death smell like something you want to be around?" His voice was incredibly calm and patient. "What do your instincts tell you?" He arched an eyebrow at me.

My instincts were telling me that he wasn't as full of shit as I wanted to believe he was. Which made it really hard for me to stay angry. "They say no, I don't." I huffed and raked a hand through my hair. "But I can't trust my instincts." I let my arm fall to my side. "They aren't even mine!" My vision blurred.

Sheppard sighed, his expression softening. "No. They're your wolf's right?"

I nodded.

He took a step closer. His toes were almost touching mine. He lifted my chin with a crooked finger, looking me in the eyes. "She doesn't survive without you," he said, and lightly tapped my nose.

I sighed. He at least meant no harm to me right now. I was certain of that, somehow.

"Listen," he said. "You and your wolf are two sides of the same coin." He fished a quarter out of his pocket and laid it flat on his palm. "Right now, you think the coin is glued to the pavement. But after the full moon, after your first change, you'll find you can not only pick up the coin, you can flip it over." He flipped the coin in his palm. "You'll realize then that it was never glued down, you just weren't paying close enough attention yet."

Two sides of the same coin. You know, I just could buy that...for a quarter.

I crossed my arms. "But how does that make any difference on what Matt said?"

Sheppard huffed out a breath. "He's not wrong." There was a deep pain in the words. "I hate when it happens. That's why I try to make a new wolf feel as welcome as possible in my pack. Then there's less to fight against, and they seem to have a better chance."

I guess that made sense. It would be harder to fight something if you felt like you belong to it.

He wiped at his face. "Matt shouldn't have just blurted it out to you. And he won't apologize for it, either. But I will. I'm sorry Lynn, for scaring you, for making you feel like your life is in imminent danger." He sighed. "But it's in our best interests if you do survive. I swear to you that this pack doesn't want any harm at all to come to you."

"How is it in your best interest? Are bigger packs better or something?"

Sheppard pressed his lips into a line and shook his head. "They are, but it's actually because of who you are that makes you a huge asset to our pack."

I rolled my eyes. "Sure. A lonely copy-editor who lives paycheck-to-paycheck is exactly what your pack needs. I'm practically indispensable, really." I couldn't keep the sarcasm from my voice.

Except it didn't feel like he was making light of things.

He gave me another fatherly smile. "I had Matt follow you and protect you from the vampires in this town because of your bloodline —because of who you're related to."

"I never did one of those DNA mapping things," I said. "You'll have to spell it out for me."

"You are what is referred to as *consanguinea*," Sheppard said. "It means that you are a direct descendent of the family of Christ."

"Like hell I am."

But there had been certainty in his voice when he said it. Even if I had trouble believing it, I was certain he did. And then the world seemed to tilt, the air too thin.

Sheppard caught me before I lost my balance, but my vision was unfocused.

"This is too much," I whispered. "I'm just a girl." The tears flowed freely from my eyes.

He brushed my hair back and kissed the top of my head. "You have never been just a girl, Lynn. That's why Matt had to watch out for you. I wanted him to make sure you never had to know about any of this."

Now that I was steady on my feet, he held my face and brushed a tear away with his massive thumb.

"I'm not sorry for what happened," he said gently. "You are far safer with pack than you could ever be alone." He released my head and grasped my hands. "This is who you are now, Lynn, and you deserve to understand the whole of it."

I sighed, staring at nothing where the curb met the road.

Sheppard placed a gentle hand on top of my head and something stirred deep in my gut. Something inside me was waking. Warmth from his hand spread through every limb of my body and I breathed it in as it displaced the crisp November air. My breath caught in my throat as I felt her. My wolf. She was there—steadfastly leaning into me, lending me her strength. I would never be alone again.

In that moment, I realized that when Jonathan had been flirting with me, I hadn't felt butterflies. I had felt my wolf, nudging me. The pull in my gut after I showered yesterday was her lending me her strength. The panic of what happened to me—and the fear of what my life was to be—crumbled away beneath our combined power. Suddenly I felt so undeniably strong.

My vision refocused, and I found myself staring the alpha straight in the eyes. It took me a moment to realize it was a clear challenge. Not what I wanted to do. I pulled my bottom lip between my teeth, looked down, and thumped my head into his chest as he hugged me.

"Welcome to the pack," Sheppard whispered.

7

SHEPPARD STEERED ME BACK TO THE PACK. THE REST OF THE DAY blurred for me. Something inside me was certain he hadn't been lying. My wolf. She was sure of the truth of his words. Still, I replayed them over and over in my mind until I was certain the story was written on my bones.

But I just had so many questions. They tumbled into and over one another in my mind. I couldn't even pick out the words to a question without arriving at three more.

At some point, I must have made my way up to my room and fallen asleep. I awoke with a grunt as my shoes landed on me sometime soon after dawn.

"Up and at 'em, pup," Matt said, tossing me a pair of my sweatpants. "Let's go."

Not exactly my ideal way of waking up. I squinted at him in annoyance. He was decidedly more bright-eyed and bushy-tailed than I thought should be legal for this time of morning.

I rubbed the sleep from my eyes and stretched, a yawn escaping me. "Go where? What for?"

"Every morning, for as long as I was watching you at least, you went running," Matt explained. "It was your morning routine. Time to regain some normality."

He looked at me expectantly and I realized he wasn't taking no for an answer, nor was he interested in allowing me any privacy.

"Excuse me, then" I said, eyeing the door to my room.

Matt looked confused, and then he got it. "Hah. Get used to skin, little lady, everyone here has seen everyone else naked. Lots. Clothes don't play nice with the change."

And then he stood there, fists on his hips.

I pursed my lips and narrowed my eyes at him. I was determined to keep at least a little of my modesty around this relative stranger. I brought the sweatpants under the blanket and squirmed my way into them. Swinging my legs out over the edge of the bed, I took the socks he handed me and tugged them on, followed by my running shoes, which were bloodstained but intact despite the attack. Gingerly, I put my feet on the ground and stood, but there was no pain.

I sighed in relief before following him downstairs.

Jamie lazily eyed us from where he and Ian laid on the couches in the living room, but neither said anything. Matt and I stepped out into the crisp morning air, but said nothing.

Dew clung to the grass and a light fog swirled around our legs as we walked around the neighborhood and out onto the main road, where we broke into an even-paced jog. Mostly, we ran in companionable silence, our footfalls matching in rhythm. Running cleared my head, letting all my questions go silent for now. A soft sigh of contentment moved through me. My wolf, I realized, was also grateful for the activity.

"So the wolf that changed you really must've had it out for your face," I said in a careful tone. Only way to find out if it's a sore topic is to touch on it, right?

Matt frowned for a moment, then smirked. "Nah, the wolf that changed me left scars here," he gestured to his right thigh and hip. "And on my back."

His back? He must have been taken completely off guard by the wolf that changed him.

He gestured to his face. "This was from a bear." He smirked again. "Pretty sure I deserved it really."

"Remind me not to run through the forest with you."

"Good luck with that," he said flatly. "I go to the forest nearly every time one of the pack does."

"Why is that?"

"Because I'm the best fighter," he said. "That's why Sheppard chose me to watch you."

"What does being the best fighter have to do with it? Aren't you guys—" I caught on my words. "I mean, aren't we the apex predator out there?"

"Minus the vamps, yes," he replied. "And I wouldn't want any of us going up against any number of vampires without backup. Pack looks out for pack."

I nodded. "So if you're the best fighter, how come you're not the alpha?"

Matt chuckled. "Have you paid any attention at all, girl? I'm too hot-headed for it." He paused a moment. "And I'd be bad at it. I've watched Sheppard care for the pack through good and bad. It's a pain in the ass. Frankly, the power he has scares me. I'm just a fighter, and I'm good at killing vampires. I'm happy to be a part of his pack."

We ran the rest of the way back to Sheppard's in silence, walking the last couple of blocks to cool down, though I wasn't even winded.

The smell of eggs and sausage made my mouth water before we opened the front door.

Inside, the house was abuzz with motion. I caught the scent of Jonathan and found him in the kitchen. He tossed a bottle of water my direction without quite looking at me.

"Thanks," I said, catching it. I guzzled down the water like I'd just left a desert. Something wasn't quite right with his scent. It was sharper than it should have been, more electric. Something growled in my gut. I could have sworn my wolf was saying "mistake." I felt eyes on me and saw Chastity glancing between me and the eggs she scrambled in the pan. Her already unobtrusive scent seemed muted. I felt like I was catching on, and my wolf nudged me to comfort Chastity.

"I'm sorry," I blurted out as I put a hand on her shoulder. Why did I say that?

Matt's spicy scent had a sharp edge to it as well as he stepped into the kitchen. Lightly running a hand down Chastity's arm, he kissed her forehead and she smiled, her scent returning to normal. I furrowed my brow.

"Shower's open," Ian called from upstairs.

"Ooh!" I put my empty bottle on the counter next to the sink. "Dibs!"

I darted up the stairs and into my room. Grabbing clothes, I stepped into the bathroom and shut the door behind me. My leg ached dully with the exertion of the run, but it was negligible compared to how it felt even yesterday. With my shirt off, I could see that nearly all the scabs had become fresh skin with a little pink scarring. Many of the marks that had been pink just yesterday had lost much of their color. As I scrubbed myself clean under the shower, what few scabs I did have, came off. The warmth of the water soothed the ache of my leg and I resolved that I would get some answers as soon as I was clothed again.

8

AFTER I DRESSED, I CALLED DOWN TO INDICATE THE SHOWER WAS FREE and scented out Sheppard. It didn't take long—he was sequestered in the office at the end of the upstairs hall.

"Come on in," he called as I knocked.

I stepped in and gently closed the door behind me. The whole room smelled of old books and leather with a hint of electronics. To my right, a pair of leather chairs sat on either side of a round dark wood coffee table. A dark wood bookcase filled with leather-bound tomes stood against the left wall, their gilded titles glinting in the light streaming from a window opposite the door. Sheppard sat at a desk of the same dark wood directly to my left, hands resting over the keyboard. He frowned at a block of text that was open in his email window. He clicked 'send' and then looked at me expectantly.

"Can you prove it?" I asked.

"*Consanguinea?*" he replied.

I nodded.

"Of course I can." He opened an application on the computer. "We've been tracking them for centuries, technology has just made it that much easier." He stood and gestured for me to sit in the chair.

On the screen was a highly intricate family tree. He moved the cursor and highlighted where my name and birth date fell on the diagram. Scrolling back, I found my own immediate family, of course, but also well-known names like Elvis Presley, Albert Einstein, and Leonardo Da Vinci. I skipped past entire sections, but on and on it went for generations and generations, all tracing back to the siblings of Jesus himself.

"Holy…" I whispered. "How on Earth do you have all of this documented?!"

"Well it was all rather painstaking and hard to see on the whole before this database was developed," Sheppard explained. "This just took a lot of the guesswork out of it. Interestingly, none of the popes have been on this chart."

"So my father is this, con-sang-ee-"

"*Consanguinea*," Sheppard corrected.

"Con-sang-win-ay-uh," I sounded out. He nodded. "Then my father is too, right? What does that mean though, exactly?"

"Only that your lineage goes straight back to the family of Jesus of Nazareth." Sheppard shrugged. "It means either your mother or father and then either their mother or father was the son or daughter of someone else whose mother or father was a direct descendant of the bloodline. It sounds confusing, but that's why we mapped it out like this." He inclined his head toward the screen.

Confusing is right. I can't even imagine the sort of logical leaps they had to make to try to keep track of it before the application on the computer.

"Jesus had four brothers and two sisters," Sheppard said. "Each of their firstborn was *consanguinea*, as were the firstborn of each generation after."

I stood as the realization dawned on me. "My father's in danger too!" I exclaimed. "I have to warn him!" I mean, sure, he and I hadn't spoken since his last check-in with me months ago, but I didn't want him to get killed!

Sheppard gestured to a phone similar to Jonathan's: the latest and greatest model, a sleek black thing, placed on the corner of the desk. "It has the card from your old phone in it."

Great. I'd worked hard to stay away from these stupidly absurd things since their inception, but now he was just giving me one. It'd probably be rude to tell him I didn't want it. And if I was pack...well then, they probably wanted an easy way to reach me. I picked up the phone and pressed the button on the side. The screen blinked on, and though it took a few tries, I found my contact list and scrolled to my dad's number.

"Call if you must," he said, "but just hear me out first."

My finger hovered over the call icon, but I looked to Sheppard.

"It's unlikely your father is in any real danger," Sheppard explained. "The vampires seek to right themselves, but—as far as we know—they haven't figured out how to track *consanguinea*. So they just take blind shots in the dark. Most of the time, they get it wrong. It's far easier for them to make a drunk college student at a bar disappear than someone like your father."

My wolf growled at the thought.

"So they like easy prey." I sat back down.

"It's the only way they stay under the radar," he replied. "Just as the world isn't ready for werewolves, it's certainly not ready for vampires. At least we're not overtly threatening." He grinned in a way that was decidedly predatory, and I squirmed in the chair. "But we're scary enough that the general populace would still be afraid. No one is particularly fond of things that go bump in the night."

"So you had Matt follow me because I was the sort of easy prey the vampires would like." Peachy.

"No." Sheppard shook his head. "I smelled you in a bar back in March. But then the military came to me about a month ago with news of a *consanguinea* in my territory. I knew who they were talking about. That's when I had Matt start watching you."

"It's been..." I did some quick math, March to November. "Eight months since you smelled me in that bar." March had been my birthday. It must have been one of the times I went out with Jenny and Steph.

"How did you connect my smell from back then to who the military talked to you about seven months later?"

71

He looked me square in the eye, "I never forget a *consanguinea*."

That was uncomfortable. I looked away.

"But wait," I said, hooking a strand of hair behind my ear. "This is just a family tree." I gestured to the computer screen. "You could have made all of this up and I wouldn't know the difference. This doesn't actually prove anything."

He smiled at me then, his golden-brown eyes glittering with an approval that was almost tangible. Nodding, he pulled his phone from his back pocket and leaned against the desk. "The only reason you're not sitting there like a strung-out junkie looking for their next fix is because of your bloodline."

I furrowed my brow. "What the hell do you mean by that?"

He took a slow breath, his face calculating. "What do you know about your friend? The tall man with the dark hair."

I cocked my head at him. "You understand that's kind of my type, don't you?"

He smiled. "Frederick was the name Matt overheard. Have you ever seen him in the daylight?"

What the hell kind of cheesy question is that? Had I ever seen Frederick in the daylight? I mean, come on. He was my friend—a great dancer, and far better conversationalist than me. We had gone out clubbing with my friends a number of times. But I thought about it.

"Well, no," I said, "but that could just make him a goth."

Which I had always assumed he was.

"Did you ever wake up with a stiff neck in the morning after going out with him the evening before?" Sheppard asked the question like he already knew the answer.

I froze. It had happened a number of times, actually. With the what little free cash I was able to squirrel away now and again, I had been cycling through brand after brand of pillows trying to find one that *wouldn't* make my neck stiff.

He tapped the screen of the phone in his hand a few times and then turned it so I could see a picture of skin with two neat little puckered pink scars. I stared, uncomprehending.

"That's on the back of your neck," he said growling. "That worthless bloodsucker had been feeding on you."

No. That didn't make any sense. It wasn't like it was a logical leap to agree that vampires were real if werewolves were, but that my friend is one? And he *fed* on me?! My heart thumped against my ribcage.

"T-there—" I stuttered. "That's just a picture you pulled off the internet."

He gestured toward the door. "The bathroom's down the hall. Go see for yourself if you don't believe me."

There was a seething anger to his words, but it was tempered with restraint. He was pissed, but I was relatively certain he wasn't pissed at me.

I raced to the bathroom and turned on the light. I leaned my head, craning my neck so that I could use the mirror on the medicine cabinet door to catch my reflection in the wall-to-wall mirror above the vanity. A cold shock ran down my spine. Right there, behind and below my left ear, closer to the back of my neck. The same pinprick puckered scars that Sheppard had just shown me. I ran my fingers over the slightly raised scars. I couldn't recall when the first stiff-necked morning was. Tears welled in my eyes, and my heart pounded. Self-conscious, I covered them with my hand as I slowly walked back to the office at the end of the hallway.

Sheppard hugged me as I returned and closed the door to the office, shutting us in. Tears streamed down my face.

"That was another thing we had hoped to protect you from," he said slowly as I wiped at my face with my hands.

He guided me to the chair and handed me a box of tissues from one of the shelves. I pulled my knees to my chest, setting my bare feet on the edge of the chair.

"Another thing we *failed* to protect you from."

I pulled a couple of tissues from the box and dabbed at my eyes.

The quiet anger was back in his voice. "The club that vampire—Frederick—frequents is a stronghold in the city. Our pack isn't large or strong enough to raid it yet."

I squirmed in the chair and looked away, balling up my used tissue, as I tried to push swarming thoughts into order so I could ask questions.

"But these," I gestured to my neck. "What does being fed on have anything to do with me being *consanguinea?*"

Sheppard closed his eyes, composing himself. "Humans get addicted to being fed on. The vampires make them forget, but it doesn't matter. Something in their bite makes a human—a sheep— seek out the vampire that fed on them over and over until the blood-sucker eventually kills them."

My wolf lurched in me at that. It was a sensation I didn't under-stand, but I knew there was something she was trying to say.

He met my eyes, and I was certain his were more golden then they had been moments before. "But that doesn't happen to *consanguinea*. The blessing within their bloodline protects them." He nodded at me. "You've been fed on enough by that vampire that you should be antsy and agitated, looking for whatever way you can escape to go to him, so he could feed on you again."

"But I'm not," I said. "Because I'm *consanguinea*."

"Exactly."

I let the silence stretch a moment. I couldn't keep focusing on the scars on my neck—the violation. It was too much. Swallowing around that stupid lump in my throat again, I blew out my breath slowly, trying to compose myself. "What does being *consanguinea* have to do with this 'cure' the vampires are looking for?"

Sheppard leaned against the windowsill. I turned the chair to face him.

"They think that because they were made from the blood of Christ, they can use direct descendants to fix the monster they became. As far as we can tell, they think the accident of their existence is that they can't walk in the day and that they can't reproduce without exchanging blood with a human."

"How did a few drops of Christ's blood create such monsters?" If I'm going to be thrown into this fight—and it looked like I was, no matter if I wanted it or not—I had better understand why.

"It wasn't just his moment of doubt," Sheppard replied. "As Christ suffered on the cross, he took on the weight of all the world's sins from now until the end of time—the evil of all those sins—so that they may die with him and be forgiven. In his moment of doubt, he was guilty of every sin humanity could ever conceive. But with his death, the blood was cleansed, and the sins were forgiven."

I leaned forward, resting my elbows on my knees. "Sounds like that puts you and your pack firmly on the 'unwavering loyalty to the church' side of things."

Sheppard laughed without humor, the sound rumbling in his chest. "Not anymore. Every member of this pack is someone who used to be human, someone who used to have a life and a path all of their own, yourself included. I wanted Matt to protect you because you deserved to live your life as you wanted to live it. When the church found out I was tracking a *consanguinea*, they tried to order me to change you and bring you in to them so they could train you exactly as they'd like you to be trained."

I can only imagine how that would have gone. Likely something like the first day I woke up here, but maybe with a lot less pain. Except he had said the attack had to almost kill you, right? So maybe not. I pressed my lips into a line.

"As if they had a right to tell me what to do in my own territory." He shook his head. "No, the dogmatic packs are much more militaristic. They have a strict structure and hierarchy that isn't up for discussion. The hierarchy of my pack is fluid because it is what makes us a pack. Regular wolf packs know which member is best for which situation and work accordingly. The dogmatic packs leave no room for questions of who outranks whom. Anyone who would dare question that is pushed down the ranks or pushed out."

The hierarchy is fluid—except I got the feeling that Sheppard's authority as alpha was uncontested.

He paused for a moment, regarding me in what felt like a very paternal way. My wolf reveled in the feeling.

"If you survived their training," he said quietly, "you'd be placed in a pack of their choosing, your family would be notified of whatever story they'd made up for you, and your entire life would be left behind. You would be expected to do as you're told or you would be disciplined in whatever way the alpha saw fit."

I rolled my eyes. "That sounds just wonderful."

"They fight a good fight," Sheppard said. "The same good fight that we do. They are at their best when they've caught the scent of a brood. Dogmatic packs eliminate vampires with precision, and they still keep humanity safe. They just seem to have left all of their own humanity behind as they do it. Still, it's true that we owe all that we are to the church."

"So the vampires want *consanguinea* to fix themselves, but they want the ones that are easy to take to keep themselves hidden so that y—" I caught myself again. "Us wolves don't come and wipe them out. You knew I was *consanguinea*, but left me alone until I started spending time with a vampire. So what happens to *consanguinea* that fall victim to the vampires?"

Wow, I really just asked that question. Vampires and werewolves were real, I'm a werewolf, and I'm actually related to the Jesus of Nazareth. Great.

Sheppard shrugged. "There's no telling, really. Torture is certain though—and for a long while without the clean release of death. Odds are good they wouldn't chance the blood losing its potency."

I suppressed a shudder. "So how come they haven't found their cure already?"

"They weren't even looking until about 150 years ago." He anticipated the question on my face as he continued. "That was when a vampire was temporarily able to walk in the daylight after feeding on what was presumably a *consanguinea*. We don't know for sure, but ever since then, the vampires have been trying to get their hands on them without making it *look* like that's what they're doing, They don't seem to have a good handle on where to find *consanguinea*, though, they just keeping looking in a sort of spiderweb pattern from where they found the last."

Consanguinea blood could let a vampire walk in the daylight. That seemed less than ideal to say the least. "Does that happen to any vampire who drinks *consanguinea* blood?"

Sheppard pressed his lips in a line and thought for a moment. "Probably not. It's hard for us to know exactly what the vampires know, though. They aren't exactly forthcoming with their enemy."

My head swam again. How had I managed to get myself into all of this? Why did it have to be me that the crazed wolf attacked? I was just a girl. My eyes filled with tears and my head fell into my hands. A sudden warmth brushed against my shoulder and spread through me. Like yesterday, she was there again—my wolf—leaning her strength against me. I took a struggling breath and my vision cleared. Sheppard kept his hand on my shoulder.

"I was never just a girl," I whispered.

"No," Sheppard said softly.

"That wolf was always supposed to have attacked me."

"Truly, that was something we weren't quite prepared for." He released my shoulder and crossed his arms. "We knew you did work for the news station sometimes, and we were pretty sure you weren't a reporter, so when you decided to go hiking off the running trails on the reserve, Matt had to improvise. He couldn't follow quite as close as he would like. He wasn't supposed to let you get hurt, but there was only so close he could follow without scaring you."

I mean, with a face like Matt's, who could blame him? It's a wonder I hadn't ever noticed him myself. Scars like that would definitely have stuck in my mind's eye.

He shook his head. "He's phenomenal in a fight and a great tracker, but he's not the stealthiest of us."

I sighed and bit my lip. "So if all of the pack used to have normal lives," I said slowly, "then they all had a circle of friends and family before they became pack." I looked at Sheppard's feet. "Do any of them still?"

"Of course," he said. "Daniel's a big-shot lawyer. He takes cases all over the country to help corporations out with their international contracts. He's got friends in every major city. Chastity's family lives in the mountains. Every month she takes a weekend and spends it with them. Ian is actually so close with his circle of friends that we hardly ever see him, but he always comes back to us to recharge, and he's always there when we need him."

I looked over my shoulder at the latest and greatest phone on the desk. "What happens if I tell my friends what I am?"

Sheppard shrugged. "I can't stop you from telling them, but they wouldn't believe you anyway." He pushed off the windowsill and put his hands in his pockets. "And if they did happen to believe you, I would question their sanity."

Well, he was probably right about that one at least. I stood from the chair. "I think I have a few phone calls to make."

Sheppard smiled and stepped over to the door. "Take whatever time you need," he said, opening it. "I just recommend you stay here with us, since that vamp insists upon hanging around your apartment. I am certain that one's tied to the cave on the reserve somehow. I can feel it in my bones."

I opened my mouth to ask another question, but he made a shooing motion with his hand.

"Make your phone calls," he said, stepping from the room. "The vampires will still be there." He winked at me and shut the door.

9

I STARED AT THE BLANK SCREEN OF THE NEW PHONE. FREDERICK WAS A vampire? My hand went to the scars on my neck. And he fed on me? Though my inner truth-o-meter practically screamed that what Sheppard said had definitely not been a lie, I couldn't help but wish it was made up. I scrolled through the contacts and found Frederick's number.

"Hullo?" He sounded tired, like I had woken him up.

It was just past noon. I furrowed my brow.

"Hey Frederick," I said. "It sounds like I called too early in the day. Do you have a minute?"

"Grace," he said. There was a smile in his voice now. "I've always got time for you. You sound troubled."

"Well, it's just that there's something I want to ask you. Something that'll probably sound a little crazy."

"Crazy doesn't scare me," he said. "What's on your mind?"

I took a slow breath. How do you ask someone if they're a vampire? "I'm not sure how to word it."

He laughed. "Just ask it."

"Are you a vampire?"

The sudden silence on the line made my ears ring.

"What a strange question. Why don't you come here, and we can talk?" There was a strange tone to his voice, an intensity I hadn't heard from him before. It made me uneasy.

"I'm, uh, kind of with some friends right now," I said. "I can't really get away."

"Come on, Grace. Come to me, and we'll talk it out." The tone was more insistent, but still odd. It didn't sound like him.

I leaned forward in the chair, propping my elbow on the desk. "Could you just answer the question please? I know it's silly, but just humor me."

"Come to me." Something about the way he said it this time sent a chill down my spine.

"No, Frederick," I said. "Just answer the question. Please."

He was quiet a moment. "No," he said finally. "I'm not a vampire." But his tone was wrong.

My eyes went wide. "You're lying." I was certain of it.

"Dammit! You're one of those filthy, mangy mutts, aren't you?" His voice on the line was loud enough that I had to pull the phone away from my ear.

"What?" How the hell did he know that?

"I should have turned you when I had the chance."

The line went dead. I stared at the phone.

Holy shit. Frederick was a vampire, and now he knew that I was a werewolf. I somehow doubted anything good would come of that. Dammit.

That definitely didn't go as planned. I'm not sure what exactly I had planned anyway for that phone call, but whatever it was, *that* wasn't it. I ran a hand through my hair. Well, it was probably only a matter of time before he found out about what I am now anyway, right? I mean, Colorado Springs is only so big.

I slumped in my chair, but then I remembered Jenny's dinner. I better at least try to call her while I've got a moment. But what do I say? 'Hey Jenny, sorry for bailing on girls' night, got turned into a werewolf, but it's cool now, we can hang.' I shook my head and sighed, realizing a lie would have to do because—as Sheppard said—the world just isn't ready for werewolves. I knew he was right on that one at least. Most of the world would have a field day with their shoot-first-ask-questions-later mentality. Taking a deep breath, I pushed the button on the side of the phone and scrolled through the contacts to Jenny's number.

I cleared the air with Jenny, giving her a lame excuse about a writer's retreat I forgot about. Well that wasn't so hard, lying to a friend. At least she hadn't dug into my story much.

I called Steph next, but she didn't answer, so I left a message before checking my own voicemail.

It was empty—as usual.

Taking another look at the family tree still up on Sheppard's screen, my mind drifted. All those connected lives, and I somehow fit into it all. I was a part of it. I thought of my dad and what I'd end up having to tell him—or *not* tell him. If I ever saw him again.

Sighing, I closed the application and turned to head downstairs. Opening the door to the hallway, I smelled breakfast and the sounds of yet another action movie drifted up from the living room. Food sounded like a good idea, so I headed downstairs.

Jamie and Ian were playing a videogame—some futuristic shooter-type game. Sheppard was seated at the dining room table, the same spot he had been at dinner the other night. He scraped the last of some potatoes and eggs from his plate. Kaylah and Chastity were in the kitchen, rinsing plates and loading them into the dishwasher. Through the window, I could see Matt and Daniel out in the back-yard. It looked like they were sparring.

"Grab a plate," Sheppard said, gesturing to the kitchen. "There should be some scraps of breakfast left."

I did as he said and sat down at the table, my plate piled with bacon, sausage links, eggs, and toast. Werewolf scraps were still pretty substantial. I sandwiched some eggs and bacon between two slices of toast and took a bite.

"So," I said around my food. "Doesn't being a werewolf kind of interfere with a stable income? I mean lawyers make enough that it's probably irrelevant, but what about the rest of you?"

"I have my own mechanic shop downtown," Jamie said, not looking away from the TV.

"The neighborhood here is almost entirely vacation rentals," Sheppard said. "I run the management company and most of us keep them running and clean in between guests."

The sound of a car engine grew louder as it neared the house.

"New renters today?" Ian asked, also not looking away from the TV.

"No," Sheppard said as he stood and took his plate to the kitchen.

He moved quickly through the house, reaching the door right as the bell rang. He opened it wide, letting in a cold, earthy scent. The newcomer. He was a tall, skinny, blonde young man in wireframe glasses and army fatigues.

"First Sergeant Langley," Sheppard smiled. "Good morning."

I couldn't explain it, but I was sure his smile was a ploy.

Langley kept his face neutral and didn't return Sheppard's greeting. "Five days ago," he said. "We lost the signal of the *consanguinea*'s phone out on the reserve. We picked it up again this morning, here, in a new device."

I stood from my seat and stepped into the living room. Ian and Jamie's game paused, Jonathan appeared at the top of the stairs, and the back door to the house opened and closed.

Sheppard's smile didn't falter. "Of course, she's here." He gestured over to me.

Langley's icy blue eyes met mine and I saw his nostrils flare and his chest expand. He was smelling me. He was a wolf!

"She's been turned," he said.

I took a step closer to Sheppard.

"She was attacked on the reserve five days ago," Sheppard said flatly, the smile fading. I sensed a tension in him and raised my chin, not taking my eyes off First Sergeant Langley.

"She's ours then," Langley replied, holding his hand out to me.

I narrowed my eyes.

Sheppard laughed. "My pack is not yours, pup."

Langley dropped his hand. His tone was incredulous as he asked,

"You would name her pack before you even know if she'll survive the full moon?"

"She was pack before you ever knew her name," Sheppard countered. "Your commanding officer knew what he was doing when he came to me about the *consanguinea* in my territory. He knew who I was then, and he knows who I am now. I and mine do not fall under your jurisdiction, Langley. You would do well to remember it."

He broke into a feral smile and gestured toward me. "Let her choose."

Sheppard's hand clenched into a fist and his jaw tensed. I stepped closer to him, positioning myself behind his left shoulder.

Langley met my gaze again. "You would be stronger with us than you could ever be with them. Your talents will be wasted here. We would ensure you reached your full potential and would ensure you did not lack anything you needed."

"Talents?" I asked.

"*Consanguinea* wolves are cut from different cloth, Ms. Cartwright," he explained, pushing his glasses up on his nose. "If you survive your first change, you will need help and guidance with the power that being of the blood will grant you."

"Of the blood is the literal translation of *consanguinea*," Sheppard said over his shoulder. "The Latin term is the more formal title, and—frankly—rolls off the tongue better." He turned to face me. "His choice is a ruse. They will take you to Rome, to the Vatican, and no one you have ever met will ever see you again. They will turn you into a weapon while you figure out for yourself what it means to be a wolf." His voice softened, and he placed his hands on my shoulders. "They will only ever value you for what you can do for them, and though you would undoubtedly do great things—you would never be more than their weapon."

Langley had gone completely still—the blue in his eyes resolved into steel. The whole house seemed to be holding its collective breath.

"I would never hold a wolf that didn't want to be here," Sheppard continued. "I will not try to stop you if you wish to go with him." He squeezed and then released my shoulders.

I gave him a small nod. I had never thought of being that strong. Langley spoke as if I could be some kind of warrior-princess. But there was no warmth to him. I inhaled again. Only cold dirt, canvas, and shoe polish contrasting sharply against Sheppard's warmth. I could pick out most of the rest of the pack now too: Jonathan's electric woodsy-ness, Matt's spice, Jamie, like motor oil…

I locked my gaze with Langley and lifted my chin. My heart pounded in my eardrums and against my sternum. I took a step toward him, raising my hand. He extended his own hand, reaching for mine. I settled my hand against his chest and gently pushed him back a few steps, away from the doorframe. I softly closed the door in his face.

As the latch clicked into place, I closed my eyes. I wasn't ready for his offer. I couldn't just turn away from this pack. I wasn't sure I made the right choice, but I wasn't ready to leave with him. Sheppard meant for me to have a life as true to myself as I could manage—I could feel that truth coursing through me. There would be a time for great things after I figured myself out.

I turned and put my back against the door only to be immediately swept into a hug from Sheppard. Over his shoulder, on the stairs, Jonathan smiled at me and stood. The gold flecks in his eyes were pronounced in the daylight.

I heard what must have been Langley's car pull away from the house as Sheppard released me.

"His commanding officer will be by after the full moon, I'm sure," Sheppard said. "General Buckheim doesn't like to take no for an answer." He met my eyes. "And you may change your mind."

I scoffed. "Good food, soft bed, keys to my car and my apartment?" I shrugged. "Hell of a package to try to beat. Besides, if I wanted to be in the Army, I'd have signed up when all of my friends did."

Jonathan laughed. "I can see it now," he said, waving a hand in the air. "Corporal Cartwright, taking no crap and beating up the enlisted!"

"God, don't call me that!" I shook my head, but couldn't help smiling along with him. "Just stick to Lynn, alright?"

Kaylah fished a set of keys out of the bowl on the fireplace mantel.

"Supply day," she said cheerily. Looking at Sheppard she asked, "Mind if I take Lynn along?"

"Of course not," he said. "That's a fantastic idea."

Kaylah jangled the keys at me. "Gitcher shoes on, missy. We're wastin' daylight."

My shoes were upstairs. Jonathan was on his way down as I turned to the steps. I paused to let him get down, but he paused too, leaving one foot on the stair behind him. There was mischief in his eyes as he quirked an eyebrow at me. Smiling, he pressed his back to the wall, spreading his arms out to be as flat as possible. He was mocking me.

"I'm not touching you," he said in a sing-song voice. "I'm not touching you."

I rolled my eyes and let out an exasperated breath. Behind me, Kaylah sighed too. I marched up to pass him on the stairs, smiling despite myself, and reached a hand to his hip.

"Yea," I said, "but I'm touching you."

His smile brightened. "Well fine," he said, placing a hand on my lower back. "Then I'll touch you too."

The next step, my left leg pressed against his and his left hand came up to stabilize me, brushing against my hip. My breath caught at his touch and I leaned closer to him. His smile disappeared. We weren't playing anymore.

"Sorry," he said, his voice barely above a whisper. He raised his hands and backed down the next step. "Sorry," he repeated more firmly as I turned and hurried up the rest of the stairs to my room.

What the *hell* just happened?! I took a breath and sat on the floor to pull on my shoes. I heard quiet, firm voices from Sheppard and Kaylah as I pulled the laces tight. Ian and Jamie's game resumed.

When I came downstairs, Sheppard and Kaylah were in the kitchen with Jonathan, whose back was to the living room. His shoulders were slumped, his head bowed. Sheppard had a hand on Jonathan's shoulder.

Kaylah smiled at me. "You ready?"

Jonathan took that as his cue and turned to leave the kitchen,

I returned Kaylah's smile and nodded. "Yep."

Jonathan pulled his keys from the same bowl on the fireplace mantel and stalked past without looking at me. He opened the door and closed it firmly behind him as he left.

I looked to Kaylah and Sheppard. I'm sure the question was clear on my face as a car engine started in the driveway.

The car sped off and Kaylah hooked an arm through mine. "C'mon hun," she said, steering me to the door.

10

Outside, there was a space between the cars lined up along the cul-de-sac where an olive green hard-top Jeep had been.

"He'll be back," Kaylah said. "He just needs to clear his head."

She unlocked Sheppard's Ram and got behind the wheel as I slid in the passenger side.

"Did I get him into trouble?" I asked, buckling my seatbelt as Kaylah started the truck.

"Naw," she replied. "He should know better than to confuse you like that before yer first change."

I guess that made sense. "Well where did he go?"

She tossed her blonde hair over her shoulder. "Probably jus' to some muddin' trail. Or to our runnin' spot. No tellin' really. He jus' needed to stop pushin' on ya."

"He wasn't being pushy." I mean, it just got a little too serious on the stairs is all. I was so drawn to him, but I wasn't sure he and I were even on the same page, let alone whether I'd actually want to try to be with him.

She pursed her lips in thought for an exit or two, and I waited her out. "Look, right now, you an' yer wolf are kinda sep'rit things in th' same body. Right now, yer wolf wants ya t' do things, but yer humanity kinna questions it." She hurried to add, "It's not like yer wolf wants anythin' *bad*, mind ya. It's just that the two a'ya ain't really *one* yet."

"Okay," I said. "But what does that have to do with Jonathan?"

"He should know better than to go stirrin' up yer wolf afore yer all together!" Kaylah asserted. "Ain't nuthin' wrong with flirtin' and wantin', so long as it's all a ya that wants it. You *and* yer wolf."

That made more sense. "So you and Sheppard are angry with him for being pushy before you think I'm ready. You're worried I don't really want any of this."

In a way, that'd be right, I suppose, but there was this feeling spreading through me that all of this was exactly how things were supposed to be for me. This was my life now, and this was my path. Goosebumps prickled my skin, like it had the last time I thought about how events brought me to the pack.

"Well yea," she said. "He's gotta give you space to breathe and figure y'self out. *Then* you can be sure if y'want him y'self or not." She exited the highway. "Till tomorrow night, ain't no way you can be sure."

We drove a little in silence. Then Kaylah said, "I'm lookin' forward to havin' a extra hand in the kitchen. What's yer signature recipe?"

"Recipe?" I asked.

She nodded.

"Um, I don't cook," I said. "Unless Cup Noodles count."

Her face lit up. "Ooh, fancy noodles. That'll be a nice change a pace!"

I waved a hand and shook my head. "No, no. Microwave noodles in a cup. Like the college kids eat?"

I had graduated last spring, but I wasn't making enough to eat much better. I had never been much of a cook, really. I often left my noodles too long in the microwave, leaving me with mushy noodle soup.

"That's alright," she said with a wave of her hand. "You can help us with the laundry then."

I laughed. "Only if you don't mind it all going in together. Some things will end up pink though, and I never seem to get socks white again."

She deflated. "Well what *can* you do then?"

I shrugged. "I'm not really the domestic type. I grew up learning what I needed to get by, but my mom wanted me to just be happy. She knew cooking and cleaning didn't exactly cut it for me, so she taught me some shortcuts."

"Well, how in God's creation are ya s'posed to find a good husband or mate that way?" She was incredulous.

So was I. "What timeline did you grow up in?! I don't need a man to get by! Sure, if I find love, I'll be happy for it. I'm just not cut out to be a meek little housewife."

Kaylah sobered and took a breath. "I forget how times change sometimes. My parents passed away over a hundred years ago. I stopped countin' my birthdays." Her eyes were haunted again, like they had been the day I met the pack.

"What happened?" I asked.

"To my parents? They just got old, I guess." She shrugged. "Daddy had a bad cough 'n Mama had the shakes. They just never got better. Mama forgot my name at the end, wettin' herself every couple a hours 'cause she forgot where to go."

Alzheimer's or dementia then. How awful for her.

"What happened to you?" I prodded.

"Oh goodness, me?" She pressed her fingers against her chest. "I jus' fell in with the wrong pack at first is all. Buncha born wolves that didn't take too kindly to a little turned girl. I slowed 'em down—kept 'em from bein' as good as they coulda been—and they resented me for it. I tried to make up with keepin' houses clean and cookin', but the alpha eventually got sick of me bein' too slow and weak. I was holdin' 'em back. He reached out to Sheppard, who brought me here. I didn't know much about what it *really* meant to have a pack afore this'un." She sighed heavily. "But it's in the past now and we'll figger out a place fer you yet, don't you worry none. Sheppard's pack ain't like my old one." She smiled at me. Her eyes weren't haunted anymore. "We're family. You'll find yer way."

89

We pulled into the parking lot of a big-box, buy-in-bulk store. Kaylah pulled into a spot and cut the engine. As we entered, I had a hard time focusing on any one thing. The store smelled of packing material and boxes and wooden pallets. And then there were the people. I hadn't realized how much people and werewolves smelled different. People smelled like soap and deodorant, sweat and shaving cream. Kaylah's sweet, flowery smell had an underpinning of something wild. I suppose that's the best way to put it. But I hadn't been able to tell that there was even a difference until I passed a person who lacked that wild scent. People just smelled bland by comparison. It was no wonder we were always preening with deodorant and body sprays.

They. It was no wonder *they* were always preening. I'm not human anymore. I sighed.

"Knock it off," Kaylah said, lightly tapping my bicep with the back of her hand. "Y'look like a serial killer, sniffin' everyone like 'at."

I looked at her. She had three bulk packs of undershirts in her hand, all of them black. She tossed them into her cart and turned to the folded stacks of grey sweatpants. Grabbing some in a few different sizes, she dropped them in the cart as well.

I furrowed my eyebrows. "Who the heck is all that for?"

"Them boys are all hard on their clothes," she answered. "They go through this stuff like crazy. You're lucky most of 'em are even wearing shirts. Plus they keep scatterin' it all to the four winds, stashin' 'em all over town, so we always seem to need more."

I guess it made sense. If the guys were always playing that game from the other night, I could see how it happened.

She turned down the detergent aisle and I had to cover my mouth and nose with my hand. The scent of all of the cleaning agents and fabric softeners was so strong and so sharp that I could taste it in the back of my throat. It made my eyes water.

Kaylah hurried through the aisle, picking up unscented detergent and dryer sheets and adding them to the cart. We rushed to the end of the aisle and around the corner, where the air cleared and I could move my hand away from my face.

She hadn't covered her face.

"How did you manage that?" I wiped at my eyes in turn, trying to clear them.

She rolled a shoulder. "Ya jus' breathe lightly. Or hold yer breath. I prolly shoulda said som'n afore we went down th' aisle."

Another few steps and the air just smelled like boxes and packing material again. I sucked in a lungful of cleaner air. "That'll take some getting used to."

She nodded and then whipped her head around, turning to look behind us.

A pair of college-aged girls were hanging out by the aisle with the shirts and sweatpants. They were the only people in sight who didn't have a cart. Except for a guy over by the batteries. How odd.

"I smell sheep," she said under her breath. "You smell it?"

I sucked in another lungful of air, trying to pick through it. Something made my skin crawl, but I couldn't place it. "What do sheep smell like?" I matched her quiet tone.

She tossed her hair over her shoulder. "Like vamps, but not as strong. Rot and dead things."

I breathed deep again. There it was. I nodded. "I smell it now."

She nodded gently once, turning back to the cart before she started walking again. "I think it's them college girls. Some vamp's keepin' tabs on us."

"I think the guy by the batteries is with them," I said, matching pace with her. "Sheppard said there was a vamp watching my apartment. Maybe they're with him?"

"Prolly. Let's see how far they follow. Sheep ain't a threat. They're jus' people."

"But they serve vamps," I whispered.

"Well sure, but they're humans—jus' like th' rest a th' people in this fine establishment." She dropped her voice to a whisper. "They're just addicted to bein' fed on is all. They're like druggies. You get 'em help, not kill 'em for their mistakes."

"So what do we do?"

91

"Nuthin'. Let 'em follow a borin' ole supply run. Ain't worth it t' call attention t' anythin' unless they make a move."

I kept looking over my shoulder as we turned into the aisle with the paper goods.

"Quit'cher rubberneckin'," she said. "They ain't gonna leave jus' 'cause we know they're there. Besides, y'c'n hear them followin' if y'jus' stop thinkin' so hard 'bout it."

Really? How had I missed that? But I tried to do what she said as she grabbed some paper towels and napkins..

She was right. I could pick out the three sets of steps that only moved when we did.

Then there were only two.

Kaylah stopped the cart. The guy had placed himself in our way. No one was in front of us. I turned to look behind us. The aisle was empty.

Well shit. Looks like they were making a move.

"Things will go much smoother for the pack if the girl comes with us." The man said in a quiet voice that seethed with menace.

My heart pounded.

"Not a chance, hun," Kaylah replied. "Sheep don't get a say 'n what pack does."

One of the college girls came around the corner from behind us, all legs and sultry walk. "Don't say we didn't warn you." Her voice was low and almost sing-song in its taunt.

The other girl came around the front of the aisle and draped an arm on the guy's shoulder.

"Don't say we didn't give you a chance to make it easy." She met my eyes and gave me a wicked smile.

I took a step toward her as a low growl began to rumble in my throat.

Kaylah's hand hit my chest as she turned to face me. "Not here. Too public."

"Oh come on, little girlie," the guy said. "Let's play."

I narrowed my eyes at him.

"S'what they want," she whispered. "Sheep wanna make a display.

If th' wolves out themselves, then th' vamps can take th' fight to broad daylight."

"Vamps can't go out in the daylight," I said, not taking my eyes off the two in front of us.

She looked over my shoulder. "No, but th' sheep can. N'when they get th' humans involved, everything goes nuclear."

"She doesn't have it in her to play," said the girl Kaylah watched behind us.

Kaylah smiled. "Oh, she plays jus' fine, don'tchu worry yer pretty little head none. She jus' won't be playin' wit' you lot."

"Make a move." The words were out of my mouth before I knew that I had even said them. They came out as more of a growl than actual words, but I'm certain the two in front of me understood them.

The girl lifted her chin at me, but hooked her arm in through the guy's.

"Ya know ya don't stand a chance agains' e'en one'a us," Kaylah said. "Best run off t' yer master now. Yer overdue fer y'fix by now, ain't ya?"

The girl in front slapped her free hand to her neck, covering the tiny pinprick scars. I balled a fist tightly at my side, knuckles cracking as I resisted the urge to touch my own.

"I don't wanna fight them," the girl whispered into the guy's ear. "He didn't say anything about fighting them."

The guy brought his hand up, batting her away from his ear. "If she doesn't come with us," he said. "Then things are about to get ugly for the pack. Starting tonight."

The full moon.

Kaylah smiled and turned her back on the sultry girl behind us. "He ain't gonna hurt us tonight," she said. "Now run along home now. Shoo." She matched the words to the shooing motion of her hands.

I kept my eyes on the guy as the sultry girl's footsteps brought her in a wide circle around us so she could join her companions. There was a sharpness to their scent, something underpinning the subtle rot and death that Kaylah had pointed out. My eyes flicked to hers, which were wide, though her demeanor suggested she was ready to fight. But something was off.

They were afraid.

I smiled at them as they turned to leave.

We finished grabbing what we needed from the big-box store and checked out. We loaded everything into the truck bed and began the drive back to pack central.

"What was that about?"

Kaylah shook her head. "I dunno. Sheep ain't usually that aggressive." She thought a moment. "But they ain't gonna do anythin' to hurt us tonight. S'th' full moon! Your first run!"

I bit my lip. I wasn't sure how I felt about this run. But then eagerness filled me. My skin itched, and I rubbed at my shoulder to keep myself from fidgeting like I was covered in ants.

I took a breath. "What is the deal with all of this 'get used to skin' business? How do you get used to just getting naked in front of strangers?"

Kaylah gave me a knowing look. "We ain't strangers, we're pack. Ain't a one a 'em that gives a rip about whatcha look like under the clothes—'cept maybe Jonathan, a course."

Heat rose in my cheeks and I looked away.

"Look," she said. "When changin', ya gotta get out a yer people clothes, or you'll tear 'em all t' shreds. Maybe even hurt yerself." She laughed. "This one girl n'my old pack fergot t' take'er bra off when she's changin' n'she got her paw stuck on th' strap." Her laughter overtook her. "Poor girl looked so silly hoppin' around on three legs tryin' t' get r'self outta th' bra."

I laughed too then. "Did you help her?"

"Well sure! Once she stopped hoppin' aroun' n'let us, one a us who still had thumbs unhooked it fer her. She darted off int' th' woods in embarrassment," her laughter died off. "But she ne'er did it again." Kaylah thought for a moment. "Actually, m'pretty sure th' poor girl stopped wearin' bras altogether. S'why th' pack likes quick change clothes so much. N'why they keep squirrelin' it away all over God's creation."

"So since you have to get naked for a run, no one even bothers worrying about being naked otherwise?" That seemed hard to believe.

"It's not like we go runnin' around th' house nekkid all a time. Jus' the boys don' like wearin' shirts, 'n all a us like stuff that's easy t' get on an' off." She looked over at me. "Ain't you noticed we all run a li'l hot?"

Now that she mentioned it, it was warm, though the heat wasn't on in the truck. I hadn't even grabbed a coat for our shopping trip, but half the town was in layers, and it was cold enough outside that you could see your breath. I should have been colder in just a long sleeve shirt and jeans. Guess I didn't need my winter coats anymore.

11

_____

BACK AT THE HOUSE, CHASTITY HELPED US UNLOAD THE TRUCK, BOTH showing me where to put away the supplies. We told Sheppard about the sheep at the store, and though he was concerned, there wasn't really anything to be done about it.

My head buzzed with more questions I couldn't quite put words to, and before I was fully aware of it, the sun dipped below the horizon and cars were being packed for the drive to the preserve. I rode with Sheppard in his big black truck. Ian and Jamie rode with Jonathan in his Jeep. Bringing up the rear was Matt's '69 Camaro, packed with what seemed like entirely too many people for a rumbling muscle car: Matt, Chastity, Daniel, and Kaylah.

Once we got to the reserve, we drove out past the campsites and parked in some brush near an old park ranger shack. There was still enough light from the dusk to see by, and the air was crisp and cool. When we got out of the cars, Sheppard took sure steps that led us along a path that—to me—was indistinguishable from the rest of the spaces between the trees. As it got darker, the light of the full moon shone bright through the trees and I felt a pull in my gut.

My wolf. She was anxious to come out and play.

The less I could see, the more I found I could sense the things around me. I followed the pack along the path more by scent and sound than by sight.

The trees thinned, and we stepped into a clearing. The moon hung just above the treetops, and I couldn't keep myself from staring at it. My gut clawed at me.

No. My *wolf* clawed at me, itching to break free and run wild. My skin felt too tight, my clothes too restrictive.

"Hun," Kaylah's soft voice murmured near my ear. "Now'd be a good time to keep yourself from ruinin' the clothes you came in." Her flowery scent filled my nostrils as she put a hand on my shoulder. Her face was turned skyward.

Blinking my gaze away from the moon's spot, I looked around, rolling my shoulder as Kaylah released it. Most of the pack was shirtless, including Kaylah and Chastity, and a couple of the guys were already out of their pants too.

No one was staring at anything but the moon.

I kept flicking my eyes back to the moon, but I couldn't stop looking back at the others.

They all had scars—viciously nasty ones that should have easily killed any of them when they were human. Instead, something about the attacks had changed all of these people into being more than they were before. None of them were human any longer.

I was surrounded by werewolves, and I was as much a part of their pack as they were mine.

Another pull at my gut and my skin felt it had shrunk a full size too small for the rest of my body.

Sheppard watched the pack. He met my eyes and nodded, looking pointedly at my shirt and pants. The ones I kept pulling at to try to make comfortable. Everything itched and pulled, even my joints ached. I knew the clothes were holding me back, but the moon was so bright. With a fierce growl that felt distinctly less than human, I peeled off my clothing, dropping it in a pile at my feet. It was all the invitation my wolf needed.

An indescribable amount of sharp, breaking pain slammed into the whole of my body. It felt like each of my muscles cramped all at once, and did it hard enough to break the bones underneath. I yelped and hit the ground. I forgot how breathing worked, and my lungs burned for air. I think my heart was still beating, but with the pain in my chest, I couldn't be sure. Red spots danced at the edges of my vision. I wanted to just black out, to let the agony take me.

Arms covered in faint scars wrapped around my aching chest. Warm skin pressed against my back. I fought against it at first, but stopped when the arms loosened enough to simply hold my body against theirs. My skin was on fire, but—somehow—the added warmth soothed me. The heartbeat against my back grounded me from the rising panic that maybe I'd get stuck in some painfully misshapen half form.

A calm, quiet voice in my ear echoed in my head. "Just let go, Dreamer."

Jonathan. His scent was still as woodsy as ever, but more electric than I had smelled thus far.

Through squinted eyes, I could see the contortions of my pack-mates becoming wolf. Their shapes transforming from human to canine. My gut twisted again, tearing a guttural yell from me.

"Let her free," Jonathan whispered, "like your dream."

With a growl that transformed into a howl, she and I became one.

I was a wolf.

Every cell in my body froze and my heart stopped for a breath of a second.

Sneezing dust from my elongated snout, which now ended in a light brown nose surrounded by white whiskers, I looked at the ground beneath my...paws. They were creamy white, like an arctic wolf. I looked between my legs at my creamy white belly and saw a pale golden-brown patch of fur waving lazily behind me. My tail. With an effort, I waggled it. My breath came out in little clouds, but I didn't even feel the chill. Then, like a puppy who must go everywhere all at once, I bounced into the air and darted off through the forest, the pack trailing behind me.

An iconic timber grey and brown wolf caught up to me, his scent warm. Sheppard. He nudged my heels to direct me and then lead the way for our run.

Looking around as we ran, I was surprised to find I could pick out the others too. Matt's spicy musk belonged to a timber wolf in darker shades of black and brown. The one that jumped off the rocky outcropping beside us. Chastity ran alongside him, her rust-colored wolf keeping easy pace with her mate.

As we changed direction to run along a ridge, I caught wind of the flowery sweet Kaylah and the cinnamon-and-clean-laundry Daniel. The former was a grey wolf with a white belly, while the latter was a black wolf. Ian's orange chocolate scent trailed behind them, his coloring more like a coyote than a wolf.

Another black wolf rushed past me, the scent of motor oil indicting it was Jamie. Chasing him was a familiar wolf, whose coloring was almost raccoon-like. Jonathan. I remembered the day I had first seen Jonathan's wolf—the day I first woke up in Sheppard's home—and my tongue lolled out of my mouth in a wolfish grin as I sped up to chase after them.

Jamie had found a rabbit, and we couldn't help but give chase to the little patch of brown fur racing along the cool earth and decaying leaves. The crisp night air was filled with the scent of tree sap and the occasional wild herb. Moonlight sparkled between the branches of the trees, lighting little patches of ground here and there. Things brushed past my face and I twitched my nose at the new sensation that whiskers introduced. I flicked my ears around at the sounds of the reserve that felt more amplified now that I had the proper ears to hear them.

The best part was the sound of my pack's huffing and footfalls around me as we ran, their breath coming out in tiny puffs of exertion as we followed the natural trails. I found that if I concentrated, I could feel something pulling us together. It was strongest when I was closest to Sheppard. Instinct told me it was because he was our alpha, but it ran through all of us in the pack—tying us together in a way that no human bonds could match.

I don't know exactly how long we ran or how much ground we

covered. It didn't matter, I had survived. My wolf and I weren't fighting to be in control of one another. We were one—no longer two pieces, but a whole. The coin had flipped. I stopped in a patch of moonlight and howled my appreciation to all of creation. Or at least, all that could hear. The pack answered me. I thought my heart might burst out of my chest with happiness at the sound. Had I been human, I was sure it would have brought me to tears.

Sheppard steered our run back to the clearing, all of us piling over each other as we flopped to the ground, chests heaving from the exhilaration. Jonathan nuzzled under my chin, and Sheppard lay with his back against mine. We all dozed lightly in the cool night air before we roused to chase another rabbit that had come across our pack. We rushed after it, following the little patch of grey fur until it darted into its burrow. We flopped to the ground again right there and dozed. I was curled against Jonathan's belly when I realized that time no longer mattered. Pack was pack, and the time spent together was so much more important and valuable than the way people—humans—typically measured time.

It was still dark when Sheppard roused us and led us back to the clearing where the night had started.

Everyone changed back, stretching as they reoriented to two legs and pulling their clothes from the pile. I tried not to stare at anyone, but my eyes kept wandering back to the back, shoulders, and arms of a certain dark-haired joker who was pulling his jeans on. The pants did nice things to his rear end.

I shook my head, snorting the clear late-night air out of my snout. Still, I had no intention of reorienting to two legs for a while. I wasn't even sure how I had actually accomplished getting into wolf form. I certainly had no clue how I was going to get back into human form.

Sheppard pulled his jeans on and knelt in front of me, shirt in hand. "It's alright if you don't want to change back here." He rubbed my head. "I'll bet you'd love to get a good look at yourself anyway. I know I wanted to when I first changed."

I leaned into his touch, closing my eyes in contentment.

"Jonathan doesn't mind fur in his jeep," he said. "Ride back with him. You can get a good look and a little rest back at the house before we hunt Frederick."

I wagged my tail at him—a strange thought—and paced over to my clothes, now the only ones left in the pile. Everyone was gathering at the edge of the clearing toward where the cars were parked.

I pawed at my clothes to get them collected together and then nosed them in Jonathan's direction, letting out a little yip. It turns out that wolf mouths don't make words.

Jonathan looked to me, another of his signature smirks on his face. His shirt was in his hand and I realized that none of the guys had bothered to put their shirts back on.

"Ridin' with me, huh?" he said.

I nosed my clothes toward him.

"Hard to do people things without thumbs, isn't it?"

I rolled my eyes, planted my butt on the ground, and sighed.

"Alright, alright," he said, picking up my clothes. "Come on Dreamer," he added quietly.

I padded along beside him as we walked back to the cars.

"She's a manual, so try to keep your nose out of the way of the shifter, alright?" He smiled and lightly tapped my snout with a finger. I snorted.

Jamie saw us approaching the Jeep and nodded, something unspoken passing between the two brothers. He spun on his heel, turning to face Sheppard. "Mind if I ride with you and Ian? The Jeep's a little crowded." He hooked a thumb in our direction as he winked at me.

Sheppard looked at Jonathan, who was opening the door for me and chortled. "Sure."

Jonathan put our clothes on the passenger seat and I hopped up into the Jeep. He closed the door and I caught a flash of white in the rearview mirror. Matt's Camaro roared to life as I maneuvered around to gaze at the face of the white wolf in the mirror. I moved my head side-to-side and the reflection followed. The wolf was beautiful. I was beautiful? Pale golden-brown spread along the back of my neck and presumably along my back, but the mirror was too small to tell for sure.

"I'll catch up," Jonathan called to Sheppard.

I heard the rumble of the Ram start up and pull away, but it felt distant.

"That mirror's too small to do you any justice," Jonathan said softly as he waved his phone. "I can take a few pictures of you now for you to see before we even head back." He quirked an eyebrow at me, but my tail was already wagging. "Y'know, if you're the impatient type."

I pawed at the door handle and he opened the door to let me back out of the Jeep. I bounded a couple of steps away as Jonathan opened the camera on his phone.

1 2

"THE OLDER WOLVES IN OUR PACK, LIKE SHEPPARD AND MATT, SEEM TO forget that these phones do more than just make calls." Jonathan's eyes sparkled at my bounciness as I shifted my weight from paw to paw. "They tend to be pretty useful." He pointed the back of the phone toward me and a light laugh escaped him. "You'll have to sit still if you want any of these to come out clear."

With a huff, I sat down. A flash of bright light blinked from the back of the phone and dots swam in my vision. I snorted and shook my head.

"Sorry about that. The full moon isn't enough light for these things. How about I take a video walking around you and maybe you can keep your eyes closed?"

I yipped an approval and bounced to my feet. The flash came on again and moved in a slow circle around me. I couldn't help but follow it with my eyes anyway, though I kept it in the edge of my vision, trying to see Jonathan too. My tail waved side to side with excitement.

When he was done, he knelt next to me and played the video, but I couldn't make out anything other than a white blob in the middle of darkness thanks to the dots still swimming from the flash. I guess my eyesight had changed as well. I shook my head, squeezing my eyes shut. When I opened them, I still couldn't see the images on the screen.

"I think your wolf form is causing you trouble here," Jonathan said, pausing the loop of the video. "If you change back, you may find it easier to see."

With another huff, I sat down again. Well okay, but how do I get back to my other shape? I closed my eyes and thought about the release of shifting back. My skin crawled a little and my toes curled, but otherwise nothing happened. I huffed in mild frustration.

"You have to think of it as the reverse of how you got into your wolf," Jonathan said. "It's like remembering that you're put together differently—your bits belong elsewhere."

I grumbled and closed my eyes to try again, this time thinking harder.

"I'll try to help you," he said. "Sheppard uses this one phrase to help new wolves change back: *sarcina eiusdem sanguinis.*"

It sounded like the Latin from a Catholic church.

I felt a pull on that same sense that I felt when running with the pack. The connection that bound all of us together. My skin crawled again, but nothing actually changed. My whole body shook with the resulting crawling itch.

"You felt that," he said. "Right?" He shifted around to face me. "It's pretty normal to have to fight your wolf to be human again the first few times. Maybe if I touch you and concentrate."

He put a hand on my shoulder, spreading his fingers into my fur. He took a long, deep breath, letting it out slowly. With a quiet murmur, he repeated the phrase.

"*Sarcina eiusdem sanguinis.*"

Nothing more than the skin crawl happened again. Maybe I could help with some concentrating of my own. I locked eyes with him. His heart pounded. I took a slow, deep breath like he just had. Then another. On the third, his breathing matched mine and he murmured the phrase again. I willed myself back to my human form, trying to push my body into shape with my mind.

My skin crawled, but then it grew tight, and my joints felt like they were in the wrong places. Like before, sharp, breaking pain caused me to yelp and curl to the ground in front of him, my head landing on his thigh as my bones shifted. I watched my paws lengthen and become fingers, the fur giving way to skin as my nose shortened and paled to its human form. As the last of my body changed back, I was curled on the ground, eyes squeezed shut and breathing hard.

The pain was nothing, however, compared to my elation at having survived the night.

As the pain receded, I looked at Jonathan, who was also breathing hard where he knelt. His eyes were closed, and he was using both hands to steady himself, the phone curled into his white-knuckled fist on the ground. I moved closer to him and touched his shoulder, my heart still pounding. Despite what should have been a cool night, his skin was warm, hot even, but he wasn't sweating. He trembled almost imperceptibly at my touch. I ran my hand along his shoulder and up to his jawline, moving my own face closer to his. The woodsy electric scent of him was intoxicating. I closed my mouth against his and breathed his scent in.

Squeezing my shoulder, he pulled away from me. His eyes were wide, focused on mine, the question plain on his face. I pulled my bottom lip between my teeth.

"Lynn?" His green eyes searched my own.

I closed my eyes, put my forehead against his, and whispered, "No questions. Just kiss me."

He chuckled against my mouth. "Gladly."

His hand tangled in my hair as I pushed him back against the leaves and dirt and moss on the ground. My knees were on either side of his hips, but when my breasts pressed against the heat of his chest, my breath caught in his mouth. His other hand brushed against my bare hipbone and my skin erupted in goosebumps. I pressed closer to him, my kisses becoming more urgent as I reached for the button and zipper of his jeans. I released them one-handed and ran a hand along his waistline and over his butt. It felt as nice as it had looked. I smiled against his mouth and giggled as he picked me up and placed me on the ground under him. Together, we worked the pants off his hips and I could feel his hardness press between my thighs.

He stopped kissing me then. "What on Earth am I supposed to do with you now?"

Like the heat he pressed against wasn't telling enough.

With a mischievous smile, I pressed a palm against his lower back and my hips against him, curling a leg around his suggestively. "You can't tell me you don't already know."

"Mmhmm," he replied. He pressed into me and I threw my head back, moaning in pleasure. "I just needed to be sure." He placed a gentle kiss on my exposed throat.

A short time later, we were lying spent and naked on the forest floor, our legs still tangled together. I twisted a section of his hair around my finger as he ran his hand along the line of my body from shoulder to hip. The scent of him clung to my skin and I reveled in his touch.

He shifted away from me and grabbed his cell phone. "You never got to see the video clearly, did you?" he asked. He tapped the screen a few times and then turned it to me. "Here."

Taking the phone from him, I sat up. The wolf on the screen was beautiful. She had pale golden-brown fur along her spine and top of the tail that faded to a creamy white on her belly and paws. I recognized the face from the mirror on the Jeep, and tears welled in my eyes.

"She's beautiful," I whispered.

Jonathan sat up behind me and kissed my shoulder, his lips brushing against the scar there. "*You're* beautiful," he corrected. "That's you."

I became hyperaware of my skin and scars and my heart pounded in my ears. I wiped my face and shook my head lightly, pulling my knees to my chest. "I'm just me." I thumped my chin onto my knee.

Jonathan guided my hand to the scars crisscrossing his chest and I could make out the faint ones on his arms in the moonlight. I gently traced the smooth skin with my fingertips. He watched me for a moment before hooking a finger under my chin, tilting it up so I met his eyes. "You are beautiful, Dreamer," he said softly. "And I will spend the rest of my life proving it to you if that's what it takes."

I sucked in my bottom lip. What the hell did he mean by that?! I took a breath. Then another. Then a third. "We should probably get back before everyone gets worried."

Something flickered across Jonathan's face, but then his smile appeared. "You just want to get back so we can make use of a bed."

I smiled and shouldered him. "Well now that you mention it," I said, planting another kiss on his mouth. "I am pretty sleepy."

And I was definitely not ready to think about the rest of his life—or even my own, for that matter. I just wanted to get back to familiar ground.

He laughed and stood, pulling me to my feet with him. He stepped over to his discarded pants, shook them out, and pulled them on. I opened the door to the Jeep and brushed the leaves and dirt from my skin.

My bare skin.

It was November in Colorado.

I may have been born and raised here, but I still should have been cold to be outside, buck naked, in the middle of the night. But I wasn't. A cool breeze sent goosebumps flowing along my skin, but even that wasn't uncomfortably cold, just cool.

Kaylah wasn't kidding when she said the wolves ran warm.

I pulled on my own clothing, sitting in the seat of the to pull on my socks and shoes, Jonathan's discarded shirt in my lap. He got in the drivers' seat and started the drive back to Sheppard's. I watched and smelled him as we drove in silence for a mile or two.

"You shouldn't really need the full moon to change now that you've changed the first time," he said quietly, almost absentmindedly. "But it helps. The more often you change, the easier it will be for you. Sheppard will probably take us on nightly runs though for a couple of weeks to help get you used to it."

A thrill shot through me at the thought of running through the forest again with my pack. But then something else hit me.

Jonathan.

I had just slept with him. Or did my *wolf* just sleep with him? My gut jumped.

Mine.

The thought came so forcefully into my head that I startled and growled softly. But weren't my wolf and I one and the same now? I mean, clearly, Jonathan wanted what just happened. Didn't I want that too? God, I didn't even want to *think* about what he meant by 'spend the rest of my life proving it to you.'

I wasn't really paying attention to how hazy everything was as we approached Sheppard's neighborhood, but with a start, I realized that the smoke I was smelling on the breeze coming into the jeep was stronger than any fireplace chimney would warrant. We were close to pack central.

As we rounded a corner onto the cul-de-sac, reality slammed into my gut like an 18-wheeler going 70 miles per hour.

Sheppard's home was ablaze.

13

ANGRY RED AND AMBER FLAMES LICKED THROUGH THE WINDOWS ON THE front of Sheppard's once-beautiful home. Clouds of thick grey-black smoke billowed onto the wraparound porch and into the night air. It blotted out the stars, and everything in the area was hazy. Firefighters sprayed the house with two huge jets of water, causing more smoke that was lighter in color than the house smoke. But the upstairs had already collapsed. There would be no salvaging the house. Pack central was going up in flames—literally, and I couldn't look away.

Jonathan pulled his Jeep alongside the curb a few houses down from Sheppard's. His heart thumped hard in his chest. So did mine, for that matter. He pulled his shirt on over his head as we exited the Jeep and looked for the rest of the pack. I couldn't smell anything but the smoke, but I could make them out close to one of the fire trucks.

Matt stormed over to us. "Where have you been, Jonathan?!"

He took a deep breath in through his nose. His expression changed, and he narrowed his eyes at me before turning back to Jonathan. "You should have been here sooner! The pack needed you!"

Why the hell was he so angry? It wasn't like the fire was our fault.

"You're letting her," he jabbed a finger at me, "make you lose your focus on what is important! She's not even sure she wants pack yet and you're rutting in the forest with her like you have claim to her! Meanwhile, our home is burning down!"

Jonathan's gaze turned to steel, and his fists were balled. "I have my own place across town, Matt," he said, quiet anger roiling in his voice. "You know that." His voice got louder. "And even if we had made it back sooner, what—*precisely*—do you think we could have done?!" He shouted the last line, moving so close to Matt that they were almost touching noses.

I wanted to run, wanted to hide. But I was not going to give Matt the satisfaction. Rutting in the forest? What kind of chauvinistic piece of—

"That's enough." Sheppard's voice washed through us along with a shimmer of the sort of power I was coming to expect from him. He came over and placed a hand on Matt's shoulder. "The smoke's covering the smell now, but it was vampires that set the fire. Once the fire's out, you'll be able to smell it again, and we can track it."

That broke my chain of thought. "Vampires did this?"

Sheppard nodded. "They must have known we were out with you for the full moon. After your encounter with their sheep earlier, they must have wanted to retaliate."

I stepped back. "It was because of me?"

My voice was barely above a whisper. Cold fear ran down my spine.

"They wanted me, in the store, but they didn't get me." My voice trembled. *I* trembled.

"No," Sheppard said.

"Now, they've burned down your house."

"Lynn..." Jonathan reached for me, but I jerked away.

"It's my fault!"

Run!

Sheppard and Jonathan both called after me—Matt too—but I didn't hear what they said. I ran toward my little purple car, still in the driveway and unharmed by the flames. Maybe I was faster than them, maybe I wasn't. It didn't matter, I had a head start and was fast enough. Certainly, faster than the firemen who tried to block me. I didn't have the key on me, but my dad had shown me long ago where he had zip-tied a spare key to the frame in case I ever lost mine.

I slammed to the ground in front of my car, the heat from the burning house like the coils of an oven at my back. The metal of the undercarriage was hot, and it took me a moment to find the hidden key.

Multiple people were shouting. The fire roaring in my ears drowned them out. My eyes were tearing up from the smoke. Or from the panic. I wasn't sure.

RUN!

The firemen were coming close, but I yanked at the key, breaking the zip tie with one hand. I clambered up and into my car, my hand stinging from the hot metal. The little four-cylinder engine of my Del Sol didn't make much noise as it came to life, but it had more horse-power than was necessary for such a small car. My radio blared some country ballad or another from the late-night radio station and I scrambled to just turn it off. It was too much noise right now.

I got my car out of the driveway and maneuvered around the firemen waving their arms. Sheppard had his right hand pressed to Jonathan's chest, his left to Matt's. The three of them watched me pull away from the burning house. Once I was clear of the throng, I slammed the pedal to the floor, switching through the gears of my five-speed manual transmission fast enough to impress a street racer.

I got out onto the main roads and sped toward my apartment. It was three in the morning, so there was no traffic. I was so caught up in the new experience of driving with heightened hearing that I didn't even turn my radio back on. The engine rumbling and the road noise, which I was already attuned to in order to catch the best time to shift gears and lanes, was so much more pronounced than I was prepared for. It took me a moment to adjust to the experience and another to orient myself once I got on the highway.

My phone buzzed in my back pocket. I ignored it. I didn't have words anyway. If Sheppard's home burning down was my fault— which it clearly was—then the pack couldn't afford to keep me around anyway. Maybe I could contact that guy that came by Sheppard's house—Langley, was it? Maybe the military would be able to protect me.

I rolled my eyes. Yea right. I had to get home. I could think better there.

My mind was racing so fast I nearly missed my exit and had to swerve from two lanes over.

I pulled into my usual parking space, but my housekey would have been on my keyring in the bowl on the mantel in Sheppard's house. Dammit. By the time the fire was out, it would be just a hunk of useless metal. I ran up to the stairs to my front door anyway.

The phone in my back pocket buzzed again. I still didn't have words.

I gripped the doorknob, which turned, but the deadbolt was set. Well of course it was, I was the last one here. That was days ago. My vision blurred. I just wanted to be in my own home.

Sheppard said werewolves were stronger, right? It's not breaking in if it's my own place, right? I set my shoulder against the door and pushed. The door gave way with a noisy crack of splitting wood.

Werewolves were decidedly stronger than humans.

The smell of home engulfed me, and though the air was stale, it was a welcome relief. My home. *Mine.*

I turned the deadbolt to the unlocked position and shut the door. It wouldn't latch, but it didn't matter. I put my back to the door and sank to my carpeted floor as I pulled in another deep lungful of the scent of my own home.

My heartbeat pounded in my ears as I hugged my knees to my chest and sobbed. This was just entirely too much. Really. Related to Jesus, able to turn into a huge wolf anytime I wanted, and hunted by vampires? That's just too much for one person. I needed normality.

Maybe if I emailed my contact at the paper, I could pick up some extra work to make up for the week or so that I had lost. I didn't know what in the world I was going to do about the vampires, so I guessed I'd just have to deal with them when they showed up again.

Except the silence in my home was…heartbreaking. It felt empty. I had only been with the pack for a handful of days, but the sudden lack of their constant presence was uncomfortable. Well dammit. I couldn't just go back to them.

A car pulled into the parking lot of the apartment complex. No. Not a car, a truck. A warm scent tinged with smoke from Sheppard's house fire wafted in through the cracks of my doorframe. There was a heavy sigh on the other side of my door.

Tears filled my eyes. "Go away." I didn't have to shout. He'd heard me.

Sheppard's voice was damnably patient. "Why should I?"

"I'm just going to keep putting you all in danger." My voice threatened to crack. "The vampires want me, and they want me so bad they're willing to burn down your home."

I choked on the last words, the sobs threatening to overtake me again. Tears rolled down my cheeks.

An amused sound rumbled from the other side of my door. "This isn't the first house of mine that they've burned down," he said quietly, "or the second, or the fifth, or even the tenth."

Something brushed the door—his hand, I thought.

"What happened tonight, to the house, is not your fault. It's all insured, and everything's replaceable. I'm just glad no one was hurt."

I sighed and stood up, wiping the wetness from my face. If we were going to talk, it was rude to make him keep talking at me through the door. I pulled it open and looked up at him.

"It sure feels like it's my fault." I gestured with an open palm to my apartment.

He stepped inside, flicked on the lamp next to my desk, and pulled a chair from my table over to me. "I can understand why you might feel that way." He sat in the chair. "But you'd be wrong."

I closed the door and resumed sitting on the floor, where I could hold the door of my apartment shut.

"This is what they do," he explained. "They fight dirty. They hit where they think it will hurt us most, never realizing what the rest of us already know: for us, home isn't a house—pack is home. It doesn't matter where we live, it's that we're together that makes it home." Then he said that phrase that Jonathan used, "*Sarcina eiusdem sangui-*

nis," and power washed over me, igniting the strands that I felt while running with the pack on the reserve.

My breath caught in my throat and I closed my eyes to keep the tears from flowing again. Golden threads spiderwebbed out from me, the thickest one connecting me to Sheppard as he sat across from me, while others reached farther, back in the direction of the pack. The threads that were stretched far and long twitched and glinted like they were catching sunlight behind my closed eyelids.

"I don't even know what that phrase means," I said lamely, opening my eyes.

Amusement lit his face. "It's Latin. It means 'the blood and the pack are one.' Simply put, we're in this together." His phone buzzed from his pocket.

I sighed. "Even if it means that everyone's house burns down?"

"It's part of the fight," Sheppard replied, fishing his phone out of his pocket. "The vampires are a plague on the world." He thumbed the screen of his phone. "It's our job to wipe them out. They know that's our goal." He tapped out a message. "Just as we know that they will do all they possibly can to stop us from succeeding." He looked at me with his golden-brown eyes. "Make no mistake." His voice hardened and rumbled with a restrained anger and his eyes flashed amber. "They will pay for burning down my house. They will pay for feeding on pack. They will pay for so flippantly maintaining a club downtown that they use for their own feeding pleasures."

I believed him.

A thrill went through me. Which didn't make any sense. I'm not a fighter. I had to agree though. *They will pay.*

"Okay," I said. "So, what about my door? And where is everyone going to stay tonight?"

I looked around my studio apartment. There was no way the entire pack would be able to sleep here unless everyone slept on the floor.

Sheppard followed my gaze around the room with a bemused smile. "I own a number of rental houses in that neighborhood. You don't really think that I just happen to like playing the real estate market, do you?"

I smiled meekly. "I suppose not."

He waved his phone. "We'll stay at one of the rental properties. Ian has the supplies he needs to fix your door jamb tonight, so your apartment doesn't have to stay open to the world all night and day. Tomorrow, we'll get a new set of locks installed and a copy of the key made for you to give to your leasing office."

"You guys are prepared for something like that?" I couldn't keep the incredulousness from my voice.

"Of course we are," Sheppard replied. "I've been fighting vampires for over five hundred years. You learn a few things when you've been fighting them that long."

"That's an exaggeration." I wasn't sure if I was asking a question or hoping I was right.

Sheppard thought for a moment. "Five hundred and twenty-seven years, to be exact."

"Werewolves live that long?" I asked. "Are you—am I—are we immortal? Are vampires?"

"Vampires are, yes," he said. "But we are not. Just very, very long-lived. Like I said before, the church wanted us to eventually have access to heaven, once our fight was done."

Oh yea. He had mentioned that in the diner. "Well, how long is 'very, very long-lived?'" I asked, using my hands to put air quotes around the words he used.

Sheppard raked a hand through his sandy blond hair and sat back to think a moment. "It's hard to know what the top end is for us; fighting vampires cuts so many lives short. The oldest werewolf I know now is over 800 years old, but I've known of others who lived to be well over 1,000."

I mouthed a 'wow' and whispered, "How old are you?" I wasn't sure I wanted to know the answer.

"Five hundred and forty-one," he replied, taking a deep breath. He leaned forward and looked me in the eye. "I want you to come back and be with the pack tonight."

I looked down and away from his gaze. My apartment was my home, but it didn't quite feel right anymore.

"Ian is on his way here now. Why don't you follow me back, and we can all get some rest?"

There was power in his words. It wasn't as strong as when he lit up the strands tying me to the pack, but it was there. I could have said no if I wanted to. But I wasn't sure I wanted to.

At my hesitation, he added, "I told you before that I would never hold a wolf that didn't want to be there. I still won't, but it would do you well to be with the pack—to know that they don't blame you for tonight either."

How was he able to put words to my hesitation so well? He was right. I was nervous the pack would blame me. But I also desperately wanted to feel those ties again like I had when we ran on the reserve. I had felt more alive than I had felt in probably my entire life. Goosebumps erupted on my skin again at the memory.

"Are you sure?" I asked, looking back up at him. "Matt seemed pretty pissed."

His eyes were gentle. "Matt's a hot-head. Always has been; always will be. Believe it or not, he's actually calmed down over the years."

I didn't want to think about what that meant for how quick to anger he must have been before.

"Chastity was...distraught about the house fire. He was simply looking for a target for his anger."

I sucked in my bottom lip for a moment. "Okay." I stood up.

Sheppard put my chair back but left the light on.

I followed him out of my apartment, closing the door as gently as I could to try to make it less obvious that there was literally nothing holding it closed. A strong breeze would probably push it back open again. I didn't like it, but I reminded myself that Ian was on his way to fix it, and that would have to do.

14

I FOLLOWED SHEPPARD'S TRUCK BACK TO THE OTHER SIDE OF TOWN. WE stopped for some fast food on the way, but there was no way I was going to get any of my burritos down while driving a manual transmission. At least, not without making a mess all over my car. They'd probably be cold by the time I got back, but that was better than no food at all. Still, the smell made my mouth water and my stomach growl.

Sheppard made a different turn in the neighborhood than the one that would have taken us back to his house, and we pulled up to a boxy, modern home with lots of windows. It was set farther back on the lot with trees and bushes strategically planted in the yard for privacy. It was beautiful in its own way, but it lacked the homey charm that Sheppard's house had. He had a spot on the driveway, as he had at his home, but the only spot left for my car was along the curb across the street.

I munched on a burrito as I entered the house. I had been too hungry to wait to sit at a table. The smells inside were a near-nauseating mix of fast food—tacos, burgers, and fried chicken—along with the scents of the pack. The now-familiar voices carried and echoed lightly off the walls and the tiled floor. Some of the tension left my shoulders.

"Lynn!" Kaylah exclaimed. "I'm so glad you made it!" She wrapped me in a hug, her flowery sweet scent soothing some of my frazzled nerves. Tears stung my eyes.

Sheppard caught my eye as she released me, the I-told-you-so clear on his face.

I placed my bag of burritos on a side table just in time for Matt to toss a wrapped burger my direction. I caught it and looked at him.

"Glad you made it, kid," he said with a smile. He held Chastity against him, her vanilla scent mixing with his own spicy musk. She seemed almost serene now, leaning against him.

She smiled gently at me between bites of her already half-eaten burger, tucking a long auburn curl behind her ear. "I think we all are," she said, her hazel eyes meeting my own.

Woodsy electric warmth invaded my senses. "I know I am," Jonathan said quietly, offering me the half-empty bucket of fried chicken in his arm.

"Thanks," I said, taking a drumstick. I pulled a burrito from my bag and offered it to him.

"Ooh!" His eyes glittered as that infectious smile of his returned. He took the burrito from my hand. "A trade! How fair of you, my lady." He bowed at the waist, careful not to dump out the fried chicken, as I shook my head with a smile and rolled my eyes.

I slumped onto a couch next to the side table where I had deposited my burritos, placing my burger in the bag with the last two burritos and tearing into the fried drumstick in my hand. I crossed my legs under me and let out a sigh. It had been a long night.

I thought everyone would be more upset about the fire. I thought they would blame me. But they weren't, and they didn't. They were just glad that I had made it through the night.

Sheppard handed me a bottle of water and sat in a recliner near one of the couches, finishing a burger of his own. "There bedrooms and couches all over the place in this house, including an office and couch in the basement. I'm in the master, but find any other sleeping spot that's comfortable for you, and it's yours."

"Thanks," I said, offering him one of my remaining burritos. He smiled and took it, placing it on his thigh while he finished his burger. Jonathan sat on the floor next to my left knee. Jamie sat on the other couch in the living room.

"We should be celebrating your run with us tonight," Sheppard said, his golden eyes meeting my own. There was a sad edge to his voice.

I looked down at the fried chicken in my hand. I was still practically ravenous. They really weren't kidding about being able to eat anytime food was available.

"But that celebration will have to wait. Tomorrow," he said, raising his voice.

The pack stopped their conversation and stilled, listening to our alpha.

"In the morning, we'll go through what remains of the old house to see what's worth salvaging. We'll lock what we don't immediately need in the shed and bring the rest here." He looked to Kaylah, whose hand was clasped with Daniel's. "Kaylah, tomorrow afternoon, I want you and Chastity to resupply again."

Kaylah smiled at Chastity, who nodded her head in response.

Sheppard was in full alpha mode. His voice carried the weight of authority without so much as a shimmer in the air. It was like he had gone through this a hundred times before and had the routine down. Just how many homes had he watched burn thanks to vampires?

"Daniel," Sheppard continued, "I need you to call in our insurance policies and get started with whatever we need to do to clear the land and build a new house there."

"The adjuster will meet us at the house tomorrow at 3pm," Daniel replied. "I called tonight to get things rolling. First thing in the morning," he continued, "I'll drop by the safe deposit box to pick up what spare keys and documents we have there and then go to the insurance office to fill out paperwork for the claim."

Wow. Talk about being on top of things. I wouldn't have even known where to start.

"Thank you," Sheppard said, genuine relief in his voice. "Matt, I need you to track those vamps." His voice hardened again. "We need to know where those bloodsuckers came from so we know where to hit first."

"Gladly." Matt's smile was feral and cold, and I could smell the change in him—the thrill of the hunt building in him. It made me glad he was on our side.

"Don't start any fights," Sheppard warned, wagging a finger lazily in Matt's direction. "Just find them. When you do, come back here and we'll put together a plan of attack. I am done playing quietly with the vampires in this town." Sheppard crushed the wrapper to his burger in his fist. "We are going to wipe them out."

A thrill went through me then, like it had when he made the similar promise in my apartment earlier. I believed him. But more than that, I actually wanted to join Matt in tracking them down.

"As for the rest of you," he added. "Do a security check of your interests around town, including any friends." He looked pointedly at Ian. "We're escalating to fighting dirty. Daytime attacks, starting with the ones responsible for the fire. Once we start poking around with the vampires, they aren't likely to stay put."

Sheppard talked like this was all just business as usual. Sure, he had aggression directed toward the vampires, but these guys were like a well-oiled machine. I think I was glad to be coming in to a well-established pack.

"For tonight, the best that any of you can do is to get some rest. It may be the last chance for real, solid rest that we'll get for a while." He unwrapped the burrito I had handed him and took a bite, crumpling the wrapper in one hand.

"We'll take the other bedroom down here," Chastity said, hugging Matt's arm. Her vanilla scent was subdued and mixing pleasantly with Matt's spice. He patted her hand and kissed her forehead.

"Why dontcha take one o'the upstairs bedrooms, Lynn?" Kaylah said. "Daniel'n I will take the other one. Lord knows the rest of the boys can manage on couches. Let the ladies have proper beds, huh?" She touched my shoulder and smiled at me.

Privacy for the new girl, huh? I mean, sure I had a room to myself at the other house, but I had also been recovering from a near-death experience. This was different. I had expected I'd end up on the couch in the basement or something.

I returned her smile and looked at Jonathan and Jamie in turn. "As long as you guys don't mind?"

"Not at all!" Jamie smiled. I had thought before that his and Jonathan's eyes were the same shade of green, but I could see them better now. His eyes were actually paler than Jonathan's, but he still had the same golden-amber flecks.

Jonathan smiled at me, mischief in his eyes, and then turned to his brother. "Dibs on the sectional upstairs!"

"Take it." Jamie waved a hand. "I'm gonna stay on one of the couches down here. It's closer to the fridge and late-night snack opportunities."

I think Jamie got the better end of the deal.

"Leave some for Ian," Kaylah said. "I bet he stopped on th' way hisself, but still. Pack." She said the last word like it was all the explanation needed. I supposed it was, really.

I finished the last of my food as Matt, Chastity, Kaylah, and Daniel all went to bed. Jonathan's warmth still radiated against my left leg from where he sat by the couch. Jamie found some blankets in the linen closet in the hallway and brought them to the other couch downstairs. He then grabbed another couple of burgers from the kitchen and plopped one down next to the bag that held my discarded wrappers and chicken bone.

I smiled at him as I unwrapped the burger. That I still had room for food amazed me.

"Changing and running takes a lot out of us all," Jamie said. "It's why you're eating so much so fast."

"This is still a lot of food for one person," I said. I raised the hand holding the burger. "This is the second burger for me, and I've already had two burritos and a drumstick."

"I told you we eat a lot," Jonathan said, smiling at me.

I returned the smile and took another bite of my burger. I wasn't sure what to say to him, and I couldn't fathom why. I mean, sure we just slept together in the woods like two wild animals. But then we came back to this raging house fire and then I ran away and then tomorrow—or maybe the next day—we were apparently going to go vampire hunting. I scrunched my eyes closed.

"What the hell kind of normal is this, anyway?"

I hadn't intended to say it, but it came out, exasperated, around a mouthful of burger.

Jonathan placed a hand on my knee and rubbed it with his thumb. My racing thoughts slowed and I opened my eyes.

"The only real kind of normal we can find," Sheppard replied quietly. "I told you, hunting vampires is what we do. We get down time while we try to strategize how best to handle things in an area." He stood from his chair. "But vampires kill people. We're the only ones with the kind of strength it takes to stop them. So we do." He walked into the kitchen, threw away his wrappers, and then paced down the hall, presumably to the master bedroom for the night.

Watching him, I could see his age—the full weight of his years and the fight weighing on him. He needed the pack just as much as the pack needed him.

The house fell quiet as I finished my burger. Jonathan stood as I crumpled the wrapper and picked up my bag of trash from the side table. I followed him into the kitchen, where he placed the bucket of leftover chicken in the refrigerator and pulled out two bottles of water. I deposited my wrappers in the garbage and took the bottle he offered me with a small smile. Leaving the kitchen, I went upstairs, Jonathan on my heels. At the top, he went to the left, where I assumed the den with the sectional was. I went to the right, passing the room where I could smell that Kaylah and Daniel had retired to.

The other bedroom on the floor was all in grey, black, and chrome. It looked like something out of Modern Living magazine. It smelled musty from disuse, and had a clean, cold feel to it. There was a marble and chrome side table next to the bed, with a chrome and black lamp atop it. I put my water bottle and phone down next to lamp.

It was already four-thirty in the morning, a time I pretty much only ever saw if I had a deadline article that the newspaper wanted me to have ready for the morning edition. I sat on the edge of the bed, which was piled high with grey and black pillows and covered with a soft, black comforter. After taking off my socks and shoes, I curled my toes into the soft, plush carpet and thought about earlier.

Would it really be so bad to have Jonathan around for forever?

A small voice, deep in the back of my mind, whispered *Mine.*

I sighed. I wasn't sure I was ready to even think about something like that. My history with guys hadn't exactly been stellar, but it hadn't been as bad as some girls had. None of my exes had ever cheated on me, and none had ever tried to hurt me. I just hadn't been what any of them had really been looking for. Maybe I was too mousy, or too sarcastic, or too intellectual. But I guess none of them had been what I really wanted either.

Another whisper, *Mine.*

I shook my head. His smile was intoxicating, and all I wanted to do was touch him again. God knows I had never really found any peace or real belonging with anyone. But I just couldn't wrap my mind around how so much upheaval could possibly bring me peace.

Mine.

And the pack. I ran a hand through my hair. God, the pack. Being here with them just felt so right. It felt like I had finally found where I was meant to be.

I tugged my pants off and pulled the covers of the bed down. I put my shoes next to the grey upholstered chair in the corner, my pants on the seat, and crawled into the bed. The light flicked off in the hallway, and the house fell quiet.

It was strange. Usually houses have some sort of ticking clock in some forgotten hallway or on a mantelpiece. This one didn't. Instead, I could hear the wind rustling the trees outside.

I stared into the darkness. Moving a foot, I marveled at how loud the sheets were, though they felt so soft to the touch. I wasn't really tired.

Actually. I was tired. But sleep was hiding somewhere in the house. I sighed. And I was pretty sure I knew where.

The voice in my head was still quiet, but more insistent this time, *Mine.*

I pulled the blanket and sheet back and kicked my leg over the side of the bed. As I stood, I balled up a section of the comforter and dragged it off the bed. I didn't bother to put my pants back on as I padded from the room and down the hall to the left of the stairs.

Jonathan didn't move when I entered the den, but I was pretty sure he knew I was there. His heart thumped in his bare chest though his breathing was slow and steady.

Maybe that was my heart thumping.

I closed the distance to the sectional where he was laying and paused a moment laying down against him. He moved to give me more space and I threw the comforter over the two of us. His hand combed through my hair, his fingertips brushing my neck and then staying there. A growl quietly rumbled through his chest and against my back.

He had found the pinprick scars that Sheppard had shown me. His growl told me he knew what they were. Well of course he did; the pack hunts vampires.

I reached for his hand, tangled my fingers in his and gently pulled his hand to my lips. I placed a light kiss there and the rumbling stopped. He pulled his hand free and wound it around my waist, pulling me tightly against him.

"Never again," he whispered into my hair. I believed that too.

15

Ian poked his head into the den just as the night gave way to dawn to let me know that my place was closed up. I sleepily thanked him and drifted back into easy slumber against Jonathan's warmth. A few hours later, I woke to Jonathan shifting and the pack moving around in the house. Though I probably could have slept for longer, I didn't actually feel tired. I sat up and looked at the scars on his chest, visually tracing up to the dark goatee and meeting the gold-flecked green eyes studying me.

"Mornin'," Jonathan said.

I smiled. "Morning."

There was that voice in my head again. It whispered, *Mine.*

I yawned and stretched my shoulders. Jonathan propped his head on his elbow. His eyes scanned the room and took in my legs. "Where'd you leave your pants?"

"In the other room up here," I replied, waving my hand in the direction of the grey and black room. I jutted my chin toward his chest. "Where'd you leave your shirt?"

He fished a piece of cloth out of the cushions behind his elbow. "Right here." He plopped it onto the couch next to me. "Would it make you more comfortable if I put it on?"

I pulled my hand into my lap. I had been tracking the scars along his torso, watching how they moved over his stomach muscles as he breathed—and apparently reaching for them. I guess I wanted to run my fingertips along them more than I thought I did. Dammit.

Mine.

He sat up quickly then, startling me. But it was the movement of those abs of his that was making it hard to breathe. He gently touched my hand, then brushed his hand up my arm, to my shoulder. When he hit the sleeve of my shirt, he brought his hand to the side of my face, pushing his fingers into my hair. I leaned into his touch and closed my eyes. Electricity crept into his woodsy scent, and I was again reminded of a forest after a thunderstorm. His lips brushed mine, gently, tentatively.

I leaned into the kiss and turned toward him, bringing my hand up to touch his cheek and hair.

Mine.

I wanted him then, and my mouth against his became more urgent. I repositioned myself, straddling him on the couch as his hands, sure and strong, slipped under my shirt to grip my waist and hold me to him. I could feel him under me, his warm hardness straining against his jeans.

"I take it that's a 'no' then?" He said, mischief in his tone.

"Hmm?" I pulled back, skeptical of his tone. What game was this?

"The shirt," he said. "I take it you don't need me to put it on to make you more comfortable?"

I snorted. "Only if me putting on pants will make you more comfortable."

He laughed, a rich sound that made my heart dance, but his expression was impish. "It might make my own pants fit a little better."

"Well if it's your pants that are the problem," I replied, "maybe we need to remove them." I slid my hands to the waistband of his jeans, moving toward the button and zipper. My heart kicked like a bass drum in my chest.

He clasped my hands in his, interrupting me, as a chuckle rumbled from his chest. "You are truly a treat, dear Dreamer," he said, his voice husky and soft. He brought my hands to his lips and kissed my fingers. "But maybe we should slow down a bit."

I tilted my head to the side. "Slow down?"

"Well," Jonathan said, raking a hand through his hair. "It's not that I don't want this." He released my hands and clasped my hips, his hands warm. "Because I definitely do." His grip tightened, and his eyes rolled into his head for a moment before returning to mine.

I sat still. What was he getting at? Did this have something to do with how Sheppard and Kaylah wanted him to give me space until the full moon?

"But you only just had your first change. And what we did in the woods last night was wonderful." His hands released my hips and dropped to the couch.

Oh god. I had just thrown myself at him, hadn't I? That kind of stuff made me look like the needy, desperate type. Dammit.

"But there was a lot that happened last night. Maybe, as things settle, you'll come around to a place in here," he tapped my forehead, "where you don't want any of this."

Unlikely. The pull I felt toward him? I hadn't felt that with anyone else. Maybe that had something to do with the fact that I had never been with anyone that was a werewolf—as far as I knew, at least. Maybe it had something to do with him being a werewolf.

Maybe that was his point.

But the gentle way his fingertips traced my cheek to my chin, was a sweetness I wasn't sure I ever wanted out of my life.

Dammit. I've got it bad for him.

He closed his eyes and sighed, his head falling against the back of the couch as his hand fell to his lap. Which I guess was my lap, really.

I pulled my bottom lip in between my teeth and studied the lines of his throat. He had a point, though. Our time alone in the woods last night was...well, it just kind of happened. And it was a lot of fun. And I had definitely wanted it then, just as I definitely wanted it now. But was it only fun?

No, the voice in my head whispered, *mine*.

I scrunched my eyes closed and wiped at my face with both hands. Probably not. I sighed to keep myself from growling as my mind circled back around itself.

So I changed the subject completely. "Do you only call me that because of that dream I told you about?"

He made a face and looked at me again, his eyes searching my own. "Dreamer?"

I nodded.

"You don't like it?"

"I do like it," I replied. "I've just never had a nickname before."

His voice dropped to a conspiratorial whisper and his brow wrinkled. "Isn't Lynn your nickname?"

I made a face. "No, it—" My confusion made me sit up. "Didn't Sheppard tell you my full name?"

His eyes continued searching my face. "When Sheppard found out you were in his territory, he learned what he could and told the pack about you. But he just told us your name was Grace." He paused for a moment. "I think Matt knew more, but he was the one looking out for you."

"So, let me get this straight. You all know my real name, but have been calling me Lynn anyway?"

Jonathan shrugged. "Sure. What do we care what you want to be called? Sheppard named you pack, so if you wanted to be called Twinkle Toes, we'd have just gone with it. It wouldn't change anything."

I laughed. "Twinkle Toes." I shook my head and sighed, looking at him again. "Lynn's my middle name. And I suppose, knowing that, it doesn't really matter then if you choose to call me Grace or Lynn or Dreamer."

His grip returned to my waist and he shook me a little, a smile tugging at the corners of his mouth. "But which would you prefer?"

I thought a moment. "Well, you might as well all stick to Lynn. But you." I leaned into him, my lips brushing against his as I whispered, "You can still call me Dreamer if you want." I felt his lips curl into a smile as I closed my mouth on his again. His hands spread up my back as my hands tangled in his long brown hair.

The smells of breakfast wafted upstairs: bacon was quickly joined by potatoes and eggs. My stomach growled at the scents and I was pretty sure I heard his do the same.

What if he was right, though? What if, when the dust settled, this was all just base urges? What if I only wanted him because he made me feel like I finally belonged somewhere? Well, so what? What if I *did* only want him because he made me feel like I finally belonged somewhere?

Mine, insisted that voice in my head.

"Maybe we should go and get breakfast while it's hot," I murmured against his mouth before pulling away to look at him. The gold flecks in his eyes were more pronounced, and there was a heat in his expression that I hadn't noticed.

"Good idea." He nodded. His heart thumped in his chest, its rhythm matching my own. "We have time. Let's not rush into something just because all our instincts are telling us to."

God bless him for being so damn rational.

"We have time," I echoed, resting my forehead against his. I closed my eyes and took in his electric woodsy-ness, the warmth of his hands against my skin, the hardness in his lap pressing against me.

Mine.

Maybe. Not yet. But maybe. We had time.

But our mouths found each other again. We stayed that way for a long moment, my arm wound around his shoulder and my other hand tangled in his hair. His hands were strong against my back as they pressed me to him.

With a quiet growl in his throat, he wrapped an arm around my waist, the other under my thigh and stood, placing me gently on my feet in front of him.

I let out a quiet whimper at the break in contact.

He smiled and placed another kiss on my forehead. "Now, now, Miss Cartwright. No whining." He lightly tapped my nose with his pointer finger and wrapped the comforter around me. "You go back to your room now, and put your pants back on. Then come and join me for breakfast." He winked. "I'll save you a seat. Besides," his voice dropped to a throaty, husky tone. "I want to be sure to take my time with you."

There was a promise in his words that sent another wave of heat through me.

God, did I ever have it bad for him.

I pouted at him, holding the blanket to me so the weight of it didn't fall off me. "What good are these instincts then, if we can't follow them?"

"You're not wrong," he replied darkly, "but we have time."

"I'll hold you to it, you know," I said, stealing another kiss from him.

His eyes glittered and a corner of his mouth quirked up. "I should hope you would."

I shuffled down the hall to my room and tossed the comforter on the bed before grabbing my pants from the chair. I pulled them on and shoved my phone in the back pocket, ignoring the notification light blinking from its corner.

Downstairs was abuzz with motion and sounds.

"Good morning, Lynn," Sheppard said as I came into view of the dining room. He was seated at the head of the table: an oval-shaped, black granite thing with flecks of iridescence within the surface. The pack sat in white leather chairs at the table, though—as promised— there was an empty seat next to Jonathan. I smiled and waved as I approached my seat.

Chastity and Kaylah were still in the kitchen, but they alternated bringing out plates of food. Sheppard had nearly cleared his plate, but reached for seconds as I sat down.

"Mornin' hun," Kaylah said, touching my hair with one hand while the other placed an empty plate down in front of me. "How'd'ya like yer eggs?"

"Ooh, scrambled with cheese, please," I replied. I reached for a pitcher of milk on the table and filled the empty glass at my seat.

Next to me, Jonathan had potatoes and bacon heaped on his plate.

I stole a piece of his bacon and munched on it while I filled my plate. My arm brushed his a number of times as I did, and he lightly elbowed me back every time, a smile fixed on his face.

"Thanks again for fixing my doorframe, Ian," I said, catching his eye across the table and taking a sip of my milk.

"Not a problem," Ian replied, smiling. "We'll go pick up new locks after we get done digging through the old house."

I sobered. It wasn't like I had forgotten that we were all going to do that today, it just still felt like it was my fault. Or at least, that it wouldn't have happened if it weren't for me. "I'm sorry you guys all have to do that because of me."

"Not as sorry as those God-forsaken vamps are gonna be," Matt retorted, shoveling a forkful of potatoes into his mouth.

"It's not your fault," Chastity added from the kitchen. It was the loudest I'd heard her be. "Those bloodsuckers don't know the hornet's nest they just stirred up."

Daniel smiled at me. "We're all alive and safe because we went running with you. We don't yet know how many vampires there were last night. Maybe there was only one, maybe there were twenty. It was too hard to tell for sure while the smoke billowed from the house. Had we not been out on the preserve, you could argue that someone would have likely gotten hurt when the vamps came to start that fire. Therefore, if anything is your fault, it is simply that none of us were injured—or worse."

Talk about a lawyer's argument. I could see why he was as successful as Sheppard said.

"'Zactly." Kaylah scooped fresh scrambled eggs from a pan onto my plate. "We're all safe on account 'a you." She kissed Daniel's forehead and returned to the kitchen.

I hadn't thought of it that way. Sheppard caught my eye and the corner of his mouth turned up as he stood to take his plate out to the kitchen. Another I-told-you-so. I smiled back at him. Message received. Pack doesn't blame pack for matters outside of our control.

Kaylah took Sheppard's plate as Chastity brought another plate of bacon to the table. I shoved a forkful of cheesy eggs into my mouth.

They were delicious, of course, creamy and yet somehow fluffy at the same time. I followed the eggs up with a forkful of potatoes.

"You guys finish up," Sheppard said. "I'm going to take the truck over and start seeing what's salvageable."

Jamie stood up. "Hang on a sec, and I'll ride with you." He shoved the last two pieces of bacon from his plate into his mouth as he stood and handed his plate to Chastity.

"Mmm." Ian took a gulp of his milk. "Me too." He also handed his plate to Chastity, who deposited both in the kitchen sink.

The three of them headed out the front door. The engine of the Ram rumbled to life and then faded down the street.

"When you're done," Jonathan said to me as I crunched into a crispy piece of bacon. "We can head over in my Jeep." He looked to Daniel and Matt. "You guys wanna ride along as well?"

Matt shrugged. "I'll wait and bring Chas along after breakfast."

"I'll ride over with them, darlin'," Kaylah said to Daniel. "You go on."

Daniel smiled at Kaylah and scooped the last bit of his eggs onto his fork with a small piece of his slice of buttered toast. He stood when he was done and took his plate to the kitchen, where Chastity waited to take it from him, her hand on her hip.

Jonathan finished his last piece of bacon and did the same. Chastity also grabbed Matt's empty plate when he was done, but Matt stayed seated. He leaned back in his chair, clasped his hands behind his head and closed his eyes. Clearly, he was going to just sit there and wait for Chastity to be done cleaning up after breakfast.

I furrowed my brow, alternating looking at Chastity and Kaylah, who were cleaning up after breakfast. "Why not help them, Matt?"

He raised an eyebrow and opened his eyes. "I'm not going in there." He hooked a thumb toward the kitchen. "That's their domain. The ladies have this well in hand."

I pursed my lips. "So you're just going to sit there?"

"Yep." He closed his eyes again. "If you think you could actually be useful in there, why don't you go help them?"

I snorted. "My version of 'doing dishes'," I put my fingers up in air quotes around the last two words, even though he wasn't looking at me, "involves throwing them all into the dishwasher, rinsed or not. I don't do dishes."

His clear brown eye speared me, though his head had only turned a fraction in my direction. "How is that any different than what I'm doing?"

I opened and closed my mouth a couple of times. I didn't have an answer for that.

Matt snorted and closed his eyes again. I shoveled the last of my eggs and potatoes together and washed them down with my milk. Then I stood and took my plate to the kitchen with a piece of toast in hand.

"Thanks, Kaylah," I said as she took the plate. I took a large bite of the toast.

"Don't you worry 'bout it none," she replied. "You folks get on." She made a shooing motion with her free hand. "We'll be along in a bit."

I sprinted up the stairs and pulled on my socks and shoes before rejoining Jonathan and Daniel at the front door. Outside, Jonathan rolled the windows of the Jeep down while I finished my toast and we headed over to the burnt husk of Sheppard's former home.

16

It was one thing to know that a house had been burned to the ground. It was another thing entirely to see the wreckage of that house in person. A uniform, ash-and-black mottling covered everything I thought I would easily recognize. It was disorienting, and bewildering.

Daniel finished taking video of the demolished home as we arrived, and then took pictures of some of the less damaged areas. But nothing was left untouched by ash.

Sheppard directed us on where to start, and though I initially balked at the first piece of fallen timber I moved, I lifted it with ease. The sheer physical strength of being a werewolf astounded me.

The smell was the worst of it, really. It started as wood smoke, but as we moved beams and pieces of wall or ceiling to get at what was underneath, we were struck with this awful choking, burnt chemical scent that stung the eyes.

I found the bowl of keys from the mantel. Or at least, what it used to be. The bowl was smashed, the keys warped and barely recognizable. The couches in the living room were just charred boxes with winding s-shaped springs across the top.

The stairs were not stable, what was left of them. But it didn't matter, the entire upper floor had caved in. I tracked where things fell to see if I could find where any of my own belongings from my room would have landed among the wreckage. I moved a beam and a small section of the roof before I found something strange: a perfect circle of unburnt carpet.

And in the center of that unburnt circle? My completely undamaged rosary.

The air felt thin again. I'm not a devout anything by any stretch of the imagination, but I have faith in God, and that definitely looked like His handiwork.

Sheppard stepped up next to me and looked at the spot. Daniel snapped a picture.

I spun to face them. "You can't show that to the insurance company! They won't believe it's not edited!"

Daniel smiled. "Of course not, but I almost don't believe it myself."

"Blessed," Sheppard murmured, kneeling to peer more closely at the carpet.

"Hmm?" I knelt beside him and reached toward the unburnt circle.

"Your rosary." Sheppard gestured to the spot. "It was blessed, wasn't it?"

I nodded in wonder as I gingerly touched and then pressed my fingers to the carpet next to my rosary. It wasn't even soggy from the water of the fire trucks.

"Can we make a whole house out of that?" Daniel whispered.

Sheppard's mouth turned in a wry smile. "That's not how it works." He met my eyes and hooked a thumb toward the rosary. "I don't suggest you try going anywhere without that."

My teeth were clenched so hard my jaw ached. I sighed and grabbed the untouched rosary.

"What are we looking at?" Jonathan chirped from the wreckage of another room. There were only burnt beams between him and us.

I held up my rosary and pointed to the spot where it had been lying. "Some minor sort of miracle, apparently."

He picked his way over to us and stared at the spot. "If I hadn't seen it myself," he said, "I'd have been sure you were making it up when you told me about it afterward."

"Yea?" Matt tromped over in heavy boots. "Well she's not. It happened. It's real. Let's get back to work already."

I sighed and mumbled, "Jerk," as I walked away from the spot, looping the rosary around my neck and tucking it into my shirt.

He just snorted at me.

As I moved other bits of burnt timber to look for things worth saving, I found myself next to Chastity, who was sorting through what must have been Sheppard's office, judging by the shapes of burnt books.

"You're wrong about him," she said.

"Who, Matt?"

She nodded. "He's not actually a jerk, or a chauvinist. He just shows off that way." She shrugged a shoulder and dropped her voice to a whisper. "Behind closed doors he's a complete softie." Her voice resumed its normal pitch and volume. "That man wouldn't hesitate to give his life for any of the pack. In fact, he's already put his life on the line for you twice over." She pointed a finger at me, poking it at my shoulder as she spoke. There was a hardness to her then that I hadn't yet seen in her.

Matt had put his life on the line for me? "What? When did he do that?"

"Don't you remember him pulling you out of that vampire club downtown?" There was anger in her voice now. "He said you were high that night, but his face is kinda hard to forget!" She made a clawing motion over the left side of her face, where Matt's scars were. The golden in her hazel eyes became more prominent, and there was a sharpness to her vanilla scent. "Never mind that he also killed the crazed wolf that attacked you and brought you here to us!"

Wow. I had never heard so many words from Chastity. She was angry. Her mate had been in danger because of me, and I clearly needed to be more grateful about it.

I wanted to get defensive about it, wanted to shout back at her. But she had a point, and I was certain she wasn't making any of it up. I'd been so caught up in all these changes that I wasn't really thinking about how much it affected the individuals of the pack. I sighed.

"You're right," I said. "I didn't know, or even think about it being him that pulled me out of the jam with that wolf. Jonathan had mentioned that Matt brought me in. I just hadn't thought about it." I gingerly touched her shoulder. I didn't know how ready to fight she could have been. "There's a lot of this that I'm still figuring out, okay Chastity? I didn't know about the club. I remember having gone there a couple of times with my friend Frederick, but I don't remember ever seeing Matt there. I didn't know it was a vampire club."

She closed her eyes and took a breath. "No. Of course you wouldn't have known. It's not like vampires go around telling everyone what they're up to."

"They certainly don't advertise it to people who aren't yet addicted to being their sheep," Ian said. "Hey look!" He lifted a misshapen metal box out of the soot and ash. "It's Shep's computer. Hopefully the hard drive's still good." He wandered off to place the computer in the back of the Ram.

"Aw man!" Jamie exclaimed from the wreckage of the living room. He held up a small black box, but it was warped, and sludge dripped out of the back corner. "We're gonna have to start our game completely over, Ian!"

A growl escaped Ian. "I had just gotten that ultra-rare sword too!" He sighed. "Stupid vampires."

"Hey," Kaylah said from where the kitchen used to be, "leas' th' pots 'n pans are salvageable, along with most a th' silverware." She looked to me. "Hey Lynn, be a dear 'n fetch me a crate outta th' shed?" She hooked a thumb toward the metal structure in the back corner of the backyard.

"Sure," I replied.

I trudged picked my way through the rubble to the backyard, where the grass was clear, if not a little soot-stained. A couple steps past the rubble, I smelled it. That same sickening dead smell that was from the front door of my apartment when I had first visited. The smell Sheppard and Matt had labeled vampire. There was a soft rumbling sound, and with a start, I realized it was me, growling. I was actually growling at that disgusting scent, at the thought of the thing that it came from. I shook my head and continued.

The shed was filled with all the normal landscaping tools you'd expect, along with a workbench and a standing tool chest. Crates were stacked in the back corner with a handful of crutches leaned against them. The top crate held what I considered to be very serious first aid supplies: sutures, gauze, epi pens, and the like—all neatly arranged and sealed in plastic to keep them sanitary. My own first aid kit at home had simply consisted of a half-empty box of band-aids that were something in the realm of two years old. The three crates underneath the first aid crate, however, were empty. I grabbed two of them and headed back to the rubble.

On the way back, I saw the football the pack had been playing with the other night. Smiling, I tossed it into one of the crates.

"Here you go," I said to Kaylah once I got back, handing her one of the crates. I placed the other one down near her, taking the football out.

"Hey Jonathan," I called, catching his eye across the rubble. I held the football up.

His eyes lit up when he saw what I had in my hand. I chucked the football to him and he caught it. "Hey, awesome! I'm glad this made it." He headed to his Jeep, tossing it into the backseat.

"Looks like the grill is salvageable, too," Sheppard said. "But I think everything else is a wash. I'm glad it's all insured." He picked up the grill—which would have only barely fit in the bed of his truck if the tailgate was down—and took it over to the shed. He put it down inside and turned back to the rubble. Kaylah had the two crates I brought her filled with pots, pans, and silverware. She stacked them on top of each other and took them over to the Ram, placing them in the bed as well.

Then we all gathered together in the backyard, where that sickening dead smell was. Sheppard looked meaningfully at Matt, who nodded and started to pull his shirt off. Sheppard put a hand on his shoulder, stopping him. "It's broad daylight, Matt," he said.

"And the scent of them heads straight from here, off into the hills, and onto the reserve," Matt waved a hand to indicate the direction he was talking about. "It'll be faster to track them in wolf form. If I get too close to civilization, I'll stop at the abandoned park ranger shack, pick up some clothes and keep tracking in town." He rubbed a hand over his head, spiking his blond hair with soot from the house. "We need to know where to start this thing."

Something dangerous spiked his tone, and again I was glad he was on our side.

"Be careful," Sheppard said.

"Come back to me," Chastity said, kissing him as he resumed getting undressed.

I turned away and Jonathan rolled his eyes at me.

"People clothes don't fit wolves," he said, chuckling.

I rolled my eyes right back at him.

"C'mon, Lynn," Ian said. "Let's go get the locks for your place." He looked to Jonathan, "You mind driving? We can check on your place and mine afterward."

"Sure," Jonathan replied. "You comin' too, Jamie?"

"Yep," Jamie answered, heading toward the Jeep.

1 7

WE STOPPED AT THE HARDWARE STORE AND PICKED UP A SET OF LOCKS for my apartment. Remembering how Kaylah had chastised me in the big-box store, I tried not to obviously sniff at every person that passed. It was hard. They all smelled different shades of the same handful of scents. But even that didn't compare to the vibrancy of the scents of my packmates.

Ian had taken a picture of my existing door handle and lock so that we could pick something that matched. I followed Jonathan as he led the way through the store. At the checkout, I reached into my back pocket, realizing belatedly that my wallet was in my purse, which was on the floorboard of my car.

"No problem." Ian pulled out a black credit card. "Pack," he whispered as he swiped the card for payment.

"I can't let you guys buy everything for me!" I crossed my arms.

They didn't reply until we were in the Jeep again.

"Pack takes care of pack," Jonathan said as he pulled out of the parking lot.

"But buying everything for everyone?" I arched an eyebrow at him.

Jamie leaned forward from the backseat and put a hand on my shoulder. I met his pale green eyes. "Shep's got a lot of old money tied up somewhere, so does Daniel. And they have investments too. There's more than enough."

"And we all take care of each other," Jonathan said. "Shep doesn't ask for money from any of us, but we usually all end up just buying things for the house and for each other." He shrugged a shoulder. "It's no big deal."

I sucked on my bottom lip and thought about that. The pack was like a family then. More than that, though. I was so content just to be around them—more content than I had been even with my parents at any point in my adult life, and certainly more content than I had ever felt around Jenny and Steph. I closed my eyes and filled my lungs with the soot-covered scent of the three packmates sharing the Jeep with me.

Jonathan's warm hand fell onto my knee and I could smell that we were closer to my side of town—the motor oil smell that seemed to accompany older cars, the old trash scent that accompanies shared dumpsters, and the unmistakable skunk of marijuana that always seemed to hang around the apartment complexes in my area. I hadn't even taken the time to really take it in since...well, since I was attacked.

But then there was that sickening scent again and my eyes snapped open. The tension in the Jeep ratcheted up as Jonathan pulled into a space near the stairs.

"That's fresh," Ian said. "I didn't smell them when I was fixing the door jamb last night."

Them? I inhaled. There was a distinction amongst the sickening dead smells. Them. There had been three of them. I practically flew from the Jeep and up the stairs to my apartment. Three vampires had come to my front door last night between 4 a.m. and dawn. The handle to my apartment turned easily. My stomach turned. The smell of my home was tainted with death. One of them had been inside my apartment. Red seeped into the edges of my vision, and my skin started to feel tight and restrictive.

My chest rumbled with the growl coming from my throat. My lips curled back from my teeth. Arms snaked around from behind me, holding me in place with a strength that was startling, but I struggled anyway, my skin pulling even tighter as my joints started to ache.

"Whoa," Jonathan's voice came softly in my ear. "Easy, Lynn. Take a breath. Not out here." Soothing calm dripped from every word.

I stopped fighting against him and glared at my door through narrowed eyes, my mouth still set in a silent snarl.

"There's no vamp in there," he murmured. "The last one left probably just before dawn. Once you get up close and smell one that's in your face, you'll get a better feel for how I know."

"How *we* know," Jamie corrected.

"For now, just trust me," Jonathan said. "Even if there was a vamp in there, you'd have him dead to rights, easy." His arms around me loosened.

"One of him," Jamie said. "Four of us."

"Unless the vamp is old as dirt," Ian said quietly.

Jonathan's head snapped to Ian. From the corner of my eye, I saw Ian's apologetic look.

"If you rip that door off its hinges," Jonathan said. "You're going to cause a lot of noise and someone's gonna look into it. Just breathe."

I filled my lungs with that sickening dead smell, scenting through it to find Jonathan's woodsy warmth tinged with electricity, Jamie's motor oil scent, and the sharp citrus-lined cocoa scent of Ian. Closing my eyes, I could feel the tension in all of them and could almost see it along the strands that Sheppard had shown me before. They were as ready to fight as I was, but they were calm, steady. I took another deep breath, bringing my face closer to Jonathan's arm around me, hoping his scent could erase some of the death pricking at my nose. The red faded from my vision, but my heartbeat hammered in my ears and my skin still felt tight.

"This is why we stick together," Jonathan said, his voice barely perceptible. "Vampires set off all of the alarm bells in everything we are. Our instincts make us want to destroy them because we know and understand that their only purpose is to kill. But the world isn't ready to see us as we are yet. If their first view of us is violence and destruction, they will never accept that we are only trying to protect them." He relaxed his hold on me entirely, moving his hand over mine on the door handle.

Well I definitely wanted to kill the thing that had violated the sanctity of my home, that's for sure.

I looked over my shoulder at Ian and Jamie, meeting their eyes in turn. Each nodded once to me and I pushed my door open as gently as I could manage through the anger, keeping my hand on the handle as Jonathan's hand shifted to rest lightly on the door itself. The door didn't bounce into the wall, so I must have controlled myself pretty well.

The normally welcome scent of my home had been tainted by death, however. It brought me no relief as I stepped in. Jonathan stepped in to my right and Ian to my left. Jamie stayed in the doorway.

I remembered how Matt had methodically checked my apartment a few days ago. There weren't a lot of places to hide in my apartment, but Ian checked my kitchen while I checked the bathroom and Jonathan checked my walk-in closet. Once we had moved away from the front door, Jamie gently pushed it closed with a small click and stood with his back to it.

With a start, I recognized the cologne mixing with the dead scent.

"Frederick," I spat.

Jamie looked at me. "Who?"

"Frederick," I repeated through clenched teeth. "A friend of mine. Or he was. Sheppard tried to tell me before that he was a vampire. I didn't want to believe him, but then I called him, and he all but confirmed it. And that's his cologne." I waved my hand, gesturing to the air.

"That's who bit you." Jonathan's comment was less a question, more a statement of fact.

I nodded, pressing a hand to the pinprick scars were. "That's who bit me."

Jonathan reached an arm around my shoulder, pulling me closer to him. I inhaled his woodsy electric warmth and listened to the steady rhythm of his heart, trying to force myself not to think about Frederick.

"You called him?" Jamie's voice was incredulous. "As in, you called him after Sheppard had already told you what he was?"

I squeezed my eyes closed and nodded. Calling Frederick was definitely not one of the smartest things I'd ever done.

Jonathan released me slowly and I opened my eyes. "Why would you call him?"

"Because I thought he was my friend." It sounded lame even to my own ears. "Because he was one of the few friends I actually had in this town. Because I thought maybe Sheppard could be wrong." My voice cracked, and I closed my eyes to keep tears from spilling. "That he hadn't only been using me as a source of food."

Jonathan pulled me against him again.

I took steadying breath and pushed back the tears. Frederick was clearly not worth tears. I should have listened to my instincts about him better. Something had always seemed a little off about him. But I guess that's why hindsight is always 20/20.

"Well," Ian said. "Then he probably knows you're a werewolf now, so what was he doing here?"

"He probably wanted to confirm it in person." Jonathan's voice resonated through his chest.

"Couldn't he have known that anyway?" Jamie asked. "If he started the fire last night?"

"If he set the fire last night," I said. "Then sure. But maybe that's why he came here after. To see if the fire would draw me here." I pulled away from Jonathan and paced across my apartment as I thought. "The sheep at the store with Kaylah wanted to take me with them. Maybe he came here to ambush me."

"What good would taking a newly-turned werewolf hostage do for him?" Ian asked.

"Bait," Jonathan said with a growl, looking to me. "He would have used you as bait to try to get the rest of the pack to act. With all of us on edge after the fire, maybe we'd slip up and his brood would get the chance to overwhelm us and take us out."

I balled my hands into white-knuckled fists. Frederick used to be my friend. But, it turns out, all he ever wanted was to drain my blood.

And now that he knows I'm a werewolf, he wants to use me as bait to kill the pack. Great.

I rubbed at my face with a small growl of my own. "So what do we do?"

Ian moved toward the door. "Well first, I'm going to grab my stuff from the Jeep and change these locks." He stepped out of my apartment.

"Why don't you shower while you're here," Jamie suggested. "Matt's tracking the vampires anyway, so we'll work together later today to get a plan of attack."

"Frederick can't hide from us," Jonathan said. "He can bolster his brood all he wants, but we'll still get him and make sure he stops hurting people."

I took a breath. "Okay," I said, walking over to my closet. I looked around my apartment as I opened the closet door. "You guys stay off my furniture, alright? You're all covered in soot and ash, and I don't have any clothes that would fit you."

"We're heading over to my place next anyway," Jonathan said with a shrug as he stepped toward my little kitchen. "I have a shower and some extra clothes for the rest of us there."

My fridge door opened as I pulled clothes from the closet to put on after my shower. I grabbed a towel from the tiny linen closet next to the bathroom and then shut and locked the bathroom door.

I caught my reflection in the mirror. My hair was a stringy mess, and there were blackened sections with bits of ash stuck in it from digging through the wreckage of Sheppard's house. My forehead and face were streaked with ash and soot. There was a light scar on my left cheek leftover from the attack. I touched it as I remembered Jonathan's hand brushing it back at Sheppard's old house, and how I had startled like a spooked deer then.

That had been just three days ago.

Sighing, I reached over and turned on the shower and looked under my sink for any extra shampoo or conditioner I might have since I had taken mine to Sheppard's place. I found a little travel pack in the back corner of the cabinet, with shampoo, conditioner, and a small bar of soap. I was pretty sure it had been under my cabinet for over a year, probably from that time I traveled for the big book convention in Chicago.

It felt like an eternity before the shower water ran clear, but once it did, I washed my hair and ran the bar of soap vigorously over my body. The ache in my joints receded, and I felt some of the tension leave my muscles under the hot water.

Bait. Frederick wanted me to get to the pack. Dammit. When would I stop being a danger to them? And why would they want to keep me around if I was?

I put my head under the shower and watched the water run down the drain for a few moments as I tried to just quiet my thoughts. I turned off the water and dried myself before pulling on underwear and a pair of loose jeans. My favorite pair had been lost in the fire. Dammit. With pursed lips, I tugged a faded black t-shirt over my head and opened the bathroom door to let the steam out. I grabbed the rosary from where I had left it on the bathroom counter and jammed it into my pocket. I also grabbed a comb from my bathroom counter, and though it wasn't my favorite way to detangle my hair, I quickly ran the comb through a couple of times as Ian tightened the last screws on my door.

"Good as new," he said, turning to me. "And just in time."

I smiled at him. "Thanks, Ian. I appreciate it."

"Sure," he replied. "Just maybe try not to make a habit of breaking into your own place, okay?"

"We usually keep spare sets of keys for everyone in a lockbox," Jonathan said. He had a glass of water in one hand and a half-eaten piece of bread in the other. I didn't even know I had bread that hadn't gone moldy. "We should probably put a copy of your key in there too, now."

I stepped over to him and pulled a piece off the bread in his hand. He smiled as I popped it into my mouth.

"Maybe let's just leave a copy with my leasing office for now," I said, swallowing the bit of bread.

"There's not really much of a point to having your own place anyway," Jamie said.

Jonathan shot him a look, and Jamie put his hands up in a placating gesture.

"I just mean that Matt and Chastity, and Daniel and Kaylah don't even bother with a place of their own," he said.

"Yea," Ian said. "But they're also all 150 years old at the least." He shrugged. "Privacy was never really a thing for them."

"They're not all that old," Jonathan retorted. "Daniel and Chastity are both only a hundred or so."

"So wait." I sat in a chair from my dining table to pull on a pair of socks. "How old are the three of you, then, if they're so old?" My tennis shoes followed the socks.

Ian screwed up his face in thought. "It's only been like 12 years since I was turned, I'm 36."

"Yeah," Jonathan said, running a grimy hand through his sooty hair as he took a breath. "But Jamie and I were turned about 50 years back." He bit his bottom lip and his gold-flecked green eyes met mine.

"I, uh," I stammered. "You're."

My eyes unfocused and I was glad that I was already sitting down. Blinking, I ran a hand through my damp hair.

Fifty years, plus the twenty or so that he appeared to be. But even if he was barely more than a child when he was turned, I had slept with a man who was old enough to be my grandfather. I ran my fingers along my cheek and lips before curling them around my mouth and chin. And I knew that wasn't true, not if he fought off the wolf that attacked him and his brother like he said before. Sure, Jonathan looked like some laid-back college student. But...

"Fifty years ago?" My voice sounded foreign to me. "So you're like three times my age?"

Jonathan winced.

Jamie busied himself looking at the books on my bookshelf.

"Cradle-robber." Ian elbowed Jonathan's bicep. He stepped past us and into the kitchen. "Where do you keep your glasses, Lynn?" He opened and closed cabinets as I simply stared at Jonathan.

"Just about," Jonathan said quietly, ignoring Ian. "Yeah. Seventy-two."

"Nevermind," Ian said from the kitchen. "Found 'em."

The kitchen faucet turned on and, a moment later, back off.

More than three times my age then.

I sucked on my bottom lip and let my eyes lose focus again while I thought.

I had slept with a man who was old enough to be my grandfather.

I rubbed my face in my hands. Ugh. We were here for a reason. Locks and a shower. They needed showers too. We had to move. Fine. I had a backpack in my closet, I could put some clothes in there to take along with me. I sighed and stood, stalking over to my closet.

"Lynn—" Jonathan reached a hand toward me.

I stopped and faced him, my expression stopping his hand before it touched me. "Look, my whole life is different now." There was no hiding the frustration from my voice. "Nothing about any of this is familiar, and all I have is whatever fantasies those authors made up." I gestured to my two bookshelves. "Along with whatever you guys tell me to guide me through any of this."

"Lynn—" Jonathan started again.

I balled my fists at my sides. "You're entire generations older than me, Jonathan!"

He closed his eyes and looked away.

I squinted my eyes closed and put a hand to my forehead, "And I slept with you!"

Jamie's eyes went wide. "Whoa," he said, his hands up again in that placating gesture. "And ew." He looked around my apartment. "Um, look, not all of that is made up." He inclined his head to the books. "Some of those authors are werewolves and vampires themselves, they just can't say anything about it."

Ian set his glass down in my kitchen sink. "Sheppard will guide you through everything. And he'll answer any of your questions, any time you ask."

"And I'll answer any I can in the meantime," Jonathan said, his voice calm and level in stark contrast to the turmoil I felt. He didn't look at me, but his heart pounded. He followed Ian into the kitchen and put his glass in my sink too. A moment later, he came back out and stood in front of me as I came out of the closet with my backpack of clothes.

I focused on a point in space over and behind his left shoulder, the direction where my door was.

"I'm sorry Lynn," he said. "It doesn't occur to me to talk about how old I actually am. I don't think it occurs to any of us, really, since it's just this side of irrelevant to us. Pack is what matters."

"*Sarcina eiusdem sanguinis,*" Jamie murmured.

"The blood and the pack—" Ian said.

"Are one." I nodded, pursing my lips as I looked at Jamie. "Right. Which is why I'm still here."

I met Jonathan's eyes, arched my eyebrows, and looked pointedly at my door as I slung my backpack onto my shoulder. "So, let's just go already."

1 8

THE GUYS WAITED IN THE JEEP WHILE I DROPPED OFF THE NEW KEY AT the leasing office. As I climbed into the passenger seat, Jamie reached forward from the backseat and squeezed my shoulder before buckling his seatbelt.

I stewed with my arms crossed as Jonathan pulled away from my apartment.

Sheppard said the oldest werewolf he'd ever known was over a thousand years old, so Jonathan, at 72, was really just a pup by that standard. But that's still a long time to be alive.

I watched him from my peripheral vision. His hair brushed his shoulder as he checked his sideview mirror and changed lanes. A man who was old enough to be my grandfather had no business looking as young—and as hot—as Jonathan did. I rubbed my face with my hands again.

At least Sheppard, at well over five hundred, looked like he was in his forties, though it was a wonder he didn't look so much older than that even. But Jonathan, at less than a fifth that, still looked like he was in his mid-twenties. Jamie and Ian too, really. God, even Chastity and Kaylah didn't look any older than Jonathan and they were twice his age!

There was a snickering laugh behind me. I uncrossed my arms and looked over my shoulder. Jamie was laughing, and Ian was pointing out the driver side window at a gas station.

Kum & Go.

"Really?" I rolled my eyes. "You guys are how old and you're making this joke?"

But the corners of my mouth turned up, and as I turned back around, I saw Jonathan's had too.

Maybe it was silly to be so frustrated about all of this.

It's just that every time I thought I had some of the mess sorted out, something else came along. I just wanted to get my head above water for a moment. And I had a lot to learn about this werewolf stuff.

Well fine. Sheppard clearly wanted me to stay with the pack, and the only way I was going to figure any of this out anyway would be to watch them and listen. So fine. I crossed my arms and settled back in my seat again.

But we were already in the parking lot of another apartment complex. I hadn't even been paying attention to where we were headed. The buildings were all finished with old stone façades, and they all had a vintage, historic feel to them. Ivy crawled up the sides and corners of the buildings, almost staining the walls with its red and gold fall colors.

As we exited the Jeep, I inhaled deeply, trying to smell whether vampires had been by. If they had, it hadn't been anytime recently. At least, not that I could smell.

Jonathan led the way to one of the first-floor apartments and unlocked the door.

We stepped into a crisp white hallway with dark hardwood flooring.

"There should still be some cold sodas and water in the fridge," he said. Help yourself to whatever you'd like. There may even be some snacks in the pantry, but I'm not sure how long they've been there."

The apartment smelled a little musty, but there were also faint hints of perfume along with Jamie's motor oil and Jonathan's woodsy warmth. I tried to shake the feeling that I was intruding on the space. Maybe the woman I smelled was a girl Jamie was seeing.

Mine, whispered that voice again.

But he wasn't. Not really.

What if that perfume belonged to some girl Jonathan was seeing? Was he the type to sleep with someone else if he already had someone?

God, what was wrong with me?

I growled and tried to clear my head. I needed to talk to him, but I wasn't sure I wanted to do that in front of the others. Maybe pack didn't keep secrets, but it still felt like something you don't just air in front of everyone.

Jonathan stopped at the entryway closet and handed Ian grey sweatpants and a white t-shirt.

"Thanks," Ian said. "Dibs on the first shower!"

He brushed past me into the living room down the hall—a living room that might as well have been the size of my whole apartment. There were a pair of black leather sectionals set opposite each other in that huge room, with a couple of grey throw pillows on each. A flat-screen TV was on a stand set on a diagonal across one of the corners of the room, and a stone fireplace framed by dark wood that matched the floorboards occupied the other open corner. There were no ashes in the fireplace, though a couple of logs waited for the next cold night.

There weren't any pictures on the mantel or TV stand, nor on the walls. Weird.

The dining room to my right was small, compared to the living room, but it held a chrome table topped with smoky glass and four black leather dining chairs.

Ian ducked into what I presumed was a bathroom through a door off the living room and the water turned on.

"My room's over there," Jonathan gestured to a door on his left, opposite the entry to the dining room. "Jamie's is to the left through the dining room. Why don't you watch something while we get our showers done?" He handed me the remote from the TV stand. "I should still be logged in to stream movies."

Jamie had disappeared, presumably to his room, and Ian was still in the shower. I met Jonathan's eyes as I took the remote. "Can we talk? Maybe let me get my head wrapped around some of this?"

Jonathan's eyes softened, and a smile played at his mouth. "Sure. Follow me. You can sit outside the bathroom door and talk to me while I shower. Unless this is the sort of conversation that merits me staying covered in ashes?" There was mischief in his eyes again.

The thought of water dripping down that body had my face getting warm, along with other parts of me.

I shook my head, hoping he didn't see the color in my cheeks. "No, no. Clean up, for sure. I'll come talk with you."

I suspect he did though, because he peeled off his shirt and then turned to open the door to his room.

To the right, the door to the en-suite bathroom stood open. I followed him into the bedroom, where a king-size bed with crisp white sheets and a grey and black duvet dominated the room. Despite that, there were two black leather armchairs around the room that would have matched the sectionals in the living room. One was next to the door of the bathroom, the other was in a corner facing the foot of the bed. He closed the door bent to remove his shoes before stepping into the bathroom.

I turned my back to the room when I heard the zipper. He had made no effort to close the door. The rumble of Jonathan's laugh came as soon as my back was turned.

"You've already seen me naked," he said, mirth filling his voice. "You've even slept with me, but you're still going to turn your back as I undress."

It was dumb, but his laugh made my stupid little heart sing.

"I'm just trying to give you some privacy!"

I felt the warmth of him close behind me then, the smoke-covered woodsy scent wafting over my shoulder.

"I need no privacy from you, Dreamer." His voice was husky in my ear. "I have nothing to hide."

My heart pounded in my ears. I was certain he could hear it. But, at least his heart was pounding too. I took a breath and tried to ignore the warmth of him.

"Then who—" I swallowed "Who's perfume is that?"

God, I just asked that question like a jealous girlfriend. Dammit.

Jonathan's forehead hit my shoulder.

"Some girl from one of the clubs downtown," he said, his breath warm against my shoulder blade as he spoke to the ground. "Elaine. She was just looking for a good time; I needed to blow off some steam. We had a fun night, but never even exchanged phone numbers."

He lifted his head, but I didn't turn around.

"You aren't even sure you want me, and yet here you are riled up about some weeks-old perfume in my apartment?" He sighed and then kissed my shoulder. "You territorial little thing." The mirth was back in his voice. "That was weeks ago."

The good thing about this internal truth-o-meter I had somehow developed upon turning into a werewolf, was that there was something liberating about just *knowing* something is true.

I sucked on the inside of my bottom lip. "Would you still have slept with me if you were still talking with her?"

"Lynn." He tugged at my shoulder, turning me to face him. "We can't really have worthwhile relationships with regular people. We can't say anything about being a werewolf, so there's always this distance. I don't know if you know this, but people don't like to be kept at an arms distance all the time. Particularly not if they want to be in any kind of meaningful relationship with you."

I tried to keep my eyes glued to his face, but they kept drifting south. After one or two course corrections, he smiled at me. The smug bastard.

I echoed Sheppard's words to me: "People aren't ready for werewolves."

He nodded. "Exactly."

"That doesn't actually answer my question, though."

His green eyes met my own. "No. I wouldn't have still slept with you."

I could feel the stupid truth to that too. Well at least there was that.

Something mischievous glittered in his eyes. "But I definitely would have ended it with her as soon as I got the chance, so I could try."

I gasped at him in mock surprise. There were butterflies in my stomach and something warm settled between my thighs.

He winked and disappeared into the bathroom. The water turned on immediately after.

He still hadn't shut the door.

"God," he said a moment later. "No wonder you took such a long shower! I forget how this soot clings!"

"You forget?! How many of these house fires have you helped clean up after?" I sat down on the closed toilet. If he wasn't going to shut me out, then there was no point to shouting throughout the apartment.

Not that I really needed to shout anyway—when he replied, I could hear him clearly despite the water running. "This is at least the third. They try it in nearly every town we go to. I guess since we wipe out the brood that does it, word can't exactly travel at how ineffective it is."

"Doesn't it get expensive to keep moving like that?"

"Of course it does," he said. "But remember, the pack has money tucked away for things like this, and Sheppard always gets the highest level of homeowner's insurance he can get."

"He said Daniel's a big-time lawyer, too, right?"

"Yep," he replied, "and Daniel fights tooth and claw to make sure the pack is never shorted on claims."

I fell quiet again, thinking.

The water started up in the other bathroom. I hadn't even heard when Ian finished his shower. The steam filling this bathroom was heady with wood and warmth. His soap and shampoo added another layer to his scent, reminding me vaguely of the detergent aisle in the big-box store, but his scent floated above it on the steam.

Mine, declared that little voice again.

I sighed. "You could have said something sooner about your age, you know."

The water turned off and Jonathan's scarred arm grabbed the towel from the rack.

"When would have been appropriate? Between telling you that your bloodline goes all the way back to the family of Jesus and Matt letting slip that your first change could mean you have to die?"

The shower curtain opened and gold flecked green eyes bored into mine. The towel was tucked around his waist.

"You say that like you actually did plan to say something."

He ran a hand through hair that looked black with the water. "You're right. Like I said before, it truly never occurred to me."

Water dripped down his chest and those stomach muscles, tracing the lines of his scars.

He rolled a shoulder. "Not that there would have been any good time to mention it even if I had planned to."

The warmth returned between my thighs and the butterflies settled into the pit of my stomach again. I licked my lips and stood, taking a step toward him before I stopped myself and closed my eyes, trying to clear my head again.

Why did I always just want to throw myself at him every time I saw him? I took a breath, but it was filled with his woodsy warmth and practically crackled with the electricity between us. And why did it always feel like that was exactly what I was supposed to be doing every time?

He took a step toward me then, closing the distance between us.

"You're going to outlive those friends of yours, Lynn," he said, his voice low and soft.

They weren't really my friends. I mean, I guess they were the closest things I had. But I didn't really fit in with them. And I always got the feeling they were only inviting me along for things because they felt sorry for me.

One of his arms curled around my waist and pulled me closer to him. His other hand brushed my cheek.

"You'll outlive practically everyone you know now. But not us, not pack." He bent his head and closed his mouth over my own as his hand tangled in my hair.

The kiss tingled through my entire body, right down to my toes, settling in that warm spot between my thighs. He was hard against me, and I wanted nothing more in that moment than to rip my own clothes off and lay with him there on the bathroom floor, nevermind that there was a perfectly serviceable bed only steps away. His heart hammered in his chest, its rhythm matching my own.

I wondered then if Kaylah's ever matched Daniel's, or if Chastity's ever matched Matt's. It was a silly thing to wander through my mind at that moment and I smiled against his mouth.

He pulled back then, looking at me. There was a heat in his eyes like there had been on the couch this morning. "We really don't have the time now." There was a sorrow to his voice. "Not the kind of time I'd like. Not for this."

I pouted at him. "It's a wonder if we ever will have the kind of time you'd like."

I ran a hand down his back and over his butt, releasing the towel from his waist. I kissed him again as my other hand wrapped around his hardness.

He inhaled sharply at my touch and twitched in my hand. It only stoked the heat in me and I ran my hand up and down his length. He growled and picked me up, sitting me on the bathroom counter, and took a step away from me, effectively placing his hardness out of reach. His hands were on the counter, on either side of my thighs, and he rested his head against my forehead.

"I want you so bad I could crawl out of my skin just to take you," he said thickly, sending yet another wave of heat through me.

My heart hammered in my ears and at my throat.

"But I'm also not willing to rush things before I know you really want this." His eyes met mine, the golden flecks had grown so that hardly any green remained. His heart beat just as hard as my own, the rhythm continuing to match. "I just want everything to be perfect with you. As perfect as it can be. I know life is messy and what we are is messy. But you..." He closed his eyes and pressed his lips to my forehead. "God. There is nothing more that I want than to give you the entire world if it would just make you smile." He placed his head

157

against my forehead again. "And I'm ready to tear apart anyone who could stand in the way of that."

A shiver ran through me.

"And that terrifies me," he continued, his voice quiet, but husky with need. "It's scarier than anything I've ever known."

I swallowed around a lump that had suddenly formed in my throat. Biting on my bottom lip and sucking on it, I raised my hands to his head, tangling in his hair as I brought his face up to meet mine. I stared into those too-golden eyes for a long moment.

"I'm trying to give you the space you need to decide for yourself what you want," he said.

I closed my mouth around his, tangling my hand in his hair as the other wrapped around his shoulder. We stayed like that for a long moment before I pulled back from him.

"If we are as long-lived as you say," I said. "As long-lived as Sheppard says, then there is time for us. If there is ever to be an us, there is time for it. I just need to figure you out first. Maybe this pack and wolf stuff too. But definitely you." I closed my eyes and placed my forehead against his, rubbing his nose with my own. "It's pretty obvious that I want you too, you know. And that's pretty scary for me too. It hasn't exactly gone well with anyone I've dated in the past, and what you're talking about sounds so much more serious than just dating."

"And that's what I mean about coming around to a place in here," he pulled his head back and gently bumped it into my forehead again, "where you don't want any of this."

"That's not at all what I mean." I placed a quick kiss on his mouth. "It seems to me to be pretty obvious that I at least want part of this. I just haven't yet decided on the rest." I met his eyes, a smirk pulling at my mouth. "Maybe you'll have to convince me."

He kissed me, and I could feel the relaxation flow through him. Which, again, set my stupid little heart to singing.

Mine, declared that insistent little voice. And maybe, just maybe, it was right.

19

IAN'S PLACE WAS THE BASEMENT APARTMENT BELOW A RETIRED LADY'S
Victorian-style home on the west side of town, in Old Colorado City.
He mentioned on the drive that since he showered at Jonathan's, he
only needed to pick up a few changes of clothes from his place. There
was no hint of the scent of vampires here, just as there hadn't been at
Jonathan's.

Ian wanted to make it a quick stop, so we didn't follow him in. He
came back to the Jeep a few moments later with a black duffel bag,
presumably full of his clothes. As he settled back into the backseat,
clicking his seatbelt into place, Jonathan's phone buzzed. Then mine
did the same, and Jamie's, and Ian's. It was a group message.

Sheppard: *Matt's back. Waiting on you.*

I didn't even know I had his number, though I guess I just missed it
scrolling through my contacts before.

"Glad we made it a quick stop here, then," Ian said, tucking his
phone back into his pocket.

Jonathan: *On our way.*

Jonathan's reply buzzed around the phones in the Jeep before he was back on the highway. I apparently had his number too. I scrolled through the contacts in my phone; all of my old contacts were there, but Sheppard must have added all of the pack's numbers when he activated this phone with my SIM card. Well that was handy.

The freshly cleaned scents of Jonathan, Jamie, and Ian were relaxing. Jamie's motor oil scent was now tinged with a lemony freshness, the same lemony freshness that seemed to enhance Ian's citrus-y cocoa scent.

I wasn't ready to think about long-term stuff with Jonathan, but I saw no problem in spending time with him in the meantime. Besides, it would help me to decide, right? Maybe I would just get sick of his face.

He caught me watching him again and smiled at me.

Or maybe I'd just keep awkwardly staring at him for the rest of my apparently long life. I rolled my eyes at myself and turned to look out the window.

Jonathan's warm hand fell on my knee and, aside from shifting gears at the appropriate time, stayed there until we reached Sheppard's house. It only stoked the song in my stupid little heart.

These guys felt more like home than anything I had been able to produce since moving out of my parents' house four and a half years ago. It was bizarre, but comforting.

At the box-like glass house, Jonathan was left parking on the street. A white Mercedes was parked next to Sheppard's black truck, with Matt's gorgeous red and black Camaro behind it. My purple Del Sol was on the street in front of the house, with a blue Ford Mustang in front of it.

Chastity pulled a huge package of paper towels out of the back of Sheppard's truck as Jonathan parked in front of the blue Mustang. We got out of the Jeep, and she pulled another huge package, this one of toilet paper, out of the truck bed. Jonathan opened the door to the house for her and we followed her in.

Sheppard, Daniel, and Matt sat at the dining room table, water bottles in front of them. Sheppard looked grim at the head of the table, but smiled gently at us as we filed in. To his right, Matt was leaned on the table, chin in hand. He looked bored, but his musky scent was sharp, something I had come to learn meant an agitation of some sort. But his heartbeat, when I listened for it, was steady—as was everyone's in the house. The comfort of that steadiness washed through me as I came to sit at the table, close to the end on Daniel's side. Daniel, on Sheppard's left, had a stack of papers in front of him, which I assumed were insurance and other legal documents. I had never dealt with the ramifications of a house fire, but I saw the mountain of paperwork that went into my parents selling their home before they retired. I didn't envy Sheppard.

Jamie and Ian sat across from me at the table. Jonathan grabbed a couple of water bottles from the kitchen and sat on my right, leaving an empty chair between Daniel and me.

In the spacious kitchen, Kaylah stuffed packages of meat into the freezer and stacking other packages of meat into the fridge. I did some quick counting—there was easily over 100 pounds of meat between the freezer and the fridge. They would have practically cleared out anything a grocery store had.

"Where do you guys get all of that meat?" I asked Kaylah. It was hard to imagine a store being happy with getting cleared out on any sort of regular basis.

"There's a butcher on th' north end a town 'at we like," she replied. "Sells bulk packs a meat fer a reasonable rate."

And I thought I had been doing well before when I got two-pound packs of ground beef on manager's special at the end of the week. I used to mix it with rice and eat off it for a week or more. Sometimes, I'd even add shredded cheese. It was what I would splurge on when I had a little extra in a paycheck. Now, I was pretty sure what used to seem like so much food would end up being a meal for two at best.

Chastity headed back outside after dropping off the paper towels and toilet paper in the corner of the dining room. She came back in a moment later with two huge bags of the good charcoal—the kind that was basically pre-burned chunks of wood. She had a bag slung over each shoulder as she came through the house. I jumped up to help her, but she speared me with a look as I got close to her.

"These aren't heavy, Lynn," she said, continuing past me. "They're just bulky. I don't need help. Thank you." She placed them down next to the back door.

I sat back down. Matt smirked at me, but when I caught him, he folded his arms behind his head and leaned back in his chair. I caught Jonathan's eye; he smiled at me too. I sighed as Chastity came and sat in the empty seat next to Matt.

Kaylah washed her hands when she was done putting away all of the meat and came to join us at the table, taking the empty seat between Daniel and me.

I closed my eyes for a moment, my heart swelling at the sound of the pack's heartbeats and the intermingling scent of them all. As I concentrated on the feeling, reveling in it, I saw the strands of the pack illuminate again behind my closed eyes. I could see the tied strands of Kaylah and Daniel, and those of Matt and Chastity. Even if I didn't know where Sheppard was at the table, I could have simply traced the thick bright cord in my mind's eye to him. My own strand was thin, but it reached toward Sheppard and tied in with the knot that was the pack.

Matt took a breath to speak and I opened my eyes. "The vampires that set the house on fire came from the same cave where we found the caged werewolves." He pulled a folded trail map out of his pocket and took Sheppard's proffered pen. "The cave is here." He marked the map. "And there are human sheep guards patrolling out to here." He made an arcing line on the map. "There's fresh blood on the walls of the cave. Fresh werewolf blood." The hand holding the pen curled into a fist "But it's not enough blood to cover the scent of the old blood mixed there. There was a new wolf in a cage, bringing the total of caged wolves to three, but the new one was just as crazed as the others."

I swallowed around a hard lump in my throat as red seeped into the edges of my vision. Kaylah grabbed my right hand, squeezing it hard. I wasn't sure I was ready to be thrown into this fight, but I also wasn't about to let the vampires get away with all they had done. Burning the pack house was one thing, holding crazed wolves hostage was another. I didn't understand it, but I was angry.

"We'll hit the cave hard in the morning," Sheppard said, "a few hours after dawn. How many humans?"

"There were three on patrol at the time," Matt replied. "But I could smell that as many as ten had been patrolling recently."

"And how many vampires could you smell?"

"At least five." Matt placed the pen down in a deliberate, controlled action. "But you and I both know that means there's more than that."

"Why?" I blurted. "Shouldn't you be able to smell all of them?"

Matt opened his mouth, but Sheppard put a hand up, stalling him.

"The older a vampire gets," Sheppard said, "the less of a scent they have. You already know what relatively new vampires smell like. Older vampires don't smell like anything except where they just came from."

"And it's hard to smell anything past fresh blood," Matt added as Sheppard's hand came back to rest in front of him. He gestured around the table. "There's enough wolf in all of us that instincts matter."

I nodded. "But why wait till morning? Why not just go now?"

Though Matt's scent had softened some when Chastity sat beside him, the edge was back and prickled my nose.

Matt's palms hit the table. "What kind of idiot tries to attack a vamp stronghold at night?"

"Matt," Sheppard said, a note of warning in his tone. "She's new."

Matt closed his eyes and huffed out a frustrated breath. The words came out slow and measured, like a practiced speech. "Attacking vamps at night is dumb. They sleep during day and are active at night. At night, you hit a den, and maybe they aren't even there. Then you've blown your plan of attack. In the daytime, vamps usually just have sheep guarding them. They know sheep don't stand a chance against wolves, but they also know we won't kill sheep, which slows us down. But if we're careful, with a good daytime attack, we can get the drop on a brood's den and take them out without losses."

"And killing sheep is never an option," Sheppard said, "unless they're trying to kill us. Sheep on patrol for a vampire are so addicted to feeding and addled in the head that they cannot possibly understand anything more than what they're set to do."

"So we hit the cave in the morning," Daniel said, jutting his chin toward the map. "Who do you want on point for the sheep?"

"I'll knock them out and get them restrained," Sheppard said. "Kaylah, with your medical training, it's probably best if you help with checking them in at Blood of the Cross. They know you over there anyway."

"Sounds good to me," she said. "Daniel, hun, can you rent us one a them big vans for tomorrow?"

"Sure." Daniel nodded. "I'll get it after we're done here."

"Wait," I said. "Blood of the Cross is a rehab center, isn't it? What good will drug rehab do them?"

"Being fed on is an addiction like any other," Ian explained.

"And that center is run by the Catholic church," Matt said.

I thought a moment. "So that means some of the staff there know about vampires, possibly werewolves too, and will get the people the care they need." The words were slow and measured, coming out as I connected the thoughts in my head.

Sheppard smiled patiently at me, Jonathan reached over and squeezed my knee.

"Okay," I said. "So what about the 'world isn't ready for werewolves'?" I used my hands to make air quotes around the last phrase.

"They're not," Sheppard said. "We're just using resources that are already aware of us."

"Then who all knows about us?" I asked.

"Well," Sheppard said. "Certain high-ranking members of the Catholic church, of course." He held up his hand, pointer finger extended. "Then there are the other werewolf packs, as you'd expect." He extended his middle finger too. "Then certain sectors of the military." His ring finger extended as well. "The vampires know about us, obviously." His pinky finger joined the other three. "And odds are good that certain members of occult societies have us figured out."

"But they wouldn't dare blab to the world or we'd be in a heap a trouble," Kaylah added.

"Humans shoot first and ask questions later," Matt said. "Even the sectors of the military that know about and have werewolves within them don't advertise that fact to the rest of them. They know their own tendencies as well as we know ours."

"But we've gotten off topic," Sheppard said, gesturing to the map. "So, we'll attack the cave tomorrow in the morning. Kaylah and Daniel will help with the sheep. Everyone else is on cleanup detail. Vampire bodies burn readily in the sun, so once they're immobilized, just pull them out of the cave and the sun will take care of the rest."

My stomach felt a little queasy at the thought of that.

"Lynn," Sheppard continued. "In the meantime, I need to know what you're actually capable of." His tone was fatherly. "So, I need you and Matt out back today, sparring."

I was glad I wasn't trying to drink anything, or I probably would have spit it out. "You want me to fight? And you want me to fight Matt?!"

I was practically a limp noodle compared to the football player physique Matt had.

"No one gets left behind on hunts," Sheppard said. "It leaves us vulnerable."

Matt leaned his elbows on the table. "The best way to learn how to fight a vamp, is to actually fight one."

Sheppard looked at me. "Matt's our best fighter. I trust him to judge your abilities. Like it or not, this is the war we fight. People's lives are on the line, Lynn, and we are what stop the things in the night from eating them alive."

2 0

MATT WAS GOING TO CRUSH ME. I TOOK A DEEP BREATH. THEN another. I didn't want to fight anyone. I just wanted to curl into my chair under a cozy blanket and read books. I hadn't fought anything a day in my life. I mean, I ran sometimes, and I won a raffle through the newspaper for a few free months of a kickboxing class, but I had never actually fought anyone. Except for that wolf that attacked me, I guess. But even that nearly killed me.

"So," my voice cracked, and I swallowed. "So what do you want me to fight him with? A knife? A gun?" My brain latched on to the last one. "You mean you want me to go to a shooting range with him, right? You just shoot…"

Everyone was looking at me like I was a poor lost puppy.

"Vampires are about as bulletproof as we are," Jonathan said quietly. "We fight with teeth and claws. It's what we were built to fight with."

"But Matt's huge! He's going to kill me!"

"He will not," Sheppard's voice was stern. "He wouldn't dare." His voice softened. "He is likely to be quite a bit better than you, of course. But he isn't going to do any actual harm to you. None of the pack would. Nor would he harm anyone in the pack."

"At least," Matt said, "nothing you won't heal right away. If I go too easy on you, I'll never know what you're actually capable of."

I wiped a hand across my forehead and down the side of my face before pushing it back up and into my hair. My heart was slamming into the backside of my sternum so hard I was certain werewolves two counties over could hear it.

"It's not that bad," Ian said, shrugging a shoulder. "It's more like our own version of a physical."

"Matt beat the tar out of me," Jamie said, something grim in his expression.

"Yea, but you kept thinking he was going to go easy on you," Jonathan replied. "You never stopped and took it seriously." He looked to me and shrugged. "Matt's a fighter. You have to think about it like you're fighting a fighter. The vampires know you're there to kill them. So they fight like you're there to keep them from seeing another night."

I sighed and squeezed my eyes shut, swallowing around the lump of fear in my throat and the dread in my stomach. I took another deep breath and tried to calm myself and met Matt's eyes as I stood up.

"Then let's just do this now and get it out of the way."

Matt's face was unreadable as he stood. His heartbeat was damnably steady. Of course it was. He wasn't afraid of me. I'm just a girl.

He was going to crush me.

I followed Matt to the back door of the house, where he held the door open for me. Sheppard followed both of us into the spacious backyard.

"The houses on either side of us are empty this time of year," Sheppard said. "But let's not let anything spill into those yards anyway."

"We'll start with hand-to-hand like this," Matt said, gesturing at himself. "Then you'll go wolf and I'll find out what your instincts are like. Like Sheppard said, I'm not going to kill you, but I'm not going to go easy on you, either. The vamps wouldn't."

I brushed my hand up my forehead and into my hair again. "Let's just do this."

And then Matt's fist jabbed square into my mouth so hard my eyes watered, and I staggered a few steps backward. Dammit. I hadn't even seen him move.

No one had ever hit me before. What the hell?

I was still reeling from the shock of having actually been hit when he jabbed me in the face again. Stumbling still more steps backward, I tasted blood and wiped at my mouth and chin. My fingers came back stained red and I spit what blood I could from my mouth.

I hadn't seen him move that time either.

Worse, he was still coming at me, lashing out with a foot toward my stomach. I dodged to the left, still reeling from the punches, but at least he missed. He followed me with a couple of quick steps until he overtook me, placing his leg behind mine as he shoved me hard to the ground. Dammit all to hell. I hit the grass and dirt with an audible crack in my shoulder and stars exploded in my vision as the air was forced from my lungs.

I thought fighting someone would leave me scared, or at least anxious. I thought I'd want to just curl up and cry or run away until I lost them. But as I lay there on the ground with an agonizing ache in my shoulder, I didn't want any of that. And I wasn't scared. I was mad. I was angry. I was absolutely furious, actually. And I wasn't sure who or what I was mad *at*.

The fight was over fast. Faster than I'd thought it would have been. If that had been someone actually trying to kill me, I'd be dead. I didn't even know what it was exactly or how to describe it, but I wanted to beat the crap out of him for it.

I was ready to beat the crap out of him.

I stood up, reaching for my aching shoulder with my other hand. As I moved it, something cracked back into place.

Had he seriously dislocated my shoulder when he shoved me to the ground? Had I seriously just reset it?

Matt was talking, but I didn't hear his words. I licked my lips, expecting to taste blood, but my mouth had apparently healed. Wow. My face still ached, though.

I balled a fist and aimed it for his nose. He sidestepped easily, deflecting my punch and pulling me in to his knee, slamming it into my gut in a single fluid motion. The air rushed from my lungs as I doubled over. Matt's elbow followed, cracking into the back of my skull, driving my face into the dirt.

At least he wasn't going easy on me.

His voice came from above me as I tried to regain my senses on the ground. "I told you. Stop. Thinking!"

Red seeped into the edges of my vision as my fist curled around a handful of dirt and grass. I threw it into his face as I rolled over, sweeping his right leg out from under him as he tried to clear the dirt from his eyes. I took that moment to scramble to my feet.

I stopped being angry then. Squaring off against Matt, as he rolled back and used his hands to launch himself to his feet, I wasn't scared, or mad. I was eager. Hungry. Ready. The red settled along the edges of my vision as a wolfish grin split Matt's face. His heartbeat was as steady as it had been when we started, and while mine had been hammering away in my chest, it was slowing. I doubted my heartbeat would ever match his, but they were syncopated cousins of each other.

Matt's hand came toward my face again, but I dropped below it, only to find his other fist coming at my face. I took a quick step to the side, avoiding the attack and pushing his arm away with my hand. But I was lined up then. I slammed my elbow hard into his gut and the air whooshed out of him in a grunt.

"Excellent," he chortled.

I turned to smile at him in time to see his fist connect with my temple, driving me to the ground again.

I groaned with exertion as I stood up, blinking to clear my vision.

"Good," Matt said. "Now clothes off, wolf out. Let's see what you're really made of."

The rest of the pack was lined along the back side of the house, watching us.

"Out here?!"

Matt rolled his eye. "Yes." He crossed his arms. "Out here."

But I hesitated, my head throbbing, and Matt narrowed his eyes at me. I still couldn't be sure how much vision he actually had out of that milky left eye.

"I suppose," he said derisively, "if you're still too modest for that, you could go inside and change, but a vamp wouldn't wait for you."

The red seeped back into my vision again.

Jonathan's whisper carried over to me even from where he stood alongside the house. "It's just skin."

I scanned the pack and met Sheppard's eyes. He nodded, the motion almost imperceptible.

I growled. "Fuck it." I turned my back to the pack and pulled my shirt over my head as I stepped out of my shoes. "Let's just do this." I unhooked my bra and tugged my pants and underwear off my hips in a single motion. It was uncomfortable to be naked in such an open place, but this was my pack. I belonged here just as much as any of them. I took a breath and tried to clear the nervousness from my head.

But I didn't have a clue how to get into wolf form again. I clenched my eyes shut and tried to remember the feeling from the night before.

God, it had only been the night before when I had first changed into a wolf for the first time.

"No, no," Matt said, derision still in his tone. "It's all right, we'll all just wait while you figure it out."

I didn't open my eyes, didn't look at him.

Dammit. How the hell do I do this?

The pack was quiet, but I could feel the tension in the air.

"Like your dream," Jonathan whispered.

In those silly dreams I had before I was attacked, I simply had to stop fighting the change to make the change happen. Okay. So I just had to let go.

I took a deep breath and just envisioned letting go of my need to walk upright. My gut wrenched hard, driving me to the ground as I cried out. I pushed harder on the sensation, trying to push myself into the wolf and trying to let go of my human form. I was a werewolf. That meant I needed to be a wolf sometimes. My gut wrenched again and my joints ached, causing me to cry out again.

But I wasn't wolf. Not yet. And after the wrench passed, my too tight skin tingled with the want for a different shape, and there was a lump in my throat. I wasn't sure I could do it. I wasn't sure how to get any closer to wolf by myself.

A warm hand fell on the back of my head.

"You can do it," came Sheppard's quiet voice, his power washing over me. "Don't think so hard about it. Just be. *Sarcina eiusdem sanguinis.*"

Stop thinking. Matt had said the same.

I took a gulping breath and…let go. I just stopped trying any of it. I decided I needed to be wolf and my body did the rest. With the same sharp, breaking pain as before, my body rearranged itself to accommodate my new form.

I shook when it was done and snorted out the last of the ache from my nose.

Werewolves are big. I hadn't realized that during our run on the reserve. I estimated my chin to be just above Matt's waistline.

"Well?" Matt said.

I lunged for his face, but he caught my head in two meaty hands. Launching off his chest, I propelled myself backward with all four paws, wrenching my face from his grasp.

"Good instincts, but that won't work," Matt chided me. "I could have snapped your neck there, and any vamp would be glad for the opportunity. You're dead." He pulled a knife from his belt. "Vamps usually have knives, big ones—some even carry swords. They get a good, solid hit to your spinal column and you're done. Try again."

Well, shit. Alright. I darted to his right, drawing his attention like I was going for his knife hand. As soon as he stepped that direction, I cut left and opened my jaws to grip his leg, catching meat and bone below his knee as I pulled his leg out from under him with all my strength. The flesh tore easily, his blood flowing into my mouth as the pressure crunched through bone.

Matt shouted in pain through clenched teeth. The strands I had seen of the pack lit up like fireworks behind my eyes and I let go.

I had hurt pack.

Gravity continued the motion I had started with Matt, pulling him to the ground.

I hadn't ever had anything's blood in my mouth but my own, let alone another person's. I didn't even like my steaks all that rare. It was disconcerting.

The pack was laughing, but Matt was clearly hurt. With a whine, I planted my butt on the ground as Kaylah hurried over to examine Matt's leg.

He ignored her and smiled at me.

Why was he smiling?

"Good job," he said. There wasn't any pain in his voice, and the approval in his tone spread warmth through me. "That worked because I thought you were going for the knife."

"Geez, Matt," Jonathan called. "If I knew that was all it took to take you down—"

Matt didn't look away from me; he just held up a fist in Jonathan's direction, middle finger extended as he kept talking.

"You should always disarm a vamp when you have the opportunity to, but your speed at pulling me to the ground worked too." He made a sour face as Kaylah moved his foot, squeezing his clouded eye shut. "You can overpower them once they're down, so use what works for you. Speed is good."

Kaylah's fingers pressed along Matt's shin. "Fibula's fractured, but reset. Muscle's torn, but healin'. You'll be fine by dinner."

Fine by dinner. His leg was broken, but he'd be fine by dinner. Jonathan hadn't been kidding when he said we were damn near bulletproof. I stared at Matt's leg, which had already stopped bleeding.

"And don't let go once they're on the ground," Matt continued, shaking a finger at me. "A vamp won't stop trying to kill you just because they're down. They know you're there to end them. So end them."

He looked over his shoulder to Sheppard.

"She's fast enough that vamps'll have a hard time getting their hands on her," he said. "She's scrappy enough to keep fighting after a couple of good hits. She's not all that strong on two legs, but as long as you don't leave her out on her own, she'll be fine in a fight."

He looked back at me as Kaylah pulled him to his feet.

"Good job," he said. "Now get your clothes back on."

I eyed my pile of clothes and huffed. Being wolf felt good. This form was comfortable and wild and safe. Four legs are much more balanced than two—it's no wonder I took Matt to the ground so easily.

"C'mon, hun," Kaylah said, her fingers brushing my head. "You got a lifetime to enjoy bein' fuzzy. The sooner you come back to us, the quicker we can eat." She winked at me.

My stomach rumbled at the thought of food. We hadn't actually eaten anything since breakfast. I felt like I could eat a whole cow, now that she mentioned it.

Well, I wasn't going to do it in this form. Thumbs are supremely helpful for manipulating utensils. So I tried to reverse the process. I decided it was time to be human again and just...let go.

Sharp breaking pain heralded my return to humanity. With a yelp, I closed my eyes and tried to focus on my breath through the change. It hurt. God, it hurt. But I could endure it. And when I was human again, I hurriedly pulled my underwear and pants back on, checking to be sure the rosary hadn't fallen out of the pocket. I hooked my bra behind my back again and pulled my shirt over my head. I didn't bother with my shoes.

"Sorry about your leg, Matt," I said lamely.

He looked at me then, his expression uncomfortably gentle despite the nasty scar. "I signed up for that." He threw an arm over my shoulder. "And I underestimated you."

We headed back toward the house. He limped mildly on his hurt leg, and I saw him wince out of the corner of my eye once.

Most of the pack had already filtered back into the house, but Jonathan came into my field of vision, the football from Sheppard's old house in hand.

He smiled at me and waved the ball. "Wanna play?"

21

THE PACK FILTERED BACK OUT THE DOOR THEY HAD JUST GONE INTO, expressions eager. Ball was apparently what they called the game of catch and tackle that I saw the day I met them. I shook my head at the realization that it had only been three days since then. It certainly felt like longer, and the pack played the game with me like I had always been there.

Because of this, I learned some interesting things. For one, Matt actually played the game, despite limping on his hurt leg; though as the game progressed, he limped less. For two, the pack was conscientious of Matt's injury without babying him about it—we tossed him the ball if he was open, and we tackled him from the other side to avoid landing on his hurt leg. Beyond that, Chastity never hesitated to try to take me or anyone else to the ground if she was closest—even if that person was Sheppard. Daniel was more calculating, preferring to watch when the ball was likely to land in someone's hands before making the move to tackle them. And Jonathan? Well, Jonathan liked to take more than one of us down at a time, so that we all had to scramble to untangle ourselves before we could get back upright. I had to admit, it was pretty funny, and the weight and warmth of my packmates in a dogpile was more comfortable than I thought it would be. Kaylah was quick to help me up if I went down, as was Ian. Jamie preferred to not have the ball at all, getting rid of it quickly so as not to get tackled. Sheppard was an equal opportunity player: if one of us hadn't had the ball for a while, or hadn't been tackled, he was sure to send the ball our way.

Most interesting to me, however, was that most of the pack had trouble getting me down before I was rid of the ball, not for lack of trying—I was simply able to dodge them better than I expected. Except Sheppard, of course. If I hesitated to throw the ball, he was usually the one who took me down.

The game was over relatively quickly as a collective rumble of stomachs asserted their need for sustenance. Warm and sweaty, despite the chill of late autumn, we flowed into the house. Kaylah and Chastity stopped to wash their hands before Kaylah pulled huge packages of lunchmeat out of the fridge and brought them to the hulking granite table on a platter. Chastity followed with three loaves of sliced bread and placed them next to the platter of lunchmeat. It was the fancy kind of bread that comes shrink-wrapped in the bag. The kind I had only hoped to one day afford because surely the double wrapping meant it tasted better. We had our choice between white, whole wheat, and rye bread.

Fancy.

Sheppard sat at the head of the table, and Matt had taken up the spot to his right, though there were seats open to his left. I moved around behind Sheppard to grab one of those seats, and Jonathan followed. Ian, Jamie, and Daniel sat toward the other end of the table, leaving the two seats closest to the kitchen open for Chastity and Kaylah, who brought the condiments and plates, respectively.

Kaylah looked around the table then at the rest of us, placing a fist on her hip. "Nuh uh." She shook her head. "Not a one a ya washed yer hands afore comin' to the table." She looked at each of us in turn, her crystal blue eyes hard.

"Aw," Jamie said, his shoulders slumping. "Come on Kaylah! You know germs don't bother us anyway." He spread his hands, palms up toward her. "What's the point?"

"Nuh uh," she said, shaking her head. "Th' *point* is, yer all dirty 'n' sweaty from playin' outside. Th' least yuh c'n do is wash yer dang hands afore you go gettin' yer mess all over each other's' bread 'n' lunchmeat. It's jus' polite!"

"Dirty food spoils quicker," Chastity added, pointer finger in the air.

"So, ya know th' drill," Kaylah said, hooking a thumb over her shoulder. "Git!"

At that, everyone scattered to do as she said.

When we returned to the table, Chastity had already taken her seat, her hands neatly folded in her lap. Kaylah came around behind us, placing round white plates in front of everyone. Sheppard unwrapped the lunchmeat: ham, roast beef, turkey, salami, and prosciutto, and Matt opened the loaf of rye bread. I grabbed the loaf of white, opening it and placing six slices of bread on my plate before passing the loaf to Jonathan.

I used to be the sort who would only eat one sandwich, but I could apparently pack it away like a champ these days. And I was positively starving. The smell of the lunchmeat had my mouth watering more than I felt was appropriate, but I kept swallowing it down until I could manage to get my sandwiches together.

Matt passed a handful of slices of rye bread to Sheppard, before pulling a handful more for himself and returning the bag to the middle of the table. Between the two of them, the loaf was half gone already. Sheppard then placed a little bit of each meat on top of three of his slices, and when Matt did the same, it triggered a tangle of limbs across the table as the pack reached for bread, condiments, and meat.

Sitting closer to Sheppard—and therefore the pile of lunchmeat—I managed to get to the roast beef and turkey while there was still plenty, piling slices on top of three pieces of bread, topped with mayo. I mushed another slice on top of each, grabbed one of my completed sandwiches, and took a bite. It was gone in just five. Wow.

Jonathan elbowed me gently. There was mirth in his eyes as he held up his sandwich—white bread with lots of ham. A mix of mustard and mayonnaise dripped from a corner and onto his plate.

"This lunchmeat is much more appetizing than you were when you came in."

He was referring to me being lunchmeat after the crazed wolf attacked me?

I squinted my eyes and brushed my shoulder against him, a smile pulling at the corner of my mouth. "It's not like you tasted me then, so how would you know?" I locked eyes with him and took a bite from my second sandwich.

"She's got you there." Ian took a swig from the water bottle in his hand. His sapphire eyes glittered.

Jonathan laughed, setting my stupid heart to singing again, and tipped his water bottle toward me. "Touché."

The rest of the pack smiled too, and the comfort of their presence was almost tangible around the black granite table.

"You're pretty quick, Lynn," Chastity said between bites of her own sandwich of turkey and roast beef on wheat bread. "Have you always been light on your feet?"

I guess I had been fast. I certainly hadn't expected to get inside Matt's guard, and that I'd actually hurt him? It seemed impossible. And though I had been a less than ideal player the first time I played ball with the pack, this time, I had held my own pretty readily.

"I don't know," I said, shrugging. "I haven't been trained in anything."

Matt snorted. "That much is obvious. But your instincts are good."

"That thing that happened though." I looked to Matt. "When I bit you. It jangled in my head like fireworks in a metal shed. What was that?"

Sheppard smiled. It crinkled the corners of his eyes. "That's pack. We all felt it. Just not as quite as strong as you did—you were closer."

"So then, you always know when pack's in trouble," I said, thinking aloud again. "Or when they're hurt."

"We all do," Daniel confirmed, his mouth full of bread and meat.

"It's pretty handy," Ian added around a bite of his sandwich—turkey and ham on wheat with mayo, by the smell of it.

So, if the pack can always know when one is hurt, then it stands to reason that they could know other things about each other too. Which could explain why Matt was able to tell so readily what Jonathan and I were doing in the woods the night of the fire.

My cheeks heated at the thought of all of these people being privy to my private life.

"What is that about?" Chastity asked. She was looking at me.

I made a face that was something like a wince. "I was just thinking about what that could mean. And why Matt said what he did when Jonathan and I came on the scene at the house fire."

Jonathan's hand brushed my thigh. His quiet voice was almost sing-song. "Pack doesn't keep secrets."

Or rather, they *can't*.

"Wait." Chastity swallowed the last bite of her sandwich as she leaned an elbow on the table and pointed at Jonathan with an upturned hand. "You're embarrassed that you slept with Jonathan?!"

Her voice was either incredulous or sarcastic. I couldn't tell for sure. Jamie laughed, and Ian joined him.

With a wince, I sat up and glanced at Jonathan, who had put his second sandwich down. He rested his elbow on the table and his chin in his hand. He was clearly waiting for my reply and was just as clearly not going to be any help.

"I'm not embarrassed," I said quickly.

Sheppard looked at me and raised an eyebrow. Okay, that was a lie.

"I mean..." I slumped against the back of my chair. "I guess I am embarrassed." Electricity crept into Jonathan's scent. "But it's not like I go around talking about who I've slept with and how often and when."

Then it hit me. Chastity was poking fun at Jonathan. And I wasn't terribly sure how best to diffuse that.

I sat up again, placing a hand on his knee. "It's not that it's Jonathan." I furrowed my brow. "It's that I don't usually talk about what happens in my bed. It's never really been anyone's business."

"It's not anyone's business," Sheppard replied. "And that's not how that works."

"I knew what you two were up to because I could smell it on you," Matt said. "You smelled like each other. You still do."

Really? I sniffed at my shoulder. Sure enough, a certain someone's woodsy scent faintly lingered there. I hadn't even noticed, but it made me smile.

"But it's not like it's hard to tell who's sleeping with who in the pack," Ian said.

"Could we please stop talking about my brother getting laid?!" Jamie asked, exasperated. "What he does in the bedroom is nothing I need to know about!"

Uh oh. I saw Jonathan's eyes glitter before he even opened his mouth.

"It was in the woods," he said over the sandwich in his hand. "On the ground next to my Jeep." The electricity in his scent dissipated, but a darkness crept into his tone. "And it was good."

I felt his last line in the pit of my gut.

Jamie slammed his sandwich to the plate, snapping the white ceramic in two. "Aww, dammit, I broke a plate!" His face was instantly apologetic as he looked to Kaylah. "Sorry, Kaylah."

My face was on fire, but I couldn't help but smile. It *was* good with Jonathan.

"JONATHAN!" exclaimed Kaylah. It sounded exactly as it had when she had chastised him the day I woke up. "Yer brother oughta be used t' it by now, but yer makin' th' poor girl uncomfortable!"

She stood and grabbed another plate from the kitchen, taking it to Jamie. He picked up his sandwich gingerly and placed it on the new plate, stacking the pieces of the old one to the side.

"Accidents happen, hun," Kaylah said, kissing Jamie lightly on top of his head. "Don't you worry 'bout it none."

I closed my eyes and shook my head, swallowing the last bite of my second sandwich. "It's fine, Kaylah." I nudged Jonathan with my shoulder. "It's not like Jamie didn't already know."

Jamie squinted his eyes shut. "But I don't need the details!"

I narrowed my eyes at him. "Jamie, you're only a handful of years younger than Jonathan, right?"

Jamie's pale green eyes met mine, his expression quizzical.

"Two actually," he said, "just two. Why?"

"Well," I said. "If you're only a couple of years younger than Jonathan, then you're *also* old enough to be my grandfather, so why does it gross you out that your brother slept with anyone?"

Jamie's head fell back and his arms fell to his side. "Because he's my *brother*, Lynn!" He looked back at me. "Do you want to hear about your brother's sexual exploits? Why do you think our apartment has the rooms separated by the living room like it does? You think I wanna hear any of that?"

"Ew," Ian said, taking a bite of his last sandwich.

"I don't have any siblings," I replied. "But I suppose that's fair."

But wait. Ian was the youngest in the pack, according to what Jonathan had said back at my place. All of the pack members used to be human except for Sheppard. And, aside from Ian, they were all multiple generations older than me. "So where are the kids?"

22

"WHAT?" CHASTITY ASKED.

Sheppard's warm scent had a tingle of electricity to it. I was beginning to wish I had a better understanding of how these scents worked.

I spoke slowly, my eyes on Sheppard. "If practically all of you are multiple generations older than me, where are the kids?"

Matt sat back in his chair with folded arms. Chastity's gaze fell to her lap.

Kaylah pursed her lips and took a slow breath before she spoke. "I hope you din't have many planned, hun."

Was she saying that werewolves can't have kids? But Sheppard was born a werewolf, so that couldn't be right. I mean, I hadn't ever given a thought to whether I wanted kids or not. I always figured that part would sort itself out when I found the right partner.

"While it's certainly not impossible," Sheppard said, "werewolves who were made later in life have a hard time bearing children. Born werewolves don't suffer the same difficulty."

"So then, what's the point of having a mate, if you were changed?" I asked.

"Turned," Matt corrected. He blinked at me, his clouded eye going through the same motions as his clear one. "And I guess there isn't one."

Chastity looked up from her lap. Her hazel eyes blazed at me for a moment before she turned them on Matt. "Just what do you mean by *that?*" Her vanilla scent was so sharp and electric it stung my nose.

Wow. I did *not* want to tangle with her.

Ian rolled his eyes and took a gulp of water from his water bottle.

"Chas," Matt said, wrapping an arm around her. "You're mine. I don't want anyone else to have you. So, you're my mate. It's just that simple."

Chastity relaxed against him, but crossed her arms and pressed her lips into a line.

"And mates are for life," I said. "Right? It's like getting married?"

"Usually," Sheppard replied. "Though there have been cases of mates separating. It usually happens if a mated pair lose a child, or if there's a heavy shift in the leadership and direction of the pack."

"Sometimes," Kaylah added, "a pack gets 'em a new alpha who's got differin' ideas from the alpha afore him. Sometimes certain members of the pack disagree with the new alpha 'n need to find a new pack. Stands to reason, then, that doin' so might break up a mated set a wolves."

"But most of the time," Daniel said, gripping Kaylah's hand in his own, "mates are for life." He kissed her knuckles.

"Long as that may be," Kaylah replied.

"Most mates never bother with getting married," Sheppard added. "There's no need. Packs know mates, and pack is what matters."

"Well okay." I took a breath. "But if you don't have a mate, don't you—" I made a vague gesture toward my gut with my hands. "I mean —people have urges—don't you guys?"

I have no idea how Matt managed to have such a flat look on his face with half of it scarred all to hell like it was, but he managed it. "Are you seriously asking if we want to fuck like everyone else does?"

Jonathan chuckled quietly at my side, his arm draped over the back of my chair. My cheeks were burning again.

"I guess when you put it like that," I said, dropping my gaze to my lap.

"It's not like it's hard to find someone for the night," Ian said, laughter in his voice.

It made me look up. He was putting together another sandwich from what remained of the lunchmeat.

"So, you just rely on one night stands?" I met his eyes. "Or short-term flings?"

Chastity speared me with a look. "When was the last time *you* had a meaningful relationship?"

Ouch. She had a point. My last 'relationship,' if you could call it that, had apparently been with a vampire who was simply using me for my blood. Before that, there was the cowboy from the club with all the country music. He had wanted me to move out to Montana with him after only a couple months of dating. Except he hadn't so much as left a toothbrush at my place by then.

Kaylah gently placed a hand on Chastity's arm—an absentminded gesture of comfort.

"It's not like we can tell anyone what we are, Lynn," Jamie said, reaching for some of the remaining slices of bread.

"Even if they believed us," Daniel added with a shrug, "it would put us at risk."

"I'd question the sanity of anyone who believed us right off the bat," Jonathan said.

"And even my friends don't really know anything at all about what I really am," Ian said. "I certainly couldn't keep a relationship going with that kind of secret."

Empathy stabbed at my heart. My voice was quiet. "Isn't that lonely?"

Ian's sapphire eyes met mine, and a smile lit his face. "Not at all. I have pack. And they know the real me. My friends are just a fun change of pace. I love spending time with them, and I'm pretty sure I usually spend more time with them than I do with pack, but my heart is here with pack."

Matt still watched me, his expression unchanged. "What do you think people would do about us if they knew the truth?"

"Go nuclear."

The answer was out of my mouth almost before I had even thought of it. But it was true. I knew people were prone to panicking and a 'kill it with fire' mentality for anything that isn't *them*. We even tried it in Salem back in the day. Which made me sit up.

"Witches," I said.

Matt just stared flatly at me. I looked around the table, and pretty much everyone had some level of confusion on their face—except Sheppard.

"What?" Jamie asked.

"Witches," I repeated, watching Sheppard. "You mentioned before that you're pretty sure some members of occult circles have were-wolves figured out, so what about witches?"

"What about them?" Kaylah asked, still clearly confused.

I met her eyes. "Are they real?"

Kaylah's face scrunched up as she shook her head. "Naw. Hist'ry jus' don' like progressive women."

Sheppard's gentle smile appeared, and his warm hand fell to my shoulder. "There are some who can do things that only faith can explain. Faith in something different than Christians, perhaps, but faith all the same." He released my shoulder.

"So they're real too, then," I said, trying to gain some clarity.

"Yes and no. Most people who adopt the moniker of witch have a faith of some sort and try to influence the world through that faith in some manner or another." He shrugged. "But it's not really any different than what the church did when they created werewolves."

"So really," I said, working through the thoughts aloud, "witch is just a name like priest or secretary. The more accurate question would be, 'is magic real?'"

Sheppard's smile widened. "That's an apt question. And it's one you already know the answer to." There was fatherly approval in his tone.

"Of course magic is real," I said slowly. "Some sort of ritualistic, faith-based magic is what created werewolves in the first place—since the church used the nails and the cross and whatever blood they could pull from it at the time."

Sheppard nodded.

"And don't forget that what science can do today is something people in ancient times would call magic," Chastity said.

"Chastity is a bit of a scholar," Jonathan said. "She tends to pick subjects and obsessively learn about them, though her choices are pretty random."

"Just because you can't follow the logic doesn't make them random," Chastity replied. "Everything is connected to everything. It's just not always obvious how."

"To get back to what I think the crux of your question was before, Lynn," Sheppard said. "It's not easy to balance a normal human life with being a werewolf." His voice was patient and measured.

"But it can be done," Ian added.

Sheppard nodded. "It can. And there have been instances of wolf-human mates. Though those are uncommon, and mostly within the military packs. We focus on making sure the rest of the world doesn't know. It helps that people don't like to believe in the scary things that go bump in the night. They like to think they're just scary movies and old folktales. Most never consider where those stories came from."

"Speaking of stories," Jamie said, looking at me. "What's with the four books you have turned backwards on your bookshelf?" There mischief in his expression that reminded me of Jonathan's smirk.

Shit.

I sat back in my chair and wiped at the side of my face, my other hand falling to Jonathan's leg. His fingers danced along the back of my hand, brushing across the knuckles with an almost distracting gentleness.

Jamie meant those books with the sparkly vampires. I hadn't completely disliked them, but they definitely weren't among my favorites. So, I kept them with their spines to the back of my shelf so I could just kind of forget they were there. And so that they weren't easily identified by anyone who just stopped by my apartment. But I guess maybe turning them backwards on the shelf like that only made them stand out more.

I pressed my lips into a line and rolled my eyes. "I got them because they were popular. I finished the series because I kept hoping it would get better. I kept them because I didn't want to throw them away. I didn't dislike them *that* much. They just weren't my favorites."

Looking for an escape, I saw Matt's trail map peeking out from under loaves of bread and condiment bottles and thought about the plan the pack had for tomorrow morning.

I wasn't sure I *could* kill a vampire. I mean, Matt sure seemed to think it was possible—Jonathan too, judging by his words at my apartment earlier today. But the violence of it all, I wasn't sure it was for me.

And then, I was sure that it was. I squinted my eyes closed and shook my head at the conflict in thoughts. This must have been what Sheppard meant about two sides of the same coin. My wolf and I seemed to be whole, for sure. But she nudged at my instincts, guiding me when I might otherwise hesitate. Rolling a shoulder, I realized that I was looking forward to the morning. I was looking forward to fighting whatever vampires were in that cave.

I looked to Sheppard again. "Is it always like this?" I leaned forward, gesturing to Matt's trail map. "When you go kill vampires, I mean."

"A hunt," Matt corrected, "when we go on a hunt."

I nodded. "A hunt then."

"Not usually," Sheppard said. "We tend to prefer to hunt them in small groups at a time. We can take down a brood of twenty vamps pretty easily." His chest puffed with pride.

"It's safer for the pack that way," Jonathan said.

"Yea," Kayla said, "but we go through a helluva lot more bandages."

Daniel squeezed her hand.

"But I suppose that's better 'n losin' someone," she added.

"There's a hell of a lot more than just twenty or so bloodsuckers in the dens under the Chateau," Matt added.

"Which is why we can't move on it yet," Sheppard said. "We have to figure out a way to separate them."

"Divide and conquer," Chastity said.

"But you're always hunting vampires," I said. "Never any peace?"

Sheppard looked at me again, and I was beginning to wonder if he had any mode other than paternal. "That's why we exist, Lynn," he said in a patient tone.

I guess maybe mine would be too if I was over 500 years old.

"Now that you're a werewolf," Matt said, "When you finally come across a vamp, you'll see. It's impossible to ignore."

Chastity nodded. "There's no point in denying it."

"Vampires kill people," Sheppard said, a hardness creeping into his tone. "We stop them."

Jonathan touched my shoulder, making me turn to face him. "We're stopping known murderers. It's a good fight."

It was a different tone than I was used to hearing from him.

"And there's never any saving them?" I couldn't help but be hopeful. I mean, vampires used to be human, right? So there had to still be a shred of humanity left to them, right?

Matt's voice was sharp and steely. "We save the sheep by killing the vamp that was feeding on them and get them help afterward. That's all we can do."

Sheppard put a hand up, stopping the conversation. He took a deep breath and looked at me, warmth radiating from him. I could feel it wind through the pack.

"You're still working into who and what you are now," he said. "Just give it time—you have plenty of it. You haven't seen a person in trouble, yet. It will all lock into place when you do. Trust me. You will understand it in time."

I sat back in my seat and Jonathan's hand fell to my thigh. I suppose Sheppard was right. If werewolves could live as long as they all said, I clearly had at least another few hundred years to see for myself whether there was anything worth saving in vampires. But I could already feel the truth of the matter: vampires had to be stopped, and the only way to stop them was to kill them. I wiped at my face with my hands.

23

I LOOKED AROUND THE TABLE—EVERYONE'S PLATE HELD ONLY CRUMBS and drips of condiment. Kaylah stacked her plate on top of Daniel's and stood, clearing the table of everyone's plates as she stepped into the kitchen. Chastity grabbed the leftover bread and what little was left of the lunchmeat and packed everything away, while Kaylah loaded the dishwasher.

"What do you guys do then when you have time to kill between hunts?"

Jonathan looked at me, hunger in his eyes as he winked. It made my gut jump, but I felt my face getting warm again. Sheppard had to have seen that, likely Matt had too.

"I mean other than play ball and eat," I said.

"Woofball," Jonathan said.

"What?" I turned to face him more directly.

"Woofball," he repeated.

"Oh not this again," Matt said, throwing his head back.

"That's what he calls it," Daniel supplied for me. He looked at Jonathan. "But the rest of us just call it ball."

I laughed. "But it's so appropriate!"

"Exactly!" Jonathan lauged too. "We are all *wolves* after all. You've

188

heard the noises we all make when we're trying to communicate while we're all wolfed out. We may be playing the game on two legs, but it is *decidedly* a dog's game."

Ian and Jamie joined in on the laughter.

"I am never going to call it that," Matt said, crossing his arms and sitting back in his chair. There was a smile pulling at his mouth, though.

"That's fine," Jamie said through his laughter, "but I will!"

Sheppard's laugh was a warm rumble throughout the house. I could almost see it in the air. Something sparkled in his golden-brown eyes as he clapped Matt on the shoulder. "Let the pups have their fun. It is a fitting name to the game, after all."

"I'm with you, Matt," Daniel said. "It's silly. And there's nothing wrong with calling it ball anyway."

"Don't fix what ain't broken," Kaylah added from the kitchen.

I eyed Matt and Daniel, glanced at Sheppard, and then met Jonathan's eyes. God I could get lost there.

Shit. I took a breath.

"Well, I will totally call it that," I said softly, pushing my shoulder into Jonathan's.

Jonathan's hand fell to my knee and he rubbed up my thigh, the laughter still in his eyes, though I could see the mischief creeping into his gaze.

"Aw man, it's getting mushy in here," Jamie complained.

"Come on, Jamie," Ian said, "I grabbed my system while I was at my place. We'll have to log in on your account and re-download the game, but we might not have lost any progress."

"Why don't we watch a movie instead?" Sheppard said, standing. "I believe it's Jamie's turn to pick a movie anyway." He started for the living room.

Jamie looked to me. "Let Lynn pick, he said. "She's new."

I waved my hands. "Nah, I need a shower. You pick this one, I'll pick the next one." I stood up and pushed my chair back under the table. I brushed my fingertips along Jonathan's shoulder as I passed behind him on my way to the front door.

Sheppard nodded and grabbed the remote from the TV stand in the living room. He handed it to Jamie.

I stepped outside to grab my backpack from the Jeep and returned to the house. Jamie was scrolling through the movie options on the huge television. Upstairs, I started the water in the shower and found a towel under the sink.

I may have just showered earlier that day, but it felt so much better to be getting the sweat and grime off after fighting with Matt and playing woofball.

I smiled. It was an appropriate name. God, but what was I going to do with Jonathan? Of course I wanted him, that much I was sure of, but maybe we could just take things slow. I just didn't want to end up trying to make life with this pack work if he and I didn't. I couldn't imagine a scenario where that would be anything less than awkward.

Besides, I didn't know anything about him. Not his favorite food, or song, or really *anything*. I didn't know where he came from or what his family was like. God, and he didn't know anything about me! Or did he? How much did the pack actually know about me anyway?

I turned off the water and stepped out of the shower stall, wrapping the plush towel around me as I did. My rosary on the counter caught my eye. Blessed. It had been blessed by the priest who had provided the service for my mother when she passed, and somehow, it had managed to not get burnt in a raging housefire. Man, if that wasn't proof that something supernatural was at work in the world— besides the werewolves and the vampires, that is—then I don't know what is.

The pack was reacting to the movie they were watching— comments of "uh oh" and "oh man" floating upstairs as I padded into my room. I placed the rosary on the bedside table and ran a comb through my hair a few times before scrunching the drips out of it with a towel. Then I threw on a pair of jeans from my bag along with a grey t-shirt and went downstairs to join the pack.

It was a Keanu Reeves movie that they were watching, but it definitely wasn't one of the Matrix films. Everyone was sprawled out across the room, relaxing as they watched the movie. Ian, Jamie, and

Jonathan were all so engrossed that they moved craned their necks around me as I passed in front of the TV and came behind the couch where Kaylah was sitting.

"You guys have popcorn," I whispered to her. "Right?"

She turned her head to me. "Of course!" She started to get up and I placed a hand on her shoulder.

"I can handle popcorn," I said, "as long as it's the microwave kind. If you tell me where it is and where a bowl is, I'll bring enough for everyone."

"Hun," she said, "that's prolly four or five bags."

Matt shushed us from the other couch, and when I looked over at him, he gestured to the TV.

I nodded. Right. Watching a movie. I leaned closer to Kaylah's ear. "It's fine, I've already missed the setup of the movie. Where is the popcorn, and where are the bowls?" I tried to make my whisper as quiet as possible, hoping the werewolf hearing would make up for it.

Kaylah put her hand to cover her mouth as she told me where to find everything in the kitchen.

I nodded and squeezed her shoulder in a gesture of thanks before padding into the kitchen. As I expected, everything was where she said it would be. I tossed the first bag in the microwave and pulled out my phone. My mouth watered from the scent wafting from the bag of popping kernels.

I leaned on the counter. I had a text from Steph. It was jarring to think that just a handful of days ago, I had been looking forward to going out with her and Jenny.

As I read the text, which chastised me for not letting them know I couldn't make it to the dinner, I realized that I didn't even actually miss them any. Jenny and Steph had been coworkers of mine, loosely speaking—they worked at the news station. Steph had been in the mail room, but was offered a receptionist position at a marketing firm and had left the news station a few months back. She and I used to grab coffee on Tuesdays. Jenny, on the other hand, had finally gotten promoted to the mid-day weather broadcasts. And why shouldn't she? She had long blonde hair and bright blue eyes and legs for days. She had an obsession with her gym membership and kept trying to get me to join and do some dance aerobics class or another. I think she called it Zumba? I pursed my lips. I'm sure the midday broadcast ratings had gone up since she took over.

But they only ever seemed to invite me to things if I happened to be around when they were planning. We didn't actually have much in common, and though we always had fun while we were out at the club, I always kind of felt like an outsider.

The pops from the microwave had slowed enough that I knew it was time to take the bag out and start the next one. Thirty seconds left on a four-minute timer. The popcorn must have been a bit stale, but it smelled delicious as I dumped that bag into the first bowl. I tossed a couple of kernels into my mouth. They tasted fine. I shrugged and started the next bag popping.

Three bags of popcorn later, I had all four bowls ready to take out to the living room and carefully stacked them up. After walking back to the living room, I handed a bowl each to Kaylah and Matt, and then crossed the room to hand one to Sheppard. Jonathan scooted over where he sat against the couch to make room for me between him and Jamie. He grabbed a handful of popcorn from the bowl as I sat down, settling my back against Jonathan's side. He wrapped an arm around my shoulder, and it was like I was always meant to be there. My stupid little heart thrummed some silly little song and I rolled my eyes at myself.

"So, which movie is this?" I whispered to Jonathan as Keanu fought his way through a red and blue club scene on screen.

"John Wick," Jonathan replied, not looking away from the TV. His breath was warm on my ear. "Ever seen it?"

I shook my head.

"Well, to put it simply," Jonathan whispered, "that guy," he gestured to Keanu Reeves, "is pissed off because the Russians killed his dog." He grabbed another handful of popcorn, and I did the same. "He used to be a hitman, but he quit so he could be with his lady. But then she got sick, died, and left him the puppy—which then got killed."

"Poor guy," I said. "No wonder he's so pissed."

Jonathan nodded as I settled in against his warmth.

As the movie wore on, there were less comments from the pack and I realized many of them had fallen asleep. My own eyelids had grown heavy too, and, before I knew it, Jonathan was gently shaking my shoulder and the TV was back at the menu screen. I blinked at him, trying to clear the sleep-fog. How long had I been asleep?

Jonathan jutted a chin toward the stairs. "I hear sleep works better in a bed or on a couch than it does on the floor leaning against some crusty old werewolf."

There was so much mischief in that last phrase that I had to stifle a laugh, even through the haze of sleepiness.

Jamie was laid out like a starfish on the living room floor, his head resting on my calf. I gingerly cradled his head and pulled my leg out from under him. Jonathan grabbed a pillow from the couch and placed it under his brother's head as I laid him down.

With a barely restrained grunt, I pushed up from the floor with my hands. It wasn't like it was hard, I just didn't want to actually move or go anywhere. My hips ached dully, but as I stood, they stretched and the ache melted away. I plodded over to the stairs and realized that Sheppard, Matt, and Chastity had already disappeared to their rooms. Ian had stretched out on the couch that Matt and Chastity had been on. Kaylah and Daniel were beginning to stir awake too.

"Two fit better on a bed than on a couch." I glanced upstairs and then met Jonathan's eyes. "The room I'm in is probably more comfortable than that sectional in the den."

Jonathan gathered the popcorn bowls. With a feigned gasp, he pressed his fingers to his chest. "Why, Miss Cartwright," he said, imitating a prim and proper southern belle, "are you inviting a man into your bed? How immoral!"

"Well, if you really think so," I replied, shrugging my shoulders, "then sleep on the sectional." I winked at him as I went up the stairs. "Your call."

I heard the bowls hit the kitchen counter a moment later along with hurried footsteps on the stairs.

2 4

JONATHAN'S ARM SNAKED AROUND MY WAIST AS I OPENED THE DOOR TO my grey room, his warm hand spreading along my belly under my shirt. "I can't just let you wander into the dark all by yourself," he said, the warmth of his tone settling somewhere decidedly below my stomach.

"I'm a big girl." I turned to face him and lazily draped an arm over his shoulder. "I don't need some crusty old werewolf to protect me."

I placed a slow, deep kiss on his mouth, and the warmth spread throughout my body. I couldn't help but want him. I felt so drawn to everything about him. It didn't make any sense at all, but I wasn't going to fight it.

"Ahem." Kaylah cleared her throat from the top of the stairs. "Hallways are fer walkin.' Get a room you two, yer blockin' traffic."

I smiled and backed a step or two into the room, watching to be sure Jonathan was following, then turned and headed for the lamp on the bedside table. I reached for it, but stopped before I turned it on and looked around the room. My arm fell to my side. I could see fairly well with just the moonlight from the window. Certainly better than I had ever been able to see in the dark before the attack.

Jonathan shut the door to the room with a quiet click. Water ran in the bathroom for a moment and then the door to the other bedroom closed. I sat on the bed, and Jonathan stepped closer to me. Our heartbeats were in sync again—his thudding in his chest just as hard as mine was in my own.

He took my hand gently in his own and guided me to my feet again. There, his hands fell to my waist, pressing my body against his as he closed his mouth against mine. I guided his hands under my shirt to the button and zipper of my jeans, and his breath caught in my mouth before he hungrily worked the pants off my hips.

He stopped short as the waistband of my jeans fell to my ankles and took a breath, resting his forehead against mine. "I don't want to push you."

I turned down the blanket, sat on the edge of the bed, and pulled my jeans the rest of the way off. Why are women's jeans always so clingy? His were so loose around his hips and legs.

"No one's pushing anyone. We're just two adults giving in to something we both want." I took his hands and gently tugged him to the bed. "I'm not thinking about forever."

I met his eyes, and could see the gold flecks clearly even in the otherwise dark of the room. "I just know what I want right now."

I leaned toward him as he closed the distance again, pressing his soft lips against mine as his hands tangled in my hair. God, he was so warm! And my head was simply buzzing with how much I wanted him, which was a curiosity in and of itself. I hadn't ever wanted anyone as much as I wanted him.

The hardness in his jeans was already pronounced, and—this time —he didn't stop me as I worked the button fly of his pants. A throaty noise escaped him as I ran a hand along his shaft, gripping it as he hardened in my hand. It redoubled the warmth spreading through me and added to the wetness growing between my thighs.

I definitely hadn't wanted anyone more than I wanted him then, and I replied to the noise he made with one of my own as the pressure from my kiss eased him back on his heels. I repositioned myself on the bed and worked the underwear from his hips. Jonathan may have been a couple of generations removed from me, but the shaft at attention in my face clearly indicated a much younger man. I pushed the number out of my head. That's all age really was, anyway, right?

I glanced up at him as I wrapped my hand around his erection. I was sure the smile on my face was wickedly promising, but he only would have had the chance to see it for a moment before I lowered my head to wrap my mouth around his cock.

"Oh shit." His words were breathy, but thick with need and his hands fell to my shoulders. He gathered my shirt into one fist and pawed at my head and shoulders with his other hand as he twitched in my mouth. I pulled him deeper into my throat and his resulting breathy growl of pleasure sent warmth and wetness straight to my core. God, I could almost come just from the sounds he made. The scent of him clung to my nostrils and my own low moan rumbled around him as my tongue worked his shaft.

I caressed the back of his thighs, clutching him to me as I slid my mouth along his length a few times. He was getting even harder than he already was and precum coated the tip of his cock.

With a groan, he released my shirt and slid from my mouth. He pushed me up so that I sat on the edge of the bed again and pulled the shirt from my torso as he stepped out of his pants and underwear. He wrapped his arm around behind me, trailing electric fingers up my spine, and my skin erupted in goosebumps at his touch. With a flick of his fingers, he unhooked the bra I wore with one hand and used the other to guide it off my body, depositing it on top of my shirt on the floor.

His mouth met mine as his warm palm cupped my breast, his thumb flicking over my already pointed nipple. I arched my back toward him and tangled my hand in his hair, feeling the heat radiating from him as my tongue greedily explored his mouth. His other hand was still pressed between my shoulder blades, but as he kissed me, he guided me down to the bed and shifted that hand lower, spreading warmth against my lower back. His other hand left my breast and he lifted my hips, pulling my panties from my waist in a single, smooth motion. I giggled lightly as they fell to the floor. His fingers danced along my shins and up my thighs, leaving tingling fireworks in their wake. He paused at my hips, and I swear I could see him calculating.

"Well, now what are you going to do?" I couldn't keep the playful taunt from my tone.

A lock of dark hair fell over one of his green-gold eyes, and he broke into a dark, hungry smile. I swear I nearly came from that look alone. In answer, he simply gripped my thighs and spread them open as he pressed his face against my folds. My eyes fluttered closed as a pleased sound escaped my throat and I balled the blankets into my fists. His tongue and mouth set my core on fire and I bit my bottom lip to keep from making too much noise in the house full of were-wolves. Releasing the blankets, I clenched his hair into my needy fist.

I pulled his face into me and ground my hips against his mouth. I was going to have to be quiet if I didn't want the whole house to hear us, but I wasn't about to try to hold back the first orgasm that crashed into me, suffusing my body with blissful endorphins. Odds were good they heard me anyway. A chuckle rumbled in his chest. His blessed mouth didn't stop until the aftershocks began to subside, and I was left gasping for air.

With a quirk of his lips, he drew a line of kisses across my stomach and latched onto to each of my nipples in turn, swirling his tongue around each and nipping them gently with his teeth as the heat built between my thighs again. Scooping me onto the bed, he positioned me under him until his hardness exerted gentle pressure against my now quite sensitive sweet spot. I jumped at the renewed contact and his smile could have lit the Colorado sky. I returned his smile, my heart singing again, and pulled my bottom lip between my teeth. He leaned down, claiming my mouth with his as he pressed just the tip of his rock-hard erection into my entrance. I groaned into his mouth and squirmed against him, my hands clawing at his hips as I tried to wriggle more of him inside of me.

"You impatient, delicious Dreamer," he said, dark playfulness resonating through the words. "What if I make you wait until later for the rest, hmm?"

He propped himself on his hands and withdrew from me then, and

I couldn't help the desperate little whine that escaped me.

I ran my hands up his back and curled a leg around his thigh, settling myself against his hardness again.

"Hmm," I mused, tilting my head to the side. "But you want me just as bad as I want you."

I wriggled my hips some more, but he matched my movements, keeping himself only barely in contact with me. His eyes glittered with the fun of the game, and the flex of his lean muscles as he moved was tantalizing.

"So there's no point—" I thrust my hips against him, hoping to pull him in. It didn't work. "In denying it." I stopped wriggling around and raised an eyebrow at him. The game's no fun when you can't win, but there was still an infectious playfulness dancing in his eyes.

"Now there," he replied, pressing the head of his cock inside me, "you have a point. I do want you."

He slowly slid his length into me as his eyes rolled back into his head—or at least, they started the motion before mine did the same. A low rumble shook his chest and I could feel it along the shaft penetrating me. I was still deliciously sensitive, and he felt warm and full and hard inside me. He lowered his weight onto me, his body solid, but surprisingly comfortable. His mouth found mine again as he started moving. I spread a palm along the side of his strong abs, feeling them flex as he moved. I swear I saw stars dance across the ceiling. His breath hitched in his throat, and I recognized the ecstasy in his voice as he thrust into me.

Our hips fell into an easy rhythm. He was skilled. Or he was at least experienced. He felt so good inside me that I didn't care which. He clutched at the back of my knee, his other hand on my breast, and pumped into me with a force I would likely have found painful a week ago. Instead, it felt just this side of divine and I writhed around his cock, unable to get enough of it as he rolled my nipple between his thumb and forefinger. Despite the simplicity of what we were doing, this sex was easily among some of the best sex I'd had, though my own bedroom adventures previous to this had not exactly been numerous. Still, I wanted more.

I rolled over on top of him and arched backward, rolling my hips along his length over and over. His warm hands held my thighs and his brows furrowed as he bared his teeth. His canines were ever so slightly more pronounced than seemed strictly normal. I ran my tongue along the line of my teeth. Mine were the same. A wonder I hadn't noticed them before now. A smile crept across my face as I threw my head back, driving myself closer to the edge of another orgasm. Werewolves.

His hips bucked in a counter-rhythm to my own, and I could feel him swell inside me. He was getting closer too. His fingers found their way to my hips, gripping me hard enough to draw blood from shallow, crescent-shaped wounds that healed as soon as they were opened. Then his breath caught and was released in a growling rumble of ecstasy that I could feel throughout his body. I closed my eyes as stars exploded along the strand of the pack threads that tied me to him, drawing the next orgasm out of me in a nearly perfect tidal wave of bliss. He pumped into me and I followed the pulsing of his cock with my hips, riding the reverberations until his twitching subsided. Closing my mouth against his, I realized that the cord between Jonathan and I—the one I could see if I closed my eyes and concentrated—had thickened and thrummed like the plucked string of a bass guitar. Well, if the pack didn't know what we were doing before, they certainly knew it now.

Languor suffused my body as the final waves of pleasure rolled over me, and he was warm and comfortable. With a little squirming and repositioning, he pulled the blanket over us. The pounding in his chest mirrored my own as I curled against him, and he placed a gentle kiss atop my head. I trailed my fingers across his chest as he buried his hand in my hair, his fingers brushing against my scalp.

"I think I could get used to this," I said softly.

His heartbeat quickened at that and I smiled. "Oh yeah?"

I nodded. "Mmhmm."

"I think I would like that," he replied, placing another kiss on my head.

25

I woke to light streaming in the window, bathing the grey room in a sunny glow. I was still wrapped against Jonathan's warm body under the blankets, his breathing slow and steady. He wasn't awake, yet. A smile tugged at the corner of my mouth as I reached and brushed a lock of his hair from his face.

Mine, whispered that damnable voice in my mind. And I was starting to feel like maybe I agreed. Maybe.

I pulled my lip between my teeth and lay my head back down on his chest, listening to the even, steady pace of his heart. Sighing, I reminded myself that you can't fall for people you don't actually know much about. I mean, sure, werewolves were pretty clearly the good guys in a battle of good versus evil—but not all good guys were actually good guys. Some just wanted to win.

Ugh. But that didn't even ring true in my head for Jonathan. If anyone in the pack felt likely to only be in it to win, it'd be Matt. Except his gentleness with Chastity and his apparent selflessness at saving me—twice—told me even that was unlikely.

And then it hit me. It was morning. Today was the day the pack was going to go hunt vampires. I was pretty sure that meant I was going to be expected to actually *kill* a vampire.

Today.

I sat up and pulled a knee to my chest as I ran a hand across my face. God, I wasn't even sure I could do such a thing.

Something surged in my gut, hot on the heels of that thought. Of course I could do that. I could kill a bloodsucking vampire. I had to. If I didn't, people would die. Innocent people. And I simply wasn't going to allow that.

Something pinched my butt and I damn near jumped out of my skin with a loud yelp.

"So that wasn't a dream," Jonathan said, his green eyes glittering.

I narrowed my eyes at him and rubbed the spot he pinched. "You're supposed to pinch *yourself* to confirm that!"

I reached and pinched his bicep in retaliation.

"Is that how that works?" He grabbed my elbow and pulled me down to the bed. I landed on top of him and he closed his mouth on mine.

I relaxed against him. Maybe you don't fall for someone you don't actually know much about, but I'll be damned if everything with him didn't feel like it was exactly how this was supposed to be.

Mine, asserted that voice in my head again.

There was a light knock at the door.

"C'mon pups," came Matt's gruff voice. "Plenty of time to fuck later. We're leaving for breakfast in five."

Smiling against Jonathan's mouth, I snorted lightly and pulled back. I rested my forehead against his. Now that Matt mentioned it, I noticed the hardness against my thigh. Jonathan was, uh, *ready* for another round. Y'know, or it was the fact that it was morning. It didn't make a difference to the warmth spreading through me.

"We'll be down in a moment," Jonathan called. "Keep your pants on."

He gripped one of my thighs in each hand and resettled me on top of him—settling his hardness against me, which sent another wave of heat through me.

"Just put on your own and get downstairs so we can go already," Matt replied, and he tromped back down the stairs.

I was definitely getting wet against Jonathan, and we decidedly did not have time now for the things I wanted to do, but I couldn't stop myself from reaching down and pressing him into me for just a moment. I bit my bottom lip as his length slid inside.

"Mmmm, nope," I said. "This is definitely not a dream—or if it is, it's a damn good one."

His wicked smile and mischievous chuckle made me even wetter around him as he sat up and spread strong, warm hands along my lower back. The motion caused him to twitch inside of me and my eyes fluttered closed as I rolled my hips along him a couple of times.

"You are fucking amazing," he whispered, tangling a hand in my hair and pressing his forehead against mine. He wrapped his other arm around my waist. "We will have more of this," he punctuated the word with a thrust of his hips against mine, "later today, after the hunt."

I stilled. The hunt. How on Earth could I concentrate on that when I wanted him so badly?

He pulled back and met my eyes. The gold flecks had become more pronounced again. "Let's get breakfast before Matt drags us there naked."

"He wouldn't!"

"He might," Jonathan replied. "Besides, we're gonna need the fuel."

I sucked on my bottom lip and sighed. God, he was right. "How the hell do you manage to be so damn rational all the time?"

"It's easy when you know you basically have all of the time in the world," he replied, rolling a shoulder.

His eyes hungrily traced the lines of my body and I tried not to let the hyperawareness of my scars settle against me. He took a deep breath and let it out slowly.

"Come on." He patted my thigh gently. "Breakfast."

Reluctantly, I shifted off of him, letting him slide out of me as I turned and kicked my feet off the edge of the bed. My pants were still in a pile on the floor.

Jonathan shifted around and sat next to me. He looked down at my pants. "You're going to want something looser than those jeans. We're probably heading to the cave straight from breakfast, and quick-change clothes are usually the easiest."

I took a deep breath. I had a feeling the day was going to come at me faster than I was prepared for it to. "Okay."

I stood and rifled through my backpack until I found the stretchy brown pants I had packed.

"Well I have these," I held them up. "They should work for that."

"They don't have any buttons or zippers?"

I shook my head as I came back to the side of the bed where my panties had fallen. "Nah, they just stretch. I have enough hips that they don't seem to fall off."

I had enough hips for most of Colorado, really.

"I happen to like your hips," he said, stepping into his jeans. His abs were positively mesmerizing.

I smiled at him as I pulled my pants on. "Well I'm glad to hear that. I don't think I would know how to change them if you didn't."

He grabbed my hands then and pulled me to him, his expression suddenly serious. The gold flecks faded from his eyes so that only the rich green bored into me.

"I would never want you to change a thing about yourself. What we have will either work as we are, or it won't. There is absolutely nothing wrong with you," he pressed a kiss to each of my knuckles as it got harder to swallow around the lump in my throat. "There never will be."

Tears welled in my eyes. I had no idea what the hell to say to that. Everyone always wanted me to change. His intensity cut straight to my heart, and I sucked on my bottom lip as I tried to keep my breathing even. But I could feel the wetness on my cheek. Dammit. I squeezed my eyes shut and turned my head away, pulling my hands from his as another tear fell. I wiped at my face and picked up my bra and shirt from the floor. I could feel his eyes on me as I hooked the bra closed and tugged the grey shirt over my head. I took a breath and tried to collect myself.

"Lynn," he said quietly.

I don't think I had heard him use the name to actually try to get my attention before now. It felt good to hear coming from his lips. Dammit.

"I didn't mean to hurt you."

I turned to look at him, my eyes focused on the scars on his chest. "You didn't. I just—" I wiped at my face and met his eyes. "It's been a really long time since I felt like I belonged anywhere. But now, with the pack, and with you, I can't imagine how I could possibly fit in anywhere else. And it just doesn't make any actual sense. It almost feels like a dream that is sticking to just enough parts of me to make me believe it's real. But I don't really know any of you, not really."

"What's there to know?" He shrugged, spreading his arms, hands palm up.

"Well," I said, "there's a lot really. Like what your favorite dessert is or where you grew up or what you like on your pizza. The simple things—and the not-so-simple things. Like what drives you to get up in the morning or how you make sense of the world."

He smiled at me, but there was still concern in the expression. "Tell you what. You get your shoes on so we don't miss breakfast with the pack, and I'll answer as many of those as I can on the way to the diner. Deal?"

Nodding, I sighed. "Deal."

His smile grew and he placed a light kiss on my forehead. He stepped past me to get to the door as I pulled my socks and shoes on. I grabbed the rosary from the bedside table before we headed downstairs.

In the Jeep, I hung the rosary from Jonathan's rearview mirror, looping it a few times so it didn't tap against the dashboard. He watched it dangle for a moment and then smiled at me.

"Just till I get the time to hang it from the rearview of my own car." I shrugged. "Sheppard thought I should probably keep it close."

Jamie and Ian rode with us to the diner, sitting quietly in the back-seat as Jonathan answered my questions. Pecan pie, Tallahassee, and meat-lovers (of course) were the simple things I had asked about. I told him I preferred apple pie, I grew up in Colorado Springs, and that I liked to add pineapple to a meat-lovers pizza. By then, we were pulling onto the highway, and the typical argument ensued about whether pineapple had any business being on a pizza.

"Sheppard," Jamie exclaimed as he jumped out of the Jeep at about the same time as it stopped moving.

Sheppard looked over as he closed the door to his Ram. Matt and Chastity came around from the other side.

"Tell her!" Jamie gestured emphatically to me. "Pineapple doesn't go on pizza!"

He was almost whining like a little kid.

Sheppard smiled. "I would, Jamie," he said with a shrug. "But it's pretty tasty."

"Thank you!" Ian crossed his arms with a satisfied smile.

"Look," Jonathan said. "You guys can like it all you want, I just don't want it on my own pizza." He used the same placating gesture his brother had at my place yesterday.

I laughed. "Then we'll have to get meat lovers pizzas with half pineapple!"

"Ha," Matt barked. "Like half a pizza would be enough for either of you."

"Then put it on the whole thing and whatever Lynn doesn't eat, I'll finish," Daniel said, closing the door to the van he had rented for today as Kaylah came around from the far side. It was a white, 12-passenger van—the kind you see little league teams go to neighboring town games in. He beeped the horn to lock it, a sound loud enough to make me flinch.

When we walked in, Dolores ushered us right back to the pack's normal table in the secluded corner of the diner.

The strangeness hit me again—it had only been two days since I ran in fear from this pack after Matt told me that sometimes the first change makes you crazy. Only I hadn't gone crazy. I had survived the change, and they were my packmates, just as much as I was theirs. I had nothing to fear from them, just as they had nothing to fear from me.

I couldn't focus on breakfast, but I know we had the same steaks we had the first time I joined the pack at the diner. The time blurred for me. And the excitement among the pack was an almost tangible thing. They were going to be at my back as we attacked a stronghold of creatures. Creatures that killed people like Dolores and the others in this diner simply because they could. There was tension and the anticipation along the strands of the pack. I was as eager for the coming fight as the rest of them.

Today, the vampires would pay for burning down Sheppard's house. Today, they would pay for following me all over town and tainting the safety of my own home. Today, they would pay for the lives they had taken.

I couldn't wait to tear into them.

26

THE RIDE TO THE RESERVE WAS QUIET, AND I TRIED TO FOCUS ON WHAT we were doing. We drove into a section on the north side and hiked to a rocky outcropping hidden behind a copse of aspen trees whose red leaves still clung to the branches. Wolves move quieter than people do, so we changed there—except for Sheppard, who stayed on two legs. It took all there was in me to not nip at the heels of the pack and set us on a run through the forest, but Sheppard's power as alpha wafted along the breeze, the warmth of his scent contrasting with the cool fall air.

"This way, I'll be better able to concentrate on grounding you through the bloodlust the cave will incite," Sheppard explained, his voice a low murmur, "and I'll have thumbs free to do things wolf paws can't manage." His golden-brown eyes met mine, "And I'll be able to direct you better." He reached into the Jeep, pulling my rosary from the rearview mirror and looping it over my head. "You never know what protection it'll offer you here." He looked across the pack, meeting each wolf's gaze. "Let's go."

The power in the words radiated along the strands of the pack. It was not a request.

I shivered in anticipation as the pack emerged from the aspens.

The surrounding trees had dropped their leaves already, and I was sure our footsteps through the terrain were not likely to be silent. Surprisingly, we were quieter than I would have guessed as we made our way to the cave Matt had indicated on the map. I marveled at my own nearly silent footfalls across the fallen leaves and pine needles. And Sheppard made much less noise than I thought possible. I focused on him. His footsteps were easy but deliberate, landing more often on the fallen needles of the countless conifers than on the crunchier fallen leaves.

The cave's scent hit me long before it came into view, its natural wet-stone scent mixed with blood and gasoline, as well as fur and wild things. The hackles along my shoulders rose.

People, just normal people, walked around outside the cave. No. They were patrolling a perimeter around the mouth of the cave. They wore the same camouflage that the local deer hunters used and carried rifles on straps slung over their shoulders. But there was a hint of death to their scent.

"Sheep," Sheppard whispered.

He threw a hand out, palm down, in the direction of the pack. Power washed over me. Stay.

I lowered my head and watched as Sheppard crept around behind each of the four sheep in turn, swift and damn near silent. In a single move, he wrapped an arm around their throat, locking it into place by grabbing his opposite shoulder as he kicked the back of their knee, lowering them to the ground as they lost consciousness. It took only seconds for each. Once they all were out, he picked up the unconscious bodies and brought them all together, back to back around a tree trunk. He pulled long black zip ties from his pocket and tied their hands together behind their backs. He intertwined the ties so that one couldn't get up unless the others were up as well.

"Kaylah. Daniel." Sheppard's voice was barely above a whisper, though Daniel and Kaylah had already moved closer as Sheppard finished tying. They were beautiful side-by-side—Daniel in black with silvery grey lining his shoulders and belly, and Kaylah in mostly grey that faded to white on her face, belly, and tail. They took up opposite sides of the tree, facing each other and the tied guards, who were already coming to. Sheppard pulled the walkie talkies from their belts and turned them off before hurling them into the forest. He then fished their cell phones from their pockets and hurled them as well.

The eyes of the guard facing roughly my direction went wide as he resumed consciousness and noticed his bound status. His heart thudded hard in his chest and I could smell the fear rise in him. The body language of the rest of them as they came to indicated the same level of healthy fear.

"Staying quiet keeps you alive," Sheppard said quietly to the waking guards, crouching beside the hulking black and grey wolf that was Daniel. On cue, Kaylah and Daniel pulled their lips from their teeth in a silent snarl. "And I suspect you'd much rather be alive than a meal for these guys." He patted Daniel's shoulder as he stood. He was bluffing, of course. I was sure of that down to my bones. But the guards didn't know that.

Looking back at the rest of the pack, he jerked his head back toward the cave.

We stalked closer, and the not-safe scent of dead things crept into the mix of blood, stone, and fur. The red on the edges of my vision threatened to cover all I saw, but the presence of the pack at my side and the weight of my alpha's power were a blanket of relative safety.

Growl and snarls drifted from the cave. Creatures who were just like the packmates moving alongside me were in pain, and angry. Red clouded my vision as rage slammed into me and a quiet growl burbled in my throat. Then, warmth spread over me and some of the red cleared. I looked to Sheppard, who met my gaze and nodded. The grey wolf that was Jonathan brushed alongside me, helping to ground me. It pushed some of the anger away, but that only made me aware of the fear that was balling into the pit of my stomach. I had no idea what I was doing here. I had no idea what I was going to do when I actually saw a vampire.

Sheppard's hand fell on my shoulder. Of course I knew. I was going to kill it. I took a breath and closed my eyes, watching power flow along the strands of the pack. My pack. The pit of fear shrank, and I opened my eyes again.

There was a bright work lamp at the back of the cavern, the kind you see on construction sites, and a large generator nearby provided power with heavy cords running off it. It was on, despite the daytime, providing more light than necessary and obscuring my vision of anything behind it. Bolted along one cave wall were four cages, only one of which was empty. The other three held snarling balls of fur as large as I was, their jaws snapping at the thick iron bars and chewing until wounds opened and knit closed.

I slowed as I passed them, marveling that there was a cage strong enough to hold them. A cage strong enough to hold us. Those could have been my packmates. I shook my head and snorted, trying to clear the stench of blood from my nose. I would kill the thing that had done this.

The dark timber wolf that I recognized as Matt nudged my heels, urging me to quicken my pace as we stalked past the cages. I didn't need more encouragement than that. The smell of humans and vampires alike was getting stronger the further we went in.

Past the light, I was finally able to see a hallway that had previously been obscured. It was like an old trick from a haunted house—except any jump scares here would be deadly. And we were on the vampires' home turf. Great.

There was a split in the cave ahead. Sheppard put a hand out, palm facing us, and we stopped. He pointed to Jamie and then to Matt and nodded his head toward the left branch of the cave, where a vaguely antiseptic smell entered the sickening mix. I pulled my lips back in a silent snarl and we walked down the right branch, where the scent of sweat and people got stronger.

The cave opened up into another chamber where five cots were arranged around the room. Small camp lights were on the floor of the chamber, one each on either side of a metal shelf. Only three of the cots were occupied, but neither of the men nor the woman stirred as we entered. Sheppard pointed at the woman, pointed to his ear, and then placed a finger over his mouth. I looked back at the sleeping forms—they all had bright orange pieces of foam in their ears. Well no wonder the snarling of the wolves in the front chamber didn't bother them.

That same unsafe dead smell of vampire wafted in as Sheppard made a nearly silent hiss at the far end of the chamber. He held a heavy curtain away from where the cave narrowed to another hallway. As we padded over to it, Matt brushed past me. Sheppard nodded to him, and I looked over my shoulder to see Jamie had rejoined us.

I guess there was nothing to see down their hallway. Well. That only confirmed what the smell was telling me—the vampires were all ahead of us.

Sheppard held the curtain for the pack as we all came into the hallway and took the lead again. We moved quickly down the almost black hallway and through another curtain into a room that held three massive four-post beds and an ornate couch. The deathly vampire scent prickled at my nose it was so strong in here. Pillows and blankets were piled all around the cave floor, on top of plush rugs, and another heavy curtain was hung at the far end of the chamber.

But there were no vampires. Jonathan, Ian, and Chastity checked around and under the beds. Matt checked behind and under the couch. It was just us.

A familiar voice called out, "I smell mangy mutts!"

Frederick. I was certain of it.

The red bled further into my vision and the ball of fear in my stomach turned to ice along my spine. There was the hint of an all-too familiar cologne amongst the death and blood.

Sheppard moved to the curtain at the far end of the chamber. "You smell your death!"

He jerked his head toward the cavern hallway beyond the curtain. The stench of vampire and death grew even stronger back that way, and—for a moment—I was torn about whether to follow the pack. I paused while the rest of the pack went forward.

Was I really ready to face a vampire? But the pack was sure, and power radiated from Sheppard along the strands I could see when I closed my eyes. With a shake that melted the ice along my spine, I hurried to catch up. I was ready for anything as long as I had the pack by my side.

As we cautiously approached the next curtain, a scrabbling, snarling noise came along behind us. Jonathan, who was ahead of me, turned and pushed past me in the hallway, back the way we came. His hackles were raised, and a growl rumbled in his chest. Jamie, nearly invisible in almost all black, followed his brother as I turned to face the way they were going.

Frederick's laugh echoed from the chamber beyond the curtain now behind me.

"We'll see who dies today, alpha" Frederick called.

His tone was different than I had ever heard from him. Colder. Angrier perhaps. I didn't have time to question it, the snarl-scrabbling had gotten closer.

Matt leapt over me in the cave and shoved me with his shoulder back the direction of the rest of the pack.

I looked to Sheppard, whose grim face also somehow held a hint of eagerness. It was infectious. He pulled aside the curtain and gestured with his head for us to go through. Power washed through me with the gesture—another command that I found myself eager to follow.

Beyond the curtain was a large chamber littered with plush rugs. A single four-post bed that somehow dwarfed even those in the previous chamber was the focal point of this room. A desk with a laptop sat along the far wall. Something smoldered smoke out of a metal trashcan next to the desk. Curtains and tapestries covered the walls of the chamber. Something that smelled of rot and decay was wrapped in a heavy sheet of plastic along the wall next to the opening into the hallway. Looking closer at it, I saw cloudy eyes and heavy makeup on a head of long, dark hair. My stomach flipped, and my heart caught in my throat.

That was a dead body.

There was a dead woman wrapped in a tarp. Red seeped into my vision again. A monster had killed her.

I whirled on the chamber, ready to fight.

And in the center of the room stood a single figure in the dark, his lanky frame somewhat more imposing than I had remembered. He speared me with blackened eyes.

"Why, Grace Lynn Cartwright," he said, drawing out my name with a voice like bloodstained silk.

It felt like claws raking along the inside of my skull and I barely repressed the shiver along my spine. I don't know how he recognized that it was me, but it didn't matter anymore.

"It is such a shame you have fallen in with these mutts." He had fangs. Actual, honest-to-God fangs. Like you see in the movies: white, pointed, and damn near gleaming. "But it won't matter soon. Once I kill them—"

Kill it.

He kept talking. I didn't hear it. The whole of the cavern was bathed in crimson. I wasn't going to let him hurt anyone or anything ever again. I leapt at him and felt power wash through me as a whistle sounded in the cave. He reached for my throat and I whipped my head side to side to get him to release me.

The crucifix from my rosary smacked into his wrist and the smell of burning flesh prickled my nose.

He did release me then, hissing with the pain as he covered the burnt wrist with his other hand.

But I didn't hesitate. I leapt at him again, and the world became a blur.

Something jangled in my head, like when my jaws clamped onto Matt's leg during our sparring match, but I ignored it. Frederick was an unnatural thing that must be ended, and I was going to end him before he harmed a single member of my pack.

2 7

"How are you doing this," burbled a weak voice from Frederick, "to me?"

My jaws were clamped where his neck met his shoulder, and I clawed and raked at his chest like a cat with a toy. He had fallen to the ground, pinning someone under him with me on top. He had claws dug into my sides, but the pressure from his fingers eased and released me as the wounds closed. He was weakening. Every fiber screamed my victory over my prey as the chamber fell silent.

Frederick's skin turned to leather in my mouth, and then to ash as my still raking claws crushed through his ribcage, cutting the clothing he had been wearing to ribbons and opening cuts across the chest of the creature underneath him. The jangling in my head got noisier.

Hands clamped on either side of my face and I thrashed to release them, trying to get my jaws around one of the arms they were attached to. The hands held firm, however, and power washed through me like a tidal wave, nearly stealing my breath. The red bathing my vision cleared, and then sharp breaking pain left me human, naked, curled into my alpha's arms.

I looked down, but couldn't make sense of what I was seeing. There, under where I'd been pinning Frederick down, was Sheppard

—my alpha—lying on the floor of the cave. And where Frederick had been...there was nothing. Just mounds of a fine, grey powder—ash—and the clothing he had been wearing. I retched around the dusty piece of bone in my mouth, spitting it out with a disgusted scream as I scrambled to my feet. Sheppard brushed what had been Frederick's clothing along with the ash off himself as he stood. He had four wide scratches oozing blood through tears in his shirt.

Oh God. I had hurt my alpha.

I backed a number of steps away across uneven plush rugs.

Ash.

Frederick. That was just his clothing there.

Oh God help me. I had also just killed a man who used to be my friend. My vision lost focus. I wasn't sure which was worse. Ice snaked along my spine.

Run.

Yes. Perfect.

With another round of sharp breaking pain taking me back to four paws, I fled the chamber, the colors of the fur of my packmates blurring as I passed. I had hurt our alpha. I had killed a man who had been my friend.

Run!

"Grace!" Sheppard's voice rang in the cave, the authority echoing down the hall.

There were bodies too, strewn about the cave floors. Fleshy, mangled ones covered in blood with gleaming pointed teeth and blackened eyes, their necks and spines at odd angles. Unlikely they were a threat anymore, but I wasn't stopping to find out.

My paws couldn't carry me fast enough through the cave, past the room full of lavish beds, past the room full of cots, and out into the chamber with the snarling wolves in cages. Red clouded my vision again. I needed to get away from here. Somewhere safe from what I had done. Somewhere not full of the dust of a former friend of mine. Somewhere away.

RUN!

Outside of the cave, the sun was bright enough to make me squint.

I blinked a number of times and shook my head as my vision changed again. The trees of the preserve were outlined in grey and everything was bathed in shades of white. I couldn't think.

RUN!!

I didn't need to think. I let my paws carry me across the ground. I passed trees and rocks and something that smelled like old blood and fur and teeth. Something that smelled like the cave.

RUN!!!

I shook again and ran so fast I practically flew across the ground. I passed houses and sheds, cars and trucks.

And then the burnt husk of a place that felt like home.

And then a glass house that smelled of pack.

I didn't have a key.

I found a corner with a clear view of the front door and curled myself into it, balling myself as tightly and as small as I possibly could, my tail curling over my nose.

I had killed a man who used to be my friend.

I had hurt my alpha.

28

AN OLIVE-GREEN JEEP CAME INTO VIEW AND MY HEART FLIP FLOPPED.

Jonathan.

A strange mixture of eagerness and dread filled me as he approached. Part of me wanted to run to him, but another part was hopeful he wouldn't see me.

He parked the Jeep in the empty space on the driveway, behind Matt's Camaro, and cut the engine. I balled tighter into my corner. Until I was sure which I preferred, it was probably better if he didn't notice me. Would he reject me for hurting our alpha? Would the rest of the pack?

I should have known better. His eyes landed on me almost as soon as he had exited the Jeep. He sighed and pressed his lips into a line, but that may have been a smile? Pulling his phone from his back pocket, he tapped out a message with his thumbs as he stepped to the front door. The intoxicating woodsy warmth of him crept along the breeze.

"Matt went to check your place," he said softly.

I barely heard him over the rustling of the trees and bushes along the house.

"Kaylah and Daniel took the sheep to Blood of the Cross." He unlocked the front door to the house and opened it wide. "Sheppard and the rest of the pack are still at the cave, pulling the bodies of the dead vamps out into the sun so they can burn."

His eyes met mine, and the gentleness in them stabbed straight into me. I was glad I wasn't in my two-legged form then, I wasn't ready to cry.

"Come on Dreamer," he said. "Let's get inside where we can talk."

I wasn't sure I was ready to go inside. I wasn't sure I was ready to talk.

Jonathan looked down the street and then back at me. "It's gonna be a while before everyone gets here anyway. And if anyone sees a huge white wolf in this neighborhood, someone's gonna poke their nose in pack business. So, if you'd rather sit in silence, we could. Just maybe inside, okay?"

Fuck me, he was good at anticipating my feelings.

He jerked his head toward the inside of the house, a gesture not unlike the one Sheppard had used to direct us through passageways in the cave. "Come on."

With I sigh of my own, I uncurled myself and padded toward the door, my tail firmly between my back legs and my ears pulled against my head. It was strange to feel that much control over parts of myself that, a week ago, I didn't even have.

Once I passed the threshold into the house, however, my stomach roiled, and I dashed to the downstairs bathroom. I slammed the door shut as I painfully changed back to human. Funny how that was getting easier, just as Sheppard and Jonathan had said it would.

There had been a dead woman's body wrapped in that tarp.

Crawling across the floor, I barely got the toilet open fast enough to keep my vomit from exploding across the nearly black wood of the bathroom floor.

I had held the bone of a former friend in my mouth as he died and turned to ash.

Between heaves of sickness, I locked the bathroom door.

I had run through puddles of blood and stepped over mangled bodies of things that once had been human.

I shook with the fear and realization of it all as what little was left of my breakfast and bile poured into the toilet.

When the worst had passed, and all that was left was dry heaving, I fumbled with the cabinet, hoping for towels under the sink as they had been in the other house. They were.

I pulled a washcloth out and wiped the sick from my face as I flushed the toilet. I ran water in the sink, rinsing the washcloth and pressing it to my face as I pulled my knees to my chest and leaned back against the bathroom door.

I never even bothered to turn the light on.

The worst part was the knowledge spreading through my bones that I would do it again if it meant keeping people safe. Of course I would. I could only pray that killing monsters would get easier in time.

There was movement outside the bathroom, something fabric plopped to the ground, and woodsy warmth wafted under the door.

"There's sweatpants and a shirt here," Jonathan said softly. "For you."

The floor creaked ever so slightly as he backed away from the door, and I put my weight on my feet, keeping low in a crouch as I slowly turned the door handle. I cracked the door to find a black shirt folded atop a folded pair of grey sweatpants. My rosary sat on top of the clothes. It must have fallen off when Sheppard...

I grabbed the pile with one hand and hastily pulled them into the bathroom, firmly closing the door once my hand and the clothes were clear.

Sheppard had pushed me to change back to human. I was certain of that now. As a wolf, I had gone so wild with the victory over Frederick that I hadn't even recognized it was Sheppard getting torn up. My vision blurred.

"I'm here Dreamer." Jonathan's voice came from the living room. "When you're ready. I'm not going anywhere."

I wiped at my face with my hands. Looping the rosary around my neck again, I pulled on the shirt and pants. The shirt was a bit large for me, but the pants were actually a bit short, so I rolled the bottom cuff to mid-calf. I took a breath. I couldn't hide in the bathroom forever, and I didn't know what had happened with the rest of the pack in the cave. I hadn't seen the fight that left all the mangled bodies. I needed answers, and I wasn't even sure what all of the questions were.

Except for one.

I swallowed around a sudden lump in my throat as I stood and opened the door.

Jonathan stood from one of the couches as I padded into the living room.

I met his eyes. "What have I done?!" My vision blurred again.

Jonathan moved closer to me, his hand reaching toward my shoulder. Frederick's body turning to ash flashed in my mind and my eyes went wide in alarm.

"*DON'T!*" I sprang away from him. "What if it happens to you too?"

"You mean what if you turn me to ash?" The corner of his mouth quirked up, but his eyes were soft and gentle, without a hint of gold.

I nodded.

He made a placating gesture and smiled. "We've touched a hell of a lot since you were turned, Lynn." There was no malice, no blame in his gentle tone. "I think I'm safe."

Safe. I wasn't sure anyone was safe from whatever the hell it was I did to Frederick.

"You can't know that. I don't know what did that to him. How *I* did that to him." I pounded my sternum with a closed fist as hot tears ran down my cheeks. "I can't turn you to ash too!"

That opened the floodgates. Sobs wracked me so hard I could barely breathe. Fear, guilt, and shame all warred for loudest voice in my heart. Fear at the overwhelming desire to kill when I was in the cave. Guilt over the death of my former friend, monster or no. Shame at having attacked my alpha.

I could still see the open wounds on Sheppard's chest.

I could practically taste the ashen bone in my mouth.

Bile rose in my throat again as I raced back to the bathroom, nudging the door shut with my foot as I dry heaved at the toilet. But I had already thrown up all that was in me.

I crept over to the sink, avoiding my own reflection. I couldn't look at myself. I wasn't even sure how Jonathan could look at me. I ran the water and slurped some out of my hand, trying to get the taste and texture out of my mouth.

I still hadn't bothered to turn a light on.

I sat back against the door to the bathroom again, my knees pulled to my chest. I crossed my arms over my knees and laid my head down, letting the tears fall to my sweatpants.

Jonathan sighed. "Oh, Dreamer." His tone was sorrowful. His phone buzzed near the bathroom, and I felt the weight of him sag against the door and slide to the ground.

"Listen," he said. "Sheppard will be here soon. We'll get this sorted out."

And still, I believed him. Dammit.

I don't know how long I was in there—staring blankly into the dark bathroom—but sometime later I heard the front door open and Jonathan's weight shifted away from the bathroom door.

A light pressure against the door soon replaced his weight, followed by the light thump of a finger tapping against the door. The warm scent of Sheppard wafted under the door.

"Grace Lynn Cartwright, come out of there at once." Sheppard's quiet yet authoritative voice held power that washed through the door.

I clambered to my feet and opened the door, my head down and eyes on the floor. My shoulders shook as fresh tears fell. I folded my arms across my stomach and slithered past him in the hallway, trying to get as far away from someone who undoubtedly was very angry with me, no matter how much restraint his voice held.

From the corner of my eye, I saw Sheppard reach for me as I passed him, and my eyes went wide as I rushed away from his hand.

"Don't!" The sobs wracked my chest again. "Please," I whispered. "I'm sorry."

Sheppard scrunched his face, pressing his lips in a line. He seemed puzzled. No. That didn't make any sense.

"It's alright, Lynn, just come speak with me." His voice was soft as he gestured to the dining room.

I looked at the hulking black table and back at him, my vision still watery. I nodded meekly.

He stepped past me and pulled out the chair next to his spot at the head of the oval table before taking up his usual seat. He looked at me and gestured to the empty chair. I expected a wash of power to accompany the gesture. None did.

I pulled my bottom lip between my teeth as I sat in the indicated chair anyway. Jonathan took up a seat near the end of the table.

Sheppard watched me and let the silence stretch. His heartbeat was steady, and I sensed not even a hint of anger from him. So, either I was completely wrong about how angry he was, or he was just that good at controlling his emotions.

I guessed maybe I would be too if I were over five hundred years old. His hands were folded in front of him on the table, and his shirt was different than the one he had been wearing. Now, he had on a black button-up shirt, the collar button open.

I remembered the mangled bodies of dead vampires, their blackened eyes staring at nothing in the cave.

"None of the other vampires died that way," I quietly blurted into the silence.

Sheppard shook his head almost imperceptibly. "No."

"The others," I continued, taking a breath. "They were all just torn apart," I made a gesture with my hands, like pulling a small ball of taffy. "They were...still fleshy. Not dust and rot and empty clothes."

The image of a rotting, desiccating Frederick flashed in my mind. His skin had shifted from fleshy to dried leather to ashen and his black hair had turned grey and stingy before turning to ash along with the rest of him. His clothes had practically deflated, like a balloon. I squinted my eyes shut, trying to clear the image, but that only made it worse. I could still hear the gentle crunch of his dried bones turning to ash as my paws crashed through his ribcage. Bile rose in my throat, but I swallowed around the lump and forced myself to sit still. There was nothing left to throw up anyway. I took a deep breath.

"Truly," Sheppard said, his voice pulling me from the replay. "I have never seen what happened in there before."

I watched his hand creep across the table, like he might place it on top of my own. He stopped short.

Ouch.

That was my alpha, and though I didn't want him to touch me, watching him stop himself from doing so hurt in a way I wasn't prepared for. God, what would the rest of the pack think?

Sheppard pressed his lips in a line as he shook his head. "Not like that, at least. I have trapped vampires in the sun and watched them turn to ash. But, that's not what happened. Frederick didn't just ash, he turned to a corpse that then decayed before our eyes."

"Is this—" My voice cracked, and I swallowed around another lump of bile. Maybe it was the same one. "Is this what Langley meant when he spoke of my power?" I spread my hands, the First Sergeant's voice ringing in my head. "Is this what kind of *talent* comes from being *of the blood*?!" I couldn't stop my voice from rising as I put air quotes around the last phrase.

"*Consanguinea* are always a little more than just another werewolf," Sheppard said, his voice staying level and even, despite my own hysterics. "So yes, this is almost certainly related."

His golden-brown eyes met my gaze and I wanted to look down and away again, but stopped myself, balling my hand into a tight fist against the cold black table.

"Beyond that, I do not have any real answers for this, Lynn," he said quietly. "I wish I did. Odds are good the military hasn't seen anything like this either. But I am not as old as my friend, Kristos, nor have I seen all the things he has. I have called him, left him a message. He should have answers when he gets back to me."

His quiet calmed me more than I thought possible, and I did drop my gaze then, pulling my hands into my lap. "Do you know anything at all?" My voice was soft and low, but I couldn't keep the hopeful tone from it.

"Only that you had no effect when you landed on me," he said simply.

I bit the inside of my lip. "Maybe that's because you're the alpha."

Sheppard nodded, his sandy blond hair waving with the motion. "Maybe because I'm the alpha. Maybe because I'm a born wolf."

"Or maybe because whatever that was with Frederick doesn't work on werewolves at all." Jonathan's voice startled me.

I had almost forgotten he was there.

Sheppard's eyes darted to meet Jonathan's, though Jonathan ducked his head as soon as it happened.

Sheppard nodded again. "Or maybe because it doesn't work on werewolves."

29

Sheppard's phone buzzed, and he fished it out of his pocket. It seemed small in his hands—something I hadn't noticed before. He stood as he tapped out a reply to a text message.

"I need you two to clear space in the basement," he said, shoving the phone into a pocket of his loose jeans. "Daniel and Kaylah are done handing off the sheep, so I'm headed back to the cave. We'll get the last two crazed wolves that were in the cages loaded up, and bring them here."

My eyes went wide. Again. "Two? I thought there were three wolves in cages?" I shook my head. "And what are you going to do with them here?!"

Sheppard's expression turned somber. "The vamps let one loose to try to flank us in the cave. It took Jamie and Ian by surprise. We had to kill it, so it didn't kill any of us." He shoved the phone back into his pocket.

Well that explained the jangling in my head and all the bodies on the ground in the cave. Pack members had gotten hurt in the fight, but the vamps paid for that with their lives. And I was so caught up in my need to destroy Frederick that I didn't even know it happened. Dammit.

"As for what to do with the remaining two, well...crazed wolves have no place in this world. They are as much a danger to themselves as they are to people. I'm going to see if I can calm them down after being in that cave for so long. Maybe they aren't actually crazed and it's just the bloodlust. But, if I can't calm them down," his expression hardened, "then there's nothing to be done for them. I will have to kill them."

"You can't just kill them!" I stood from the dining room table so fast it nearly toppled my chair. "They can't even understand what—"

Sheppard speared me with a look of hard resigned sadness that told me he had been through this argument a thousand times.

"No," he said. "They cannot understand what's happened to them, and it is no fault of their own that they cannot make peace with what they have become. But if they are that far gone, there is nothing to be done for them."

"But it's barbaric!" I slapped my palms to the hulking black table. I couldn't believe he could just kill them, even though some strange part of me agreed that they were lost causes.

"No Lynn," Sheppard replied. "It's humane. As quick and painless as possible."

"There's nothing to be done for crazed wolves," Jonathan said quietly, drawing my attention to him. "They know nothing but death and destruction. It's why we all hoped so hard that you would be alright after the attack."

Certain details were clicking into place—like what Matt had said at the diner the morning after I met the pack.

"And why it didn't matter how much you told me before the full moon." I pushed a hand into my hair.

Of course they didn't care what I knew about them. If I didn't go crazy, then I was a werewolf and needed all the knowledge. If I did go crazy...well. My eyes went wide. Then it didn't matter, they would have killed me, like Matt said at the diner.

How could I have been so blind to such an obvious euphemism?!

"That's what you mean about surviving the change! Everyone

survives it, but not everyone stays sane!" I backed away from the table, but my back hit the wall.

"But Lynn," Jonathan said, his expression earnest. "Listen. Crazed wolves are dangerous, chaotic, violent things. They don't change back to human. They only know wolf. And that wolf only knows to rampage."

"Matt's our best fighter, and even he couldn't stop the crazed wolf from turning you." Sheppard's eyes bored into me. "That's how dangerous they are. That's why we have to stop them just as much as we have to stop the vampires."

A car horn sounded outside, the double beep of someone trying to get the attention of another.

Sheppard looked toward the door and then back to me. "I need you to breathe right now." The faintest hint of power washed over me, and calm invaded me. "You have survived." His voice was calm and precise. "Yes, it is simply a saying, and you're right, it didn't matter how much we told you before the full moon. If you went crazed, you weren't ever going to return to a form that could do any real harm to the pack."

Squeezing my eyes shut, I took a slow, deliberate breath. I saw the strands of the pack. My pack. The pack that I only had because I *had* stayed sane.

A hand closed around my shoulder and I yelped out a scream as my eyes snapped open. Sheppard had closed the distance between us. His hand gripped my shoulder, but I flinched away. Maybe I didn't affect him before, but I had no idea how what happened to Frederick happened.

"You are safe now," Sheppard stated simply, power in the words.

He was right. Of course I was safe. I was with my alpha. Who had somehow managed *not* to turn to ash when I killed Frederick. I took a steadying breath.

"I remember you having to go through this with Ian too," Jonathan said.

He was talking to Sheppard, and I could hear the age in him then. Or maybe it was just the experience of having been a werewolf for most of his life. But then he looked at me, and the softness in his gaze stabbed into me.

"That's probably the hardest realization of pack. That you're only there because you managed not to go crazy when you turned into one of the things that goes bump in the night." He closed his eyes tight for a moment, balling a fist at his side. He took a deep breath before he continued. "I swear to you, Lynn, all of us are beyond glad that you made it. And pack is never going to turn its back on you."

Dammit. I believed that too. My vision got watery again.

His hand still on my shoulder, Sheppard looked to Jonathan. "I need you to make space in the basement. Just push everything up against walls and clear as large of a space as you can. If you need to, move things into the garage. I need enough room for two of those cages down there with plenty of space between them and anything else, including each other."

Sheppard met my eyes again. "Matt's outside with my truck. I think you should come along and see for yourself what crazed wolves are like." Once again, I was ready for a wash of power that never came. "You'll understand better that way."

I nodded and followed Sheppard to the garage, where he grabbed some rope and a couple of those big white painters' drop cloths.

He held them up. "We'll need these to cover the cages."

I raised an eyebrow. "Won't they just claw and tear through those?"

Sheppard shook his head, his sandy blond hair brushing his shoulders as he pushed the button to open the garage door. "They'll probably tear some holes, but they can't get enough of their claws or teeth through the bars of those cages to shred them. Especially not on this short of a trip."

Matt hopped out of the big black truck as Sheppard approached, leaving the door open and the engine running.

Sheppard put a hand up. "It would be best if you drove, Matt."

I followed him around to the passenger side.

Matt shrugged and got back into the driver's seat. "It's gonna be tight getting everyone back in just your Ram and Daniel's Mercedes."

Sheppard sat in the center of the bench seat. "We'll make it work.

Maybe I'll sit in the bed with the cages. If it gets too tight, Jamie and Ian can run."

Matt's eyebrows rose as Sheppard shifted to make enough space for me to close the door, but whatever he thought, he kept to himself. It was probably better that way, odds were good that I mostly looked like a teenager who'd just gotten into trouble for breaking curfew.

The ride back to the reserve was quiet, aside from the rumble of the Ram's engine. I wondered what on Earth seeing the crazed wolves in cages was going to do to convince me killing them would be okay. But there was that nagging feeling that Sheppard was right. Dread welled in my stomach.

We pulled off the path and right out onto the reserve, all the way to the cave mouth. I was sure any park rangers would have a conniption if they caught us. Or rather, they would until they saw those cages and what was in them.

As soon as Matt cut the engine and opened the door, Sheppard's power started pulsing again as it had before. I closed my eyes and watched that power roll along the strands of the pack like a veil of fog. The wolves in the cages paid him no mind and continued to tear and bite at the bars of the cages, opening and reopening fast-closing wounds on themselves. The metallic scent of blood from the walls of the cave hung in the air, clinging to my nostrils as I breathed. It left me on edge even more than I already was, and I was glad Sheppard was there.

Chastity had a laptop under her arm, along with a leather-bound notebook. Her curls were pulled back with a hair tie. She walked over to the truck as I clambered out, Sheppard right behind me. She placed the laptop and notebook on the driver's seat and placed a light kiss on Matt's cheek.

"We'll need to check what he was up to," Chastity reported. "There was medical equipment in the cave. Kaylah said it was like the kind blood banks use to process donations. I don't know what he was up to in there, but I don't like it."

"Let's get these cages onto the truck," Sheppard said, another pulse of power washing over us. "There will be time to dig through whatever you found tonight."

The wolves in the cages were nothing but violence. Ian, Jamie, Matt, and Sheppard lifted the first cage, the wolf inside tearing at their hands and arms as they moved the cage toward the bed of the truck. Chastity hopped in the truck bed and motioned for me to do the same. I did. When the guys got the snarling cage to the truck, Chastity squatted down and grabbed an edge, pulling on the cage while the guys lifted it into the truck. Her arms were getting torn at too, though all of their wounds were closing almost as soon as they opened.

"Stop being useless and help me," Chastity barked.

I stared at her. She wanted me to help pull the cage into the truck. With a wild crazy thing tearing at my arm as I tried? Really? I shook my head and waved my hands in front of me. Either one of those wolves would gladly kill any of us simply for being here. I didn't want to get any closer to it than I already was.

And then it howled. It was a broken sound, coming from the throat of a broken creature, and icy claws rent down my spine. With a shiver, it was all I could do to just get out of Chastity's way as she pulled the cage onto the truck bed.

Matt hopped up once the cage was stable, looking for all the world like he didn't even hear the thing howling next to him.

"You help with the next one, pup," he said to me, hooking a thumb back in the direction of the other cage.

"Lynn." Sheppard's voice broke my shock. "There's still one more. Let's go."

I hopped down from the truck and followed Sheppard to the other cage, Ian and Jamie on my tail. The wolf inside circled as we surrounded the cage.

"Grab the corner, near the bottom," Sheppard said as the wolf snapped at him. Power washed over us, and the wolf snorted at him before turning its attention to Ian.

"But what if I," I wiggled my fingers at the snapping wolf.

Sheppard looked at the snarling mass of brown and white fur and back at me. "Then it's no worse off than it already is. Odds are good they're too far gone anyway, Lynn, like I told you before. Grab a corner and help me keep it stable."

I didn't want to. I knew I would heal just as quickly as the others did when that thing ripped into my arms, it was just the matter that it was absolutely going to rip into my arms that I was distinctly unenthused about.

The wolf's pale gold eyes met my own as I bent to pick up the bottom of the cage. I tried to ignore the rumbling snarl coming from its chest as I lifted in sync with Jamie, Ian, and Sheppard. I just wanted this to be done. I wished the wolf would just stop being crazed and calm down. I wanted it to be okay. As we took the first step, the thing lunged at my corner, tearing into my arm. I yelped as my blood flowed hot over my skin. Dammit that hurt. The wound was already knitting closed, but the heat remained, tingling as it traced up my arm and into my chest as the creature struck again with the next step.

Only it was weaker this time.

The scratches didn't even bleed. And the cage was becoming lighter as I watched the fur melt away to reveal a young woman.

A naked young woman.

She was maybe college-aged, curvy and tall, with tanned skin and long, raven-black hair. As her form shifted, she lost balance and fell onto her side. Her eyes fluttered closed, though her breathing was steady.

The broken howl sounded again from the wolf in the bed of the Ram.

Jonathan's words echoed in my head: crazed wolves don't go back to their human form.

Holy shit.

Whatever it was I could do, whatever it was that I had done to Frederick, some part of it worked on werewolves too.

Holy fucking shit.

30

SHE DIDN'T EVEN SMELL LIKE A WOLF ANYMORE. THE SAME HINT OF wild that was the underpinning of every wolf's scent—or at least, every wolf I had ever met so far, including Langley—was simply gone from her. She just smelled like sweat and blood.

My vision lost focus and I dropped my corner of the cage. It was a good thing Sheppard, Ian, and Jamie had lowered their corners as soon as she started to shift. Their eyes were wide and staring.

Oh God. It works on werewolves too.

She wasn't dead and rotting and turning to ash—thank God—but I was certain that what had just happened to her happened because of me.

I looked at my hands. They were just normal hands. Okay, normal werewolf hands, but still, just hands. I turned them over and traced the faint scars from the attack that turned me into a werewolf. There weren't even scars from where she had scratched me just a moment ago.

The snarling and growling resumed its violence from the cage in the bed of Sheppard's truck.

I looked back at the naked woman curled at the bottom of the cage. She smelled human, but she used to be a wolf. She used to be a werewolf. She was crazed, sure, but now…now she was just a person. Just a woman. I stumbled over my own two feet. She was never going to be able to turn into a wolf again. Oh God.

Matt and Chastity were staring at me too from the truck bed.

Holy goddamn shit, it works on werewolves too.

Run.

I balled my hands into fists and steeled myself against the instinct, squeezing my eyes shut again.

I was still part of this pack. My alpha was here. I didn't hurt him this time. If anyone could help me understand what the holy hell had just happened, it would be him. I stepped closer to him, keeping just enough distance that he didn't accidentally touch me as he moved.

But I couldn't stop staring at her.

"Jamie," Sheppard said, his voice all business. "Grab some clothes from behind the seat in the truck." He turned his head to the truck. "Matt, help me pry open this cage."

Matt hopped off the truck bed. He came between me and the cage, and—together—he and Sheppard managed to pry a side of the cage open, popping the welds of the corner seams by counter pressure.

Jamie appeared with a black t-shirt and a pair of grey sweatpants in his hands. They were like mine. It was no wonder Kaylah had picked up so many of them when we had gone shopping before. The pack really did seem to keep them stashed everywhere.

Chasity appeared then, taking the clothes from Jamie and shouldering him away. "If she wakes up naked in a cage surrounded by men, she'll scream bloody murder. Back off guys." Her hazel eyes met mine. "Get over here, Lynn. You did this to her, you help her."

I put my hands up in a placating gesture and shook my head. "Unh-uh. Her scratching me turned her human again."

Yea, *that* was a sentence I just said. God help me.

"If I touch her myself," I swallowed around something in my throat, "on purpose, she might turn to ash like Frederick did. I have no idea what just happened."

Panic was rising in my chest again, followed quickly by a pulse of calm from Sheppard.

"She's got a point, Chas," Sheppard said, reaching into the open cage and lifting the girl out of it. "I'll hold her. You get the clothes on her. I've already got a phone call in to Kristos, to see if I can't get some answers."

Chastity bent to roll the sweatpants onto the girl's ankles.

"Yea," Matt said, rolling his eyes. "Because that asshole is *so* accommodating."

Sheppard speared him with a look and Matt looked down and away, scratching at the back of his head.

"Lynn," Sheppard said, turning his gaze to me. "Go grab the drop cloths." He jutted his chin toward the truck. "We need to get the other cage covered so we can get that one back to the house."

I nodded and headed toward the truck.

Once the pants were on, Chastity pulled the shirt over the girl's head, shoving her arms through the sleeves like a rag doll.

"Why not have Lynn just change that one too?" Ian asked, hooking a thumb at the other cage.

I shook my head, trying to clear it as I pulled the drop cloths from the floor of the cab and brought them alongside the bed. I didn't want to try to change the other one, I wasn't even actually sure how I changed the first one.

I began unfolding the canvas material, shaking each drop cloth to their full size. Dust fluttered in the air, tickling my nose. I tried to focus on what I was doing. I couldn't freak out right now. I had to hold it together. The pack needed my help.

"Because this one is unconscious right now," Sheppard replied, glancing at the girl in his arms. "Assuming she wakes up, she may not be sane." He took a breath and blew it out slow. "We have time. I want to understand what happened to this one before we do anything with the other." He stepped over to the nearest tree and set the unconscious girl on the ground next to it, propping her weight against the trunk so she sat upright.

The wolf in the other cage hadn't ceased snarling and biting. I tossed an end of the drop cloth over the bars, and Ian pulled it down on the other side. Sheppard hopped into the truck bed and started tying down the drop cloth with heavy strapping.

Red spots speckled the cloth near where the creature's head was. They spread into wider, wet red stains. Blood. From where it was tearing itself open to get out of these cages. It was like a train wreck that I couldn't look away from.

Daniel's white Mercedes pulled up, crunching along the dead leaves and pine needles as we finished tying the first drop cloth to the anchors of the truck bed. I barely noticed the arrival as I tossed the second drop cloth over the snarling cage. As we secured it under strapping, I was almost mesmerized by the movement of the violent creature underneath.

"Oh good," Sheppard said. "Daniel, I need you and Kaylah to take this one to Blood of the Cross too."

"How on Earth'd we miss one?" Kaylah hurried over to the woman.

"You didn't," Matt said. "Lynn changed her."

Kaylah's crystal blue eyes met mine as she knelt beside the tree.

I nodded at her, trying to shrink as I pulled my bottom lip between my teeth. God, would the pack ever forgive me for doing that to another werewolf?!

"See if you can pull on some of your connections while you're there to get updates on her status," Sheppard said. "I want to know when she wakes up, and how stable she is when she does." He turned back to the caged wolf.

Kaylah nodded and looked back at the girl. She pinched her wrist between her fingers for a few moments before picking her up and walking her over to Daniel's car. Daniel opened the door to the backseat and Kaylah placed the girl gently down in the car.

"Chas," Kaylah drawled. "Why don'tcha join us so she dun't wake up screamin'?"

"Sure." Chastity opened the door to the truck cab, gathering the laptop, cord, and journal she had placed in there. She then got into the backseat of the Mercedes as Daniel started the car. Kaylah sat in the front seat, and they rolled away.

It was almost like they had never been there.

Sheppard's focus was still on the snarling cage under the drop cloths. He sat on the raised section of bed over the passenger side wheel. The power radiating from him was like a warm, comfortable blanket.

"I wish I hadn't left my bike back at the shop," Jamie said.

"We can get all cozy," Ian said, stepping toward the cab of the Ram.

"You guys ride up front," I said, not taking my attention away from Sheppard and the roiling mound of drop cloth. "I'll ride in back with Sheppard."

"Plenty of space for you two beanpoles," Matt said as I closed the tailgate and climbed into the truck bed.

Sheppard glanced my way as I sat with my back to the tailgate, my legs crossed under me.

The snarling and biting and clawing didn't stop the entire drive back to the glass house. I don't know why I expected that it would have. I guess the power I could feel radiating off of Sheppard gave me hope for the poor creature. But I could still hear its broken howl. Even that sound had held a promise of violence to any that heard it. I shuddered. Sheppard was right. If this wolf couldn't be calmed, there was nothing to be done for it. Whoever it was may have once been human, but violence was all they knew now, and violence was all they wanted. Killing them would be a mercy.

I wiped tears from my face as we pulled up to the glass house. It was late afternoon already—the day had practically flown by, and it wasn't even over yet. Matt opened the garage door with a button press and backed up to the garage. I helped Sheppard to loosen the straps that held the drop cloths down, and it wasn't long before Sheppard, Matt, Jamie, and Ian had the cage down.

Jonathan came outside as Matt pulled the truck away from the garage door enough to let the door close. He looked around at us and then looked outside before turning back to Sheppard. "Are Kaylah, Chastity, and Daniel tracking the other one? Did it manage to get loose?"

"It didn't get away," Sheppard said. "It's just not a wolf anymore."

"You got it to change back?" Jonathan's tone was incredulous.

"Lynn can apparently change them back to human," Ian said.

I met Jonathan's eyes. "It works on werewolves too, just not the same."

His mouth fell open, and his eyes went wide. There was shock on his face, or fear? Oh God. He was afraid of me now. I had to look away. And why shouldn't he be? I don't know how I had managed not to do anything to him before now, but I hadn't. Thank God. I wasn't about to chance hurting him like that. He belonged with pack. But as much as I wanted to belong with pack too, I wasn't sure the pack wanted me with them anymore. And who could blame them?

"The others are taking that wol— that human to Blood of the Cross," Sheppard said.

He and the others maneuvered the cage and its snarling inhabitant through the garage and down into the basement. I followed them, noticing that the wolf avoided Sheppard the whole time. Maybe there was something to be saved there after all.

All of the furniture in the basement had been shoved against the far walls. Not that there was much to push really. Just a couch, a desk with chair, a couple of armchairs, and a TV stand with a large TV on it. The stand now had the TV facing the wall. Jonathan had even had the forethought to roll up the area rug and push it against a far wall, exposing the tile floor.

Once the cage full of violence was placed in the center of the room, Sheppard pulled the desk chair over to it and sat, placing his back to the basement stairs as he concentrated on the wolf. His power rushed over me, and I was sure the rest of the pack felt it too. I closed my eyes and could see shimmering waves emanating from the strands of my packmates. The shimmer flowed toward Sheppard's strand. He was calling on the pack as a whole to help this poor creature. The snarls died down, but the wolf's ears were still pinned to its head, and the hackles were at full attention along its spine.

Matt's phone buzzed from his pocket. He pulled it out and tapped on the screen. "Chas says they're on their way back here now."

"Well then, dibs on the shower!" Jamie darted up the stairs.

Matt nodded. "Me too." He followed.

I watched Sheppard and the now pacing wolf. Its head was held low, and it watched Sheppard with wary yellow eyes. Drool dangled from its mouth. It may be quiet, but it radiated just as much violence as it did before, and I was certain that it would attack again as soon as anyone came close.

Still facing the wolf, Ian made a face—something approaching disappointment—before he turned and tromped up the stairs.

Yea, I didn't like this situation at all either.

A moment later, the front door opened, and keys jangled as they hit one of the coffee tables in the living room.

"Go," Sheppard said.

The wolf twitched an ear at his voice, but then pinned it back again, a snarl erupting from its muzzle.

"I'll have to stay here and see if I can make any progress."

I nodded as I backed away from Sheppard and the cage. At the stairs, I turned and darted up them.

Jonathan hadn't even followed us down into the basement.

"Lynn," Kaylah called as she caught sight of me from the kitchen. Her hair was pulled up into a messy bun, and her hands were under running water in the sink. I was pretty sure she was washing potatoes, based on the smell. She nodded toward the living room. "Yer clothes 'n' phone are on th' coffee table there."

"Thanks, Kaylah." I balled the clothes into my arms. "Did she wake up?"

Kaylah shook her head. "Nah. She might though, 'n' I managed t' git one a the ord'lies to call me if she does."

"That's good." I looked at the phone in my hand. I had a missed call from Sheppard. Probably from when I ran, judging by the timestamp.

"Oh, fer th' love of…Chastity McAllister!" Kaylah had full southern momma bear in her voice, but she was smiling. "Go take that research elsewhere if ya can't focus on cookin'!"

Chastity smiled at Kaylah and closed the laptop she had in front of her on the counter, pulling the cord from the wall as she did. She grabbed the leather-bound notebook that she had laid out next to it as well.

"Thanks Kaylah," she said, placing a kiss on the other woman's cheek as she moved to the dining room table.

"What is all that, Chastity?" I stepped to the table as she plugged the laptop into the outlet behind her. She sat at the end of the table.

The spot farthest from me.

"That bloodsucker had some kind of research he was working on," she replied, flipping open the notebook again. "I found his notes. And this." She held up a thumb drive, wiggling it between her thumb and forefinger. "If I can break the encryption on this thing, I'll be able to see what he was really up to. His notes are otherwise incomplete." She gestured to the leather-bound book. "Many of the pages were ripped out, and—judging by the ash in his trashcan—he burned whatever was torn out of here."

Jonathan whistled from behind me. I nearly jumped out of my skin.

"He must've really wanted to keep whatever he was working on a secret," he said.

I took a step away from him. I didn't want to accidentally brush his arm.

Chastity nodded. "The spreadsheets on here are just numbers, so they're not terribly helpful just yet. Once I get into the encrypted files, I think I'll have a better handle on what he was doing.

"Shower's free," Jamie called from upstairs.

"Same here," Matt called from down the hall.

I looked to Jonathan.

"You take the upstairs one," he said. "I'll shower down here."

He stepped away from me as I passed him. He had to. Of course he had to. But it hurt just as bad as watching Sheppard stop himself from touching me.

I couldn't get upstairs fast enough. I pulled fresh clothes from my bag in the grey room, and just managed not to slam the bathroom door in my rush to be away. With an almost inaudible click, I locked the door.

Elsewhere in the house, the water turned on and off twice in the time it took me to shower. I let water hot enough to nearly scald me pour into my mouth over and over as I tried to get the taste of ashen bone off my tongue. But I was certain I would never forget that dusty taste and the gritty feel, even if I lived to be as old as Sheppard, or older. I scrubbed at my skin over and over with the washcloth, trying to be sure there was no ash left on me. I even lathered and rinsed my hair three times.

Eventually, I had to face the facts. The real reason I was taking so long was so I didn't have to spend so much time trying to make small talk with a pack that may not even want me around anymore.

31

BY THE TIME I GOT DOWNSTAIRS, THE PACK WAS SEATED AROUND THE dining table, a platter of baked chicken breasts in the center along with two large bowls of cubed and baked potatoes. Well, what was left of the chicken and potatoes, anyway. I had smelled the food once I emerged from the steamy bathroom, but when I caught sight of it, my mouth watered. Sheppard smiled wearily at me as I approached, but the pack was oddly quiet, aside from the movement of dinnerware.

The seat at the end of the table was open, between Jonathan and Daniel, and I sat as Daniel passed the chicken my way. He was careful to put the platter down close to me before I reached for it.

As I piled chicken and potatoes onto my plate, I was mindful of my elbows, careful not to brush Jonathan or Daniel. The usual game that had developed between Jonathan and I of brushing against each other as we reached for things was distinctly absent—no warm hand on my knee, no brush of an arm as he reached for more potatoes. Not that either of us would dare, I supposed, given the events of the day. But it hurt. He didn't even meet my eyes.

I shoveled potatoes into my mouth. Maybe if I could get the meal over and done with quickly, I could just escape to sleep.

Sheppard stood soon after I sat down and took his empty plate to the kitchen. He placed a hand on Kaylah's shoulder in thanks as he left the dining room, heading back to the basement with the caged wolf. It hadn't made a sound during our meal, but I heard the growl start soon after Sheppard closed the basement door.

I jammed a fork into the chicken, tearing a piece off and shoving it into my mouth sullenly. There still wasn't any chatter at the table, which set me on edge perhaps more than the lack of touch did. We just weren't going to talk about it?

Another forkful of chicken down.

I took a crazed werewolf and made her human again. Part of me felt like I should be really proud of that, but I couldn't get past the shock. And I guess, neither could the pack.

Yet another bite of food down.

If I had been in wolf form, I think my hackles would have been up. I felt like an outsider.

But this was still my pack, and I could still see the strands tying all of us together when I closed my eyes. That wouldn't still be there if I wasn't pack, right? Maybe I just needed to wait until we heard from that guy Sheppard called. Maybe that was all they were waiting on too. But there was an emptiness in the quiet here that was hard to bear.

I stood and took my plate to the kitchen.

"You all done, hun?" Kaylah asked as she stood. Her blue eyes were fixed on my plate.

I looked at the bits of chicken and potatoes still on my plate. I couldn't stand making them any more uncomfortable. I could have eaten more, but I wasn't going to make them suffer through my presence. My eyes watered as I placed the plate on the counter next to the sink.

"I'm fine," I lied as I hurried away toward the stairs.

I didn't turn the light on in my room. I didn't need to. I just shut the door with a quiet click and crawled under the blanket. I stared at the light coming from under the door, listening to the sounds of the pack finishing dinner as I fingered the beads of the rosary around my neck. They were still eerily quiet even as I heard the plates being gathered and cleared from the table.

Spicy musk wafted under my door, and there was a light knock.

Matt. I pressed my lips into a line. What did he want?

"Lynn," he said. "Can I come in?"

"Um. Sure." I sat up in the bed, pulling my knees to my chest. The blanket pooled around my ankles.

Light spilled into the room from the hallway as he opened the door.

"All right if I turn on the light?"

I rolled a shoulder. "Sure."

He flicked the light switch, and I blinked at the sudden light in the room.

He watched me for a moment. "Killing a vamp shouldn't bother you like this. They're monsters. All they do is kill, so we stop them." He sat on the far corner of the bed. "And every new wolf gets a little freaked out their first hunt. Most are scared they're gonna die. But that's not pack. Pack protects each other. And with that ability of yours, you have nothing to be afraid of, you can just dust them all."

I furrowed my brow at him. He thought I felt bad for killing a vampire? I mean, I suppose I did. But I was more freaked out by the fact that I had held the bone of someone that I thought had been my friend in my mouth, and then followed that up with something that should have been impossible. So much so that even my alpha couldn't do it, and he had shown to have considerable power.

"Matt, I don't even know how this works." I made a vague gesture in his direction, my palm open. He didn't move or flinch, but the widening of his eyes—yes, even the scarred one—told me that even he was afraid of my touch.

I tilted my chin down and looked scornfully at him. "None of you are willing to touch me, Matt. You're all afraid of me now. Even you. It's why no one said anything at dinner. You've all had time to consider that you have a pack member that could take all of this away from you." I made a sweeping gesture of the house, careful to keep away from Matt.

"Whoa now." Matt put his hands up in a placating gesture. "You just caught me off guard is all. We're pack. We'll get this all sorted out." His voice dropped to a dangerous whisper. "With your ability, we could kill every bloodsucker at the Chateau."

I sighed. Of course I could. And a part of me surged to agree with him.

"But I don't even know how this works. Have you ever seen anything like it?"

"No," he chastised. "But it doesn't matter. We're pack. We'll figure it out."

I turned my head away from him. "Just leave me alone." I pulled my legs closer to my chest, resting my cheek on my knee so that my face was turned away from him.

There was movement on the bed, and I snapped my head to face him. His hand was inches from my knee.

"Don't," I whispered. "Please, Matt, just leave me alone."

With a slow, deliberate movement, he placed his palm on my knee, spreading his fingers along my leg. I would have thought it a brave move of him, except there were sweatpants between his hand and my skin. It didn't stop the stillness that spread through me. What was he trying to prove here?

His eyes met my own. "I'm never going to be afraid of you, Grace."

It was odd to hear him use my proper name.

"God gave you that ability for a reason," he continued. "I'd put cold hard cash down that you can only do that to vampires and crazed wolves."

There was a resolute faith in his words that almost made me believe them.

Almost.

"Listen," he said. "Sheppard's got a call in to Kristos." His mouth turned wry. "And if any asshole is gonna know anything at all about this, it's that asshole."

I didn't even have words. I just stared at him.

"It's fine," he said. "We're pack. You'll see. We'll sort it out and everything will be fine. Don't worry so much." He squeezed my knee and stood.

He was convincing himself more than he was convincing me.

He didn't turn off the light as he left. He didn't even shut the door. I sighed.

Ian's sapphire eyes met mine as his head appeared around the edge of my doorframe. "Look," he said, scratching his head as he leaned against the doorframe. "You ran here, right?"

What kind of question is that? I shrugged. "Yea, why?"

"Well," he said. "Why did you run here?"

I blinked at him. "What?"

"Every other time you've run, you ran to your apartment. What made you run here this time?"

I tilted my head back like I had been smacked. Why did I run here? I hadn't even thought of it. I pulled my bottom lip between my teeth. I certainly hadn't even been thinking about it at the time, I was just running.

But I knew. I ran back here because pack was home. Pack was safe. Pack was where I belonged. My apartment wasn't home anymore, it was just where most of my stuff was.

"Pack is home," I said, the simple truth of the words flowing through me and humming along the strands of the pack. My vision blurred again.

"And that's what *sarcina eiusdem sanguinis* really means," he said.

I nodded, the tears spilling onto my cheeks.

"We'll get it all sorted out, Lynn," Ian said. "We're pack. All of us—including you." He pushed off the doorframe and turned to leave.

"Ian," I called.

He turned back to me.

"Could you turn off the light please?" I nodded my head at the light switch.

"Sure." He smiled and flicked the switch, then grabbed the door handle and closed my door with a quiet click.

My thoughts swirled almost as hard as they did only a handful of days ago, when I learned I was actually a werewolf. What the hell had

Matt been trying to prove anyway? But Ian was right, I had run here because this was pack. And even if they couldn't touch me, this was where I belonged. Maybe we'd all have to get long gloves so no one accidentally got turned back to human. God, but there had to be another way. How could I be sure they would even still want me around? Ian had said we were all pack, but even so. Would I just get used to them not touching me? Over and over my thoughts tumbled until the house fell quiet and dark.

That's when the worst thoughts started to swirl. Frederick had been my friend. I had killed him. Worse, I had absolutely destroyed him, in a very literal sense. I saw his face again, the skin sagging along his bones as it turned to ash. His short black hair bleaching to stringy grey. The dust crumbling away from his bones. The bones falling out of his clothes. The powdery grit in my mouth.

My stomach roiled, and I rushed to the bathroom. I managed to make it in time again. The chunks of my dinner hit the water in the toilet with sickening little splashes that only intensified the taste in my mouth and made the next heave harder.

Until there was nothing left.

I still hadn't turned on any lights.

32

I TURNED ON THE FAUCET, SPLASHED WATER ON MY FACE, AND LEFT THE bathroom. Jonathan was in the hallway, leaning against the wall with his hands in the pockets of his sweatpants. I watched him until he met my eyes in the dark hallway. He sucked on his bottom lip for a moment and then nodded toward the stairs, pushing off the wall.

"Come on," he said quietly as he turned toward the stairs.

What? Come where? Why?

He looked over his shoulder at me. I hadn't moved.

He pressed his lips into a line and sighed. "Everyone's gone to bed. It's just you and me. Come on." He gestured with his elbow toward the stairs, keeping his hand in his pocket.

I sighed and followed him. Why not?

Downstairs, I paused at the hallway. The basement was through that door on the left. Judging by the smell, Sheppard was still down there. There was silence where there had been snarling after dinner.

"If Sheppard can get that one to change back," Jonathan said, "there may be a place for them here." He stood next to me now, closer than he had been earlier. "He'll do all he can to save that one." Jonathan met my eyes. "Just as he'll do all he can to save you." He dropped his eyes and turned away. "Just like I'll do all I can."

I got the distinct impression that he was ashamed of himself, and I couldn't understand why. I wasn't even sure how to ask him. So, I kept quiet and followed him to the kitchen.

He opened a cabinet and filled a glass with some water, carefully handing it to me so that our fingers didn't brush.

I stared at the water and hopped up to sit on the counter. I took a swig from the glass, swishing the water in my mouth before gulping it down.

Jonathan rummaged around in the fridge. "My first kill was awful too," he said, his dark head emerging from behind the fridge door. He pulled out what was left of the lunchmeat, along with some cheese and mayo, and plopped it on the counter.

I didn't think I could be hungry, but the scent of meat proved me wrong.

A chrome breadbox sat where the counter met the side of the fridge, and Jonathan pulled out a handful of slices of bread. He started to assemble a couple of sandwiches.

"Vampires are awful," he said. "They talk like people. They kinda move like people." He moved his shoulders to accent the words. "They even sometimes have a heartbeat if they've fed recently."

He handed a sandwich to me. A vampire with a heartbeat? That's new. Certainly not something pop culture would have you believe about the night-dwelling undead.

"But they aren't people," he continued. "And that's hard to make peace with—at least at first." He took a bite of his sandwich. I did the same.

"You've got it worse," he said, jerking his chin toward me. "Because that vampire—you thought he was your friend."

He was my friend. I nodded and took another bite of my sandwich.

"But you don't know how long he'd been feeding on you." Jonathan took another mouthful of his own sandwich. "We don't even know how long he'd been feeding on you." A corner of his mouth pulled outward, and he shrugged. "But that doesn't make it any easier."

He was right. Frederick was a vampire, so God only knows how long he had been feeding on me. My hand floated to the scars on my neck. Jonathan's eyes followed the movement, and his chest puffed out. A corner of my mouth pulled outward then too.

He still wanted to protect me from that, even if he couldn't touch me. Well that was something. I took another bite of my sandwich.

"Matt's got it easy," Jonathan said. "He's a fanatic. He'll kill vamps and be happy about it because he's dead certain that they're an abomination that needs to be cleansed."

Something in me surged in agreement.

"He joyfully goes on the hunt for vampires and kills them with a righteous fervor." Jonathan finished his sandwich. "I sleep at night because I know that vampires are evil. They kill people. Lots of people." He met my eyes, and there was an uncomfortable sorrow in them. I wanted to fix it, but I didn't understand it. "Hunting them is a job. It's work. It's what we do to protect people, because they cannot protect themselves from this."

I swallowed the next bite of my sandwich. "Are they all killers? Do they only make friends with people to make them food?" Was it possible that Frederick was ever actually my friend?

Jonathan shook his head. "They can only live on human blood. And humans get addicted to being fed on." He ran a hand through his dark hair. "Well, most humans anyway." He nodded at me. "Sheppard said *consanguinea* seem to be immune to that. Either way, they eventually kill the people they feed on—or turn them. But I've heard their strength increases if they've recently had the last drop of someone's lifeblood."

I suppressed a shudder and hid what I could with the last bite of my sandwich. Jonathan and Matt were right. Vampires had to die if we were supposed to keep people like that poor girl that went to Blood of the Cross safe. I hopped off the counter.

But I couldn't help being fixated. "He was my friend, Jonathan. How can I reconcile the man who would take me to dinner anytime I wanted with the ashen bones in my mouth? I can remember the way he smelled, and his laugh, and what foods—"

I furrowed my brow. I couldn't remember what foods Frederick ate.

"Actually, I'm not even sure I ever saw him eat something."

Jonathan refilled my glass and gestured out of the kitchen without handing it to me. I led the way to the stairs.

"I don't think vampires get anything out of eating actual food," Jonathan explained. "I think they do it out of pretense, like when they breathe. Older vampires stop breathing altogether."

He was following me to my room? He couldn't touch me, and I couldn't touch him, yet he was following me to my room.

I ran a hand through my hair. "What was your first hunt like?"

Jonathan pursed his lips for a moment before taking a deep breath. "It was a little brood that had holed up in an abandoned mall in Dallas. They had been taking in runaways. Some, they turned. Others, they just fed on."

He followed me into my room. Well. I was just going to have to be extra careful not to touch him, then, wasn't I?

I sat on the bed, up near the pillows, and pulled the blanket over my legs. I wasn't cold, but it at least offered another layer of protection between us.

"We had staked out the place and blocked off all the entrances," he continued, setting my glass of water on the bedside table. "My first kill was a vampire that looked like she was the same age as Jamie. Most of the vamps in that brood looked young though. No telling how old any of them actually were. I guess there's never really a good time to get turned."

He waited until I was settled and tucked the blanket around me, careful not to touch me directly. He then sat facing me on the other side of the bed, crossing his legs before he continued. His eyes were elsewhere, unfocused, like they had been when he told me about when he and Jamie were turned.

"She was just a girl, but when her fangs sank into my shoulder, I snapped her neck." He blinked and was back here again. He looked at me in the darkness. "I had only ever killed rabbits and the occasional deer before that—aside from the wolf that turned Jamie and me, I mean." There was a deep pain in his voice. "Poor kids had never stood a chance against the bloodsuckers. And once they were vampires, they never stood a chance against us."

I pulled a hand out from under the covers, gingerly placing it on his knee. Panicked, his eyes met mine. "Lynn?" His skin sagged against his skull, his hair turning to stringy grey.

I jerked my hand away from him, covering my mouth to keep from screaming. Oh God, it was happening to Jonathan! "*NO! Jonathan!*"

But it was too late for him. His clothes practically deflated, and ash poured from them, covering the blanket in a dark grey powder.

I threw the blanket off myself and backtracked toward the open door, watching the pile of ash and clothes that used to be Jonathan. I couldn't! He can't! Oh God!

My back ran into something—or rather, someone—and I quickly turned. "Ian!"

But his skin was sagging too. He had touched me to try to stop me before I ran into him. His clothes sagged to the floor, ash spilling from the sleeves and bottom of his shirt to land in a neat little mound.

I screamed and ran down the stairs. "God! Please no!" I didn't care who heard me.

Downstairs, I scrambled for the basement door, throwing it open and slamming it shut behind me. I raced down the stairs. Sheppard sat in a chair at the bottom, his back to the stairs, and—subsequently— the door. Sweat beaded his brow, and his concentration and focus were entirely on the wolf in the cage. He hadn't even registered my entrance.

I grabbed his shoulder, urging him to face me. He did. Scratching wounds opened from beneath his shirt, pouring dust into his lap. He stared at the wounds and dust for a moment before meeting my eyes. I could only imagine the look of terror he must have seen there.

"They will always fear you," he said simply, his voice eerily calm. And then his jaw fell from his face as the rest of him burst into dust on the chair.

Another scream of unadulterated terror rose from my chest, and the wolf in the cage sounded its broken howl.

I ran back up the stairs, but the doorknob wouldn't turn. I was locked in the basement with the ashes of my alpha and the broken, violent creature in its cage.

"Somebody, please! Help me!" I slammed my fists against the door. "Please! I'm sorry! I don't know what to do!" I pounded at the door again. "I didn't mean to hurt anyone!" Another strike on the door. "Please someone! Help me!"

There was a voice on the other side of the door, "Lynn." I couldn't place whose it was.

"Help me! Please!" I pounded at the door again.

"Lynn!" It was Jonathan's voice? How?

"I'm so sorry! I didn't mean it!" Something jangled in my head and I shook, trying to clear it.

"*Lynn!*" Jonathan was shaking my shoulders under the blanket.

I was screaming when I woke, unsure where the nightmare had started. In a single move, I threw the blanket from me and leapt from the bed. I ran to the bathroom and splashed cold water on my face. There was no roiling in my stomach, no vomit threatening to escape me. But my heart pounded like a kick drum against my sternum, and I could feel the adrenaline racing through me.

"It was just a nightmare," Jonathan said from the door of the bathroom. "You're alright." His heart was pounding too.

I looked into my own panicked face in the mirror. The golden eyes of my wolf stared back at me.

I would have brushed past Jonathan as I left the bathroom, except he had the forethought to step back. I had to get to Sheppard, to confirm for myself that he was alright, but also to...well, I wasn't really sure. As I rushed down the stairs, the words from my nightmare echoed in my head: they will always fear you. God, that couldn't be true, could it?

Sheppard hadn't gone to bed. I could smell that he was still in the basement. I slowed my pace as I got to the door and quietly turned the knob. I didn't close the door behind me this time as I descended the stairs. Jonathan was a step or two behind me.

Sheppard was in a chair with his back to us, just as he had been in my dream, and my heart pounded harder. Sweat beaded his brow, and he lifted his head as I approached, his eyes still focused on the wolf. The caged creature was asleep, the gentle rise and fall of its chest belying the violence it promised when it was awake.

I wiped at my face. "I have to know if I'm a danger to the pack. To your pack."

Sheppard turned to me then. His shirt was open halfway down his chest now, and I could see the wounds that had poured ash in my dream. But his wounds were simply scabbed over with blood.

"Grace Lynn Cartwright," he said solemnly. "If I thought you could ever hurt this pack, I would have let the military take you long ago." His eyes and tone were gentle, and it broke my heart.

My vision blurred out of focus, and I had to swallow around the sob that threatened. I squeezed my eyes shut and saw the strands of the pack again, power shimmering along them, leading to Sheppard. I swallowed around the lump again. My own strand was just as strong as the others'. I took a breath to try to slow down my heart and opened my eyes, looking at Sheppard's wounds.

I gestured to his chest. "I thought we were nearly bulletproof. Shouldn't those have healed by now?"

Sheppard gave me a wry smile and touched the topmost scabbed injury. "Wounds from *consanguinea* take longer to heal. If I thought you were going to crash through that vamp's body like that, this probably wouldn't have happened." He shrugged. "I'm fine."

My skeptical face must have been showing.

"It doesn't hurt," he said. "And it'll heal in another day or so."

I pulled my lip between my teeth. I wish I knew what the heck was going on with me. Or how to stop it from hurting the pack. But I couldn't even put together how dusting a vampire and turning a werewolf human again were even related. It just didn't make any sense.

"We'll figure out what's going on," Sheppard said, his voice as patient as ever. "I just need to hear what Kristos knows."

253

"What do I do in the meantime?" It came out as a hoarse whisper around the lump in my throat.

"Patience is hard when you're not used to the idea of being around for centuries," Sheppard said with another wry smile. "You try to get some rest. Maybe help Chastity crack into that flash drive in the morning." He nodded in the direction of the sleeping wolf. "I'm going to keep trying to save this one. Getting it to sleep is good, but it's not enough. If I can get it to change back, then there's a chance of saving them." He spread his hands. "But the effort is leaving my pack vulnerable, and the last thing we need is for the vampires to try to come down hard on us while my focus is shifted like this. I don't have the same control, nor the same power."

"What does that mean?" I couldn't fathom what it even meant to have the kind of power being an alpha entailed.

"It means he can't keep trying forever," Jonathan said from where he sat at the top of the basement stairs. "Or we may lose our alpha."

My eyes went wide, and I snapped my attention back to Sheppard. "It could kill you?!"

Sheppard's gentle smile returned and he shook his head. "No. The exertion of power over this wolf won't kill me, but the instability could fracture the strength of the pack. And if the vampires attack, we could splinter apart. If you concentrate, you can feel the imbalance of power straining the pack bonds."

"We're stronger than that, Shep," Jonathan replied.

Sheppard nodded. "I would hope so. The pack needs my attention much more than this stray does. Pack must come first, or we lose the ability to save others."

"Lone wolves aren't effective," I guessed.

Sheppard's golden-brown eyes met mine. "Lone wolves don't survive well. We're meant for packs."

I looked to the sleeping wolf in its cage, watching the rise and fall of its chest.

"Go. Sleep." He jerked his head toward the stairs. "Help Chastity in the morning." He looked up at Jonathan on the stairs and gave him a smile that felt distinctly fatherly.

254

Reassuring warmth shimmered in the air, and I was glad I had come to bother Sheppard. I may not have any more answers about what was happening to me, but he had all but told me that pack was where I belonged anyway. As I followed Jonathan out of the basement and back upstairs, my nerves settled. Maybe there was a place for me here.

33

IN MY ROOM, I STARED AT MY BED FOR A LONG MOMENT. IT WAS childish, but I was afraid to go back to sleep. When I was little, my nightmares had always returned upon going back to sleep. Though my nightmares as an adult had been rare, I still had trouble getting back to sleep those nights. My nightmares waited for me, and I hated it.

I turned to Jonathan. "Will you—" I pushed my hand into my hair and focused on his bare feet. "Will you stay with me? Tonight, I mean?"

The electricity crept back into his woodsy scent. "I'd be glad to," he replied with a gentle smile. His heart pounded too.

He waited for me to get into the bed. When I finally got settled, he laid down on top of the blanket next to me, draping his arm across my stomach. Though the blanket was between his arm and my body, it was warm. I wanted to like it, but I couldn't get the image of me accidentally flailing into him in one of the aftershock nightmares and turning him to ash.

"What is it?"

"It's just—" I squeezed my eyes shut and took a breath. "I just don't know how good of an idea it is for you to be here in the bed." I couldn't bring myself to look at him. "What if I accidentally, you know?"

"What if you accidentally dust me, you mean?" There was a half-hearted attempt at a joke there, but it was too serious a matter for it to carry any weight.

I nodded.

He placed his hand over mine and squeezed through the blanket as he sat up.

"I still don't think you're going to affect me. Not given all the touching we've already done since your change." He waggled his eyebrows at me. "But I'll grab one of the blankets and a pillow from the linen closet and sleep right there on the floor." He pointed over me to the space in front of the nightstand and met my eyes. "Just to be on the safe side."

His face was only inches from mine. And dammit if I didn't want to just lose myself in his kiss right now.

My chest ached. I wasn't sure I was ever going to be able to kiss him again without risking losing him altogether.

He closed his eyes then, and I heard him inhale as he leaned a fraction of an inch closer. Closing my eyes, I pressed my head against my pillow, willing him not to try to come any closer—trusting him not to come any closer. Tears slipped from the corner of my eyes as he took another breath and pushed himself off the bed.

I pressed the heels of my palms against my eyes, trying to quell the sob that was trying to tear through my chest. Hadn't I cried enough over this stupid ability?

He came back a moment later with multiple blankets bundled against him with one arm, and a fluffy pillow gripped in his other hand. He folded one of the big comforters in half and laid it on the ground, arranging the pillow up near the nightstand. He then laid down on his side, facing the bed, and pulled the other blanket over him.

"Try to get some sleep, Dreamer," he whispered. "Sleep away as much time as you can until we hear from Kristos. Then it won't seem so long."

I smirked at him. "Did that line work on your brother for Christmas or something?"

He laughed then, a sound I wasn't sure I was going to hear from him again. My chest grew tight.

Dammit.

"I tried," he said through a chuckle, "but Jamie was more the stay-up-all-night type."

I put my head down on top of my hand at the edge of the bed, my knuckles pressing into my cheek. "You know, I believe it."

He watched me for a moment, hooking a strand of his dark hair behind his ear.

"What happened in that nightmare?" His voice was quiet. "Did you just go crazy and attack everyone?"

There was no malice or fear in the tone, of course, just curiosity.

I pressed my lips into a line and looked away from him. "No. I just dusted everyone. It started with you," the lump in my throat formed again, "and ended with Sheppard."

Jonathan nodded slowly. "You're so scared to hurt pack that your dreams are attacking you."

I tried to swallow past the ball of grief lodged in my throat. "Pretty much."

"There has to be something that triggers it," Jonathan said, his brow furrowed in thought. "You've probably had the ability to do that since your first change. I don't think this is something that just spontaneously develops. So why didn't it happen before? What happened now?"

"I don't think..." With a huff, I wiped at my face. "I can't think about that right now. I can't even run through what happened in the cave without wanting to throw up."

Jonathan smiled, and there was mischief in it. "It's probably gonna be a while before you can eat grilled ribs, huh?"

I threw a pillow at him. "Rude!" But I could feel the smile pulling at my face. "But yes, it's probably gonna be a while before I'm interested in having anything with a bone in my mouth."

"Well that's a shame," he winked at me. The impishness hadn't left his eyes.

I threw my other pillow at him. He caught it. "I can't even touch you right now and you're sad I can't give you head?"

"Sausage-fest, remember?" He tossed the pillow back onto the bed. It landed behind me.

I lifted my chin playfully. "You're just a horn-dog."

He sobered then. "For you."

I propped my head on my hand, my elbow on the edge of the bed. "How can you be so sure you want anything to do with me at all? You don't even know me."

"Sure I do," he replied. "Grace Lynn Cartwright; age 22; born March 20th, 1997; freelance copy-editor; drives an old Honda Del Sol, purple; mom died in a car accident sophomore year of college; dad's off in Europe; no siblings; hangs out in used bookshops and cafés; heads to the club with her girlfriends on weekends; runs the trails every morning; loves peanut butter and raisin sandwiches."

I stared at him. That was an alarming amount of specificity.

"Ew! Wait a minute! No I don't!"

His eyes glittered. "I know, I just wanted to see if you were actually paying attention."

"And my car's not that old." I rolled my eyes at him and retrieved the pillow. "That's a lot to know about me. I thought you guys had only been tailing me for a month or so."

"Well, yea," Jonathan said, raking his hand through his hair. "But Sheppard knew about you for longer, and he shared what he knew about you with us after the military stuck their nose in on pack territory."

"Are you guys really so picky about that?"

"We have to be with the military around," he replied. "They have their own werewolf program, and we're not interested in crossing with them. Those guys are ridiculously regimented, and they have their own agenda."

"What do you mean?"

"Well look." He sat up then, crossing his legs and facing me. "The military has its own pack, probably more than one, and the base is just north of The Springs, right?"

I nodded.

"So, if there's a military base crawling with werewolves right outside of town," he said, gesturing north with his hand, "then why are there still so many vamps underneath the Chateau?"

That was a damn good question. One I couldn't possibly have an answer to.

"And that's why Sheppard doesn't trust the military," he said. "There shouldn't be any vampires at all anywhere near here, but there are. And now that we're in town, the Chateau is part of our territory, so the military has lost their chance at it, unless they want to take us out."

"Would they do that?" My eyes were wide.

"Hell no," Jonathan replied, his voice emphatic. "They wouldn't dare. If they tried to take us out, the packs we're friends with would come down hard on them. It'd probably lead to so much infighting that the bloodsuckers would take over North America."

"Wow, you think so?"

"Well," he hedged, "maybe not all of North America, but it's hard to fight a war on two fronts. And it'd be just the kind of thing that the vampires would love to see happen."

I yawned. "How do you guys keep the fighting between you and the vamps so quiet? How come the whole world doesn't know?"

"Shep says the world isn't ready." Jonathan yawned too. "But I think part of it is that they simply don't want to believe." He laid back down on the blanket, propping his head on his hand. "People make up excuses and rationalize things that don't otherwise fit into their worldview. I think the world isn't ready for werewolves because the world's too busy being blind to itself."

"I'm scared to go back to sleep," I whispered as my eyelids grew heavy.

Jonathan's gentle smile returned. "I know," he whispered back, "but I promise I'll wake you if you start having another nightmare."

"Without touching me?"

He nodded. "Without touching you."

That helped, actually. I settled my head against my pillow. "Goodnight, Jonathan," I whispered.

I could hear the smile even in his whisper. "Goodnight, Dreamer."

34

MY NIGHTMARES DIDN'T RETURN FOR ONCE, AND I MARVELED AT THE peaceful sleep I had gotten. I did, however, wake soon after dawn, judging by the light from my window. Jonathan's deep, even breathing told me he was still asleep on the floor, which I confirmed by looking over the edge of the bed. He had spent the whole night on the floor of my room. Just so that he could be there for me if I had another nightmare.

With a quiet yawn, I stretched my arms over my head. It had been too many mornings since I last went for a run. A lot had been happening these past few days, sure, but I missed the routine of my morning. Nodding to myself, I grabbed my phone from the night-stand and crept from the bed to keep from waking Jonathan. At the chair in the corner of the room, I put my tennis shoes on and checked the battery of my phone. I was at forty-three percent. That should be fine for a run around the neighborhood. It wasn't like I was going to be gone all day.

Still, I didn't want anyone to worry. I tapped out a quick message, sending it to both Jonathan and Sheppard.

Taking my morning run. Be back soon. No worries.

Jonathan's phone buzzed from under the bed. And it sounded like his breathing had changed. Dammit. I looked back to his spot on the floor. If he was awake, he hadn't moved, and it certainly didn't look like he was going to try to stop me from running. Thank God.

I crept out of the house, closing the front door with a nearly inaudible click, and broke into a jog down the driveway and ran through the neighborhood. I didn't try to run through the events of the cave, and I tried not to let myself focus on the pack not touching me. Instead, I just tried to enjoy the crisp fall air. The chill of winter breathed over the mountains, a promise of snow to come. The birds woke as I ran, their chirps and caws sounding through the trees, though I didn't know enough about the wildlife to be able to identify any of them.

It felt so good to be running again, but it was almost eerie to be alone. Once I became aware of the lack of company, it pressed on me. For the past week, there had always been someone of the pack with me. There was always another presence, even if it was quiet. Now, the lack of that presence was almost a ringing in my ears, like after a loud rock concert. Like the deafening silence of my empty apartment, it was uncomfortable. I wanted pack. I had spent most of my adult life living on my own, and now, after only a week or so, I found I missed the pack so completely that my chest grew tight.

Closing my eyes, I saw the strands of the pack, thrumming with energy that fed back to Sheppard, and tears filled my eyes. It was so odd to find comfort in just seeing the strands of my packmates. And to think, a little over a week ago, they were just strangers to me.

I blinked in surprise as I rounded a corner. I was back in front of the glass house again. How had I missed running past the wreckage of Sheppard's old house? How on Earth was I back here already? I checked my phone. I had been gone nearly an hour. I must have run multiple times around the sprawling neighborhood in that time.

Shaking my head at the house, I sighed. "*Sarcina eiusdem sanguinis*, indeed."

Inside, the house smelled of waffles, maple syrup, sausage, and bacon. Kaylah and Chastity were in the kitchen, while Matt, Jamie, and Ian were eating at the dining room table. Jonathan was coming down the stairs, his hair still wet from his shower.

He smiled at me. "Good run?"

Maybe my text didn't wake him this morning. Or he was just going along with the charade.

"It felt good to get my feet moving under me again," I replied, waiting for him to get past the landing before I stepped toward the stairs. "You didn't take all the hot water, did you?"

"Nah," he said. "This place has one of those on-demand water heaters. You have to be trying to run out of hot water here."

"Well good."

"Lynn," Kaylah called.

I looked her way in time to see the water bottle sailing my direction. I caught it and smiled at her.

"Hurry back down or breakfast'll all be gone," she said as I opened the bottle and took a swig of the cool water.

I nodded and darted up the stairs, my stomach had been growling at me since I stepped into the house.

"I'll save some bacon for you," Jonathan called behind me.

At the top of the stairs, I turned and smiled at him. "Thanks!"

I didn't take a terribly long shower—I didn't need it. I just needed to cool down and rinse off. Toweling off, I pulled on a pair of stonewash jeans and shoved the rosary in my pocket. I dug around my bag for a shirt, finally settling on the olive green one. Remembering what Matt had said before, I sniffed at my shoulder. It didn't smell like Jonathan anymore. Pressing my lips into a line, I squeezed my eyes shut to clear the tears that threatened to spill from my eyes. I scrubbed at my face, pressing the heels of my palms against my eyes.

God, I had only known him for a week! What did it matter if I didn't smell like him anymore? I sighed, pushing tears away. I probably wasn't going to be able to touch him again anyway, so I should just get used to this.

"Your bacon tastes even better than mine!" Jonathan called from the dining room.

I couldn't help the smile that pulled at my mouth. For someone old enough to be my grandfather, Jonathan seemed to always have a sense of what to say to make things better. I shook my head with a sigh and wiped at my face again.

"There better be some left when I get there," I said, heading for the stairs. "Or you'll have to go into the kitchen and make me more yourself!"

"Oh no he ain't!" Kaylah exclaimed. "The last time I let one a them boys cook, we were still scrubbin' sauce offa the cab'nits three days later!"

Jamie threw his head back in exasperation. "The sauce had to simmer, Kaylah!"

She shook her wooden spoon at him. "You simmer things with a lid on 'em, mister!" Her crystal blue eyes met mine. "And that wa'n't even the worst'v it. I had t' throw out th' pot after th' spaghetti burnt so bad it glued itself to th' bottom!"

I raised my eyebrows in surprise as I sat at the open seat between Daniel and Jonathan. As promised, my plate already had a handful of bacon slices on it.

"Wow Jamie," I said. "Even I don't burn spaghetti, and I can't cook to save my life."

Kaylah clucked her tongue as she brought a fresh plate of waffles to the table. She set them down near me and grabbed the syrup from in front of Ian and set it next to the waffles.

"Milk?"

"Ooh," I replied. "Yes please."

Kaylah disappeared back into the kitchen and returned with a tall glass of milk. I didn't try to take it from her; I just let her place it next to my plate.

"Thanks, Kaylah," I said.

She smiled gently at me and sat on the other side of Daniel, piling sausage onto her plate.

Picking up a couple of waffles with my fork, I stacked them on my plate and poured syrup over them. I took a bite and noticed that Chastity, on the other side of Kaylah, kept eyeballing something in the living room as she stuffed bite after bite of her food down. I looked over my shoulder. The laptop she had brought back from the cave was on one of the coffee tables. It was open, and something was running on the screen. I took another bite of waffle and studied the screen.

"Decryption software," Chastity said flatly. I guess she saw me staring. "Hopefully it can crack that flash drive."

I crunched on a piece of bacon and took another bite of my waffles. "How'd you get that?"

"Ian knows a guy." She looked at her food, scooped a bite of sausage into her mouth, and looked back at the laptop.

"What do you think might be on that?" I asked her.

Her hazel eyes finally focused on me, and she shrugged. "No way to be sure. But his notes indicate that he thought he was getting close to figuring out the connection between vampires and werewolves." She waved her hand. "Beyond what we already know about how we both came to be."

I dipped the bacon in some of the maple syrup that had pooled on my plate and took a bite. "But what did that have to do with keeping crazed wolves in cages?"

"He was running experiments on them," she said. "I just don't know what he was hoping to prove."

The laptop dinged.

"AHA!" Chastity sprang to her feet, shoving a piece of bacon into her mouth. "Gotcha!" She darted over to the coffee table and sat cross-legged on the couch next to the laptop. It was kind of an odd sight, her sitting sideways to face the laptop over the arm of the couch.

I finished my waffles and pulled the last few pieces of sausage onto my plate, rolling them around in the leftover syrup before cutting them in half with my fork and popping them into my mouth.

"*HOLY MOTHER OF GOD!*"

I swear, I could have heard Chastity's exclamation from three counties over. I actually felt it jangle in my head—a gentler version of what happened when I bit Matt during our sparring match the other day.

Matt stood from his chair. "What is it Chas?"

She looked over at him, her eyes wide. She looked at all of us and then swallowed. Looking back at Matt, she said, "He used to be a werewolf."

Matt scrunched his face in confusion. "What?"

"That bloodsucker Lynn dusted," she said, gesturing to the laptop. "If his notes are to be believed, then he was a werewolf long before he was a vampire."

A chill snaked its way down my spine. "That can't be true."

She looked back at the screen. "It says here that he'd lost his pack in a vampire raid. In retaliation, he tore the throats out of the sheep of that brood, feasting on their flesh. That was all it took for him to lose the ability to turn back to wolf, and he found that he hungered for blood the way he knew vamps did. That's what started his experiments."

"Holy shit," Ian whispered.

Holy shit was right. A hush fell over the pack.

"How is that even possible?" Jonathan asked.

Chastity hadn't looked up from the computer. "I don't know. But he wasn't the only vamp turned from a werewolf. He somehow captured a crazed werewolf, turned some of his sheep into were-wolves, and then experimented to see exactly how many people they had to eat to turn vamp."

I pushed my plate away from me as anger surged in me. "What kind of sick, twisted—"

"Vampire," Matt said, cutting me off. "Those bloodsuckers are the only things on the planet capable of that kind of evil."

"People can be pretty bad to each other," Daniel said. "Remember, there are some wolves that were actually around when the Holocaust happened."

Matt speared him with a look, despite only having one good eye to do so. "If you think vampires weren't part of that, then you haven't been paying attention."

Whoa. That was an angle I certainly hadn't expected. Vampires were involved in the Holocaust? I shook my head. Okay, sure. I mean, why not? But what we had here, what Chastity had found, was terrifying.

"Apparently," Chastity continued, largely ignoring the conversation as she skimmed the files, "most of the werewolves fed human flesh went crazy, but from those that didn't, he found that three was the magic number."

I took a breath, trying to calm the renewed roiling in my stomach. "So what did he need all the medical equipment for then?"

Chastity looked at me for a moment, but I could see her thoughts swirling.

"Hmm." She turned back to the laptop and opened more files. "He was," she scrolled through the top document, "looking to make a connection between the vampires and the werewolves." She opened the next file in the folder and stopped scrolling. She looked at me, something altogether new on her face.

I squinted at the screen, but couldn't make it out from the angle I was at. "What?"

"He knew you were *consanguinea*," she said. "He intentionally released the wolf that turned you. He figured *consanguinea* would be a better chance at bridging that gap."

"He clearly didn't know most *consanguinea* don't survive turning vamp," Matt said.

I wasn't listening anymore. My vision had lost focus. Frederick had known I was *consanguinea*. He had never been my friend. He had only ever been trying to figure out my patterns, so he could use me in his experiments.

Numbly, I stood from the table. Things in my life had gone from simple to incredibly complicated.

Run.

My gut jumped. I wanted to. But where? There was nowhere to go. My apartment had been infiltrated by Frederick already. He may be dead and gone now, but that didn't make my apartment feel any safer. Safe was here with pack. And pack wasn't running.

"Oh my God," Chastity said, snapping me from my thoughts as she unplugged the laptop and stood. "Sheppard's gonna need to see this." She headed toward the basement door.

I followed her.

In the basement, Sheppard was still in the same chair as he was last night, his shirt damp with sweat. He turned to Chastity as she came down the stairs, wiping sweat from his brow. The cuts on his chest looked better this morning than they had last night. The caged wolf hadn't moved in its slumber.

Chastity handed the laptop to Sheppard. "Her entire family tree is in there," she said, pointing at the screen. "All of the *consanguinea's* are."

My blood turned to ice in my veins. Then the vampires knew how to figure out who was *consanguinea* and who wasn't. I didn't know what exactly that meant, but I could feel in my bones that it couldn't be good.

Sheppard looked at me, the concern plain on his face. "We have to hope that the vampires' innate distrust for one another means this information is not widely known." He looked back to Chastity, returning the laptop to her. "I heard the rest of what you found."

He fished his cell phone out of his pocket and scrolled through his contacts, touching the dial icon when he found the one he was looking for.

"Buckheim," came a gruff voice from the other end of the line.

"I have something you'll want to see in person," Sheppard said, and ended the call.

35

"Who's Buckheim?" I asked.

Sheppard had said before that pack doesn't keep secrets.

His gentle eyes met my own. "He's an old friend—and First Sergeant Langley's commanding officer. I'm honestly surprised he hasn't shown up on our doorstep already, since the military seems keen on recruiting you." He nodded his head toward me. "General Buckheim runs the werewolf operations within the military. He's going to want to see the proof that shows the vampires know how to track *consanguinea.*" He pressed his lips into a line.

Chastity swore. It made me raise my eyebrows at her.

I looked back to Sheppard and pushed a hand into my hair. "What happens if they find them all?"

"They'll kill them," Matt said, appearing at the top of the basement stairs.

Sheppard nodded. "Most likely, yes. Or they'll try turning all of them, most of whom will die. But some won't, and we'll have a handful or so of high-powered *consanguinea* vampires running around." He sighed. "But mostly it spells nothing but bad news for humanity. If the vampires figure out that the blood stays strong with *consanguinea*, then they'll just start wiping out entire swaths of people. Then they'll find out pretty quick whether a cure is even possible for them."

That was horrifying.

"Wait," I furrowed my brow. "What do you mean 'the blood stays strong'?"

Jonathan appeared at the basement door. He stepped down to sit at the top of the stairs as Ian came to lean on the doorframe. Jamie squeezed past Matt and Ian to sit next to his brother on the stairs. The two were a pretty striking pair with their swarthy skin and dark hair. The boyishness that was almost exaggerated in Jamie was simply hinted at in Jonathan, but the two were unmistakably siblings: they had the same nose and the same strong chin.

Sheppard eyed the sleeping wolf in the cage and then turned his chair to face the stairs. "Kaylah, Daniel," he called, power lightly washing through the words. "You two are going to want to hear this as well."

Jonathan and Jamie stepped down a couple of steps and sat back down, allowing Matt and Ian to sit on the top steps. Daniel appeared in the hallway. The water turned off in the kitchen, and a moment later, Kaylah came to lean on the doorframe, drying her hands on a kitchen towel. Chastity slumped onto one of the middle steps, and I sat at the bottom of the stairs. Having all of the pack so near, their scents intermingling with each other, made my heart so full it ached in my chest.

"The vampires likely know how to track *consanguinea* now," Sheppard said with a sigh, presumably repeating himself for those that weren't here.

"So I heard," Kaylah said.

Sheppard nodded then, thinking. He looked up to where Matt was sitting. "You've heard that phrase, the blood stays strong, haven't you?"

Matt nodded. "Yea, it means the number of *consanguinea* in a generation stays the same, more or less."

Sheppard nodded again. "Exactly. So if a *consanguinea* dies without having any children, the blessing passes to the eldest sibling of the parents, or the eldest sibling. Sometimes this makes it jump families, and the church loses track of it for a little bit."

"Then *consanguinea* ain't got nuthin' to do with actual genetics," Kaylah said.

"If the church loses track of it sometimes," Daniel said, thinking out loud, "then the vamps probably would too if it jumped families."

"And they would likely wipe out entire cities trying to find it again," Matt added.

Sheppard's somber look told me those were more than just good guesses—they were right. "It would be a while before the vampires realized they were killing off their food supply too quickly." He ran a hand through his hair. "But their numbers would wipe us out long before that."

Ice snaked down my spine again. "Shouldn't we tell the church then?"

Sheppard thought a long moment before answering. "Not just yet." He shook his head. "There's no telling where they got that information from in the first place. Ian, did you manage to save the hard drive from my computer?"

Ian nodded. "I'm pretty sure it'll work. I just need to get an enclosure for it and then we can hook it up to the laptop to see."

"Let's get that done today," Sheppard said. "I want to compare Frederick's file of the *consanguinea* line to ours. With any luck, it's out of date."

Jamie cleared his throat. "What good will it being out of date do?"

"Well," Sheppard said, "if it's old enough that the blessing jumped families, then they'll be on a wild goose chase for a bit."

"That just means more sheep, more vamps, or more dead wherever the former family last was," Matt said sourly.

"Then we'd better bank on their distrust for one another and hope this information hasn't gone terribly far," Sheppard said. He wiped at his face and I realized he still hadn't slept yet. The bags under his eyes were pronounced.

"Is there anything at all that any of us can do to help you?" I asked quietly, looking meaningfully at the caged wolf and then meeting Sheppard's eyes.

His tired smile broke my heart all over again. He waved the phone at me. "Just wait till Kristos calls back. That old bear will know something, I'm sure of it."

"We haven't seen that asshole in over two hundred years, Shep," Matt said, crossing his arms. "What makes you so sure he'll call back?"

My eyes went wide. "Two hundred years?" And Sheppard called him an old friend.

"If he didn't have anything to say," Sheppard replied, "he'd have texted or called right back. Kristos is a straight-shooter, always has been."

"Well, here's to hoping he's on our team this time." Matt stood and left the basement. I heard the back door open and shut a moment later.

Sheppard wiped at his face again. "Every time I push too hard on this one," he gestured to the cage, "it wakes up snarling and I have to force it back to sleep. I'm going to give it till dawn tomorrow, and if I can't bring them around, there'll be nothing to be done."

My eyebrows shot up. "You gotta sleep before then! The mind isn't good with sleep deprivation."

A chuckle rumbled from Sheppard's chest. "The rules of life as a human don't apply so well to werewolves. We can go for days without sleep or food or water. It's not comfortable, but our healing can more than make up for it." He made a shooing motion toward the top of the stairs. "Now, go on, let me concentrate again." He picked up his chair and set it down again, facing the caged wolf.

I waited until the rest of the pack had made it up the stairs before following them.

"Hey Ian," Jamie said, and Ian turned to face him. "Give me a ride to the shop when you head out to pick up that enclosure?"

Ian nodded. "Sure. Let's head out now and then we can work on a speed-run of the first half of Diablo once you get back."

Jamie smiled. "Sounds like a plan to me." He sat on the couch to pull his shoes on while Ian did the same.

Chastity set the laptop on the dining room table and joined Kaylah in the kitchen, where the two of them methodically clanged pots, pans, and silverware as they prepped meals. At least, I hope it was more than one meal they were prepping, based on the different hanks of meat on the counter. Jonathan flopped onto a couch and turned on the TV. Daniel disappeared upstairs. He was still ironing things out with the insurance company about Sheppard's other house.

The fire had only been two days ago.

Maybe I wasn't used to the idea that I was going to live for centuries, but so much had happened in just the past week, that it felt like an entire century had passed in just a week's time. I had been nearly killed, turned into a werewolf, found out I'm part of a protected bloodline, fallen in with this ragtag family of a pack, had my first change where I actually turned into a wolf, found the pack's home on fire, dug through the wreckage of that fire, fought vampires, learned my friend had never been my friend, and on top of it all, I learned that I can apparently turn werewolves back into people and vampires into dust. Oh yea, and I was apparently falling for some werewolf with mischievous green eyes that I was probably never going to be able to touch again.

I sank onto the other couch in the living room.

The Fifth Element was on, and had apparently just started. I stared blankly at the screen.

Jonathan looked at me. "You've seen this one, right?"

I nodded. "It's one of my favorites." But I could barely concentrate on it.

Sometime soon after I sat down, there was a thumping from the backyard and I looked over the back of the couch. Matt was in the backyard, chopping up a skeleton of a pine tree with a hatchet. It only took him three swings to get through the trunk. Holy crap, were-wolves were strong.

Daniel came back downstairs sometime during the movie. Right around the part of the movie where the Mangalores blow up the ship over Fhloston Paradise, Ian arrived back at the house.

I grabbed a water bottle from the fridge, dodging around Kaylah and Chastity, though their food prep mad my mouth water. There was a huge pot of what smelled like chili on the stove, and a rack of ribs in the oven. Ribs. Great. I swallowed the little bit of bile that had risen and took a gulp of cool water from the bottle. At the entry from the kitchen to the dining room, I realized that I couldn't be the only one thirsty.

"Anyone else need a water?" I asked of the guys in the living room.

Ian, Daniel, and Jonathan all nodded, almost as one. It was kind of creepy, but I grabbed three more bottles of water. In the living room, I tossed one to each, eliminating the chance that any of them would touch me and curled my feet under me on the couch to watch the tail end of the movie.

"It lives!" Ian exclaimed.

I turned to look at him in the dining room.

He gestured to the laptop, which now had a little black brick attached to it with a cord. "Sheppard's hard drive is fine." He looked to Chastity in the kitchen. "I'll leave it hooked up here, so when you're done there you can check the two bloodline documents against each other."

Chastity smiled at him. It lit up her face and was a nice change of pace from the seriousness that usually resided there. "Thanks Ian," she said.

He pulled out his phone and leaned back in the chair, tapping out a message. When the credits rolled for the movie, he stood up.

"Jamie's on his way back now," Ian said. "You guys mind if we pick up on our game?" He picked up his backpack from beside the couch and pulled a game system with cords from it, holding it aloft.

"Go ahead," Daniel said, pulling his phone from his pocket and making another call, this time to a bank. He disappeared upstairs again.

I shrugged. "Sure." But the tedium was getting to me. There was nothing I could do until Kristos called back. There was nothing to be known until then, other than whether the vamps' bloodline file was up-to-date. But I could feel that Matt was right—even if it wasn't, it only spelled death for more people, not less.

Wow. That was a thought that never would have even crossed my mind a week ago.

Ian busied himself setting up whatever system it was he had pulled from his bag.

With a sigh, I stood and looked out the back window of the dining room. Matt dragged another skeleton of a pine tree into the yard from beyond the property line. By himself. There wasn't even sweat on his shirt from the exertion. He started chopping branches off, tossing them into a pile next to a long stack of firewood that lined the wire fence that separated Sheppard's lot from the neighbor's.

A motorcycle pulled up to the house, its engine more whine than rumble. Some rice-rocket then. A moment later, Jamie came inside wearing matching jacket and pants. He looked bulkier than he should, and I realized the jacket and pants were armored.

I jerked my chin at him. "What do you need the armor for if we heal so quickly?"

Jamie looked at me wide-eyed. "Crashing still hurts!"

"Come on, Jamie," Ian said, pulling a controller out of his backpack and tossing it to him. "We've got a date with the Skeleton King."

Jamie caught the controller. "That guy was easy!" He unzipped his jacket. He only had on a sleeveless muscle shirt under that. He plopped the controller on the couch, tossed the jacket on the floor next to Ian's bag and reached for the top of his armored pants.

I turned my back to Jamie then.

Jonathan laughed. "He's not naked under that!"

I speared him with a look. Jamie and Ian laughed then too.

"It's fine, Lynn," Jamie said through his laughter.

I turned back around. "Okay, fine, so he was wearing basketball shorts under his gear, so what? I am still not interested in seeing your brother naked, Jonathan!"

"Whoa! We've kind of all seen each other naked," Jamie reminded me. "It's not really a thing?"

"Maybe not to you guys," I said.

"But it still takes some getting used to," Ian replied.

I nodded. "Yeah."

Y'know, like just about everything else that comes with being a werewolf.

3 6

I watched Jamie and Ian play their game until I dozed on the couch. I watched Matt chop wood. At some point, Kaylah pulled lunchmeat from the fridge, bringing it to the dining room with breads for sandwiches. As before, I was careful not to touch anyone while we were in such close proximity around the table. I felt like a ghost floating through the house. The wait was tedious and weighed on me, keeping me on edge and anxious.

As the sun sank below the horizon, Jonathan sat on the couch next to me, careful to leave space. "You look more than a little tense. Why don't we work out some of that tension?"

I raised an eyebrow at him. Surely he wasn't suggesting...

"You get that we're probably never going to be able to do that again, right? I can't even touch you."

He furrowed his brow at me. "That's...not what I had in mind. I'm pretty sure you're wrong on that too, but that's beside the point." He shook his head and hooked his hair behind his ear. "I thought maybe we should go on a run."

I furrowed my brow. "I did that this morning."

Jonathan rolled his eyes at me. "Not that kind of run, a wolf run."

A thrill ran through me. "Just you and me?"

God, please tell me the hopeful tone of that hadn't come out as desperate as I thought it did.

He smiled that stupid smile of his that lit up the Colorado sky.

"Just you and me," he said in conspiratorial tones.

"You know there's probably vamps out there just waiting to get us alone," Daniel said.

Jonathan nodded. "Just a run. We'll head straight back if we even smell trouble."

"I can do a run."

I stood and headed to the bathroom down the hallway to change somewhere not so awkwardly in the middle of everything. I pushed the door mostly closed, but didn't latch it. Wolves don't have thumbs, and doorknobs were hard to operate without them. I stripped down, piling my clothes in the corner behind the door, and watched myself in the mirror for a moment. There was a tone to my muscles that I hadn't noticed before. The corner of my mouth pulled up and I shook my head. Well, fat lot of good it was going to do me anyway. Maybe I looked better naked now than I ever had in my life, but it wasn't like anyone was going to get to enjoy that again.

I wiped at my face and concentrated on changing. The familiar breaking pain overtook me, bringing me to the floor with a loud grunt as my limbs rearranged themselves. I nosed the door open and met Jonathan in the hallway. He shoved his clothes across the floor with his nose and I pushed them into a pile with my own, reveling in the woodsy scent of him as I did so.

Kaylah opened the back door for us, and Matt turned as we stepped into the backyard. He wiped his forehead where a sheen of sweat had gathered and watched us. Jonathan paused at the wire fence and met Matt's eyes for a long moment. I think he was watching to be sure Matt didn't follow us?

"Hurry home if you smell a vamp," Matt said. "Where there's one, there's many."

Jonathan nodded and stepped through the wires of the fence. I followed his lead, being careful not to trip myself or get tangled. As soon as I was clear, he broke into a run, and like a pistol shot starting a foot race, I followed, the exhilaration singing through my body.

The scents flew by in a blur: rock, detritus, pine, dirt, animal. Animal. We chased a couple of startled squirrels up their tree. As dusk turned to full dark, we came across a small family of raccoons, who chittered as they scurried away in random directions. We chased after one or two, but as neither of us had any inclination to eat or kill one, it was easy prey, exciting only for the novelty of it. Jonathan trotted ahead, and we smelled some kind of large animal, but he steered us away before I could catch a glimpse of anything that could tell me what it was. Once we were away from the big animal scent, he broke into a run again and I followed, reveling in the feel of the cool night air through my fur. The fall wind rushed past my ears and filled my lungs with the night. Words failed me. I just felt so very alive.

Six metal canisters sailed over our heads, smoke trailing from one end. Jonathan turned to look at me as they hit the ground, bouncing trails of acrid smoke that made my eyes blur and thickened the air. What the hell?

He started to bark at me, but the sound came out more like a cough. He jerked his head forward and darted ahead. I followed suit as the choking smoke engulfed us. As I cleared the smoke, its effects immediately receded.

Jonathan yelped in pain. There were four vampires attacking him. I took a couple of steps toward him when two more vamps appeared from the woods. They moved so fast it was a blur.

Kill them.

Remembering my fight with Matt, I went for the closest one's leg, but he dodged. He was blindingly fast. I saw the glint of a sword streaking toward me and I tried to dodge, but it bit into my shoulder hard. I yelped in pain and jumped back as the two vampires came between me and Jonathan.

Kill them!

I lunged at the vampire again, going for its leg once more, but as the vampire brought its sword down, I redirected and grabbed it at the forearm, close to the wrist. My jaws crunched through bone as the skin fell away to ash. I sneezed the dust from my nose as the brittle bone fell to the ground.

I didn't have time to process the disgust.

I spun to face the other vamp. It had circled around behind me, but his form blurred away through the trees.

I wanted to chase it, but Jonathan snarled, pulling my attention toward him. One of the vampires sank his blade to the hilt right through Jonathan's back leg, who yelped in pain. It jangled in my head louder than it had for Matt. The one in front of him raised his sword, aiming for Jonathan's head. I pounced on the latter, sinking my teeth into his upper arm. I rode the pile of bones and decaying flesh to the ground, but the slimy texture of gooey rotted flesh in my mouth made my stomach turn. The vamp on my left turned to me then, as Jonathan tore the throat out of the one who had just stabbed him.

The one facing me lunged to my right, sweeping his axe down toward my spine, but I darted forward, sinking my teeth into his thigh before his axe could connect. His skin turned to ash, and the axe buried itself in a nearby tree.

By my count, that left one more, but he was gone.

Jonathan worked the knife from his flank as his remaining wounds closed and jerked his head in a direction as he took a few steps. I started to take off, but slowed to match Jonathan's pace back toward the house. We made a wide circle around the smoke cloud, Jonathan's pace quickening as the wound near his leg healed. The smell of vamps was still in the air, and we ran as fast as we could back to the glass house.

In the backyard, Jonathan barked.

Kaylah swung open the back door for us. "You two stink to high heav'n!"

I ran down the hall to the bathroom to change, but Jonathan stopped in the kitchen.

In the bathroom, I pulled my clothes on.

"Yea," Jonathan said from the kitchen. "We got ambushed by vamps. They used tear gas again." Matt harrumphed, but Jonathan continued, "There were six of them. Lynn killed at least two, but at least two got away."

I hurried back to the kitchen, carrying Jonathan's clothing in one hand as I tugged my shirt over my head with the other.

Jonathan was standing in the kitchen, naked, his fists on his hips. Of course he was. No one else seemed to notice or care.

I tossed his clothes at him. "How did they know we were there?"

Jonathan pulled on his sweatpants, but held the rest of his clothes in a ball.

Matt snorted. "Those bloodsuckers probably have eyes on the house."

"Do they always just know where the pack lives?" How freaking frustrating.

"It's not like we're particularly hard to find," Jonathan said. "Not if you know what you're looking for."

"And they can smell us almost as well as we can smell them," Matt added.

"So this is just my life now?" My eyes were wide. "This is business as usual for you guys?"

Matt smirked at me. "Pretty much."

"And you handled it just fine," Jonathan said. "You took out at least two vampires on your own."

The basement door opened, and the sound of a buzzing phone made its way to us.

Sheppard appeared in the doorway. "Lynn." He showed me the screen.

Kristos.

I took a couple of steps toward him as he tapped the screen.

"You're on speakerphone," Sheppard said.

"Alright Sheppard," came a deep smoky voice, "fill me in." He sounded like an old jazz singer with an accent I couldn't place, but there was an odd emptiness to his voice.

Sheppard took a breath and told Kristos all that had happened starting with the attack on Frederick's cave. The line was quiet for a moment after he finished.

"And I just killed three more with just a bite," I added.

Sheppard raised his eyebrows at me.

I shrugged and looked to Jonathan.

"She's faster than you might expect in a fight, with good instincts," Sheppard said, pride in his voice as he smiled a gentle smile at me. "But other than the dusting and turning the crazed wolf back to human, she's not anything outside of the realm of normal for a wolf."

I crossed my arms over my belly. The thought of the slimy rotted skin from the one vamp in my mouth turned my stomach.

"The dusting and turning is pretty well outside of the realm of normality," Kristos replied.

There was something about the emptiness in his voice that bothered me, but I couldn't put my finger on it.

"I never saw this power in person," he said. "But I have heard of a *consanguinea* that could do what you describe. Just one."

A thrill went through me. Someone had actually heard of this before. I leaned closer to the phone.

"The church called it *purgatum*," Kristos continued in his odd accent. Maybe it was European? "Means 'purified.' They cleansed the blood of those they encountered, turning older vampires into desiccated corpses, and fresh-turned vampires back to their human selves, though those humans went mad shortly after. When they turned a werewolf back to human by happenstance, the church took action."

There was a grim tone to his last phrase. I gasped. "You mean they killed them!"

Sheppard eyed me meaningfully. "I am not going to let that happen."

"Nor would I expect you to," Kristos said. "But you need to know how they're going to respond if they find out about her. If they get wind of this, they will come down hard on your pack."

Sheppard pinched the bridge of his nose. "And we sent one straight to them." It was more of a mutter to himself.

"What?"

"We took the former werewolf to Blood of the Cross here," Sheppard replied. "It's where we take the sheep."

Kristos harrumphed. "I suggest you pull on whatever contacts you have to make that one disappear. It may already be too late; the church leadership may already know." He sighed and lowered his voice, it practically rumbled through the phone now. "Maybe times have changed and maybe they won't kill you all, but if the church hears about her, you can be damn sure you'll never see your *consanguinea* again."

I stared at the phone. I didn't even have words. The church would just kidnap me? Would that be worse than what the military wanted?

Sheppard caught my eye. "I'm not going to let that happen either, she chose pack."

"Then your real concern is whether or not she's a danger to that pack of yours," Kristos said.

Sheppard nodded. "Exactly."

"Well, she's not," he replied. "Or at least, she shouldn't be—so long as your pack's free of douchebags like that hothead you used to have."

Matt opened his mouth, but Sheppard placed a hand on Matt's chest, stopping whatever he was about to say.

"All *consanguinea* have control over their abilities," Kristos continued. "So should she. God only knows what degree her control should be and how she learns it, but she absolutely should have control." He raised his voice, though he had to have known it wasn't necessary. "And little one, you shouldn't have to worry about doing it by accident. Whatever happened in the moments you dusted the vampires or turned the werewolf, you wanted to remove a threat, so you did."

I backed into the dining room and sank into a chair. I shouldn't be able to do it by accident. He was right. I had wanted to remove a threat every time. With the vampires, I just wanted to eliminate them —and with the crazed werewolf, I just wanted her to stop.

"Thanks for your help, Kristos," Sheppard said. "It's much appreciated."

"You take care of yours, Shep," he replied, and the line went silent.

Sheppard tapped the screen and pressed the button on the side of his phone before sliding it back into his pocket.

"That asshole has some nerve," Matt barked.

"No," Sheppard said, looking at him. "He has a point. He knows who you were 275 years ago, Matt. You were a lot quicker to anger then; you flew off the handle at a moment's notice."

Matt crossed his arms.

"You've calmed down since then," Sheppard said, placing a hand on Matt's shoulder. "You're still pretty quick to anger, but at least you think about it before flying into a fight."

Matt pressed his lips into a line, his expression resigned. "Hmph."

A thought occurred to me. "How do you know he's not making a call to church leadership right now?"

"I don't," Sheppard said. "But he and the church had a falling out long ago. He's not likely to go back to them, ever."

I RAKED MY HANDS THROUGH MY HAIR. "WELL WHAT HE SAID IS GREAT and all, but not knowing how I'm doing this is terrifying." My thoughts turned to the gritty bone and slimy skin. "And it's disgusting —the taste of ash and rot in my mouth turns my stomach. But more than that, I have to know for sure if I'm a danger to anyone here. Kristos seems to think not, and I don't seem to do anything to you, but—" I looked to Jonathan and the lump in my throat returned.

He was still shirtless in the kitchen. He had been leaning against the counter of the island, but pushed off it and took a couple of steps toward me.

"He said you should have control," Jonathan said. "And he seemed to be pretty certain of that."

Sheppard nodded. "*Consanguinea* usually do. He made a good point."

Jonathan took a deep breath and knelt in front of where I sat. He reached a hand toward my face and my eyes went wide. "No time like the present then to find out for sure," he whispered.

I sucked on my bottom lip and closed my eyes. I held my breath and willed myself not to hurt him—not to change him—as Jonathan's fingers gently brushed my cheekbones. I released the breath I was holding slowly as his palm flattened against my face. I leaned into his hand as I breathed in the electric woodsy scent of him.

Then his mouth was against mine and my eyes snapped open in alarm. His eyes were closed, and his scent remained unchanged.

He wasn't changing.

The kiss deepened, our tongues finding each other as I wrapped my arm around his warm, bare shoulder. I had lost my concentration, but it didn't matter. I could touch him. He was safe.

He wrapped an arm around my waist, picking me up from the chair, and I let out a startled squeak, breaking off the kiss as I hooked a strand of hair behind my ear. I searched his face.

He smiled at me, his green-gold eyes glittering as he lowered me, letting me stand. "I don't taste the rot or the ash, just you."

I could touch Jonathan without any ill effects. Maybe I could touch the rest of the pack too!

Matt elbowed him. "Yeah, yeah, but we all know she likes you, Jonathan. She won't change or dust you."

I looked to Matt then, but there was still a wariness in his eyes. It stung, but he had a point. I looked back at Jonathan.

Mine.

God, how I'd like for that to be true. I squeezed my eyes closed and sighed. Maybe I couldn't touch the rest of the pack. At least I could touch Jonathan and Sheppard.

Sheppard looked back down the hallway, eyeing the entry to the basement. He took a couple of steps toward the hall.

"Alright then, Lynn." He ran a hand through his hair. "You need answers and so does the rest of the pack." He hooked a thumb toward the basement. "There's nothing else I can do for that wolf. I have exerted enough control over it to hold it in sleep. It won't hold forever, but it'll hold for now."

I followed him as he walked downstairs.

"But I cannot push it to change back. They are too far gone. If what Kristos said is true, you might be able to turn this one human again, permanently—and on purpose this time."

287

I thought of the girl with the long dark hair, now at Blood of the Cross.

"But what about their choice? Didn't you say you would never try to hold a wolf against their will? How is this any different?"

"They never chose to be changed," Sheppard said. "And now, their wolf has completely taken over. The wolf cannot make peace with the humanity within it and has gone wild and violent. Crazed."

He put his hands on my shoulders and I met his eyes. There was a sadness and disappointment there that I hadn't seen in him before now.

"There is nothing for this one, Lynn. Without my control, it will kill people. That is a fact. As it is, the strain of keeping even this much control over it puts the pack at risk. Pack must come first." He put a finger up, forestalling my next question. "You need to know if you can control it, and so do they." He gestured to the sleeping wolf in the cage. "This one will never go back to walking on two legs without your intervention, and it is a danger to those we protect on four. It no longer gets a choice about the matter."

God, I could feel the truth of his words in my bones, and not even a hint of power had washed over me. I looked from Sheppard to the sleeping wolf. "You're sure it won't wake and try to take my hand off?"

Sheppard nodded. "Yes—that much I am certain of."

I bit my lip as I approached the cage. Taking a breath, I tried to simply clear my head as I reached for the sleeping wolf, pushing my hand into the dark, tawny fur at its shoulder. "Well at least just touching them doesn't do anything."

The pack had gathered on the basement stairs now. They were watching. Well, good.

Sheppard nodded at me. "Good." There was a note of relief in his tone. "Now try."

I nodded and looked back at the sleeping wolf, taking another long deep breath. I tried to distinguish the scents of my pack on the stairs: Sheppard's warmth, the spicy musk of Matt, the vanilla tinged scent of Chastity, the flowery scent of Kaylah, the cinnamon-and-clean-laundry of Daniel, the orange-chocolate of Ian, the motor oil scent of Jamie, and the electric woodsy warmth of Jonathan. I looked at where my hand was buried in the wolf's fur and concentrated on the thought of bringing this poor creature's humanity back.

A warm tingle started in my fingertips, spreading through my hand and up my arm like the pins-and-needles of a limb that has fallen asleep. Slowly, the fur under my hand became skin until a naked blonde teenager lay on the floor of the cage. She was petite and thin, with shoulder length blonde hair. A bottle blonde, her dark roots were showing. Her blue eyes fluttered open, unfocused, and closed again. She was pretty and—even in her unconscious state—I got the feeling that she was somehow wild, probably a party girl from downtown, though she was clearly below the drinking age.

Chastity appeared next to me with a blanket as Sheppard opened the cage and picked the slight girl up.

I met Sheppard's eyes and then looked down at my hands, turning them over to examine them. Now that I wasn't touching her, the tingling sensation dissipated throughout my body.

"Kaylah," Chastity called. "Grab me some clothes for her."

Sheppard nodded at me. "Good job, Lynn. You saved her life."

Holy shit I had.

Comforting warmth spread through me, but this time, it had nothing to do with Sheppard. He had been staring down the barrel of having to kill this poor girl for circumstances that had come together entirely outside of her control.

And I had just changed that.

"Frederick is a perv," Ian asserted.

"They all are, Ian," Matt said. "Bloodsuckers are only ever interested in the pretty ones.

"Then they get dinner and a show," Jonathan said.

Kaylah bounded up the basement stairs and came back a moment later with sweatpants and a t-shirt. Man. The pack just goes through clothes like candy.

"Let's get her dressed and upstairs before she's conscious," Sheppard said.

Kaylah tugged clothes onto the girl. "I figg'r we can't take 'er t' Blood o' th' Cross."

Sheppard shook his head, handing the girl to Kaylah. "No, we'll have to hang on to her here for now. I called Buckheim and expect him on our doorstep at any time. We can hand her to him. Maybe he can get her lost in the system or into witness protection."

"Because if the church hears about her," Daniel started.

"Then it's trouble for all of us," Ian said.

The pack moved to make room for Kaylah to pass through on the stairs. She disappeared down the hallway.

"What about the one we already took there?" Jamie asked.

Sheppard looked to him. "We'll have to see if Buckheim can get her released to him as well. He's the only pull we have here. Losing sheep in a mental health facility is easy. All the packs do it. But losing a former werewolf? That's not something that's done. We can hide bodies if we need to, make them look like other things happened. But there's never been anyone that survived becoming a werewolf and then actually went back to being a human. I'm not even sure Buckheim will believe me, but if I ask him to do it as a favor, he'll do all he can to make it happen."

"Oh he'll believe you," Matt said. "It'll be all you can do to get him not to take Lynn with him when he comes."

My heart lurched and the air felt thin.

"I'm not going with him." My voice probably came out more panicked than I meant it to. I shook my head, my vision blurring as the words spilled from me. "He's not home. Not even my apartment is home anymore." I gulped in air as the lump in my throat broke my words. "This is home. Pack is home." I must have sounded like a sobbing little child. "I won't hurt anyone. Never. Only vampires."

Sheppard's arms wrapped around me as the tears flowed.

"No one is going to make you go with him," he whispered against my hair.

"Sheppard, please." I sobbed into his chest. "I swear I will never ever use this to harm the pack. Never. Pack is where I belong." And with that last phrase said, I couldn't help but feel the truth of it in every ounce of my body.

Sheppard brought his hands up to either side of my face, kissing me on the forehead like my father used to do when I was a little girl.

"Shhh. I know," he said softly. "But don't swear it to me. Swear it to your packmates."

I met his eyes then, sucking on my bottom lip and swallowing around the lump.

"Your pack needs to know they can trust you," he said. "I know you'll never do a thing to hurt them, but the words are important. We are human enough that words matter."

I wiped the tears from my face with my fingers and nodded, turning to the pack on the stairs. Kaylah had come back to the basement and sat on the top step. She leaned back out the door, looking down the hall toward the living room, and then looked back at me. Slowly, she nodded to me. I met Jonathan's eyes as he wiped at his cheek. He nodded at me too.

I closed my eyes and took a breath, forcing my thoughts to slow down.

"I've never belonged anywhere," I said. "I never really fit in with the kids growing up. I preferred books to dolls. I was in an odd in-between generation with my extended family, so Christmases were always weird. On the odd year that I managed to actually get a gift, it was always for the wrong age, while my cousins opened mountains of exactly what they wanted. What few friends I made in high school moved away after graduation. And when my mom died," I tried to swallow around the lump that formed at the thought of her. "Well, when she was gone, I guess my dad and I didn't belong together so well anymore either." My voice barely supported the words.

I huffed out a breath and looked up then, meeting the eyes of my packmates one by one.

"So when I tell you that I finally feel like I belong somewhere, it comes from a lifetime of searching. A lifetime of not belonging." I rolled a shoulder. "Sure, it's not the centuries-long lifetime that you all know, but twenty-two years of not belonging is still an awfully long time." I took another slow breath. "Which is how I know—down to my soul, down to the core of my bones—that I will never do anything to jeopardize that. You all took me in and treated me like family without even a question. And maybe it was because you all knew so much about me by the time I got here that you felt safe." I squeezed my eyes closed. "But then I got this weird ability. I didn't ask for it, and I'd give it up if I could. It scares me more than I ever thought anything could." I swallowed around the sob that threatened again. "But please." Again, I met the eyes of my packmates in turn. "I'm begging you to trust me. I swear to you that I will never—*ever*—do anything to hurt this pack."

I looked to Sheppard, then. He nodded at me and I looked back at the pack.

Jonathan closed the distance to me. "I told you we were safe." He held my face and kissed my wet cheeks, brushing a thumb across where his lips had just been.

"I am never going to be afraid of you," Matt said, standing. "You won't hurt pack." He pulled me into a hug.

I looked over his shoulder, meeting Jonathan's eyes. "And I swear that will always be true." He released me and punched my shoulder lightly as he stepped away.

"Girl," Chastity said, her hazel eyes sparkling as she embraced me. "You've gone and done it now. You're stuck with us."

Was that a joke? Her curls tickled my face as she released me, and I wiped at my nose with my hand.

"Pack's pack," Kaylah said. "We're family." She hugged me too. "No gettin' 'round it." She wiped a wayward tear from my cheek when she released me, but her cheeks were wet too.

God, they were all touching me as they hugged me. I thought they'd never do that again. My heart sang with the joy of it.

"You always belonged here," Daniel said, pulling me against him. He squeezed me once before letting go and ruffling my hair like you would a small child. I couldn't help but smile.

"Sheppard knows what's good for pack," Jamie said. "He knew you belonged months ago. It was only a matter of time." He smiled at me as he wrapped lanky arms around me.

Ian wrapped his arms around both of us. "Group hug!" But Jamie wiggled out as Ian whispered into my hair, "*Sarcina eiusdem sanguinis.*"

The blood and the pack are one.

I felt the truth of those words more and more strongly with each passing moment.

I closed my eyes and the strands of the pack practically glowed.

I had finally found where I belonged.

EPILOGUE

BUCKHEIM

"Grace Lynn Cartwright; age 22; freelance copy-editor; *consanguinea*." Elias had the girl's file open in his lap.

"Werewolf," I added.

Elias grunted as he flipped through her file.

Pulling his team home from overseas had taken longer than I wanted it to. I would have preferred to show up at Sheppard's door with him three days ago, but our operations overseas were touch-and-go, and pulling a whole team out required putting another team in their place. It had been tricky paperwork, but when Langley—that arrogant brat—failed to get the girl to come in, I knew I needed a lighter touch. Elias was one of only two *consanguinea* in the program, and his healing abilities were much more extraordinary than his cousin's ability to change quickly and without pain. I needed extraordinary to be sure she would come with me.

Another page flipped in Elias' lap. "What's her dad doing in Europe?"

"Forgetting about the pain of losing his wife," I replied. "Ignoring his only daughter."

"She must feel so isolated."

I smiled. "That's why I'm bringing family to meet her."

294

Elias nodded.

I parked on the street in front of the modern glass house, noting the other vehicles present. By the looks of it, Sheppard's whole pack was home.

Sheppard stood at the open door by the time Elias and I reached the porch steps, the warmth of his scent mixing with his pack and wafting out the front door. It was a subtle reminder that I was in their territory, and a sharp contrast to Elias' antiseptic scent.

"Good to see you, sir," Sheppard said, extending his hand.

I shook it. Over his shoulder, I could see most of his pack had gathered in the living room.

"Please come in," Sheppard said, gesturing into the living room. "We can speak in the dining room."

I followed him, Elias a step or two behind me. The girl was seated to the left of the head of the table. His redheaded woman sat next to her, a laptop open in front of her.

"How many of these houses are you going to go through, Sheppard?" He'd had seven houses burn to the ground in the past 15 years alone. And those were just the ones I knew about.

He glanced over his shoulder at me. "As many as it takes, sir, until the vampires are gone."

A shame. His insurance rates had to be astronomical.

The girl raised an eyebrow at the honorific and then looked sharply at me, her steel-grey eyes meeting mine without fear. I smiled at her.

Sheppard pulled out the chair to the right of the head of the table as he passed and sat at the head of the table. "Thank you for coming so quickly."

"Of course," I replied, sitting in the seat Sheppard had pulled out for me. "It sounded important."

Sheppard nodded. "It is." He looked to the redheaded girl. "Chastity?"

The redhead, Chastity, looked at him and eyed me before spinning the laptop around. The machine reeked of vampire, but I kept my expression neutral as I looked at the screen. Where the hell had they gotten a vampire's laptop anyway? The dens under the Chateau?

I focused on the file she had open. It was the *consanguinea* bloodline.

"They know how to track *consanguinea* now," Sheppard said.

I read names and tried to recall the last time I had seen the lineage we had on file. "How up-to-date is that file?"

"It's accurate," Sheppard said. "Lynn's on it."

Lynn? Not Grace then. Interesting that she would make that change. Still, that file could be twenty-two years old. Though—admittedly—the line hadn't jumped families in the girl's lifetime.

"Hm." I rubbed the stubble on my chin. "The church will want to know right away."

Sheppard nodded. "And I knew you would know who needed this information best, sir."

"Indeed. I'll need a copy for our records."

"Of course." Sheppard nodded to Chastity, who tossed a flash drive across the table to me. I caught it and placed it in my shirt pocket.

"Who's your friend?" Lynn asked, jutting her chin toward Elias.

"Ah," I said, straightening in my seat and meeting her eyes. "Forgive my impropriety." I gestured to Elias. "This is Second Lieutenant Elias Clark. He's a doctor. You can call him Elias."

She narrowed her eyes at him, but her nose twitched. She was scenting him out. "I'm not sick."

I smiled at her. "Of course not. But he's also *consanguinea*, which makes him a cousin of yours."

Her eyes widened. Sheppard's narrowed.

"Elias has an ability that rather uniquely suits him," I told her. "He takes the injuries of others unto himself, healing them. He then heals at an accelerated rate, even for a lupine."

"All werewolves heal fast," Chastity spat. Sheppard speared her with a look and she spun the laptop back around and snapped it closed.

As she stood, she picked up the laptop and went to sit on one of the couches in the living room. She sat sideways, facing a coffee table and reopened the laptop, the screen facing away from me. I watched her with quiet amusement. Natural packs like Sheppard's ran by different rules. There was no real hierarchy within his pack, just the alpha and the rest of them.

"Elias heals faster than any lupine we have on record," I continued. "He helps people that even modern medicine would fail to save."

The girl's mouth fell open. Got her.

Sheppard folded his hands on the table. "How is your program doing these days, sir?"

I smiled at him. "We now have over a ninety percent turn success rate. Thanks to DNA mapping, we can identify which recruits would be a good match from the moment they get their physical. Through their training, we learn who has the mental acuity."

Sheppard smiled, though something hid behind that smile. "That's impressive, sir, only about half of natural crazed attacks end in a viable pack member."

I nodded at him. "Once we've turned them, we match them with an alpha and their real training begins." I looked across the table at the girl. "But *consanguinea* are a cut above. Because of their value and rarity, they are given much more freedom and leniency than any other military operative. Forget that crap Langley fed you." I made a sour face. "If you come with me, you'll never be asked to do something you weren't already willing to do, and I'll give you the training and tools necessary to make you capable of anything you set your mind to."

She smiled then. It was something feral. Perfection. She was going to be hell-on-wheels in a pack. And I was pretty sure I knew just the right alpha to keep her in line.

"That reminds me," Sheppard said. "Kaylah, could you bring Hayley down here?"

"Sure." The blonde on the couch uncurled herself and hurried up the stairs. She spoke in quiet tones upstairs. "C'mon hun, yer ride's here." She came back downstairs, her arm around a human girl, barely eighteen, with dyed blonde hair and wide set blue eyes. She wore a black t-shirt two sizes too large for her, knotted into a crop top and hanging off a shoulder. Her grey sweatpants were probably two sizes too large for her too, but at least they had a drawstring securely tied at her waist.

There were four lines of parallel pink scars on her stomach, their edges rough, like she was torn open. Curious.

"General Buckheim, sir," Sheppard said, "This is Haley Bennett. She needs to disappear. Safely." He met my eyes, his expression earnest.

Elias, gentle as ever, reached for the girl as she came into the dining room. He did a basic check to see if she was injured. The poor girl's eyes were vacant, like a drugged sheep.

"Take her to Blood of the Cross," I waved my hand vaguely. "Like you do the rest of the sheep."

Sheppard shook his head and crossed his arms. "There's a Jane Doe at Blood of the Cross that needs to disappear as well. She probably remembered what her name is by now, but she was unconscious when she left us. Neither are sheep."

I narrowed my eyes at him. The girl—Lynn—sat back in her chair and watched me. She still wore her feral smile. Gold circled the pupils of her eyes.

"What is this about, boy? Why do they need to disappear?" I gestured across the table. "Why does she look like she just ate the last cookie in front of the schoolyard bully?"

Sheppard leaned forward in his seat and folded his hands on the table again. "I'm not at liberty to discuss such matters with the military, sir." He looked pointedly at my ear.

I met his eyes, my expression hardening. His did the same. The girl folded her arms across her chest.

Sheppard and I had a long history. He was still a pup when I first met him over four hundred years ago. I had saved him then from the vampires that killed his family. He and I had been trading favors ever since. We had gotten each other out of tough spots before, and his expression now told me he was in another. Just what had this *consanguinea* done?

Sighing, I nodded once and unclipped the keys from my belt loop.

"Elias." I handed the keys to him. "Take Miss Bennett and get the Jane Doe from Blood of the Cross." I looked to Sheppard. "Description?"

Sheppard looked to Elias. "College-aged, tall, curvy, tanned skin, long black hair."

I nodded again, and half turned in my seat. "Use my credentials in the glovebox if you need to. Then take both back to the base and get their paperwork started. I'm sure Sheppard will give me a ride back to the base."

"Sir!" Elias' eyes widened. "All due respect, sir. That will leave you without backup."

I waved his objection away. "This pack's no threat to me, Elias. Go on now."

Elias pressed his lips into a line and looked at Sheppard. He then looked back at me and nodded once. He escorted the girl to the door, and the house was still until the car drove away.

I unbuttoned the top button of my shirt and removed my ear wire, making a show of disconnecting it from its power source. If history had been any indication, Sheppard needed a discussion that was entirely off-the-record. He needed to be sure the only ones in the room were me and his pack. I took my phone from my pocket and opened the back, removing the battery and leaving it beside the phone on the table.

I sighed then and pinched the bridge of my nose. "We go too far back to keep secrets, boy. What's this about?"

Sheppard smiled at me and pointed at the door. "That girl and the Jane Doe used to be werewolves."

Used to be?

"What do you mean they 'used to be werewolves'?"

Sheppard looked to the girl on his left. Lynn.

"He means they used to be crazed wolves," she said, her voice calm, "destined for a 'merciful death'." She unfolded her arms and put air quotes around the last two words.

I narrowed my eyes at her. "And you changed that?"

She met my eyes. "And I changed that," she confirmed, nodding once.

299

I had never heard of such an ability. A *consanguinea* that could turn werewolves human again? It seemed impossible.

"She can also turn vampires to dust," Sheppard added.

My eyebrows tried to crawl off my head. She could start another bloodbath, the likes of which I haven't seen since the Crusades. Only hers would be covered in dust and written in the annals of history with the chalky bones of dead vampires. I may have been a young pup then, but the image of bodies piled as high as a house flashed in my mind, clear as day. Hers would be piles of ash.

"I'm not going anywhere with you General Buckheim," she said, cool control in her voice. "This is my pack. I have made my choice, this is where I belong." Her steel-grey eyes sparkled with the declaration.

I stared at her. No. She couldn't choose this pack. The church would do all they could to manipulate her to join their side of the fight. It would be better—easier—for her if she just chose to come along willingly. And this ability she had would only make the church leadership want her more.

"The last time the church knew about a *consanguinea* like her, they deemed it too great a threat and culled it." Sheppard stood and stepped behind the girl, placing his hands on her shoulders. "But she's made her choice, and the pack will defend it."

It was impossible to miss the meaning of that last phrase. The pack would kill to defend her right to stay with them. And if she could turn werewolves to human again, nothing could stop them. Humans were chaff compared to werewolves.

"It would simply be too much trouble for the military to take her by force," I said, meeting Sheppard's eyes.

He nodded. We were on the same page. "The costs would be tremendous. You'd lose too many valuable assets."

"And you're gonna owe me a favor for helping to lose those two former wolves in the system."

Sheppard smiled and crossed his arms. "I am, aren't I, sir?" There was amusement in his eyes.

The girl's face lit up and she turned to Sheppard with a sharp intake of breath. "I know what I want to do."

He furrowed his brow, glanced at me, and then sat back at the head of the table. He canted his seat, so he could face her better.

"I want to help those that go crazed," she said, "the ones like Hayley and the other girl. The ones that wouldn't survive otherwise."

She could literally wipe the Earth clean of the existence of vampires, and she preferred to help the crazed wolves. That sort of short-sightedness would never make it in a military pack. Which means she would never make it. Any of my alphas would push her to destroy vamps instead of help the moonraged.

Sheppard placed a hand on hers. "You're sure?"

She nodded. "I am. In the diner, when Matt said that I might die the night of the full moon, I was terrified." She scooted to the edge of her chair. Her enthusiasm was nearly palpable. "But don't you see? No one has to die anymore."

Blessed Mother of Christ, she was right. Sheppard sat up and stared at her.

She glanced at me and then met Sheppard's eyes. "You couldn't push those two back into their human form." She waved toward the hallway. "But I," she placed her hand on her chest, "I pulled the wolf from them entirely."

She laid her warm hand on top of mine on the table and met my eyes. "You have over a ninety percent success rate, but what happens to the other ten percent? How many recruits do you put down because they raged at the full moon?"

Too many. Last year, we lost seventeen men to the moonrage. This year, we had already lost fourteen. I tried to keep my expression neutral, but I saw on her face that I had failed. She was right. I pinched the bridge of my nose with the hand she wasn't touching.

She squeezed my hand. "Good men don't have to die anymore, General."

I met her eyes. She meant every word of what she said. God bless her.

"No more 'training accidents,'" Sheppard said, putting air quotes around the last two words. His eyes were red, and tears had gathered. He knew.

I looked hard at the hand on top of mine. That hand could turn even me to human if she wanted to. A chill ran down my spine. Sheppard had just made a play to become the strongest alpha in North America, likely the world. Even if the church found out about her, they were going to have a hell of a time trying to get her now.

I sighed. And it was only a matter of time before the church found out, given her plan to save moonraged wolves.

"You have the right of it, boy. I'll come up with something for the report. The church won't hear about her from me or mine." I stood, collecting my ear wire, phone, and battery. "Now if you'll excuse me, I would appreciate a ride back to the base."

Sheppard smiled. "Of course. I'm glad we could come to an agreement."

I nodded and followed him back out the front door, glancing back at the girl. She was going to change the rules of the game, assuming she even knew there was a game being played.

ABOUT THE AUTHOR

Born and raised in Texas, Becca Lynn Mathis has been writing since she was a little girl, and could often be found sitting among the branches of a tree, reading a book. She even used to get in trouble in high school for writing stories after her work was done.

Today, she is a graduate of Lynn University with her B.S. in Psychology. On weekends, she plays Dungeons & Dragons (or Pathfinder) with her friends and trains with the Royal Chessmen stage combat troupe, who perform at renaissance festivals and pirate faires all across Florida.

She lives in sunny South Florida with her husband, their blended family, and two goofy dogs.

~

Be sure to visit her website and sign up for her newsletter to keep up to date about the rest of the Trials of the Blood series!

www.beccalynnmathis.com